CAPTURED

INNOCENCE

CSA Case Files, Book One

Kennedy Layne

CAPTURED INNOCENCE

Dedication

First and foremost, a heartfelt thank you to Kallypso Masters. Without her, this book would never have taken place. You are, without a doubt, the fairy godmother of love.

Vella Day and Olivia Jaymes…your support throughout each chapter helped keep me on track. Love you, girls!

Gabrielle Evans—for keeping my sanity in check!

J.M. Madden—thank you for your advice, support, and willingness to share a wonderful editor.

As always…to Jeffrey, who has forever captured my heart and soul.

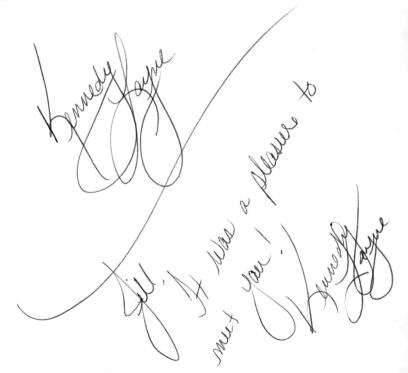

Prologue

Bzzzzz. Bzzzzz.

Crest reached out for his phone, not even bothering to roll over onto his back. It took him a few times, but eventually his fingers found the elusive square device. Holding it up to his face, he squinted at it with one eye. Who the fuck was calling at four thirty-three in the morning? He'd just fallen asleep an hour ago. Ramsey County Jail was being broadcast across the screen. Groaning a vow to castrate whoever it was, he swiped the bar and held the phone to his ear.

"Who would be dumb enough to call me at this hour?" Crest grumbled. "It's in the middle of the goddamned night."

"I need your help, Crest."

The background noise of electronic recording beeps, low voices making similar calls, and the unmistakable sound of a cell door closing had Crest opening both eyes and rolling onto his back. He recognized his best friend's voice. Terry Sweeney sounded hoarse, as if he were attempting to control his emotions. The room was dark but for a stray halogen ray from one of the city lights that was peeking in through the heavy curtains shrouding his bedroom window. He swung his feet over the side of the mattress and sat up, running his hand through his brown hair. He paid little attention to the brunette sleeping behind him.

"You've got my attention, T."

"I've been arrested," Terry said. The desperation in his voice was evident. That was soon washed away by some kind of utterance, communicating untold grief. The pain pouring through the phone was tangible. It sat on your chest and squeezed the breath from you. For the first time, Crest heard his best friend sob. "Marilyn's been murdered. I-I found her t-tied up and—"

Crest felt like he'd been punched in the gut. Marilyn Sweeney was dead—murdered. A montage started in his head of all the good times they'd had over the years. Granted, the marriage had been a little strained lately, but Terry and Marilyn were the ones that he would have bet his last dollar on could make a marriage last a lifetime, especially with Terry's childhood experience. His best friend's wife was dead. Fuck. Taking a deep breath, he mentally categorized what he would need to accomplish in the short term. Crest reached down for his black dress pants.

"They think I did it, Crest."

"Have you made any statements?" Crest snatched his shirt off of the chair in the corner, shaking it out as Terry answered him. He held his phone between his shoulder and ear as he shrugged one arm into the sleeve. "I'll be there in twenty. You listen to me carefully, T. Not one more fucking word. No matter what they promise or how they bait you, you clam up until I get you an attorney."

"She's dead," Terry whispered, as if his world had fallen apart. Crest knew it had. "What will I do without her?"

"Just keep quiet," Crest advised, reaching for his keys on the nightstand. He shoved them in his pocket and started looking around to confirm he hadn't left anything important. "I'll find out who did this. You have my word."

Crest disconnected the call and stood there for a few moments to gain some clarity. Images of Terry and Marilyn throughout the last few years played over in his head. He had no doubt that his friend wasn't capable of any kind of domestic violence and the police were barking up the wrong tree. He was convenient and since when wasn't the husband a prime suspect? They just snatched up the most expedient person. They didn't know Terry like he did.

He stood staring at the floor while he wrapped his mind around this tragic event. Crest brought his hand up and ran his fingers over his close-cropped hair. Making a swift decision, he swiped the bar across the bottom of his phone once more. Crest sent a simple text to his team, instructing them to be at the office at eight o'clock this morning. Having hand-picked five of his best colleagues that he'd come across during his time in the service, he had made sure that Crest Security Agency was staffed to exceed excellence. The team consisted of four men, one woman, and his personal assistant. With Terry's rushed arrest, it was looking as if they had their work cut out for them.

"Crest?"

He turned around. Shit. Crest had forgotten about...hell, he couldn't even remember her name. Her sultry figure was barely covered by the thin white sheet. The crevice of her ass caught the false beam shining through from the outside world, highlighting her best asset. His gaze traveled up the arc of her back, landing on her long brown curls that obscured her pillow. She was better than most of his recent encounters. He gave up trying to remember her name and looked around for his jacket. It was over by the bedroom door. He retrieved it and shrugged into the coat, all the while looking for his tie. It was nowhere to be found. He'd have to go without.

"I've gotta go. Listen, help yourself to breakfast in the morning. I'm sure there's something edible in the fridge." Gavin opened the door, other things weighing on his mind. She'd find her way out without too much trouble. "I'll call you."

Chapter One

Connor Ortega felt like hammered shit. Saturday was supposed to have been his day off, but for Crest to request the presence of the entire team, even he knew to drag his ass out of the rack. Keeping his aviator mirrored sunglasses on, he opened the door to Crest Security Agency. The firm's logo was situated front and center in between the dark, exposed beams jutting out of the ceiling. It reminded him that he needed to square his ass away. Work was exactly what he needed.

Laughter and low murmurs came from the heart of the office and he suppressed a groan as the truncated noises caused his head to hurt. Jessie wasn't at her desk, so he walked through the large, unlit open area filled with cubicles until he reached the conference room. Jax, Kevin, Ethan, and Taryn were all congregated around the heavy oval table. The throbbing in his temples became worse upon entering the brightly lit room, regardless that his shades kept the light to a minimum.

The CSA office was situated in the warehouse district of Minneapolis. It wasn't as upscale as the buildings that were located deeper into the heart of the city, but the team liked it that way. Connor felt comfortable in his jeans, long-sleeved pullover gray shirt, and brown bomber jacket he'd thrown on instead of having to wear a conservative suit as the men did in the upper scale structures. He pulled a matching battered Marines baseball cap lower on his forehead as he crossed the threshold.

"You do realize that you're inside a building, right, Ortega? Who're you trying to impress with those shades?"

Connor flipped Kevin the bird, not slowing down until he reached the coffee pot on a small metal table in the back. Someone had made the crap GI style—thick as mud. Since no one was clutching their chests from the swill, he figured that was a good enough sign. He slipped one of the Styrofoam cups off of the stack and poured the hot liquid until it was ready to overflow.

"He just doesn't want Crest to know that he was banging the state senator's daughter last night," Jax said, joining in the laughter.

On one hand, he knew that Jax was covering for him. On the other, if they knew that he'd been at some dive bar up until the damn thing closed, they probably wouldn't have believed him. Hell, he hadn't fucked a woman in months—not that he'd tell them that. Maybe that was his problem and he needed to get his ass back in the saddle. As it was, he kept letting the memory of a cheating, vile woman keep him from moving on with his life. He knew better than to think he was cut out for a long-term relationship. All women eventually cashed out. Hadn't his mother taught him that? He needed to grow a pair of balls. He disgusted even himself.

"Didn't you hear?" Kevin motioned with his hand and tongue in cheek at the same time. "The senator's daughter was caught giving head to the Love Drive's drummer over at First Avenue. It was all over the press last week. She dumped Connor's ass a while ago."

"Ignore these fuckers," Taryn said, holding out two ibuprofens as Connor took the seat next to her. Her short, spiky blonde hair fit her personality to a T. Her body was tight and she had a small heart-shaped ass that rivaled no other. Too bad she was like a sister to them. "Here. This should help get you through the meeting, at least."

Connor's head was now pounding and he gratefully took the pills. Tossing them back, he ignored the burn of the hot liquid as he washed them down. As much as they all bullshitted with each other, they were a close-knit group and had each other's six. He tried to remember that as they continued to needle him. After all, they were all sharks and there was blood in the water. It just happened to be his.

They were all private investigators working under Crest for the Crest Security Agency. The only main prerequisite was that they had to have had a military background and that they could pass muster with Crest personally. There wasn't a thing about their personal and professional lives that Crest wasn't privy to. The same couldn't be said in return, as Gavin Crest was a very private man.

Connor and Jax had been in the same infantry unit, putting in their twelve years with the Marines before Crest offered them the lives they were living now. They had jumped at the chance. Kevin had also been a grunt, but his honorable discharge came sooner than he'd wanted when he'd been wounded during a combat tour over in Afghanistan. The military didn't want a man if his body contained too many pins, plates, and screws apparently. Ethan was the youngest, having only done one enlistment as a comms tech. It was Taryn who was the odd one out. Not only was she a woman—she was former Navy Intel.

"So, what are we here for?" Connor asked, his voice still gravelly from the amount of alcohol he'd consumed. He really couldn't remember how much he drank. "Did you jack-offs do something that pissed off Crest? I know for a fact that I'm the golden child since I closed that cold case for him."

"Don't know," Jax said, tossing one of those yellow stress balls across the table to Kevin. "I know I didn't do anything beyond my normal bullshit. I've been working for that Hill woman chasing her cheating husband over half the county. I've got the photos to prove it and all I need to do now is to schedule a sit-down with the wife. She's going to toast his ass in court; that is if he lives long enough to make the court appearance."

"We all got a text that said to be here by eight o'clock," Taryn said, sipping on her own cup of coffee. Her black-rimmed glasses sat perfectly on the bridge of her nose. "Here we are."

"Did Jennifer Lynn really get caught giving head over at First Avenue?" Ethan asked, still on the previous conversation. He looked back and forth between the team members, as if gauging their responses. "I did some work for her father. She didn't seem like that type of girl when I was fucking her."

"Ethan, they're yanking your dick," Connor said, pulling his cap lower on his forehead. Why were these lights so goddamn bright? "I tied one on last night, that's all. We were supposed to have the weekend off, remember?"

"Didn't the corps teach you anything, Ortega?"

Connor looked up to see Gavin Crest walk through the conference room door. Even though his suit was rumpled, his tie was missing, and he looked just as bad as Connor felt—he commanded their respect. Crest tossed a folder onto the table, garnering everyone's attention. Business it was.

Crest had a rough exterior and wasn't what one would call handsome, although Connor had heard many women refer to him as just that. Connor didn't see it, but hey, whatever floats their boat. Taryn had, on occasion, said that Crest reminded her of the actor Daniel Craig, but Connor thought Taryn must be fishing for a bonus. Craig was a pretty boy actor—Crest was the real fucking deal. His legacy in the corps was what you might imagine a Master Sergeant to be. He had paid the price many times over and that marked a man. His bearing betrayed him for who he was. It was hard to miss.

"Always expect the plan to go FUBAR ten seconds into the mission, Crest," Connor answered, after clearing his throat. He always did like the meaning behind the acronym—fucked up beyond all recognition. That's what he felt like at the moment, too. Connor took his sunglasses off and tossed them on the table, barely repressing the need to squint at the artificial light. "What have you got for us? We're all present, for the most part."

"It's a murder case. I didn't call Jessie. She doesn't need to be here," Crest said, referring to his personal assistant. Connor didn't find that too odd, considering that everyone was privy to the underlying tension between them lately. It wouldn't surprise Connor if Jessie quit sometime soon. Crest shrugged off his jacket and draped it across the back of his chair. "Listen up. Whatever cases you're working on, I want you to brief Ethan no later than this afternoon. He's taking over all open cases until further notice."

Connor slugged more coffee, exchanging glances with his fellow teammates. Whatever happened to cause Crest to hand off paying clients to the youngest man on the team had to have been beyond the normal shit sandwich. Jax caught the yellow stress ball that Kevin had thrown back to him and closed it in his fist. He noticed that Ethan was now sitting a little straighter as well. Taryn was leaning forward, recording notes in her tablet.

"As you know, I'm good friends with Terry Sweeney." Crest opened the folder and threw six photos on the table. The entire team leaned forward to see what the images had captured—and they were heinous. Connor knew who she was before her name was ever said. Son-of-a-bitch. He'd personally seen her at the clubs around town, but that had been many months ago. "His wife, Marilyn, was murdered last night. She was tied up, tortured to death, and then left that way for her husband to find. Unfortunately, Terry panicked and tried to cut her loose."

"It's a normal reaction for the uninitiated," Connor said, grateful that the caffeine he was drinking was finally kicking in. The pictures had enough of an effect that he felt sober anyway. He took a finger and pulled a photo toward him. What a bloody mess. "It's a damn good thing they didn't have children. I take it the police questioned him? I know he's your friend, Crest, but can you be sure that he *didn't* do it?"

"I'm sure." Crest's voice broke no argument and Connor decided that he'd speak with him when they had a moment of privacy. The information that Connor was privy to…he wasn't so sure that Crest would want revealed to the team. It was rare that cases crossed into Crest's personal territory. "That didn't stop the police from arresting him. I have a meeting with the Lieutenant in around an hour."

"What evidence do they have?" Taryn asked.

"Terry said he pulled out the knife that was in her side when he found her. He used it to cut the ropes, thinking he could save her. Remember, he's a surgeon. Unfortunately, she was already dead. His DNA is everywhere and as we all know, it'll be a while before we have additional reports to confirm someone else committed the murder. After questioning Terry at the residence, Detective Morrison felt his answers were enough to warrant an arrest."

"That's one way to fuck up a crime scene," Connor said, referring to the fact that Terry had not only pulled the knife out of his wife's dead body, but then tried to use the murder weapon to cut her loose. He knew that Crest had contacts inside the police forensics lab where initial tests would be run. They'd be given a copy upon completion, along with the initial crime reports, the scene workups and any interviews that the police may have done. "Crest, do you recognize these knots?"

The only other person in the room besides Crest who probably knew what Connor was referring to was Jax. Connor and Jax belonged to a couple of clubs around the city that catered to the kinkier side, not that he'd been playing lately. The BDSM community was tight and he'd wanted to steer clear of it until *she* got her ass out of town. He caught Jax's eye and knew his friend recognized the woman in the picture as well. Marilyn Sweeney had been caught up in the lifestyle.

"Yes. The knots and style are very intricate. The killer is obviously well versed in shibari." Crest leaned back in his chair. His green eyes surveyed his team and waited for everyone to settle down before detailing more information. "Let me give you an overview of their life. Terry and Marilyn dabbled in BDSM. They usually played at home, but occasionally they would attend the members only nights at the two clubs they frequented—Masters is one, Whip is the other. I already know what you're thinking, Connor. Terry was up front with me regarding Marilyn's desire for club play. I know that she went by herself quite a bit and although that added several layers of tension between them, he didn't kill her."

If Crest said Terry didn't kill his wife, then that was good enough for Connor. He nodded his head and looked over at Jax. His friend didn't quite seem to be in agreement, but Connor was sure that Jax wouldn't trust a Jesuit priest at this point. Jax hadn't been the same since their last combat tour. The table conversation turned his attention back to the case at hand.

"Where was Terry during the time of the murder?" Kevin asked, taking one of the photos. "You said he came home to find her. I'm assuming it was their bedroom?"

"Yes, he found her in their bedroom," Crest replied. His eyes were bloodshot and Connor winced when he rubbed his eyes. "Terry had flown in from Chicago earlier in the evening—around eight-thirty. He said that Marilyn had mentioned she was stopping by Masters, so he swung by there first. From what I'm being told, she wasn't there. He stayed to talk to some friends and watch a suspension scene for about an hour. He then came home to this."

Crest had waved his hand over the photos. Connor did the math in his head. Crest said that Terry had arrived at the airport at eight-thirty last night. He gave the man thirty minutes to get through the airport and collect his luggage, then ten minutes to walk to his car. Terry would have taken at least twenty minutes to drive into the city. An hour at the club would put the time at around eleven at night.

"Where is their residence?" Connor asked. "What suburb?"

"Maplewood."

"So that would put Terry roughly at his house between eleven-thirty and midnight."

"Yes. He placed the 911 call at twelve-eleven precisely. The police responded immediately and arrived at twelve twenty-six. Each of you will be given a copy of the report once it's in my hands." Crest pushed back his chair, stood, and walked to the back of the room. He poured himself a cup of coffee, taking it black like the rest of them. "After hearing where Terry had been that evening and that Marilyn frequented the clubs by herself, they immediately assumed that Terry killed her in a jealous rage. The more he opened up about the clubs gave Detective Morrison more ammunition to build a case. It didn't help that his fingerprints were all over the weapon or the fact that he was covered in her blood."

"It's hard to explain the lifestyle to a person who hasn't been exposed to it," Jax responded, squeezing the yellow ball in his fist. "Do you know the arresting officer? I've seen him on television during interviews."

"I know *of* Detective Morrison," Crest replied, returning to his seat. "If I knew him personally, I guarantee he wouldn't have arrested Terry on such an asinine assumption, which is why I have an appointment with the Lieutenant."

"It's too late, though," Connor said, placing his coffee on the table. He pushed the one photo away and picked up another. The quality of the ropes was good. The knots and weave had the markings of a Dominant who knew what he was doing. "The damage is done. They just wasted over eight hours on an assumption. We all know that the first twenty-four hours are critical."

"You're right, Ortega. Which is why Terry has hired us."

They all just stared at Crest with blank faces. He shrugged. They all knew that he wouldn't take money from his best friend. Hell, half of their cases were pro-bono. The agency made their bread and butter through government contracts.

Kevin had just come back from some godforsaken place to bring back a known terrorist who was trying to seek asylum with a non-extradition country. Technically, Connor was up next in rotation for an overseas assignment, but he had a feeling he would be staying in the States.

"Crest, I know you're aware that Jax and I frequent those clubs." Connor shared another knowing look with Jax. If Crest wanted this as a team effort, there was no reason to keep information under wraps. "Marilyn wasn't just enamored with the club scene. She was also a masochist and word had it that Terry wasn't giving her what she needed. She had sought out some other Dominants."

"I know." Crest placed his cup on the table. His green eyes met each of theirs one by one. "This is personal. There will be no judgment on how they lived their lives or how we live ours. Terry is a good man and Marilyn was blameless. She didn't deserve to be carved up like a Sunday roast. I want this bastard caught and strung up by his balls. We're going to be the ones to deliver this cocksucker to the hardcore bangers in the state pen."

Connor could see the angst in Crest's eyes. His friend was in trouble and this was the only way he could help. Connor took one last look at the picture, knowing that every team member would have copies within the hour, and then slid it back into the middle of the table.

"This is how it's going to go down. Kevin, I want you to scour the streets. I want every informant you know questioned. If someone is bragging out there about killing the wife of a surgeon, we want to know who is saying what to whom. Taryn, you'll do your computer thing and bring me whatever you can find on similar attacks anywhere in the US in the past ten years. Put together a profile to screen your results on the search.

Also, I want you to get with our friend in the evidence locker at the department and ghost the hard drive in her laptop. If Marilyn met this scumbag online, I want the transcript—first to last of every contact. Connor and Jax, I want you to hit the clubs. They know you…personally. The members will be more willing to speak with you than anyone else in this room, but I want it done discreetly. No one is to know that we're looking for tracks. Work it from an undercover angle. Obviously, the person we're looking for is well versed in shibari. For those of you who don't know much about the lifestyle, I suggest you research it thoroughly. There's always a chance I might send one or all of you in covertly."

Connor and Jax remained silent. So much for their sexual preferences staying under the radar. It wasn't like they hid it, but it certainly wasn't office chatter the next morning. He and Jax had figured Crest was into the lifestyle as well, but they had yet to cross swords, so to speak. He was a private man, more so than most. Connor shifted uncomfortably as Taryn continued to stare at them with a cagey smile. What the hell was her deal?

"Connor and Jax," Crest said, garnering their attention. "In my office."

Well, that's one way to end a meeting. *Fucking great.* He wasn't in the mood to hear what Crest had to say. While he gathered the photos, Connor grabbed his cup and drained the contents. He swiped up his glasses and fought the urge to slip them back on. Instead, he hung them on the V-neck of his shirt.

Both men followed Crest out of the conference room and straight across the hallway to his office. He signaled for them to close the door, which Jax did before joining Connor in the two chairs situated in front of their boss's desk. The office was bare, basically looking like no one worked there. Crest wasn't a materialistic man by any means.

"I'll cut to the chase." Crest threw the folder on the desk. "I don't want the clubs thinking you two are there on official business. I want you to go and insinuate yourself within the community. Find out what you can. It shouldn't be too hard, considering you're there every weekend anyway. I'll amend that statement—since Jax is there every weekend. Connor, are you going to have a problem with this?"

"No," Connor said, ignoring the fact that Jax nudged his foot. "No problem at all. From my understanding, Ashley's left town. I just needed a break. Obviously, break's over."

"Jax, is this true?" Crest ran his fingers and thumb down his face. "I need the both of you to be on your A game. This case is too important to me for your personal issues to get in the way."

"Ashley left town over a month ago," Jax said, confirming what Connor already knew. "Connor will have no issues, from her at least. Some of the submissives have been asking about him anyway. It should be a smooth transition."

"Good. Start tonight." Crest reached for his phone. Connor and Jax stood and started to walk towards the door. "Keep me apprised every twenty-four hours. More often, should anything arise."

Jax opened the door and walked out first. Connor stopped, holding the door in his hand. He turned to see Gavin look up at him, the phone against his ear. The underlying grief in his eyes was evident. His eyebrow rose in question.

"I'm sorry about Marilyn, Top," Connor said, referring to Crest with the nickname associated with his retired rank. He received a nod of acknowledgement. "We'll get the guy who did this."

Connor shut the door behind him. He should have known that Jax would be waiting for him. He looked over at his best friend and really took in his appearance of jeans, a Nike sweatshirt, and black tennis shoes. Jax was wearing the same clothes he had on yesterday.

"You have room to talk, shit heel," Connor said, shaking his head. "At least I had the decency to change clothes."

"I wouldn't call those decent," Jax said, his usual gaff of laughter following. They made it to the large space off of the main reception area where Taryn and Kevin were debriefing with Ethan. The room was divided into cubicles, but they were sitting at the table which dominated the common area, adjoining the individual office spaces. Connor wouldn't have to stay for this part since his case had wrapped up. He turned to Jax, thinking of telling him that they could meet up for a bite to eat before heading to Masters tonight when Jax brought up Ashley. He'd been so close to getting out of here, too. "Seriously, are you going to have an issue tonight? They all know that Ashley left town to get married."

"I don't care what they know," Connor answered, his headache coming back in full force. He pulled his sunglasses off of his shirt. He slipped them on, instantly dimming the lights that were instigating the throbbing inside of his head. "Ashley liked the *idea* of the lifestyle, as well as the men who frequented the clubs. She wanted a wealthy prick to set her up in style, and she cashed up for a better standard of living. I should have known better. Thank God I found out who she was before I became the mark. I'll be fine tonight. It's no big deal. Meet me at the Uptown Diner at seven tonight."

"Deal. Now get some sleep, jackass." Jax flashed his Val Kilmer smile. The one the actor was known for when he'd been younger. "We've got a killer to catch."

Chapter Two

Connor and Jax walked into Masters. The familiar sound of Ravel's "Bolero" drifted from the speakers concealed above. Connor knew the Latin music was a staple for many clubs. However, this particular rendition just happened to be one of his favorites. It favored the Cuban dance so recognizable from his youth—his father's influence on his coming of age.

The entry hall was the picture of understated excellence. It was lit well enough to see the hostess and her obligatory security escort. The blonde flushed with recognition of Connor and Jax. He smirked, knowing she had fond memories of past fun and games with both of them. Jenny smiled her reception and nodded to the attendant, who buzzed them through into the club.

Dark English walnut adorned the walls. They were polished with orange-scented wood soap, practical in its ability to eliminate the brazen smell of sex and sweat. The sounds and scents of the club surrounded him with the warmth of an old friend welcoming him after a long absence, thus easing his way back into old well-worn habits. It was about damn time.

Connor took a moment to survey the room. The bar was lined up against the left wall, which was mirrored and backlit. The lighting was only slightly brighter in that area, giving the entire space a nightclub appearance. Sweeping away from the bar were sitting quarters consisting of booths and couches, screened with palms and ferns. This effect gave the illusion of secluded grottos all through the middle of the room.

On the right side, several play areas were partitioned off with black velvet rope slung between brass, antiquated poles. Interestingly, all of the public stations were in use at this early juncture in the evening. Everything seemed the same, although the crowd appeared a little heavier than he was used to. It should be a good evening to gain insight on Terry's visit here last night.

"Ortega."

Connor nodded his acknowledgement when a member walked by. He rolled his left shoulder, easing the tension out of the old injury. He felt slightly better after his previous night of binge drinking. Sleeping the majority of the day and a long, hot shower had done wonders for his physical wellbeing. A phone call checking on his father and shooting the shit had fixed his mental health. He was back on his game.

"I'll be at the bar," Connor said, feeling uneasy without his bag. He half wondered if they still kept it behind the bar in an alcove designed for just that purpose, or if it had been moved to another more permanent storage space. For a small fee, the club maintained his equipment and made sure it was clean and ready for use. He'd gotten into the habit of carrying his own implements years ago. Most of the regulars did. There was no sense in buying the club's provided fare every time you had a scene. Tonight wasn't about play, though. He and Jax had discussed the best tactics for gathering information. Jax would hit up the subs while he sat at the bar and reconnected with old acquaintances. "If I don't get anywhere, I'll head on over to Whip and meet up with you later to write up our SITREP."

The acronym from their past reminded them both why they were here. A common form of reconnaissance report was a SITREP, or situation report. With any luck, they could turn this place over and find the information they were looking for.

Jax nodded and hoisted his bag over his shoulder. He had issues leaving his implements behind for others to take care of and refused to let others touch his stuff. His blonde hair was disheveled as usual, but the women loved it. Already, two subs were heading his way. He bit down on his chewing gum with a *smack* and gave a farewell smile.

Connor shook his head and sauntered over to the bar. Instead of wearing his usual leathers this evening, he chose black jeans and a matching V-neck, long-sleeved shirt. He'd left his jacket in the Jeep, as he'd parked in the underground garage next door. Knowing he wasn't going to play, he'd worn his black boots in order to conceal carry. It wasn't his usual piece, but the P259 model Sig was much easier to obscure than his normal full frame P220. Both were chambered .45ACP loads. It would get the job done if needed. He always carried on assignment.

Taking quick note of the small crowd at the bar, he figured maybe three out of the seven would be of any help. These people only had a vague conception of what transpired between him and Ashley. It would be easy for him to convince them that he wasn't ready to top a sub just yet. He'd use the time wisely.

"Ortega, it's been a while," Russell said, polishing a tumbler with a bar towel. The bartender was young, probably in his mid-twenties. Connor knew that once he got the conversation rolling, there wasn't anything that would shut the kid up. "What can I get you?"

"Whatever's on tap tonight," Connor answered. He took a seat at the end of the bar where he could watch who came and went through the entrance. The mirror behind the bartender allowed him to discreetly observe the room. Jax was already sitting in an overstuffed leather chair with three submissives at his feet. "How've you been?"

"Good. The club's been busy, so Joel's happy."

"I bet he is," Connor answered, bringing his attention back to the bar.

Russell placed the tumbler with some others located behind him and then tossed the towel over his shoulder. Grabbing a fresh chilled beer glass from the cooler, he put it at an angle under the spigot and pulled the long ivory handle. Connor knew the two-drink limit was for those who intended to play— that included Tops as well as bottoms. Since he wasn't playing, he didn't have to worry about it.

"I'm still considering entering the service, though," Russell said. "I'm just not sure I'd make it through boot camp with a bunch of assholes yelling in my ear."

"Thanks," Connor said, accepting the beer.

Connor grabbed the handle of his mug and situated himself more comfortably on the stool. Russell wasn't cut out for the military, but he needed to figure that out on his own. He didn't have the heart for it. A man had to want to be a Marine in order to make the full thirteen weeks of initial training. Joel was always complaining that Russell was late and even after two years didn't know how to stock the bar properly.

"Military is the way to go, man," Connor replied, saying what he always said to Russell. "You can't go wrong with say, something like the Air Force."

"I hear Ashley left town," Russell said, making no qualms about meddling into things that were none of his business. He leaned his arms against the counter. "Someone mentioned she was getting married."

Connor looked at the members who were sitting at the bar, trying to ignore Russell's inquiries. He let his eyes travel over the mirror. The majority of everyone had already claimed their seats in the middle area. The Doms and Dommes that were at the bar were either getting something to drink for themselves because they were not playing or scoping the room much like himself. It was the ones who weren't playing he was most interested in.

"That's what I hear," Connor replied, turning his attention back to the bartender. One of the submissives cried out softly from the play area. "Speaking of gossip, I've been out of the scene for a while. Anything new? Any new subs?"

"Shit, man," Russell replied, standing up from the counter and using his hands to lean against the wood. "Jax didn't tell you about the murder last night? It was all over the paper this morning. Marilyn Sweeney. You remember her, right; the redhead who was married to Terry?"

"I remember her. She was murdered?"

"Yeah. Terry got popped for stabbing her to death or something. Maybe he finally got tired of her playing around on him. She shouldn't have been messing around with other Dominants."

"Damn. That's rough. I thought they had an agreement, though," Connor said, leading Russell right down the intended road. He wouldn't mention that Marilyn was wrapped in silk rope. If no one knew that yet, maybe the police hadn't leaked it to the press. He made a mental note to have Taryn scour the papers to see what evidence they had issued to the media. He drank the foam off of the top of his beer. "Didn't she used to play with Greg?"

"Greg stopped topping her a while ago."

Connor looked to his left. Kyle, who was one of the regulars, joined in on the conversation. He was looking Connor's way. Things couldn't get any better, Connor thought, letting them run the gossip mill.

"She was getting too close to the edge," Kyle said, shrugging his shoulders. "Greg's a sadist, but he stops before blood is drawn. She'd started to play over at that new club, Whip. I told that to the police earlier. They sent two detectives to ask around about Terry and Marilyn. They stopped in during newbie social hour and chased off this week's looky loos. Joel wasn't too happy."

Joel Summit was the owner of Masters. Connor had no doubt the man wasn't pleased that the local LEOs, law enforcement officers, were running off potential customers. Joel had the members' confidentiality to protect. Connor also knew police would have asked for a list of said members and had a warrant to back up their request. The sad thing about this situation was that they were using what information they gathered against Terry. Kyle's diarrhea of the mouth while talking to the police, dropping that Marilyn played with Greg and disclosing her predilection for pain only strengthened their case.

"I bet he wasn't happy," Connor said in agreement. Movement in the mirror caught his eye. He saw Beverly, one of the Dommes who frequented Masters, walk up behind him. He knew she would have been here last night and decided he wanted her in on the conversation. He kept talking, hoping she'd join in. "I just didn't figure Terry as the kind of guy who would have it in him to murder his wife. You said she was stabbed?"

"That's what the paper said, although the police didn't say much," Russell said. He gave Beverly a smile when she finally came to stand beside Connor. His eyes lit up. "What can I get you, Mistress?"

Connor picked up his beer to hide his smile. Apparently, Russell still hadn't figured out a way to kneel and take Mistress Bev's order at the same time. He'd been sniffing around her for the last year, but Bev was having none of it. Everyone here knew that he'd have to grovel first. Beverly was a bigger woman with an even larger following. All the male submissives wanted a chance to lick her thigh-high, shiny patent leather boots.

"Just a ginger ale," Beverly said, dismissing him with her eyes. She focused on Connor. "Well, if it isn't my favorite Marine boy-toy."

"How're you doing, Bev? Not finding your platoon of submissives challenging enough for you?"

"Just peachy. For the record, I'd love to draw you over to the dark side." Beverly placed her forearms on the counter and leaned a little his way. "Listen, I was real sorry to hear about Ashley. You're a good guy. You didn't deserve the crap she was shoveling."

"Ancient history," Connor said, wishing like hell the topic was more or less buried. He knew that he'd have to rehash this shit coming back here, but that didn't mean he had to like it. A quick glance in the mirror showed him the sub he'd heard earlier. She was hitting subspace and knew that he was bound to lose the crowd to her scene. "I was just asking Russell if any new subs joined the club when he told me about Marilyn Sweeny."

"It's a shame, isn't it? For two reasons really," Bev replied with a snarky smile. "First, Russell needs to keep his nose out of everyone else's business. He needs to learn his place around here and I'm of half a mind to show him exactly where that should be."

"And the second?" Connor asked, taking another long swallow of his beer.

"Because she was a very nice woman. I was just arriving as the police were wrapping up their nice little interviews. Joel told them he preferred that they wind things up by eight o'clock this evening to question people—before open play began. They didn't disclose much information, but I do know they also asked for a list of members and also the vendors that Joel uses. He didn't have a choice but to hand over the member list, but apparently the vendors weren't registered in the warrant. Joel told them to come back tomorrow with a new warrant if they wanted any more information."

"Why would they want a list of his vendors?" Kyle asked.

Connor wondered the same thing, until the unique rope from the pictures clicked in his mind. He knew it looked unusual. He bet it was made of Japanese silk and since the police thought that Terry did it, they probably figured he'd purchased the rope from a supplier at the club or online. Joel was known to have vendors come in at least once a week, not that Connor had ever attended. Was there a BDSM vendor in town that he didn't know about? The police would have already had Terry and Marilyn's home and business computers confiscated. Connor would have to remind Crest to have their contact ghost all of the seized hard drives, and not just Marilyn's. Detective Morrison already knew whether or not he'd bought the material online. Since the police were still looking for the source, that must mean they didn't find the transaction.

"They didn't say," Beverly said. She took the ginger ale that Russell had placed on the counter. She looked over her shoulder, obviously not wanting to miss what was happening in the play area. "The most popular vendor that Joel uses is Incandesce, and that's located in the warehouse district. I think the majority of the members have bought from there."

"Now that is one redhead I'd like to have kneel before me," Kyle said, turning around on his stool to witness the flogging scene.

Connor knew he'd lost all of them. Their attention had been dragged away, but he was pleased with the information he'd gathered. Maybe the killer had purchased the rope from one of the club's vendors, although more than likely, whoever it was had bought it online. Connor wondered if Jax had come up with anything.

Connor joined the crowd, twisting on his stool to watch the scene unfold. Beverly made her way back to her attentive gang of male submissives. Jax was still in his seat, with the same three subs kneeling on pillows in front of him. They met each other's gaze and Connor knew immediately that his best friend had some information. They would play the evening out and debrief one another later. Connor switched his attention to the Dom wielding the flogger.

The leather strands of the purple implement glided through the air. They rained down over the submissive's curved ass, which was a lovely shade of pink. Connor knew the duo. Flint and Shelley. She was his permanent submissive and they usually played here once a month. Shelley was bound to the St. Andrew's cross with her brown hair in a French braid, pulled over her shoulder to expose her back. He could see a glistening layer of sweat on her skin as well as the dripping moisture on her inner thighs when she gyrated her hips. Shelley was enjoying herself immensely.

"Kyle," Connor said, trying to garner the other Dom's attention. Something wasn't adding up with his previous ginger statement. "That's Shelley. She's always been a brunette, not a redhead."

"I wasn't referring to Shelley," Kyle said, not taking his attention away from the scene. "I was talking about Lauren Bailey, the owner of Incandesce. She's one hot little ginger, if you know what I mean."

Connor nodded, thinking over what he'd learned this evening. The police were just gathering evidence against Terry at this point. If Terry had purchased the type of rope used to tie up Marilyn, that was just a nail in his coffin. It was obvious from the statements that Kyle, Russell, and Bev contributed to their theory that Terry was a jealous husband who resented that his wife was playing with other men.

Tomorrow was Sunday, but Connor would make a trip to Incandesce and browse their inventory. If this Lauren Bailey was there, then the better it was for him to throw a few questions her way. They needed access to her client list, so Connor made a mental note to have Taryn hack into the store's computer system. The police would have it by tomorrow anyway. He wondered what the other team members were turning up in their search for Marilyn's murder. The twenty-four hour mark was approaching and so far, they had nothing substantial.

Chapter Three

Lauren stood with her hands on her hips, surveying the vast amount of deliveries that had arrived yesterday. It was Sunday morning and the last thing she wanted to do was unpack, categorize, and restock all of the various implements within, because the precious jewels alone would take her the rest of the day. Each cut had a pile of paperwork describing the stones' quantity, condition, and quality. Hanging her head, she recognized that she was just plain old tired. All she did was work, and lately she'd been restless and not sleeping. A visit to her sister's place in Florida was starting to look good by comparison.

The bell rang above the door in the shop and she was grateful for the distraction. Lauren had spent the last hour debating with the police in regards to giving out her client list until the warrant they'd produced had left her no ability to refuse them. A murder had taken place a couple of night ago. Due to her connection with the BDSM community, they apparently thought the murderer had purchased some items from her. She had arrived at the tipping point where her online business was enough to support her. Leaving this city was starting to sound better and better.

Walking through the makeshift curtain, Lauren scanned the shop to see a man in his mid-thirties. He was idly tracing his finger along the outline of each of the clit clamps that were lined up in a display case sitting on the glass countertop. They were her standard base models that were undecorated—a blank canvas if you will. A part of her didn't want the specialized order that he was probably here for. Knowing that was not like her at all, Lauren promised herself that she'd call her sister to say she was coming for a visit immediately following this transaction.

Something about this man's bearing drew her to step closer. He was dressed in jeans that fit his form in a way she could appreciate, accompanied by a brown bomber jacket adorned with unit patches from what appeared to be a military background. He was a good six inches taller than her five-foot-six-inch frame. His stance clearly stated he was a dominant alpha male. Taking a brief moment to shake off the previous melancholy that had settled over her, Lauren stepped around the counter and cleared her throat.

He turned his head in her direction and she lost her breath. The blue of his eyes were like the most pristine blue tourmaline stones found only in Brazil. His gaze cut through her like the razor thin blade in the machine she used to resize the stones she handled. Remembering she could never be with a man who needed so much control, she brought her hands up and closed her fingers around her watch to remind herself of why. Immediately, the inferno was extinguished and she felt more grounded.

"May I help you?" Lauren asked, grateful her voice came out smooth and didn't betray the confusion within her. She dealt with many Dominants in her business, so what was it about this man's demeanor that affected her in such a carnal manner?

"I'm just browsing."

He turned to face her full on and Lauren tightened her grip on her watch. The man's jet-black hair was closely cropped on the sides, yet long enough on top that it fell over his forehead. His skin seemed sun-kissed, but his color was obviously from his heritage. Maybe a mixture of Cuban and Caucasian? He had a square jaw, probably matching his personality, and he hadn't shaved this morning. Why that made him more sexually appealing, she didn't know. His lips were full and she finally noticed that they were moving.

"...town. I was at Masters last night and overheard them mention your store. My name's Connor Ortega. I seemed to have missed your vendor table at the club, although I'm usually there during play hours only."

Lauren just bet he was. Connor Ortega seemed to be the type of man who worked hard and played hard. The exact kind she stayed away from, although he was the precise type she would have gone for had she still been the naïve girl she once was in her early twenties. When he stepped forward and held out his hand, she had no choice but to reciprocate. Releasing her watch slowly, she slid her hand into his and ignored the way his warmth seemed to seep into her skin through the electric contact of his grip.

"Lauren Bailey." The second he released her hand, she stepped back. "Are you looking for anything in particular?"

"Not really," Connor said, although his eyes said something different. She retreated around the counter. "I'm meeting a friend for lunch and had some extra time to kill."

"Well, please look around. If I can be of any help, let me know."

Lauren gave him a strained smile and hoped it didn't show. As he went back to perusing the items in the various display cabinets, she leaned up against the stool that she always kept behind the counter pretending to look at a clipboard listing the shipment she needed to go through today. There was an underlying sensual impression that he seemed to leave in his wake. Feeling her irritation grow at the irrational emotions she was experiencing, Lauren put it down to the hectic afternoon she still had ahead of her.

The bell above the shop door rang once more. Lauren looked up to see one of the two police detectives from earlier walk through the door. A slight throbbing developed in her forehead. She watched as he gave an evaluating glance toward Connor, but continued to amble up to the counter. She had a feeling the rouge on his cheeks wasn't just due to the cold outside. His midsection had an extra layer it shouldn't and she wondered how far he'd walked to get here.

"Detective Hagen," Lauren replied, trying not to glance Connor's way to see what he was looking at. As soon as she was able to get both of these men out of her shop, she'd close early and head back to her apartment. "Was there something else you needed? I gave you my client list as you compelled me to do."

"We appreciate your cooperation." Detective Hagen lowered his voice as he leaned closer to the counter. It was obvious that he didn't want Connor to hear what he was saying. "Do you still keep track of those orders by client name, even if they pay cash? The items you sell seem very specialized."

"Not always," Lauren replied honestly. She'd already answered their questions regarding Terry Sweeney. He wasn't a client of hers, although the wife had purchased a few things on her own. Her death was a tragedy and she hoped that if the husband did do it, that he paid dearly for his crime. In her experience, most predators escaped their sentence. "If a customer comes into the store and buys an item that I have in stock, then I ring up the purchase as is. I went over this with you earlier, Detective."

"And you're positive that Terry Sweeney was not one of those cash purchases?" Detective Hagen reached into his suit jacket and pulled out a long piece of paper. "Do you have a security camera installed here?"

"Yes, but only on a twenty-four hour loop," Lauren answered. Now she understood why he'd come back. She was betting that the detective had put in for a warrant, but what she was about to say was going to disappoint him. "The majority of my business is through the local clubs and online. My actual store hours are so minimal that it doesn't require me to have a more thorough security system. The camera you see in the corner was installed by the previous owner. It's not going to have what you're looking for in its recently recorded memory."

"What about your inventory? Where is that kept?"

"Half here and half at my residence," Lauren answered, noticing that Connor had made his way over to the restraints. Her stomach twisted. "If I need to cut stones, I have to do that here. I have a one-micron particulate ventilation system in back that takes out the fine particles in the air. If I have easier projects that I can do by hand, I tend to do those at my apartment. And before you ask, the answer is no. There is nothing missing in my inventory. If you could be more specific about what you're looking for, I might be able to assist you more than I have. Maybe there are some types of jewels or implements that you have an interest in?"

"I see that you're closed tomorrow. Is there a number I can reach you at? I'll need you to look at some photos and help identify specific items as yours or possibly a competitor's."

"Let me write down my cell phone number," Lauren said, grabbing a scrap piece of paper underneath the counter. Snatching up a pen next to the register, she scribbled her information. "If it's something I made, I'll know instantly by looking at it."

"I'll be in touch, Ms. Bailey," Detective Hagen said, turning on his heel and walking out.

Silence seemed to descend over the small shop. Lauren clicked the pen a few times before realizing it echoed through the air. She couldn't explain why she felt so apprehensive with Connor Ortega, but knew she didn't like it. Today was just one of those days. If she didn't spend so little time here, she would have had a sound system installed for at least some background music.

"I heard what happened to Marilyn Sweeney," Connor said, startling her. He turned and walked to the counter. A pair of silver, white fur-lined cuffs that she'd decorated with emerald accents was in his hands. Why did those cuffs suddenly look so small? "All the members of Masters could talk about last night was her murder. I still can't get over that they think Terry murdered her. From what I saw between them in the past, they had certain arrangements within their relationship that allowed her to play with others. I'm sure with the business you're in, that you knew them both."

"It's hard for me to believe, too," Lauren replied. She was glad to have something to talk about instead of thinking about what his hands could do with those cuffs. Did that make her a bad person to want to talk about a murder instead of the sexual feelings he was stirring within her? "I met Terry at a few of my vendor shows at Joel's club, but he never bought anything. He seemed nice enough, but for the police to have arrested him there had to be evidence, right?"

Connor shrugged and held up the cuffs. "So what exactly is it that you do? I was under the impression that you sold rope and other items."

"I take hand-crafted implements from some of the well-known high-end suppliers and add an elegant touch," Lauren explained. She held out her hands for the cuffs. She was grateful when he dropped them in her hands without touching her. "See these emerald accents? There are matching ankle cuffs, as well as a collar with larger stones. These are silver. I can produce them in white gold and yellow gold with various size settings for larger cut jewels. I also provide them in animal friendly versions, as well as any specific fur you desire. Some of my wealthier clients ask that nipple clamps and a clit clamp be assembled with the same jewels to complement the look. If you'd like to give your submissive a gift, I take special orders."

"I don't currently have a sub," Connor responded, his blue eyes zeroing in on hers. She resisted the urge to swallow and looked back down at the cuffs in her hand. She laid them gently on the counter and then crossed her arms over her disobedient nipples. Why had she even mentioned him having a submissive? "I assume you live the lifestyle?"

"No." Lauren gave her standard answer with a small smile. She was used to people judging her. "I don't actually. The lifestyle really isn't for me. I'm just a businesswoman who saw an opportunity to sell my art. It just happened to be alternative toys, collars, and implements."

"Really?"

Her smile slipped as Connor's tone indicated that he didn't quite believe her. Lauren pushed off of the stool in what she hoped didn't come across as her being rattled. She didn't like the feeling of intrusion—it was as if he was reading her like a book. She ignored his implied question, and walked over to the large display case she had set up on the left side of the store. This conversation needed to be switched back to business.

"These are some of the clamps that I've attached to chains," Lauren said. She was grateful that her voice remained steady. She motioned over the glass with her hand at the variety of specialized items. She stood looking down at one of her favorite pieces. A clit clamp adorned with chocolate diamonds that were attached with white gold Figaro links to two matching nipple clamps. Different sized chocolate diamonds were situated in settings artfully spaced along each chain's length. Her nipples throbbed just thinking on how they would feel pinched between the pads. It was something that she would never allow herself to experience. She really needed Connor to leave. "As you can see, depending on the jewels, I have interwoven them between the lengths of chain. I have some brochures that you can take with you, should you decide to order something in the future."

"So you don't sell rope?" Connor asked, stepping beside her to look down inside the case.

"Uh, no," Lauren replied, wishing that he'd stayed where he was. She could actually feel his heat assaulting her body. It made her realize that she'd been keeping too much to herself lately. She'd look at her orders this evening and free up some time in order to go and visit her sister. Feeling better, she turned her head and met his gaze. "No rope. I know of some good websites if you're interested in a specific silk."

"No, thank you. I appreciate you taking the time to show me some of your inventory," Connor replied, the side of his mouth lifting up in a smile. She maintained eye contact, refusing to look down. "I better head out if I'm going to meet my friend on time."

"Have a good day," Lauren said, envious of the woman he was going to meet. Hell, she was envious of all the women in the lifestyle. What she would give to be able to relinquish all control. She was such an anachronism. The ache in her chest arrived that always accompanied this familiar time-traveling experience. She caught herself rubbing her wrist in remembrance and dropped her hands, as if to rid herself of a bad dream. "Enjoy the rest of your weekend."

"So why are we here and not grabbing something to eat?"

"I left a copy of those photos here," Connor answered Jax while pushing the doors open to the office. Someone was here, for the door had been unlocked and the lights were on. "Order us in some pizza. I think we're going to be here for a while."

Walking into the open area where the cubicles were, Connor spotted Taryn at her desk. Her glasses were perched on the end of her nose and her fingers were flying across the ever-present keyboard. Her staple coffee mug was in place and he knew that she'd been here a while.

"Ortega, the client list of Incandesce is on your desk," Taryn said, not taking her eyes off of the monitor in front of her. "Marilyn is listed, but not Terry."

"Thanks, squid," Connor said, using the nickname that they'd given her because of her past years in the Navy. He shrugged out of his jacket and walked around to his side of the cubicle. Throwing it on his desk, he ignored the list Taryn had left for him and opted for the folder containing the crime scene photos. Looking at the first one, the angle was wrong for what he needed. He went through three more before finding what he knew would be there. "Jax, look at this."

"Is that—"

"The police weren't trying to locate where the rope was purchased," Connor said, standing up and walking down the hallway. "They're trying to locate who customized the clit clamp to include the rubies. And that could only mean one thing."

Connor strolled to Crest's office, having no doubt that he'd be there. The door was ajar and he rapped a couple times before pushing it open. He was surprised to find Jessie standing a few feet away from the desk with her arms crossed in annoyance. It was obvious that he'd interrupted something from the tension in the air, but before he could apologize and back out, Crest waved him in. Shit, was that sexual tension?

"Connor, what have you got for me?"

Connor was still looking at Jessie. He didn't miss the hurt that flashed in her eyes or the way she straightened her back before walking toward the door. He'd previously suspected that she had a thing for Crest, but now he was sure of it. She was the youngest member of their team by at least a year and cute, with long brown hair that had a natural wave and stunning green eyes. The color reminded him of Lauren Bailey's eyes. This kid was way out of her league with Crest, though, as far as worldly experience was concerned.

"Hello, Connor," Jessie said, her smile strained. "Before you leave, I have the supplemental contact reports that the detectives filed this morning. Marilyn Sweeney wasn't raped."

"Thanks, Jessie," Connor replied in a supportive tone. He waited until she left before crossing the floor and taking a seat in one of the guest chairs. "You realize that girl has the hots for you and you give her nothing but grief."

"She's young enough to be my daughter," Crest replied, waving a hand in dismissal. "What have you got, Cupid?"

"There's a vendor that customizes high-end bejeweled implements and toys for the BDSM community." Connor leaned forward and let the photo slide across the desk. "Look closely at the picture and you'll see it. Because it's such a specialized item, the police are trying to tie Terry with the purchase. Can you have one of your contacts get a better picture?"

While Crest studied the picture, Connor couldn't help but let his thoughts go back to Lauren Bailey. He hadn't expected her to be so stunning. She wasn't normally the type of woman he'd go for, but there was something intriguing about the way she carried herself. Her hair was long with vivacious curls alit with a corporeal shade of fire red. Her green eyes were stunning and reminded him of those same emeralds she'd fastened to the silver clad, white leather and fur-lined cuffs he'd liked. There was underlying distrust between them that he'd love to be able to extinguish with his favorite flogger and the application of some quality time in his bedroom. Maybe she was exactly what he needed to rid himself of the bitter taste that Ashley had left behind these past weeks.

"I'll have a closer photo for you within the hour," Crest said, handing the picture back. "When you were attending the clubs regularly, how often did you go?"

"Usually Saturday nights," Connor answered, flicking the pic against his knee. "On rare occasion, a Friday night would be within my MO. I haven't been by Whip in a long time, so I'll stop in there next Friday. It's only been open for less than a year. If I'm seen there during the week, that'll put up red flags.

I heard last night that Marilyn had started to play over there more often."

"Terry mentioned it," Crest said, looking up from the picture.

"Do me a favor, and ask Terry if he knew of any friendships she may have cultivated there. Maybe Jax knows some of the women she might have passed the time with. Also, who did she play with that knew shibari? That design was rather intricate, so whoever it was was well versed. Jax said he was checking that angle."

"I'll talk to him today," Crest promised. "Jax play during the week?"

"Like a tomcat on the prowl."

"You work the vendor angle and anything else that comes your way throughout the week." Crest ran a hand through his hair and sat back. "Jax can continue to gather information while he's at the clubs and see what Doms are privy to shibari."

"Has Terry made bail yet?"

Crest shook his head. "He's scheduled to appear in court tomorrow morning. I was able to pull in some favors. Lou Moser will be representing him."

"He'll make bail then," Connor replied confidently. Moser was one of the best criminal defense attorneys in the state. Leave it to Crest to be able to get the man to drop everything for a friend. Connor wondered what long ago favor he was cashing in. "How's Terry holding up?"

"About as good as can be expected," Crest said, crossing his arms. Connor swore he heard the starch scratch as he crossed his arms. "Marilyn's parents arrived in town last night."

"Let me guess—they're out for blood."

"Believe it or not, they stopped by the county jail and offered their support." Crest leaned back in his chair. "They don't believe he did it either."

"He must have had a damn good relationship with them." Connor shook his head in disbelief. In his experience, even family members turned on the suspect. "What about his family?"

"I spoke with Terry's father last night. He's driving down today and should arrive in plenty of time for the bail hearing."

Connor knew enough about Crest's background to know that he'd grown up in northern Minnesota, near the Iron Range. While Crest had joined the service, Terry had stayed in his hometown and married young. They'd maintained their friendship. That was the extent of his knowledge and with Crest so private about his personal life, he was fairly sure that was all he was going to learn without a damn good reason.

"I'm going to go look at those criminal reports that Jessie put on my desk," Connor said, standing up. "I'll work the vendor angle and keep you posted. Jax picked up something interesting last night as well. The Dom that Marilyn had been playing with a few months ago? His name is Greg Winters. Turns out, no one has spoken with him for a couple weeks— not even the sub that he's been topping regularly. I'll track him down and see if I can't find out more information."

"Good. Anything else?"

"I had Taryn check out what the police released to the press," Connor said. "I thought maybe they kept the shibari thing under wraps, but that isn't the case. At least, not necessarily. The media leaked she'd been tied up, making the public think it was strictly bondage. We can use that to our advantage. Jax has quietly been checking out the Doms and Dommes who practice it regularly."

"Keep me posted. Stick around for an hour though." Crest uncrossed his arms and reached for his phone. "I'll have those photos delivered."

Connor nodded his agreement and walked back to his desk. Taryn's fingers were still flying over her keyboard, while Jax had the phone glued to his ear. Ethan and Kevin were absent. Scanning his desk, he saw the folder that Jessie had promised would be there. Sitting down, he knew that he should be concentrating on the case, but images of a certain fair-skinned ginger kept flashing through his mind. He was thinking a visit was called for, sooner rather than later. After all, they both had to eat dinner and there was nothing to say he couldn't mix a little business with potential pleasure.

Chapter Four

Lauren poured herself a glass of red wine, intending to use Wednesday evening to finally put the finishing touches on a collar that was due at the end of the week. The client was a regular, and from her understanding was giving this particular gift to his submissive at their collaring ceremony. She'd already punched the intricate pattern of holes into the thin white strip of leather. All she needed to do now was fasten the settings and insert the sapphires she'd already cut to size. Absorbed completely in her work, she left the kitchen intending to retrieve some tools from the spare bedroom where her extra machines were kept. When the doorbell rang, she stumbled mid-stride and wondered when she'd get some damn peace so she could work.

"Shit," Lauren muttered underneath her breath. Her wine sloshed over the rim and she watched as the droplets landed on her carpet. "Great…just what I needed right now."

Quickly closing the distance to the island that separated her living room from the kitchen, she carefully set the wine glass on the counter and snagged a few paper towels. Leaning down, she blotted the tiny stains as best she could. She made a mental note to mix baking soda and hydrogen peroxide to place over the stains before bed. The doorbell rang again.

"Just a minute, please," Lauren called out.

It was either Betty Finch from next door wanting to borrow more sugar or it was the police. She was kind of hoping for the detectives, because Ms. Finch could talk for hours without saying anything. Standing, she tossed the towels into the sink and made her way to the door. Swinging it open revealed the last person on earth Lauren would ever have expected to be in the hallway. It was also the man whom she'd had trouble erasing from her mind for most of the afternoon. Work had been the only cure. She found herself having difficulty forming complete thoughts without stumbling across another question in her mind. What was he doing here and how had he known where she lived?

"I hope you haven't eaten," Connor said, flashing a smile. He'd shaved, revealing a masculine jawline.

"I—" Lauren caught herself before she answered. Did she want to have dinner with him...a self-proclaimed Dominant who was currently without a submissive? Plus, it made her wary that he personally came by her apartment without calling first. She finagled her way around the question. "How did you know where I live?"

"Perks of the job," Connor replied. He shoved his hands in his jacket and gave her a pointed look. "I'm a private investigator, but I promise I didn't do a background check on you. At least not yet. I had actually tried to make it back to your shop on Sunday, but work got in the way. I was hoping you'd have dinner with me."

"I don't think that's such a good idea," Lauren said with a small smile. She tightened her fingers on the doorknob. She couldn't bring herself to release it. "Like I said, I'm not into the whole tie me up and spank me thing."

Lauren heard the faint sound of a deadbolt being released. She closed her eyes and knew that Ms. Finch was about to perform her signature move of pulling her door open with her chain attached to see who was talking to whom in the hallway. Lauren could either invite him in to avoid the after-action interrogation or leave him out there to fend for himself. Unsure of how she would answer the older woman should she question who he was, Lauren made a hasty decision.

"Would you like to come in?" Lauren asked, taking a quick step back.

"I'd like that," Connor replied, his gaze fleeting sideways as Ms. Finch's door started to open. She breathed a sigh of relief when he crossed the threshold. Lauren closed the door quickly, dismissing the sliver of guilt at knowing that Ms. Finch was now left wondering who'd been at her door. "I'd like to ask you a few questions, if you don't mind."

That grabbed Lauren's attention. She spun around and faced him. Why did her apartment suddenly seem smaller? He took his time looking around her place before turning to face her. It didn't take her that long to realize he'd only asked her out to dinner as an excuse. He'd said he was a private investigator and now he wanted to ask her questions. That took care of her initial problem of turning him down for dinner.

"About?"

"Marilyn Sweeney."

"Of course," Lauren said, throwing her hands up. How could she have been so blind?

"It's my understanding that you sold her a few pieces from your shop—a plug in which you decorated the base with rubies, along with matching nipple and clit clamps. Did she happen to mention for whom she purchased them?"

"The police came by here yesterday with pictures already. Why didn't you say something last weekend? I didn't realize that you were investigating her murder."

"I'm really not at liberty to say much," Connor said with a bit of mirth, as if knowing she would almost explode with curiosity. "If you don't want to answer my questions, I understand. It would help with my investigation though and any insight into your conversations with Marilyn would be greatly appreciated."

"You didn't have to pretend to be interested in me for that," Lauren reiterated, not sure how she felt about being misled. Why it should matter when she'd already turned him down, she didn't know. Maybe it was the principle of the thing. Walking around him, she crossed the room to grab her wine. A little alcohol might be the fortitude she needed. "I'll tell you the same thing I told the police. Joel sometimes lets me stop in during social hour to display my work. Marilyn was there a couple of months ago and said she wanted to surprise her husband with a collar. We discussed the different types of jewels and she specifically wanted rubies, saying that her husband liked the color."

"It's usually the other way around, though. It's highly unusual for a sub to buy her own collar. Did she say why *she* was purchasing it and not Terry?"

Connor took a few steps her way. Lauren could see that this wasn't going to be a one or two question and answer conversation, so she turned and walked to the small kitchen table that she'd bought at Ikea. It wasn't expensive furniture, but it definitely fit her personality. She set her glass down and took a seat.

"She mentioned that it was her way of making things up to him." Connor's blue eyes seemed to take in everything and as they landed on her wrist, she realized that she'd wrapped her right hand around it. Immediately releasing her hold, she placed her fingers on the stem of the glass and started to twirl it. "I didn't pry. That was basically the sum of the conversation."

Connor closed the distance and pulled out a chair. Lauren knew immediately that sitting down had been a bad idea. He'd chosen the seat next to her, although he'd pulled it out so that he would be directly facing her. As he made himself comfortable, she shifted her knees so that they wouldn't touch. It also dawned on her that the heat in her apartment was set a little too high. She'd have to fix that.

"How long ago did she pick up her order?"

"Winter months are always my busiest and she'd placed her order a month and a half before Christmas. As you said, the plug, clamps and collar." Lauren couldn't help but lower her gaze to his chest. Connor's brown leather jacket was open, revealing a black cotton shirt that had a V-neck collar. His neck was weathered from many hours exposed to the elements and his chest had just a hint of coarse black hair. "Um, she picked it up around two weeks ago. Right before the holiday."

"In the store?" Connor rested his arm on the table, snagging her gaze. His hands were large, with long, thick fingers. Images of him wielding a flogger came to mind, making her a little breathless. Lauren picked up her glass and took a healthy drink. She was too old to react like some schoolgirl. Thirty was right around the corner. "Did she elaborate then?"

"No," Lauren replied, shaking her head. The movement wasn't only in response, but more of a way to clear the wicked thoughts that were entering her head. "We exchanged pleasantries; she paid with a credit card and then left. That was the last I heard from her. The police were here yesterday with the same questions. Are you working for her husband?"

"I can't disclose who I work for," Connor said with a small smile. She noticed that he'd nicked his chin shaving and for some reason, the sight captivated her. Lauren finished her wine and then realized that she hadn't offered him any. "I would appreciate it if you wouldn't say anything to anyone about my inquiries."

"If it helps convict whoever murdered her, then I'm glad I could help."

Lauren pushed her chair out and stood. In a way, she was grateful for the work she still had to do this evening. It would keep her mind busy and not on things that weren't good for her mental wellbeing. An image of Rick Hastlen, the accountant in apartment 310 sprang to mind. He seemed upstanding, although his thinning hair wasn't all that attractive. Maybe she should take him up on his offer for a movie.

"Lauren," Connor said softly as he gradually unraveled his tall form from the chair. The action brought him closer than she would have thought and she had to tilt her face to look at him. "I could have easily stopped by your shop to ask you these questions. I waited for this evening because I really would like to take you to dinner."

The genuine look on his face convinced her he was telling her the truth, but it didn't change anything. Connor Ortega was exactly the type of man she didn't want to be with. Lauren went to touch her wrist when he beat her to it. The warmth of his skin burned into hers. He had a sensual aura about him that one could only be born with. Unfortunately, she wasn't the woman for him to use it on.

"I can't," Lauren replied, her voice barely a whisper. She cleared her throat and forced herself to step away. She was grateful that he let his fingers slide off of her wrist. Turning, she quickly walked to the door. "I wish you luck in your investigation. I'm sorry you wasted your time."

✧ ✧ ✧ ✧

Connor felt like he was watching a wary feline making her way to safety. It was obvious she was a strong-willed, business-savvy woman who was used to being independent. It was what was underneath the mask that he was interested in.

Lauren had used some sort of clip to keep her hair up and away from her face. Her curls ran amok and seemed to rain down around head. He couldn't help but watch the way the cream denim hugged her ass as she walked across the floor. The rich green of her silk buttoned-down shirt brought out the deep auburn color of her hair and made him want to remove the clip. The nervous gesture that she did with her wrist didn't escape his notice either. Why did he make her so apprehensive?

"Are you seeing someone?" Connor asked, not moving from his spot in the kitchen. He needed to know why she was turning him down. His chest tightened as he awaited her answer. "I apologize if I've overstepped."

"No," Lauren replied, but immediately bit her lip. He fought back a smile as she realized her mistake and welcomed the relief he felt over her response. This meant there was no reason she couldn't spend time with him. They were close in age, so what was her hang-up? "I just…don't think it would be a good idea. I'm not looking for anything permanent right now."

"Then we're on the same page. I'm not looking for any-thing along those lines either." Connor reached into the pocket of his jacket and pulled out his phone. He held it up for her to see. "If you'd rather eat in, I know a great Chinese restaurant that delivers. I think I asked you this before, but have you already eaten?"

"No, I haven't."

Again, Connor got the feeling that she recognized her answer wasn't what she should have conveyed. Did she know that her beautiful face telegraphed every emotion she was feeling? Her irritation was making itself known, but Connor felt not the slightest bit guilty for leading her to where he wanted this to go.

"Mr. Ortega, you've asked your questions and I've answered them. There's really no need to take this further."

"Lauren, it's just dinner." The more times she turned him down, the more he wanted this meal to take place. She made him want to know more about her. "And please call me Connor. Mr. Ortega is my father."

Lauren's green eyes seemed to come to life and deepen in color. She left the safe haven of what could have been his exit and marched herself into the middle of the room. At least her short-tempered reaction got her to release her wrist and confirmed the old adage he'd always heard about redheads regarding their quick temper. He had to wonder about the other saying involving sexual fire.

"Can we just face facts? Your looks alone could pay your way into any club, while I will never be able to fit into a size two. You play at the clubs and I don't. You're a Dom and I'm as vanilla as it gets. So why are we even standing here talking about this? I have work to do, as I'm sure you do as well."

"For the record, I always pay my way."

Connor could tell his injection of humor didn't go over well, but it was his way of bringing a little sanity back into his head. What he really wanted to do was close the distance between them and demonstrate to her that the chemistry between them deserved to be explored. Those red lips of hers weren't that color because of the wine she drank. They were naturally that shade and he wanted nothing more than to claim them as his.

"You know what I mean," Lauren said, the frustration she clearly felt causing her voice to rise.

Ashley's behavior had set him back, but thankfully reminded him why he wasn't cut out for anything serious. Lauren was standing in front of him saying she wasn't looking for anything complicated, but pushing her now wouldn't get her to see what they had in common. Being in the military had taught him patience that he'd never had in his younger days. Glancing down at the table, he saw a pad and pen. Picking them up, he scribbled down his information. Ripping off the top sheet, he threw the rest back down.

"Let's get your facts straight," Connor said, slowly crossing the room to where she now stood. He waited to continue until he was directly in front of her, looking down into her sea green eyes. Did she actually think she wasn't pretty? "First and foremost, regardless of me being a Dominant, I am capable of being a gentleman while sharing a dinner with a beautiful woman. The two are not mutually exclusive. Second, you *are* a beautiful woman. You're assuming I like overly thin women. I'll have you know, there's nothing more sensual than a woman's curves. Third, I suggested dining in on Chinese food—not tying you down to the dining room table."

Connor reached down and gently took her hand, which was now rolled into a tight fist. He wasn't surprised to find her pale skin as soft as her silk blouse, but what did cause him to pause were the rough calluses on the ends of her fingers. He assumed it had to do with her working with her hands, but would save that question for another time. As if handling fine china, he pulled back each of her fingers until he was able to place the piece of paper within her palm. Brushing them closed once more, he lifted the back of her hand to his lips and softly kissed her knuckles.

"When you change your mind, call me," Connor said, lowering his voice. "And let me reiterate that my wanting to enjoy your company has nothing to do with my investigation. Goodnight, Red."

Connor walked to the door without looking back. He had every confidence that she would be in touch. He couldn't put his finger on it, but there was something in Lauren's eyes that articulated her desire. Something was holding her back, but with a little incentive he was hoping she'd contact him. Hearing her say she wasn't looking for anything permanent was just icing on the cake.

Connor closed the door softly behind him. He stood in the hallway, waiting until he heard her latch the lock and swing the deadbolt home. It hadn't left his mind that there was still a killer out there and they had yet to figure out a motive. It didn't escape his notice that Lauren had ushered him into her apartment before whoever was in apartment 321 opened his or her door. What Lauren didn't know was that he got a look at the elderly woman with the curious stare. He walked down the hallway, knowing full well that the old biddy got a good look at him through her peephole. Connor winked as he strolled past. What he would give to be a fly on the wall for that conversation.

Chapter Five

Connor couldn't help but think the collar and clamps were significant. He'd been at his desk for well over two hours going through the evidence that he'd been provided. The detectives on the case were confident that Terry Sweeney murdered his wife, but having spoken to him personally, Connor was in full agreement with Crest. Terry didn't do it. Connor was glad he'd made bail, although it seemed almost as if Terry had gone into hiding. Connor wondered how much of that was his own idea and how much of it was Crest's.

"Are you heading over to Masters tonight?"

Connor looked up from the mess that now occupied his desk. It didn't compare to how Kevin looked. Wearing a ratty old white T-shirt that was frayed around the edges, along with jeans that had weathered a storm or two, he was relatively sure that Kevin was heading out for a long night on the streets.

"Jax is heading over there in around an hour," Connor replied, leaning back in his chair. "I've decided to see if I can make any headway at Whip. One of the members at Masters mentioned that Marilyn had started playing over there."

"That's a rough crowd, isn't it?" Kevin leaned against the cubicle wall and Connor waited for it to snap. Kevin was pure bulk and had the biceps to prove it. "Was she that much of a masochist?"

"Some submissives thrive on pain," Connor answered, lifting his legs and placing his feet on his desk. "If Crest sends you into the clubs, talk to me or Jax before you put in for your membership. Whip isn't rough, it's just different. We'll go over the general dos and don'ts, as well as give you a crash course in wielding some of the implements. God help us if you hurt someone."

"Do you guys have a minute?" Taryn said, taking her ear buds out and rolling her chair backwards.

"Sure."

"I just got off the phone with Crest. I gave him my SITREP. There were no other murders similar to what transpired to Marilyn—at least unsolved. A couple of years ago, a husband in California got carried away with some knife play and his wife bled to death when he nicked something vital."

"So that takes us back to square one," Connor said, linking his fingers behind his head.

"It's personal," Kevin said. "Either the person did it to get revenge on Terry for some indiscretion, or it was an intimate attack on Marilyn."

"Stabbing is a very up close and personal way to kill some-one," Connor agreed. "I keep coming back to the same question. Terry said the collar and clamps were special to them and that she never wore them to the club. Why did she have them on? Jax's visit to Whip indicated Marilyn had stopped there earlier that evening, and at the time hadn't been wearing her personal jewelry. Did the killer put them on her? Did he know that they meant something special to the couple? And he would have had to know that Terry wasn't due home until late. The only way the suspect would have known that was if Terry or Marilyn told him."

"You're assuming the killer is a him." Kevin shrugged. "I've been doing some research on the BDSM lifestyle and I've got to say, those Dommes are just as capable as the Doms."

"Don't confuse capability with talent," Connor said with a smile. Taryn rolled her eyes and then stuck her ear buds back in. His grin faded as he thought over what Kevin said. "I haven't discounted that a woman might have completed the act, but my gut is telling me something different."

"Did Marilyn play with Dommes?" Kevin asked. "I spoke with Terry and Crest earlier, and to tell you the truth, I think there was a lot about Marilyn he didn't want to know."

"All marriages have their secrets." Connor looked up at the clock and knew he'd better be heading out. It was already ten o'clock at night. The clubs would be getting busy. "I know this Dom who stopped playing at Masters because Joel has a *no bodily fluid* rule. He's well versed in shibari and since it's not an easy art to learn, thought I'd concentrate on Whip tonight."

"Whip allows exchange of bodily fluids?"

"There isn't a lot that Whip doesn't allow," Connor said, dropping his feet to the ground. "It's a newer club and I've only been there a handful of times. Let's just say it's not my style."

"What *is* your style, Ortega?" Taryn asked, looking over their way. Her music obviously wasn't turned up too loud. She smiled, taunting him like the little sister he never had.

Connor felt his phone vibrate. Shifting in his seat, he reached into his front pocket and pulled out his cell. Jax's name was displayed on the screen. He swiped the bar and placed the phone to his ear. Sounds of passing cars and honking horns could be heard.

"What have you got?"

"I overheard that your pretty little vendor lady was taken to the hospital a few hours ago," Jax said.

Connor had to have heard wrong. He sat up and dropped his feet, catching sounds of muffling. He figured Jax was walking to a place where he could talk a little more privately.

"Joel had her scheduled to come in earlier tonight during social hour to display some of her stuff. She called to cancel."

"Is she all right?" Connor asked, already coming out of his chair and walking toward the door.

"Joel mentioned that she sounded fine." Jax lowered his voice. "She was mugged packing her inventory into her van. I don't think it was a coincidence, not with evidence that's pointing toward the significance of the collar and clamps."

"I'm on my way."

Connor hit the door with his fist, throwing it open as he exited the office. He'd waited for Lauren to call him, hoping she'd eventually take him up on his offer for dinner. The call never came. That didn't extinguish the magnetism that he felt every time he thought about her. The way Lauren subconsciously circled her wrist with her fingers made him want to be the one who did that—to restrain her wrist and control her movement for just that exact moment when they exchanged glances. First, Connor had to make sure that she was safe.

Lauren signed her release papers and cringed at the twinge of pain in her stiff wrist, not to mention how awful her signature appeared. It couldn't be helped. Her hands were still trembling, as well as every other part of her body. She didn't consider herself a weak woman, but those few seconds when she thought she'd end up dead scared the shit out of her.

"Sir, wait." Lauren lifted her head upon hearing the nurse's tone coming from outside of the curtain. The emergency room was busy for a Friday night, but the staff still ran a rather tight ship. Maybe it was the police coming back to ask more questions. "You aren't allowed back—"

The curtain was yanked aside, revealing Connor Ortega. His presence never failed to leave her breathless. No man had the right to look like him. His blue eyes zeroed in on her and she instinctively wrapped her fingers around her wrist. *Ouch.* The action brought her out of her reverie for two reasons. One, it helped stabilize her feelings and two, her wrist hurt like hell.

"Connor? Why are you here?"

"Do you want this gentleman removed?"

Lauren glanced at the nurse holding her discharge papers. A frown marred the woman's haggard face. She hadn't been the most pleasant. After Lauren had discovered she was closing in on the end of a twelve-hour shift, she didn't blame the nurse for her fatigued attitude.

"No, she knows me." Connor stepped into the room. Lauren prevented herself from looking for something to throw. This back and forth between them only further fueled her irritation. She didn't need more bullshit right now. What she needed was for him to go back where he came from. He'd somehow upset the balance of her daily routine and she needed it back desperately. "Where are the police?"

"They left. Connor, how did you know I was even injured?" Lauren asked, still wondering what he was doing here.

"Left?" Connor turned to address the nurse and Lauren felt her irritation with him return. It had only been two days, but he seemed to have a gift when it came to raising her ire as well as her…maybe she had hit her head a little too hard. "Is she being released?"

"Yes."

The nurse ripped off the top sheet of her clipboard and pushed the paper into his chest in what could only be an act of dismissal. Nurse Broomhilda actually smiled as she paused before launching into what seemed like a drill sergeant impression. Lauren would have thrown her hands up in disgust if she thought she could handle any more pain.

"I'm glad to know that she won't be alone this evening. She hit her head pretty hard against the cement. We tried to get her to stay the night for observation, but she insisted she'd be fine. I can see where she learned that trick. Here are her discharge papers. It wouldn't hurt to wake her every couple of hours. No sex, buddy boy. Got that? She should eat light and there is to be no alcohol consumption. The rest of the directives are included on the discharge order and she should make a follow-up appointment with her doctor. See that she does that."

"Thank you, *Sergeant*." Connor returned her smile. Lauren resisted the urge to roll her eyes, knowing all too well it would only make her headache worse. "I'll see to it that she follows orders."

Lauren's heart skipped a beat at the double meaning of his words, but chose to ignore it. There was no way in hell he was coming home with her. She'd resisted calling him for two days and would continue to do so, for both their sakes. In her experience, as well as by observing customers on a daily basis, a true Dom didn't date vanilla girls like her. She turned and picked up her purse out of the chair, realizing that her hands were still trembling from the attack. Connor's presence didn't help anything at all.

"What happened?"

Lauren slowly faced him, and only then noticed the nurse had left. It was now only the two of them in the tiny emergency room area. Still not understanding why Connor was even here, she pulled the strap of her bag over her shoulder with every intention of leaving. Lauren couldn't help but wince when her wrist started to ache from the movement. It wasn't her issue that the nurse misunderstood why he was here. Bottom line, her mugging had nothing to do with him.

She was surprised when Connor stepped forward, crowding her space. What shocked her even more was when he laid down the papers he'd been given and gently took her hand, exposing her wounded wrist.

"Lauren, I asked you what happened."

A feeling of utter provocation overcame her at the sound of his voice and she found that she needed to get away from him before he changed her mind and she took him up on what he offered. If he would just stop coming around her, Lauren knew she wouldn't have a problem with ignoring these overwhelming feelings of longing that he stirred within her. She tried to pull back her hand, hoping that he would release it. She should have known better.

"I was mugged," Lauren said rapidly, hoping the faster she spoke, the sooner she could leave. She continued to stare down at their hands as his fingers encircled her wounded wrist, not wanting to look into his bright blue eyes and get sucked in. Her emotions were unstable and she didn't want to do anything stupid. "Someone must have heard me scream and called the police. Within moments of the guy attacking me, I heard sirens. He ran off. They called for an ambulance. End of story. Can you please move?"

"Look at me."

That was the last thing she wanted to do. Before Lauren even lifted her gaze, she felt tears sting her eyes and berated herself for it. She didn't want him to think she was some weak woman who couldn't handle herself in a crisis. And that annoyed her even more. Why should she care what he thought anyway? Unable to prevent herself from following his command, Lauren connected her eyes with his and saw his immediate sympathy. His warm grip seemed to stop time in her small world. She could only barely perceive that around her the planet continued to spin as they were trapped in this moment. Why did he care? That was all it took for a tear to escape.

"You're fine," Connor murmured, gathering her up in his arms. Lauren couldn't suppress the sob that escaped her chest. His warmth enveloped her and though she knew the safety she felt was illusory, that didn't stop her from relishing in his embrace. "I've got you, Red."

Chapter Six

Lauren didn't do the damsel in distress well. She was fully capable of taking care of herself, and after her mini breakdown at the hospital, she tried to fully convey that to Connor. He wasn't having any of it, and within the hour she was back at her place and tucked into bed questioning how that had happened. She had taken the time to change into her favorite pair of pajama pants and tank top. As she passed her full-length mirror, Lauren realized her new attire gave him a better view of her breasts, but she currently had the covers tucked underneath her arms. He didn't need to know that her nipples had hardened into pebbles as he walked into the room. His presence affected her physically and she wished she could blame it on her concussion.

"I hope you don't mind, but I rummaged through the kitchen for some tea bags." Connor sat on the side of the bed and held out a steaming cup of hot liquid. A lock of his hair had fallen over his forehead. "You look like the kind of woman who would like it sweetened, so I added some sugar. If you'd like me to make you another one, it's no problem."

"Um, no," Lauren replied. She quickly finished pulling her hair up into a hair tie, careful of the bump at the back of her head. She took the tea he offered her. She still felt a dull ache in her wrist, but she was getting used to the pain. "This is fine. Thank you."

"Is there anyone you want me to call?"

"Would that get you to leave?" Lauren asked, immediately feeling guilty for such a snarky reply. "I'm sorry. That was uncalled for. But really, you don't have to stay here. I'm fine."

"If it's one thing you'll find with me, Lauren, it's that I'm honest." Connor rested a hand on the other side of her thighs. The movement put them in a more intimate position than she was comfortable with but she didn't want him to know how much he affected her. "While you were changing, I phoned one of the officers who responded to the 911 call. He told me that they found you lying on the sidewalk in front of your shop. You were incoherent for a few moments, which was why they called an ambulance. Now, you don't have to like it, but I'm staying the night. We're going to follow the nurse's instruction. I'll take the couch and wake you every couple of hours."

"How did you even know I was at the hospital?"

"It's not important," Connor replied, frustrating her even more. He was very evasive with his answers for a man who claimed to be so honest. "Get some sleep and we'll talk more in the morning."

"Why do you think that you are even remotely responsible for me?" Lauren asked, wrapping her palms gently against the cup. The warmth felt good as it traveled to her wrist. "It was a mugging. It happens to people in the city all the time. You don't really even know me."

"But I'd like to," Connor replied, reaching up and tucking a stray hair behind her ear. "Let's save that discussion for another time. I don't want you claiming it was your concussion if you end up kissing me."

Lauren started to protest, but Connor just laughed. He stood and then leaned down, placing a kiss on her forehead. The false security she'd felt at the hospital returned and she tried to shake it off. There was no way she'd admit that having him out in the living room on her couch made her feel better. He would take that the wrong way, and at this point she didn't want to encourage him.

"If you need anything, just holler." Connor walked across the room and paused in the open doorway. Looking back over his shoulder, she noticed that his blue eyes had deepened in color. Why did that always resonate something deep within her? "Get some rest."

Lauren sipped her tea as she listened to the sound of him in the kitchen. He must be getting a glass of water. Did he know that he should help himself to whatever was in her kitchen? She didn't want him to go hungry. Connor's voice traveled through the apartment, signaling that he was talking on the phone. Was it business or personal? That question had her wondering if maybe he was here because of his investigation. He never did say why he'd been at the hospital. The more she thought about it, the more irate she became. Which didn't make sense, because one would think she would be relieved it was work-related.

Resting her cup on the nightstand, Lauren scooted deeper under the covers with every intention of sleeping. She tried. She really did, but the thought that he was only here because of some case he was working on didn't sit right with her. Her life hadn't been on an even keel since she'd met him. He flirted with her, yet she didn't quite know where he stood. She flipped back the covers. Connor needed to go.

Standing, Lauren winced as the blood rushed through her head. The throbbing increased, but she wasn't about to let that deter her from what she needed to do. In bare feet, she shuffled across the hardwood floor and out into the living room. Connor was sitting on the edge of the couch with his cell phone tucked into his ear. In his hands was an iPad or something similar. He looked at home in her apartment.

"I'll check that angle tomorrow night," Connor said, using his fingers to type something into his tablet. "By the way, I tried to track down Greg Winters. He works for a glass manufacturer and is apparently out of the country until next week. Can you do your computer thing and find out the exact day, time, and flight that he'll be on? Oh, and can you locate the street cameras around Lauren's business address? See if there is anything there for us to use in finding out who was behind her attack. I appreciate it, Taryn. You should head on home soon. You've been at it since the crack of dawn. Night."

"If you're here because you think this is in relation to your case, it isn't," Lauren replied. She kept her one hand tucked against her abdomen, not wanting to add to her discomfort. Getting out of bed seemed to make her headache worse as well. "I can get Ms. Finch to check on me. You don't have to feel obligated."

Connor took the phone away from his ear. She watched warily as he placed both devices on her coffee table. He didn't move right away and instead just sat on the couch staring at her. He did that a lot and Lauren resisted the urge to fidget. She wouldn't back down. It was time he left.

"You'd really rather be subjected to Ms. Finch overnight than me?" Connor asked, placing his hand on his chest. "I wasn't aware I had that type of affect on women."

"Wait," Lauren said, glancing toward the door. "How do you know what Ms. Finch is like?"

"I had the pleasure of meeting her while you were changing. She graciously told me what a nice boy I was for taking care of you." Connor flashed a smile. "I haven't been called a boy in a long, long time."

"What did she—never mind," Lauren said, shaking her head and then wishing she hadn't. It was apparent that Ms. Finch had knocked on her door to get the scoop. "We're getting off track. I can see that you're busy with your investigation, so you should...you know...go do that."

"I'm about to go against my better judgment here," Connor replied, gradually unfolding his frame from the couch. He walked slowly toward her and she suddenly felt like things had shifted. She should have stayed in bed. "Don't say I didn't warn you about your excuses in the morning. If you can get out of bed with what has to be a massive headache to try and get me to leave because you're cautious of what is developing between us, then you're cognizant enough to know that your reaction is real."

Lauren knew what he was going to do before his hands ever cupped her face, but for the life of her, she couldn't speak or move. No protestations fell from her lips. Maybe somewhere deep down she wanted this to happen to prove that there was no chemistry between them. If he kissed her and felt nothing, at least he would leave her alone to rest in peace and suffer in silence.

Connor's warm lips covered hers and all thought fled. Her mind shut down. Her pain receded. His hands tilted her head, giving him more access. Lauren felt his tongue glide across her lower lip, as if asking her to part them and let him inside. She granted his request and a burst of coffee and mint exploded onto her tongue. He playfully dueled before seriously exploring and caressing her mouth. The kiss was unlike any other. He slowly pulled away and she wanted to whimper.

"Go to bed, Red," Connor murmured. His thumb brushed her cheek before he let his palms drop from her face. He stepped back. "Go now, before my common sense takes a hike."

Lauren nodded, instantly bringing back the throbbing at the base of her skull. He was right. She should go to bed. Without a word, she spun on her heel and made her way back into the bedroom. She was sure that her sanity would return in the morning. It had to. Otherwise, she was setting herself on a course that would only end in disaster.

✧   ✧   ✧   ✧

Connor rubbed his eyes. He'd been staring at his tablet, hoping to go over some new reports that Crest had emailed him with regards to Terry's case, but it was useless. All he kept seeing was the arousal in Lauren's green eyes. She had tasted so fucking good. Damn it, he shouldn't have kissed her.

Swinging his legs off of the couch, he tossed his tablet on the cushion beside him. Glancing at his watch, Connor saw that it was two o'clock in the morning. He should go check on her but was reluctant to enter her bedroom. She had this sweet scent about her, almost as if she were wearing an exotic perfume. He was relatively sure it was her hair, but knew better than to bury his nose in her mane. If he had, she sure as hell wouldn't have gone to bed alone.

Connor leaned back against the plush burgundy couch and really looked around, trying to get a sense of her personality. There was something about Lauren Bailey that had crawled underneath his skin and wouldn't leave him alone. She was guarded, yet didn't have trouble articulating her thoughts on personal matters. She was attractive but it seemed as if she refused to see herself that way. She claimed to be vanilla, but Connor couldn't wrap his brain around the fact that she specifically decorated BDSM toys and implements in high-end jewelry without being curious about the lifestyle. Why would she go into a business that she had no interest in? And the way she touched her wrist…shit. Had something happened to her in the past to make her afraid of dominant men?

"No!"

Connor shot off the couch and within seconds, had reached her doorway. Glancing around, he immediately saw that no one was in her room. Lauren was thrashing around, her covers down by her feet. Her body suddenly stilled, as if her dream had been halted, but her whimper indicated it hadn't.

Quickly crossing the hardwood floor, Connor turned on the bedside lamp. He sat on the edge of her bed and placed a hand on her arm. It was cold, so he stroked her skin up and down. As if knowing he was there, she turned her face toward him. He felt his chest tighten as a tiny frown marred her forehead.

"Lauren, wake up." Connor continued to touch her, wanting to reassure her that she was safe. "Come on, Red. Open those pretty eyes for me."

A gasp of air left her lips as she came awake. At first, Connor could see that she wasn't quite with him. He let Lauren slowly take things in and as her green eyes cleared, knew that she was finally awake.

"Bad dream?"

"He said something," Lauren whispered, leaning up on her elbows. She focused on him and spoke rapidly, as if she didn't want to lose her memory. "I was loading the last box of items into my van when I felt someone come up behind me. Before I could turn, he grabbed me around the neck. *You can't say another word.* That's what he said, but I hadn't even cried out. I hadn't said anything. It doesn't make sense."

Lauren paused and looked down, as if just now realizing his fingers were caressing her skin. Knowing now wasn't the time to push her, Connor reached behind her and pulled a pillow up against her headboard. Taking his cue, she sat up. He remained quiet, knowing that she would continue in her own time.

"I heard somebody yell at him and that's when he pushed me to the ground." Lauren looked down at her hands. "I tried to catch myself, but my hands slipped on some ice. That's when my head smacked against the cement."

"Did you see him run off?" Connor asked, trying to keep her memory alive. Maybe she'd seen something that would be useful in tracking this fucker down.

"No," Lauren replied. "I looked up to see a man standing over me with his cell phone. I think he was a taxi driver. He'd already called the police."

"Okay. This is good," Connor said, reassuring her. "Do you remember what his voice sounded like?"

"Um." Lauren's brow formed a cute V as she tried to remember. "It wasn't as deep as yours."

Connor's conversation with Kevin returned. He let his eyes roam down her body and couldn't help but appreciate her curves. Her breasts were full and round, the silk tank top leaving little to the imagination. Lauren was small enough, though, that a larger woman would have been able to come up behind and easily have subdued her.

"Do you think it could have been a woman?"

Lauren slowly shook her head, although her green eyes had started to sparkle and she crossed her arms across her chest.

The movement reminded him of her habit of touching her wrist. His earlier thought that something may have happened in her past to cause her to be afraid of dominant men went out the window. The spunk she sometimes got smashed that idea into pieces. It was obvious she wasn't afraid. Connor didn't miss the hardening of her nipples and while he would have liked nothing better than to suck on them, he concentrated on the conversation at hand.

"Why not?"

"I'm not sure," Lauren answered, pursing her lips in concentration. "Just the feel of him against my back, I guess."

"You weren't wearing a coat?" Connor asked, frowning. It was damn cold out there and she should know better than to be outside without protection. "You had one at the hospital."

"The policeman got into my van to retrieve it." Lauren's frown deepened, as if she didn't like defending herself. "I was hot from carrying all of those boxes. I took it off."

Connor could tell they would only end up arguing over something trivial if he pushed the issue. He always prided himself on choosing his battles wisely. This time, it was better to walk away.

"Fine. You took it off. Was the perp wearing a jacket? Did the front of his chest feel cushioned?"

Lauren showed surprise at that but nodded her head. "Yes, he did. It wasn't too thick though. His chest was solid."

"Good girl," Connor praised, reaching down for the comforter she'd kicked away during her nightmare. "If you remember anything more, just tell me. How are you feeling?"

"You really shouldn't call me that." Lauren pulled the comforter out of his grasp.

"What? Good girl?" Connor reiterated with a smile. "Why not?"

"You and I both know that's probably how you praise your subs." Lauren didn't meet his gaze, making him wonder what she was really thinking. "I just feel it's inappropriate. And speaking of which, that shouldn't have happened."

Lauren had expertly switched topics. He let her have her way. For now.

"Our kissing? I thought it was nice, personally."

"You kissed me," Lauren said. Her pink lips pursed and she was lucky he didn't kiss her again. "I thought you said you weren't looking for anything permanent."

"I'm not," Connor replied, taken aback by her question. If that wasn't a way to slam reality down on the situation, he wasn't sure what else could. If his past had taught him anything, it was that there wasn't a woman alive on the planet who wouldn't cash out for a better situation. Even his whore of a mother had done the same thing to his father. Casual sex was the only way to go. "If I'm not mistaken, neither are you."

"I'm not. But I also didn't agree to anything more than a professional relationship." Lauren looked down at her lavender comforter and started to trace the swirl pattern that was directly over her lap. "I'm awake. As you can see, I'm healthy. I think it would be best if you left now."

"I'm going to get a complex if you keep that up." Connor stood, knowing he had better head back out into the living room before he kissed her again to keep her from talking. "Food for thought while you try and get some sleep. There's something between us. You feel it. I feel it. We're both in agreement that we'd rather have something casual. It's there for the taking and it could be damned good. Why not see where that road takes us?"

"As long as it remains casual?" Lauren asked, reiterating his earlier claim.

Lauren had stopped fidgeting with the comforter and looked up at him. Damn, she had beautiful green eyes. What he'd give to see those matching white leather cuffs around her wrists, ankles, and neck. He knew those emeralds couldn't hold a candle to her eyes, but it would complement them.

"Yes," Connor replied, turning and walking towards the door. He wasn't about to crash and burn again. "But I bet the trip will be amazing."

Chapter Seven

He sat in his vehicle, nervously bouncing his leg up and down. He didn't care that his knee kept hitting the steering wheel. Across the street was Lauren Bailey's apartment building. He'd just pulled up, not able to get here any sooner. A man in a long, black dress coat was walking toward the entrance. His brown hair blew in the wind and he squinted against the cold. The man could have been there for any of the tenants, but there was something odd about the way he carried himself, as if his bearing defined his character. Resisting the urge to follow the guy into the building, he took a drag on his unfiltered cigarette.

Had Lauren gotten a look at him as he'd been sprinting down the alleyway? Had she recognized his voice? If only that damned taxi driver hadn't interfered. It wasn't like he was going to kill her, at least, not right away. He'd only wanted to scare her into keeping her mouth shut. People were unreliable in his opinion. She might say something unintentional that could draw away the attention that the detectives had placed on Terry Sweeney. After all, he couldn't be sure that she hadn't put two and two together.

He blew the smoke out of his lungs, not taking his eyes off of the building. Smoke curled around his body. Lauren wasn't like Marilyn Sweeney. Marilyn had gotten what he had determined to be her destiny. As long as Lauren thought her attack was a real mugging instead of a premeditated attack, maybe that would take her mind off of her previous encounter with the police. No need to dwell on that. As the nicotine entered his system and calmed his nerves somewhat, he prided himself on predicting exactly how everything would play out. Yes, Lauren would be too busy fretting over a mugging instead of remembering what she'd unintentionally overheard a couple of weeks ago, while he focused on the master plan.

✧ ✧ ✧ ✧

Connor poured two cups of coffee. In one, he placed two sugar cubes and a splash of half & half. Considering the fact that she lived alone, kept a bowl of sugar cubes next to the brewer, and had a fresh quart of her favorite creamer in the fridge, it was a fair bet he had her cup nailed. He'd heard Lauren get out of the shower around thirty minutes ago. He'd hit the brew button when she started blow-drying her hair. He gave himself a pat on the back when she exited her bedroom, dressed and ready for the day, as the last bit of water ran through the filter.

"Good morning."

"Are you one of those cheerful morning people?" Lauren mumbled, making her way over to the counter. He couldn't help but smile as she took the cup he'd slid across the granite and immediately brought it to her lips. There was a hint of gloss on them and he wondered what it tasted like. She hummed her appreciation. "God, you actually put the right amount of sugar in it. You get to stay an extra fifteen minutes."

"Why's that?" Connor asked, leaning against the sink and making himself comfortable. Whether she liked it or not, he was staying a hell of a lot longer than fifteen minutes.

"To make a second pot of coffee." Lauren pulled back one of the two brown leather stools in front of the island and situated herself on it. She leaned down on her elbows, still cupping the warm mug. "When I do it, it either comes out too weak or too strong."

"How'd you sleep?" Connor asked, purposefully ignoring the chance to toy with her. The doorbell should be ringing any moment and he'd be right back on her shit list. He took a swallow of his coffee. "Headache gone?"

"It's more of a dull throbbing right now, although I'm sure the coffee will help."

"Remember anything more?"

"I slept fine after…that. And no, I don't remember anything else."

They drank in silence. Connor tried to appear relaxed, not wanting to push her any more than he already had. He'd opened himself up as much as he was going to. If she truly didn't want to engage in a casual affair with him, he wasn't going to force the issue. That didn't negate the fact that her alleged mugging might be connected to his case.

Ding-dong.

Lauren's green eyes flew to his. She didn't seem alarmed, so much as curious. It made him wonder who she would be comfortable with ringing her doorbell this early on a Saturday morning. Ms. Finch or someone else? Connor shook his head when she went to get off of the stool.

"I know who it is." Connor walked across the room and opened the door. Crest stood there in his long black dress coat, looking at him through hooded eyes. "Come on in."

"What happened to keeping the investigation low key?" Crest asked in a low voice, crossing the threshold and tossing Lauren a glance. "Your message purported to everything but."

"The detectives on the case got to her before I did." Connor closed the door and lowered his voice. "Crest, I'm not certain the mugging wasn't just that, but it seems too coincidental. Either way, I need to protect her."

Crest seemed to be gauging Connor's words, but he didn't know how to say it any clearer. He didn't want her to be a casualty in this case. In his peripheral vision, he saw Lauren stand and start to walk their way. The tension in his muscles relaxed when he saw Crest give a nod in acknowledgement.

"Lauren Bailey, please meet Gavin Crest. He's the man who runs Crest Security Agency."

"It's nice to meet you, Mr. Crest."

"Crest will do just fine." He held out his hand in greeting, waiting for Lauren to take it. "I'm sorry we have to meet under these circumstances. May we have a seat to discuss some things?"

"Of course," Lauren replied, walking toward the living room, the only area in the apartment where the three of them could sit comfortably. Connor remained standing though. She took the overstuffed chair while Crest sat on the couch. He leaned forward, openly displaying his interest in the coming conversation. "I'm not sure what I can help you with. If this is regarding the jewelry I made for Marilyn Sweeney, I've already shared the information with Connor and the police detectives."

"We appreciate your cooperation, Ms. Bailey." Crest wasn't a man to play around with words and got straight to the point. "For a city, Minneapolis can be a small one. Everyone knows everyone within certain circles."

"You mean the BDSM clubs?" Lauren asked, leaning forward and placing her cup on the coffee table.

"Yes." Crest ran a hand over his chin as if contemplating his next words. "As you're aware, we're investigating the murder of Marilyn Sweeney. Connor and certain other team members practice within the lifestyle, so for them to ask questions seems rather ordinary to those unaware of our interests. We'd like to keep it that way."

"Of course," Lauren replied, glancing toward Connor. He smiled his reassurance, although he wasn't feeling it right now. He knew that what Crest said next would either be accepted or go over like a lead balloon. "I've already given my consent to remain silent on the subject. I wouldn't want to hinder your investigation."

"I appreciate your cooperation," Crest said. "It's also come to my attention that you were attacked last night. Have you remembered anything that would be useful in catching whoever did this to you?"

"I'm not sure what Connor has told you, but the police think it was a random mugging."

"They would," Crest replied, sharing an unimpressed look with Connor. "The police who responded to the call are in a separate county from the detectives questioning you on Marilyn Sweeney. They wouldn't get the correlation unless you said something."

"I didn't even think to say anything about it. I didn't think it was related. I'm still not sure if it is. When my attacker came up behind me, he said, '*You can't say another word*'. Could that be connected to me talking to the police? Maybe. But it could just as easily have been someone who got his words mixed up as he was trying to mug me."

"Was anything taken?" Crest asked.

Connor took another drink of his coffee, listening in on the conversation but also observing. Lauren looked a lot better than she had last night. The light in her green eyes was back and she didn't seem so emotional. He also noticed that for the first time since he'd met her, she hadn't touched her wrist in the manner that she used to. He still wondered what could have been the cause of such a nervous habit.

"Nothing," Lauren replied to Crest's question. "The man ran off immediately when someone yelled in our direction, obviously seeing what was taking place."

"I have a suggestion, although the choice remains in your hands," Crest said, gesturing toward her. "To verify that this wasn't an attack against you for speaking with the police, allow Connor to stay here for a few days, just to be safe. If nothing is amiss, say by the end of next week, you both can go your separate ways. It would make me more comfortable knowing we have our bases covered, along with your physical wellbeing. Would that be all right with you?"

Connor saw the surprise in Lauren's eyes as she took in Crest's request. Her eyes flickered his way, but instead of saying anything, she reached for her coffee cup. Taking a sip seemed to provide her the time she needed.

"If someone didn't want me to speak with the detectives, what about the other people at the clubs? I know that the members were questioned. I spoke with Joel on the phone. Why wouldn't the man have targeted them?"

"That's a good question and one that we're confirming as we speak. An associate on our team is monitoring any reports of assault that might be related. It could be that this person feels you may have seen or overheard something in particular."

"Or it might not be related at all," Lauren argued, replacing her cup on the table. "I truly appreciate that you're covering all of your bases, Mr. Crest. But don't you think that if this was in relation to Marilyn Sweeney's murder, the guilty person would have tried to break into my apartment last night?"

Connor tightened his jaw to prevent himself from saying anything. She was now irritating him with her casual brush-off—and that's exactly what it was leading to. Lauren was setting it up to where she didn't want him here to protect her. He'd known from first meeting her that she was independent, but damn if it didn't get underneath his skin. To top it off, she'd gone ahead and disregarded Crest's request to drop the mister.

"Not if he or she had been watching your building and observed that Connor had brought you home," Crest answered, spreading his hands in gesture.

"I appreciate your concern. I really do, but I think my assault was random." Lauren stood up and looked his way, ignoring the fact he had practically ground his teeth down to stubs. "Connor, thank you for helping me last night. If I think of anything that Marilyn said, or someone else for that matter, that could possibly help you in your investigation, I'll call you."

Dismissal. That's what she'd done to them, plain and simple. Crest followed her lead. Although he knew Crest looked his way, he couldn't bring himself to tear his eyes away from Lauren. She stared at him as if he was just another investigator in a case that didn't involve her.

"Do that," Connor replied. He walked over to the small kitchenette and swiped his jacket off the back of a chair, along with his tablet that was on the table. She wanted him gone. He'd go. Simple. No hard feelings. "Don't forget to make your follow-up appointment with your doctor."

With those final words, Connor took the lead and walked to the door. He could hear Crest say his goodbyes, give her instructions to call should she see or hear anything unusual, and then follow behind. Within moments, they were in the hallway and making their way toward the elevator. He pushed the button a little harder than was needed.

"You know, you could have joined in on the conversation."

"If I'd joined in," Connor said, "she wouldn't have liked what I said. There's a damn good chance her attack wasn't random. I'm not leaving her unprotected."

"I'll have Ethan check in on her, but you know damn well we can't safeguard someone who doesn't want it."

"Ethan?" Connor asked. "Isn't he busy with the open cases?"

"I'm sure it will be a refreshing change."

Connor threw Crest a glance and saw that he was looking at the blinking numbers above the elevator. He couldn't be sure, but there seemed to be a slight smirk emerging on Crest's face. Blood was in the water and the first shark began to circle.

Chapter Eight

Connor pulled his jacket closed around him, a meager attempt at warding off the biting sting of the wind. Jax walked next to him, seemingly oblivious. Connor had heard on the radio earlier that a small snowstorm was blowing in from the west. Usually he didn't mind the weather, but nothing had been going his way today.

"Taryn said that Greg Winter's trip got extended," Connor said, coming to a stop at the cross section. "Looks like he's not due back until sometime next month. She's monitoring the situation."

"Do you think he's delaying on purpose?" Jax asked, frosty condensation swirling in the air with each word.

"My gut is telling me he had nothing to do with it." Connor shoved his other hand in his pocket. He'd walked out of his house without his gloves and now his fingers were stiff from the cold. "When I spoke with some of the members of Masters last week, it seemed to be common knowledge that Marilyn was traipsing a little too far over the edge for Greg's comfort level. They parted amicably."

"Speaking of parting ways, have you checked in with your pretty little vendor?" The crossing sign changed, indicating it was safe to traverse the intersection. "I heard Crest giving Ethan orders to swing by her place. I thought you had that covered, old buddy?"

Connor hadn't really had a chance to go over specifics with Jax. By the time he'd caught up on his sleep and read over the additional reports that Jessie had sent him, Connor had just enough time to take a shower and grab a bite to eat before he and Jax headed into downtown. They both lived southeast of the city, in a duplex they'd purchased during the second wave of housing troubles. The location was great and they each had their privacy.

"Lauren doesn't feel her attack is connected to our case," Connor said, knowing he hadn't fooled Jax in the least. His frustration could be heard loud and clear. "I went to the hospital after your call last night. The attacker didn't come anywhere near doing what he probably wanted, as a taxi driver interrupted the mugging. Lauren was pushed to the ground and hit her head pretty damn hard. I stayed with her overnight, but by morning she'd convinced herself it was a random assault."

"I have two questions for you," Jax said, reaching the other side of the road. They were still two blocks away from their destination and Connor knew there was no getting around the upcoming interrogation. "One: why have you let her get to you? I can tell by the way you talk about Lauren that there's—"

"Sex. Plain and simple." Connor could feel the cutting cold seeping into his bones and walked faster. "It's been a few months. Cut me a break."

"Well, then," Jax said, keeping pace, "I guess I don't need to ask the second one."

They walked one block before Connor caved, but he couldn't help himself. The silence was fucking deafening. He kicked himself for even asking, but Jax had that way of tripping his trigger.

"Fuck me," Connor muttered, crossing the next intersection and not caring that they were jaywalking. "Ask."

"So Ms. Bailey says 'no, thank you' to whatever service you may have offered, and you just walk away?" Jax shook his head as if he were disappointed. Connor fisted his hand in his pocket. Delivering a blow to his best friend wouldn't help the situation. "Shit, maybe Ashley did have you whipped. Did she give back your balls when she left?"

"What the hell does that mean?" Connor asked, coming to stand outside the door of Whip. "I don't even know her, for fuck's sake. Lauren had interactions with our murder victim and I was following a lead. I offered to stay until we had verification that she wasn't being targeted. She said no. She doesn't want protection? Fine. It's no skin off my back. Crest has Ethan doing fly-bys anyway. There's not much more to be done."

Connor yanked the door open for another fun-filled evening of questions and answers. He liked it a hell of a lot better when coming to the clubs was a personal choice and didn't involve interrogating people he'd come to know in an entirely different way. Jax walked in front of him, muttering something under his breath, but Connor ignored him and stayed where he was for just a moment as he tried to loosen his pent up frustration.

Connor looked up, seeing two submissives sashaying their way toward him. He knew exactly what those long dress coats covered and decided tonight might be a good time to get back into the game. He was a free agent, after all.

"Hello, ladies," Connor said, flashing his best imitation of one of Jax's famous smiles.

"Aren't you Master Jax's friend?" the svelte blonde said, batting her eyelashes. It was as if she'd brushed away any inclination he'd had to play. Her false disposition became more apparent and Connor suddenly wanted nothing to do with her. "Is he here tonight?"

"That I am," Connor replied in succession, answering her first question. "And he's right ahead of you."

As he and the women stepped into the club, Connor was hit with the smell of latex, leather, and sex. The same hint of orange soap fragrance wafted his way. Whip was set up totally different than Masters in that it had a separate room for play. The club wasn't as big and had limited room. In front of them was a sitting area with a small bar, which only contained non-alcoholic drinks. This clientele leaned more toward edge play, since bodily fluids were permitted, making alcohol prohibited.

"Master…" the brunette paused, waiting for him to fill in his name.

"Connor." He took his time looking around, noticing a couple of people he knew and more that he didn't. He'd allow Jax to take the lead tonight, since it was obvious any questions coming from him would appear odd. On second thought, seeing Alex Snyder by the bar might be just the thing they needed to give this investigation a kick in the ass. That man was worse than Russell when it came to spreading stories. He looked down at the brunette. "What's your name?"

"Juliet."

"Is there a reason you haven't removed your coat?" Connor asked, lowering his voice to indicate his disapproval.

"I was waiting on you, Master Connor."

Connor snapped his fingers to the hostess, who'd been flirting with Jax. It wasn't until that moment that he realized Jax must have been coming here more often lately. Was there something his best friend was keeping from him? The hostess laid a hand on Jax's arm as she bypassed him and came over to retrieve the coats from the subs.

He raised an eyebrow in question when Jax looked his way. Connor could see that maybe he'd been too caught up in his own drama to notice what had been going on around him. His phone vibrated and he reached inside of his pocket. He'd have to shut it off anyway, since the playroom didn't allow for electronic devices. Looking at the screen, he saw Ethan had shot him a text saying that Lauren was all snug in her apartment and that he was heading home for some shut eye.

"Anything important?" Jax asked quietly, as he wandered over his way.

"No," Connor replied and then shut down his cell phone. He wished he could as easily shut down his concern for Lauren. She chose this, though. He also had a job to do. There shouldn't be any distractions. "What about you? That hostess seemed overly friendly. Have you been playing here a lot?"

"No more than usual," Jax replied, turning to the two submissives that were now standing in nothing but black leather waist cinchers, laced-topped stockings, and high black boots. Both women had framed their delicate bare pale mounds with hard dark leather. The pair of them were a ready meal for any famished Dom. Jax's usual smile was absent. Connor got the uneasy feeling that his friend wasn't telling him something, but now wasn't the time to address it. "Very pretty, ladies."

"Thank you, Master Jax," the blonde replied, having already picked her Dom for the evening. She was a pro and kept her eyes downcast.

"Shall we head on into the play area?" Jax asked, taking the lead. "I think you both need to have your bottoms warmed up, so we'll see what we can do about putting a nice healthy glow on them."

"You go ahead," Connor said, indicating that Jax should take both subs with him. "I need something to wet my whistle. I'll be in shortly."

"No worries," Jax replied, glancing toward the bar to see who was there. "I'll get these little subbies up to speed."

"I bet you will." Connor laughed, keeping up the pretense.

He'd give himself five minutes and if he wasn't making headway with Alex, then he'd join Jax. Connor made his way to the bar. He held up a hand to the bartender and indicated he wanted to place an order.

"What can I get you?"

"Club soda with a twist of lime," Connor replied, knowing his voice would get Alex to turn his way.

"Connor Ortega?" Alex asked, surprise lacing his voice. "Shit, man. I haven't seen you around in months. Weren't you playing over at Masters?"

"I took a break from the scene," Connor replied, surprised that he didn't mention Ashley. "Jax and I are hitting the clubs tonight though. We might even end up over there later tonight. Anything new?"

"Other than your pal Jax learning his way around fire play?" Alex said, laughing. "Man, he did a scene a few weeks ago that people are still talking about."

Connor nodded, muttering his thanks to the bartender for the drink that was set in front of him. He had no choice but to act like he knew what Alex was talking about, but felt his temper rising that Jax hadn't handed that information over himself.

"Have you been over at Masters? I hear Joel is pissed off that he's losing clientele."

"Joel doesn't get pissed," Connor replied, knowing for a fact that the owner of Masters was as laid back as one could get. "Why? Is Gerry spreading rumors again?"

Joel Summit and Gerry Mason had been business partners for years until they had a falling out over money. They went their separate ways years ago, until Gerry somehow came up with enough cash to front another club. Where Joel was smart and knew that two clubs would only bring in more business from out-of-towners, Gerry was still in the mindset that if he stole enough members, Joel's business would close. At least, that's what rumor said. Connor had always maintained neutral ground, but preferred the clientele over at Masters.

"Hell, no," Alex replied, taking a drink of soda straight from the can. "Gerry's been lying low. I ran into Beverly the other day. She mentioned that she overheard Joel say that his numbers were low."

Connor could tell by Alex's body language that he was waiting for him to ask why Gerry had been lying low, but knew he'd get more information if he were to walk away. Knowing that drinks weren't allowed inside the play area, Connor finished off his club soda and smacked the glass on the counter.

"Masters looked busy when I was there last weekend," Connor said, taking out his wallet and leaving a few ones to cover his tab. "Jax is waiting for me with two subs that are clamoring for attention, so I'd better head in."

"Hey, you're a private dick, right?" Alex asked, lowering his voice and stepping closer to prevent Connor from leaving. Snap. And there lay his prey. He knew that Alex couldn't allow a murder that happened a week ago to go without comment. "Do you have any insight on the Marilyn Sweeney case?"

"I work shit jobs, Alex. You know, cheating spouses and deadbeat dads." Connor shrugged. "I heard about what happened, though. It's a shame. I thought Terry was a good guy."

"That's why Gerry's lying low," Alex said. Now they were getting somewhere. Connor nodded to a member he vaguely remembered from Masters as the man walked by, giving off the impression that what Alex was saying was of no interest. "The police were here asking questions about Terry. Gerry had to hand over his member list and it turns out that Marilyn wasn't on it."

Connor knew that wasn't true, as Taryn had hacked into both clubs' computer systems and garnered every piece of information they might need. Marilyn Sweeney's name had been on that list. Had Gerry taken it off? If so, why? Not wanting to appear over eager for answers, Connor reached around Alex for the peanut dish and tossed one into his mouth.

"Really?" Connor asked. He popped another peanut. "Well, like I said, I've been out of the scene for a couple of months. The way you can gather information, maybe you should be the private investigator."

Alex's chest ballooned with the fake compliment, but it did what Connor hoped it would do. Within seconds, he revealed that Gerry said Marilyn played at Whip as a guest and that he'd been trying to pilfer members away from Masters. Alex continued to drone on until Connor knew there was nothing else to gain. Taking his leave, Connor walked through the long, heavy red velvet curtain into what resembled a dungeon.

Cages were situated in each corner, holding submissives that were either being disciplined or punished. The middle of the floor held a suspension area where a sub was currently hanging and being subjected to a cane. From her cries of pleasure, it didn't seem that she had an objection. The place felt crowded, but each roped-off section had enough room for play and the dungeon monitors looked to have things under control.

Connor spotted Jax sitting on a couch, caressing the blonde's hair as it draped over his knee. They were talking in low tones and the background music prevented their voices from carrying. Making his way over, he saw that Juliet was kneeling in the correct position on the floor. Knowing he would have to do a light scene and thinking maybe this was exactly what he needed, Connor couldn't help but picture Lauren at her apartment drinking wine by herself.

"I've kept Juliet busy as she waited for you," Jax said, gesturing with his head.

Connor looked down to see that her right hand was manipulating her clit. Juices glistened on her inner thigh underneath the dim lighting from above. There was no doubt she was a pretty young thing, but nowhere near carrying the class that Lauren did. He clenched his teeth in irritation that she crossed his mind again.

"Did you make that phone call you needed to?" Jax asked, coming across as relaxed. "I told Juliet that you'd probably get called into work, but not to worry. I have plans for the two of these subs and as long as they behave, everyone will be satisfied before the lights go out."

"That's what I was coming to tell you," Connor said, taking the bait. He wanted to check out that client list and also read over Gerry Mason's statement. Him leaving had nothing to do with Lauren. "Juliet, I'm sure you'll be fine in Master Jax's care. Be warned though, I hear he does a kick-ass fire play scene."

Connor's comment didn't faze Jax in the least. It was obvious that his friend didn't want to even acknowledge that he was acting out of character. He wouldn't push the issue because Jax knew that he had an open door policy. When he wanted to talk, Connor would be there.

"Connor," Jax called out, causing him to turn around. "Check your texts."

He waited until he was out on the street before digging his phone out of his pocket and turning on the device. Walking towards the underground garage where he'd parked, he wasn't too worried about Jax finding a ride home. Connor zipped up his jacket as the cold wind snapped around him. His phone finally vibrated, indicating that it was ready to use.

Connor slowed his stride, looking at the text that Jax had sent him. His friend must have slipped out of the play area to send it. Fuck. While he'd been talking and gathering information from Alex, Jax had been doing the same thing with those two submissives. Apparently the blonde, Kimmie, had a pair of matching nipple clamps she wanted to try out with her outfit. They were similarly adorned with rubies that Marilyn Sweeney had on at the time of her death. Jax stated he tried to play it cool when she asked him if he would let her wear them and dropped them into his hand. The man who gave them to her? Joel Summit.

Chapter Nine

Connor rubbed the grit out of his eyes and then stretched his tired muscles. He'd been sitting at his desk for hours, watching his computer screen that Taryn had so graciously set up to monitor the lobby of Lauren's apartment building before she left the office last night. He'd stayed awake by reading Gerry's statement, comparing the list he gave the police to that of the one Taryn had downloaded, and keeping an eye on the lobby for anyone who looked suspicious. Unfortunately, there wasn't a traffic camera near the alleyway where Lauren had been attacked. Now that it was daytime and Ethan would be furtively checking in on Lauren, Connor needed sleep.

"Joel Summit purchased similar clamps for another submissive?"

Connor looked up at Crest as he walked toward Connor's cubicle with his dress coat hung over his arm, a folder in one hand, and a coffee in the other. He looked crisp, clean, and ready for anything. Connor grimaced and leaned over his desk, shutting off his computer. Lauren had left for her shop well over an hour before this, and he'd more or less been fighting sleep since.

"Yes, and unless we reveal that we're investigating Marilyn's murder, we're not getting answers as to why anytime soon—at least not from him." Connor ran a hand over his face, wondering if he should have one more cup of coffee to at least get him home. He knew what Crest was going to say before he said it, so Connor beat him to it. He knew what he had to do, but he didn't have to like it. "I'll talk to Lauren later today and see if she received a customized order from Joel."

Before Crest could respond, Jax strolled in with his black leather jacket, matching gloves, and his favorite skullcap that covered his dirty-blonde hair. His cheeks were red from the cold and it was obvious from the wet marks on his shoulders that the snow had started. Connor glanced at Crest and wondered how in the hell the man had avoided the snow. He was dry as a bone.

"For someone out so late, you sure do look damn good," Connor replied, reconsidering his decision to head home. Maybe he'd just catch a nap on the only couch in the office. Jax could take up the legwork. "Any more leads?"

"I always look good," Jax replied, flashing a smile. Connor could see he was back to his normal self. He came to stand beside Crest. He looked at Connor from head to toe. "Unlike yourself. You look like shit, boyo."

"I stayed up going over reports. Gerry left a few submissives off of the list that he gave the police. I think we're missing something very simple, but I can't put my finger on it."

"Isn't it always simple?" Jax asked. "Speaking of leads, Joel wasn't at the club the night Marilyn died. Crest, are we getting overtime? It is Sunday."

"You're salary," Crest said, draping his dress coat over Taryn's chair and taking a seat. "Which can be cut for missing a workday in these trying economic times."

"Duly noted," Jax said, shrugging out of his jacket. "Which is why I'm a cut above the rest. As Connor already told you, Kimmie, one of the submissives at Whip requested that I apply a pair of custom nipple clamps during our scene. They were infused with similar cut rubies that Marilyn had on her at the time of her death. When I questioned her about them, she said they were a gift from Joel Summit."

"Has she ever played at Masters?" Connor asked, not remember seeing Kimmie there, but again, he'd been MIA for a couple of months.

"No, she said it was at a private play party hosted by—"

"Gerry Mason," Connor finished, reaching for the man's statement on his desk. "I've gone over his statement and can't get why he would lie about Marilyn being a member of Whip, or the other submissives for that matter. But if Joel and Gerry aren't the enemies they are portraying themselves to be, then maybe they have something in common after all?"

"It sounds like you have your work cut out for you," Crest said, standing. "Good job. Jax, since you're in deep at both clubs, see how close you can get to Joel or Gerry. Connor, get back in touch with Lauren and see what she has to say about Joel purchasing those clamps. Maybe there is something to her attack."

"Pussy."

Connor shot Jax a dark look, not liking the judgment of his tone. Before he could say anything, his cell phone vibrated. It was somewhere on his desk, so after shuffling the files around, he found it.

"What the hell would you have me do? She turned Crest down and said no protection," Connor replied to Jax's insult. "Hello?"

"Connor? I, um, I need you. I think."

Lauren's voice hit him like a ton of bricks. Connor glanced at his dark computer screen and then pulled his phone away from his ear to look at the display. She was calling from her cell phone.

"Lauren, are you all right?"

"Someone broke into my apartment." Connor could hear her shuffling some things around. "I don't think anything was taken, but I'm thinking maybe you and Mr. Crest were right."

"Don't touch anything," Connor ordered, standing up and grabbing his bomber jacket off the back of his chair. "I'll be there in five minutes."

"Need the police?" Crest asked, pulling his cell phone out of his dress pants.

"Yes."

"No."

Connor looked at Jax, questioning why the hell his friend would say no, when he didn't have the facts. He knew his friend well enough to know the gleam in his eye. It was a mixture of pride and guilt that only Jax could pull off. That's when it hit him that Lauren's break-in had nothing to do with the case and everything to do with Jax.

"What the hell did you do?"

"Something you didn't, choir boy."

"Jax," Crest said, almost in a sigh, "my office. Now. Connor, let me know what Lauren says regarding her business with Joel. Jax might have gone about it the wrong way, but I do think she is a piece of this puzzle. And make sure you apologize on behalf of CSA."

Connor didn't bother replying as he made his way to the door. He knew he should be pissed as hell for what Jax did, scaring Lauren like that, but he was feeling anything but. She called him. When push came to shove and Lauren had felt threatened, it was him she reached out for. He didn't stop to analyze why he knew that wasn't a good thing. All he knew was that she needed him.

Lauren stood with her hands on her hips and surveyed her living room. Nothing was damaged, nothing was taken, and nothing seemed disturbed. She'd left for her shop early, needing to do some invoicing, when she realized she'd left the specialized items at her apartment that needed to be shipped that day. She'd been gone no more than an hour before returning home to find that her door was ajar.

"I still think you didn't lock up properly, dear," Ms. Finch said after sipping on her tea. The older woman was currently sitting at Lauren's small kitchenette. "I would have heard if someone had been out in the hallway."

"Not if they were trying to be quiet," Lauren replied, holding back her exasperation. She had no doubt that she'd locked her door, but Ms. Finch couldn't let it go. What would help the situation was if the older woman went back to her own apartment. "Men who are experts at this can come and go without anyone knowing."

"You mean a professional jewel thief?" Ms. Finch's eyes widened in astonishment. She then lowered her voice as if they shared a secret. "Have you checked your spare bedroom to make sure your inventory is still there?"

Lauren placed a hand on her forehead, hoping that would prevent her from snapping at the older lady. She swore that

Ms. Finch had cameras in every apartment within the building. She was a wealth of information and that's what had Lauren uneasy. If Ms. Finch didn't hear any sounds from hallway as someone picked at her lock, that didn't bode well for Lauren. Nothing was missing, which meant the person didn't find what they were looking for. Her mind went to the black SUV that had been parked across the street from her shop this morning.

"Lauren?" A rap on her door came simultaneously.

She crossed her living room and opened the door. Resisting the urge to lean against him like she did that night at the hospital, Lauren turned away. Getting that false sense of security was the last thing she needed now. She smothered a groan when Ms. Finch's eyes sparkled at meeting someone new.

"Connor, this is Ms. Finch. Ms. Finch, Connor Ortega is a friend of mine."

"We've already met, dear," Ms. Finch said in a higher pitched voice, holding out her right hand. The teacup in her hand rattled on the saucer beneath it.

Lauren had forgotten that they'd met the other night upon arriving home from the hospital. She was impressed when Connor walked straight over to Ms. Finch and shook her hand. If she wasn't so worried about the break-in, she might have even enjoyed watching the older woman bat her eyelashes at him. As it was, someone *had* broken in. She just technically couldn't prove it, which was why she'd called Connor.

"Ms. Finch, have you been holding down the fort?" Connor asked.

"I'm doing my best, young man," Ms. Finch replied, leaning forward just a bit.

"I'm so glad you called me, honey," Connor said, turning to her. Before Lauren could ask what the hell he was doing and why he would say something like that, he walked over to her, leaned down to kiss her cheek, and whispered in her ear. She barely heard him as her heart raced, causing a rushing sound to almost drown out his voice. "Go along with me."

Two things registered. His warm lips were like satin against her cheek and his whispered words tickled her ear. Lauren forced herself to look up into his blue eyes as he pulled away, and that's when she truly realized that whatever physical attraction was between them wasn't going away on its own.

"I had to stop by here on my way to work this morning because I'd left my cell phone in the bedroom," Connor said, smiling. Lauren tilted her head, thinking she had to have heard him wrong. "I must not have locked up. I'm so sorry you thought someone had broken in."

"That explains why I didn't hear anything," Ms. Finch said, setting her teacup and saucer on the table. She clapped her hands once as if she'd solved the case on her own. Lauren continued to stare at Connor as if he'd lost his mind. "I must have thought it was Lauren. You see, I might be old, but I can hear the difference between a key in the door and someone doing something that they shouldn't."

"I'm sure you can, Ms. Finch." Connor shrugged out of his jacket and walked back to the table to sling it across the back of a chair. Lauren wasn't sure exactly *what* she should do. What game was he playing? "Lauren so appreciates how you keep an eye on things, as do I. The city isn't the same as it used to be."

His comment got Ms. Finch going and for five minutes, Lauren stood there listening in disbelief as to how the older woman tried to be a good neighbor and watch out for things that seemed suspicious. Connor joined Ms. Finch at the table, listening to how Mr. Oldstien in apartment 305 had dementia, a newly married couple had moved into 325, and that she was pretty sure that Alice Trimino was secretively harboring a cat. Lauren wasn't spared a bit, either, as Ms. Finch relayed how Rick Hastlen was still sore that she wouldn't have dinner with him.

"That just means I'm doubly honored that Lauren took a chance on me," Connor said with a wink. "Speaking of which, you wouldn't mind leaving us alone for a moment before I have to return to work, would you?"

"Of course not, dear," Ms. Finch said, slowly rising from her chair. Connor held out a hand to assist her and they gradually made their way to the front door. "You have no idea what it does to my peace of mind, knowing that Lauren has such a strapping young man in her life to take care of her."

Lauren couldn't resist rolling her eyes and crossing her arms over her chest. Connor better have a damn good reason for lying to Ms. Finch and making it seem like they were in some type of relationship. She didn't even get to ream him out after they got to the door, because Connor followed Ms. Finch out into the hallway and made sure she made it safely in her apartment. Lauren stayed where she was, tapping her foot and glaring at the doorway. She should have called her sister when she'd had the chance. He finally made an appearance and closed them inside.

"What the hell was that?"

"It was the only way for me to cover what one of my asinine partners did," Connor said, walking toward her until they were a few feet away. "Lauren, I can't apologize enough. Jax knew that Crest and I weren't comfortable with leaving you here alone and took matters into his own hands."

"Seriously?" Lauren asked, throwing her hands up. "He thought by staging a break-in, I would cave on you staying here? That doesn't make any sense. Am I so important to this case that he would break the law?"

"Something like that," Connor murmured, running a hand through his hair. She ignored the sensual way it lay on his forehead and instead noticed that he seemed exhausted. That didn't stop him from asking more questions. "Joel Summit. Did you sell a similar set of clamps to him like you did to Marilyn Sweeney?"

Lauren wasn't finished discussing what this Jax person did to make her feel violated, but she would delay the conversation to answer his questions. She thought back to what Joel had ordered and although the stones were the same, the clamps and chains were distinctively different.

"He ordered nipple clamps with a Venetian chain, whereas Marilyn's was a Valentin style." Lauren couldn't see where he was taking this. "Connor, a lot of people choose rubies or ruby accents to adorn their clamps and collars. If you're implying that Joel had something to do with Marilyn's murder, I have a hard time believing that. He's a really nice guy."

"Is there a way for you to put a client list together of those who ordered something similar to what Marilyn did?" Connor asked.

"Yes, but shouldn't we give the list to the detectives as well?"

"The prosecutor thinks he has what he needs," Connor said, crossing his left arm over his chest while resting his right elbow on it and rubbing a hand over his face. "He's not going to blink at a list of people who ordered specialized items from your store...no matter how much it's related."

"I don't mean to change the subject," Lauren interjected, "but you look exhausted."

"I haven't slept." Connor yawned, covering his mouth with his hand. "Wait a second. Why did you come back to your apartment? Isn't your shop open?"

Lauren didn't answer right away, still absorbing the fact that he'd apparently been with someone last night. Why that should bother her when she clearly stated that she wasn't interested, she didn't know. But it did, damn it. Although he was a dominant male who lived the lifestyle, she didn't take him for a man who slept around.

"Lauren?"

"What?" She didn't mean to snap at him, but her tone had him raising his eyebrow.

"I asked if there was a specific reason that you came home from the shop this morning."

"I heard you and I'm opting not to answer," Lauren replied, trying to take back control of the conversation. "It doesn't really matter now that I know this break-in wasn't anything but a business associate of yours trying to manipulate the situation. And I'm still not sure why he would do that. As I said, multiple people within the lifestyle choose rubies to accent their toys—that doesn't make them killers."

"You're not telling me something," Connor said, letting his arms fall to his sides and taking a step closer to her.

"Why would you say that?" Lauren contemplated stepping back, but he might think that he physically affected her in some way, and she wasn't about to have that.

"You reached for the end of your curls that are draped over your shoulder." Connor seemed to study her, making her want to shift her body stance. "You've only done that once and that was just a bit ago when I misrepresented our relationship to Ms. Finch."

"What does that mean?" Lauren couldn't see his logic and wasn't about to admit that he might be on to something. Did she touch her hair when she didn't exactly tell the truth? "You know what? Don't answer that. It doesn't matter. It's obvious you keep coming back here for your investigation. I'll get the list of clients that purchased anything with rubies and have them sent to your office. Do you have a business card?"

"Why did you come home early?"

"No? Then stop by the shop tomorrow," Lauren said, continuing as if he hadn't asked that question. "And please tell your *friend* not to break into my apartment again."

Lauren went to walk around when Connor wrapped his hand around her upper arm and pulled her body close to his. Their mouths were inches apart and she placed her hands on his chest to keep herself balanced. It had been so long since she'd touched a man like this that the memories would have had her pull away, had he let her.

"What is it about you that drives me so fucking crazy?" Connor whispered, searching her eyes as if they held the answer.

She didn't have a response, so he could explore all he wanted…there was nothing to find. His lips descended on hers and Lauren decided then and there that as long as he was willing to keep the sex vanilla, there was nothing wrong with taking him up on what he offered. Anger morphed into hunger.

Chapter Ten

Connor couldn't seem to get enough of her. As he felt Lauren's fingers slide up into his hair, he used the opportunity to bring her closer. She was trying to control the momentum, and he suppressed the urge to take over. Hoisting her up, he wrapped her legs around his waist without releasing her lips.

Lauren now had both hands on his face and he felt her curls brush against his skin. Damn, he needed to fuck this woman. Making his way to the couch, he'd been about to lay her down when she used her foot to catch the material, causing him to drop both of them into a sitting position on the cushion. The moment Connor looked up into her beautiful face he could see her warring with her desire and the need to manage how this played out.

"No strings, no dominating, and no mistaking this for more than what it is," Lauren whispered, her green eyes sparkling with lust.

"Stop talking," Connor replied softly, brushing a curl away from her forehead.

Something deep inside of him knew if he said anything else, Lauren would pull away. There'd always been something innate within him to control a woman during sex and now was no different. He refrained from twisting her and placing her back on the couch and doing just that. It was a conversation that would be saved for another time. Right now, he didn't care how it happened, as long as he was able to have her.

Lauren searched his eyes, and whatever she found satisfied her curiosity for she leaned back down and ran her liquid tongue over his bottom lip. She was wearing a buttoned-down white blouse with a pair of faded jeans. He slowly released each pearl white key, and upon reaching the last one pulled away. Using his hands, he leisurely parted the material wanting to savor the view in front of him.

"Damn, you're beautiful," Connor murmured.

Easing the material over her shoulders, he couldn't prevent the small smile as he took in the light freckles that decorated her smooth pale skin. To him, it showed her femininity. Connor let the material drop down her arms. Leaning slightly forward, he brushed his lips over those tiny specks and reached around her. With one hand, he unfastened her white lace bra and slowly used his fingers to remove the straps. She shivered and the action had his cock twitching.

"What you do to me, Red…"

Wanting to see the treasure he'd revealed, Connor held her upper arms as he leaned back. Milk white skin appeared before him. Her ample breasts were perfect, with half dollar sized areolas and nipples the dimension of a pencil eraser. His mouth watered and his dick throbbed.

Before he had time to do what he wanted, Lauren surprised him when she let her knees slide down to the floor. Her fingers went right to his buckle, which she was now loosening in a rather swift manner. Connor didn't want this to be a quick fuck, but when she'd managed to get his jeans unzipped and her fingers wrapped around his cock, he admitted she wore on his resolve. He let his head fall back when her warm fingers tightened around him. His heart pounded in his chest.

"I need you," Lauren said, her voice taking on a husky tenor. "Now."

Lauren's body felt like someone had lit her on fire. She was by no means a virgin, but something about Connor Ortega raised her body heat to an inferno like no other man. Her rational behavior had taken a short hiatus and knew the culprit was the animal magnetism they both felt. She wanted him and would face the consequences, come what may.

Releasing his cock, she stood up. Connor lifted his head and seemed to devour her breasts with his eyes. Lauren reached for the button on her jeans and threaded it through the hole. Taking the zipper, she slid the metal over jagged edges and felt excitement as he watched her movements. It had been a long time since she'd seen a man look at her with that *hungry wolf about to have his prey* stare.

"Join me?" Lauren asked, not wanting to be the only one naked and vulnerable.

"You don't have to ask me twice," Connor replied, reaching for the bottom of his shirt. Whipping it off, he revealed his contoured chest with a sprinkling of hair. Her fingers itched to run through it. "Don't stop on my account."

As she pushed the denim and delicate lace panties over her legs, Lauren watched him do the same with his jeans and briefs. Once he'd removed his shoes and socks, discarded the articles of clothing and sat back, she couldn't prevent her eyes from going straight to his cock. It was long, thick, and hard. A vein ran up the side, keeping time with his heartbeat.

Connor moved to situate himself on the edge of the couch, much to her disappointment. She'd wanted to straddle herself over him. His hands reached out for her hips, bringing her closer to him. Lauren held her breath as the back of his finger brushed over her red curls. She caught herself before pushing her hips forward, wanting him to touch her clit but not wanting to seem too eager. She kept her mound trimmed, so it resembled more of a landing strip and she couldn't help but wonder what he thought. She didn't have to wait long.

"As much as I like knowing the drapes match the carpet," Connor murmured, his voice deep in a tone that sent shivers down her spine, "I want you bare."

Lauren lost her breath at recognizing his tenor. Her fingers closed over her wrist. While she emotionally felt the cold seep in, her body betrayed her as she felt her cream lubricate her folds. As if sensing her struggle, Connor looked up her. His blue eyes had turned a shade darker in intensity. She would have backed up had his left hand not tightened on her hip.

"We'll do it your way for now, Red, but don't think we won't revisit this."

Before she could reply, Connor bent his head and swiped his tongue through her curls. Lauren's hands immediately reached for him and she sank her fingers into the dark tangled mess his hair had become. His hands went around her thighs and when his grip indicated he wanted her to separate her legs, she was helpless to resist.

His warm tongue ran through her folds and he took his time exploring. By the time his mouth settled over her clit and suckled gently, Lauren couldn't suppress her wanton cries. God, he was talented.

"Please, Connor," Lauren said, unable to keep the slight desperation out of her voice, "I need you inside of me."

He finally pulled back, his lips glistening with her juices. Leaning down, Connor grabbed his jeans and rummaged through the pocket. Lauren saw the condom in his hand and knew this was a turning point. She could handle whatever came after, as long as he didn't try to force the lifestyle on her and kept things casual. Her body felt like one massive exposed nerve that needed soothing and knew that he was the only one capable of making that happen at this point in time.

It was fascinating to watch him roll the latex over his cock, not to mention erotic as hell. As if knowing she'd been struggling internally with his need to control, Connor sat back on the couch in all his glory. Lauren had no doubt he was waiting for her to make her final decision. She answered by moving forward and placing her knees on either side of him.

"Take the lead, Lauren," Connor murmured, reaching his hands up and cupping her face.

His tone indicated that this would be the last time it would happen. His eyes promised it. And maybe that was the way it should be. Connor might feel he could change her mind regarding her sexual preferences, but she knew that would never happen. She liked knowing she could make choices; she needed to have the upper hand, and as the tip of his cock nudged at her entrance, she relished the control given to her.

Inch by inch, Lauren's body accepted his length in rolling motions. He filled her and by the time she'd taken him fully inside of her, her pussy had started to randomly grip and release its captive. Lauren closed her eyes, shutting out the intensity of his. Her lips parted instinctively as he tilted her head and claimed her lips.

Neither moved their bodies as they resumed their earlier exploration of one another. Finally, Connor pulled away and she was able to drag in some much needed oxygen. His fingers trailed down her neck, over her chest and underneath her breasts. He cupped them, lifting them up as if gauging their fullness.

"Ride me, Red."

Connor leaned over, capturing one nipple in his mouth while rolling the other between his fingertips. Lauren followed his command, not because he'd ordered her, but because her body refused to stay still. Using her knees as leverage and placing her hands on his shoulders, she raised herself up until only his tip remained inside of her. When his teeth caught her nipple, she sank back down.

"Ah!" Lauren cried out, feeling his cock hit that elusive sweet spot inside of her. It wasn't near enough, so she lifted herself up again. "Harder, Connor."

Moving his hands down to her hips, Lauren was grateful that his mouth didn't release her nipple. His fingers tightened on her flesh as he took control and slammed her back down over his cock. This type of influence she didn't mind. Her legs were turning to jelly and she was grateful that Connor had the strength to maneuver them. Over and over he thrust inside of her, and every time his tip would glide over that area that created ripples throughout her very soul. When he bit her nipple, she teetered on the edge.

"Touch your clit," Connor ordered, after releasing her with his mouth. Lauren's body needed to come and she didn't think twice about following his command. She lowered her hand and when her fingers made contact with her overly sensitive clit, she moaned. The nodule of nerves was so engorged that her touch was almost painful. It didn't cause her to stop. Her own cream lubricated her fingers and she rubbed firm circles until she was crying out.

"Look at me." She opened her eyes to see him drinking her in with that familiar manner. "I want you to see me watching you come."

The second he said the word, Lauren's body exploded. Their eyes remained connected as her pussy clamped down on his cock in rapid succession. She hadn't realized just how vulnerable a woman was at this significant time until it seemed as if he were looking into her very center. She was grateful that he didn't leave her alone in that moment, as his lips parted and the blue of his eyes deepened into a sapphire color as he joined her in release.

"Connor," Lauren whispered, almost in question.

His hand reached up and buried in her curls, pulling her head down to his chest while pressing her firmly onto his cock while he released an endless stream of jets. He gently kissed her forehead and they lay there, catching their breaths once their orgasms began to fade. His skin was warm and she let herself relax against him, ignoring the tingling feeling of doubt that was sneaking in. As reality slowly returned, she bit her lip. What the hell had she just done?

Chapter Eleven

Connor's phone rang and he instantly reached for his nightstand. He felt nothing but air and he pried one eye open. The daylight in the room was painful and he brought his arm over his face to shut it out. The action didn't prevent him from immediately recognizing where he was. Damn. How long had he been asleep?

"It's two o'clock in the afternoon," Lauren said softly.

Lifting his arm, Connor managed to get both eyes open this time and saw that Lauren was looking down at him from behind the couch. She was dressed in the same clothes she'd stripped out of earlier, her hair was back in place and her make-up looked refreshed. He tried to gauge her reaction, but for a woman that he'd thought was an open book, she was doing a damn good job of keeping her feelings to herself.

"That call could be important." Lauren gestured toward his pants with her head as she lifted up a coffee cup in her hand. "Made you some coffee before I head to the post office. Thought you might need it."

"Don't leave yet," Connor said, although his voice cracked from sleep.

He cleared his throat, gratefully taking the coffee before grabbing his pants with his other hand. It took some maneuvering, but he wasn't about to give up the caffeine. He took a slug of the hot liquid as he searched his pants with his free fingers. Finally finding his phone, he saw that it was Jax. Swiping the bar, probably on the last ring before it went to voicemail, he held his cell up to his ear.

"Yeah."

"Crest wants everyone in the office tomorrow morning at seven o'clock sharp for a debriefing," Jax said. "I'm sure you received the text if you bothered to look at your phone, but since you weren't responding to mine, I figured you were otherwise engaged. Heads up, though. Reports are to be turned in, along with a verbal account of what's been discovered. Terry will be there."

"I worked on my SITREPs last night, so I'll be ready." Connor paused to take another drink. "I appreciate the call."

"The storm hit. Five inches on the ground and another six arriving tonight."

"Good thing the city has decent maintenance."

Connor watched Lauren retreat to the kitchen and pour herself a cup of coffee. She opened the drawer to retrieve a spoon, putting two sugar cubes into the steaming liquid from what looked to be an antique sugar bowl. Her movements were graceful, but something about the scene before him brought back a childhood memory of watching his mother do the same thing. He swung his feet to the ground, only then realizing she must have covered him with an afghan. He ignored the twinge of sincerity the gesture was made in.

"I'll touch base later," Connor said, ending the call.

He placed his elbows on his knees and hung his head. The women he usually slept with were subs at the club and they didn't expect anything except a scene and a damn good orgasm, if they deserved it. Lauren—hell, could she really go for something casual? Connor placed his coffee on the table in front of him and snagged up his clothes.

"Connor, I can stay long enough to finish my coffee, but I really need to hit the post office. The overnight box in the building only has one pick-up and I'm not sure if the driver will come due to the snow," Lauren said, walking around the island and perching herself on the stool. "I didn't wake you, because you obviously needed your sleep, but you and I both know this shouldn't have happened. I'll make sure you get the client list on who ordered the same exact settings and then we can go our separate ways."

Connor stood there with his jeans pulled on and nothing else, staring at her in annoyance and trying to figure out what the hell it was about this woman that burned him like the sun did in the desert. Lauren was telling him exactly what he wanted to hear, and yet it angered him that she thought she could dismiss him like a quick meaningless fuck. He wasn't about to be shelved as if he'd been a mistake—casual sex was what it was.

"It did happen," Connor stated, pulling his shirt over his head. "I'll go with you to the post office and we can discuss it. Or, we can hit the post office on the way to an early dinner. Your choice."

"That isn't a choice," Lauren exclaimed, tamping down her irritation. She turned slightly so that she could put her coffee down before it spilled. What had made her think it would be easy to get him to leave was beyond her. She stood from the stool and stiffened her resolve. She had enough common sense to know her anger would only escalate the situation. "We had sex. It was good. But we both agreed that we weren't looking for anything serious. So, the best route we could both take is opposite of each other."

"We agreed it would be casual." Connor leaned down and hooked on an ankle holster, making certain his weapon was secure. How she'd missed such a thing earlier, she didn't know. He put his black leather boots on and once finished, he snagged his cell phone and shoved it into his pocket. "I think we should stay on that course."

Connor's phone rang once more and from his expression, it was obvious he was aggravated at the interruption. Digging his cell out once more, he glanced at the phone and within seconds, his expression turned to one of tenderness. She was fascinated by the change and couldn't help but wonder who it was.

"I've got to take this," Connor said, although she could see his reluctance to interfere with their conversation.

"That's okay," Lauren said, knowing that she'd use this time to steal away. She needed to make a call as well. "Go ahead and answer."

Connor connected the call, walking around the couch and strolling to the window. "Hi, Dad. How was your week?"

For a brief moment, Lauren was speechless. She would have laughed had it been funny, but she just didn't picture Connor as someone's son. The manner in which he spoke showed the level of respect he had for his father. Hearing him connect with a family member made her think of her sister. She needed that link as well, and used his inattentiveness to leave.

She walked over to the door, shrugged her coat on and picked up the packages. Knowing that there was no way he wouldn't have heard her, Lauren turned to face him. He was still at the window, although he was looking at her with his finger held up, indicating that she should wait.

"I'll be back in thirty minutes," Lauren whispered, not knowing what else to say.

Without waiting for his response, she turned and walked out the door. Hurrying down the hallway, Lauren didn't want him to be able to stop her. Luckily, the elevator doors were open and she quickly entered, hitting the button for the lobby. The minute they closed, she sighed and leaned up against the panel. She needed just a minute to think.

By the time the elevator doors opened, Lauren had decided to use the mail department that was located in the apartment building after all. Walking quickly around the corner to the left, she entered an empty office that held specific slots for the different types of deliveries. She set her packages down on the counter and grabbed the appropriate mailing slips. Filling them out, along with her FedEx account number, she then slapped the stickers on them and slid them into the chute.

Exiting the room, Lauren wasn't about to go back upstairs just yet. Walking past the elevator and through the lobby, she walked to the window seat facing the street and made herself comfortable. Snow was coming down hard and she could see the plows hard at work. Taking her phone out of her pocket, she speed dialed her sister.

"Hello?"

"Sue? It's me."

"Hey, Carrot Top. Hold on a second." Lauren heard a muffling sound. "Lacey, give that to your brother. He had it first."

Lauren smiled when she heard Lacey arguing with her mother that boys shouldn't play with dolls. When Sue countered back that it was a GI Joe doll, Lacey said she needed him because he was taking Barbie to the movies. After three minutes of debating, Lacey was satisfied that Ken would take Barbie because GI Joe had to go and save the world.

"Nice save," Lauren said, laughing. It felt good to have a normal conversation and made her miss her sister. "I need some advice."

"My younger sister, after thirty years, is finally seeking my counsel? Hold on. I need to mark this on the calendar."

"Funny," Lauren said sarcastically, knowing that Sue felt she never took her advice. That wasn't true. Sue just wasn't here to see her follow through. "Seriously, I have no idea what to do."

"That's easy," Sue quipped. "Close up shop and move here."

Lauren and Sue were from the twin cities, but Sue had moved to Florida with her husband seven years prior. That was the year after Lauren had started her business and it wasn't in her best interest to transfer down south. Their parents had been older and by the time Lauren had been in her mid-twenties, they had both passed away. It was times like now that really hit home how alone she was here in the city.

"Maybe one day," Lauren said, giving her standard answer. She had a lot of those, which brought her back to why she called. "I, um, met someone."

A long pause came through the phone. "And that's a bad thing?"

"He's a—"

"Don't say it," Sue said. "Hold on while I put some Dora on to keep their interest."

Lauren passed the minute by watching a snow plow drive by the building. As the snowflakes fell, she caught sight of a vehicle parked across the street. A shiver of unease worked its way through her. It had to be a coincidence that it looked like the same one that had been sitting across from the shop.

"Okay," Sue said, breaking through Lauren's concentration. "They're occupied, so I should have five free, uninterrupted minutes. He's a Dom, isn't he? Did you meet him when he came to buy something?"

"Not exactly," Lauren said, hedging. She breathed a sigh of relief as the black SUV pulled out and drove away. Connor was making her paranoid. "He's a private investigator."

"And?"

"And a Dom," Lauren replied, admitting what her sister already knew. "I told him that I wasn't in the lifestyle, but he still wanted to take me to dinner."

"There has to be something about him that would even make you consider going out with him," Sue said.

"He's…intense," Lauren responded, trying to explain her attraction to Connor. A picture of him sitting with Ms. Finch flashed in her mind. "There are times when he's humorous, patient, and kind. He appears dedicated to his job, which I think is from his military background."

"Military, huh?" She clicked her tongue. "Doms in the making."

"He's caring," Lauren said, talking over her sister. She remembered Connor holding her in the hospital. Not wanting her sister to worry that she was almost mugged the other day, Lauren worded her next sentence carefully. "I, uh, fell the other day. He stayed for a while to make sure I was okay."

"He sounds almost too good to be true," Sue said, "with the exception of living in a lifestyle you want nothing to do with. I told you designing jeweled items for those people would limit your exposure to suitable men. Have you slept with him yet?"

"His father called just a few moments ago." Lauren grinned as she casually skipped over her sister's last question and remembered how Connor's face went from tenderness to one of irritation when she slipped out of the apartment. "They seem to be rather close."

"Oh, my God," Sue exclaimed, "you did have sex with him!"

Lauren instantly regretted sharing too much, as her sister obviously heard the truth in her voice. She winced, knowing that Sue was going to go from giving advice to telling her what to do. It was the curse of having an older sister.

"This changes things," Sue said. "If you felt comfortable enough to have sex with him, then—"

"It was vanilla sex," Lauren interjected, rolling her eyes. She might as well fess up her fear. "But I don't think that will keep him…you know, content for long."

"So tell him."

"Sue, it's not that simple. Men like him think they can fix everything," Lauren replied, irritation setting in. "I tried it before, remember? And I grew up with Phil. I trusted him just as I trust you, and look at how that turned out."

"But you—"

"Uh, I have to go, Sue," Lauren said, catching sight of Connor stepping off of the elevator and heading her way. He didn't look happy, but then again, she knew the minute she'd left the apartment without him that he was annoyed. "I'll touch base in a few days. Love you."

"We'd agreed to go together," Connor said in displeasure, walking up to her just as she disconnected the call. He held his bomber jacket in his hands. "It was a phone call I had to take, but you should have waited. Where are your packages?"

"I decided to use the apartment building's mailroom. The snow is coming down pretty bad," Lauren replied, tucking her phone in her coat. She didn't like the reprimand she heard in his voice. "And just for the record, I don't have a problem with you taking a phone call, but I have a business to run and your private or professional—"

Connor stepped into her personal space. The backs of her knees were up against the bench she'd been sitting on and she brought her hands up to his chest to keep herself balanced. His body heat immediately soaked into her front, while the chill from the window enclosed her back.

"Let's worry about our private and professional lives to-morrow," Connor murmured, his lips inches from hers. "Come back upstairs with me."

His invitation surprised her, yet didn't. Her body felt alive every time he was near and it was obvious to her that whatever attraction they felt for one another hadn't been extinguished with one round of sex. Lauren knew their time was running out. Connor wasn't the type of man to allow his inner dominant self to stay dormant for long, but in the meantime, maybe she could work him out of her system.

"Okay."

Chapter Twelve

Connor slammed the door shut with his foot. He threw his coat on the floor and then proceeded to remove hers. Lauren helped, and within minutes they were both naked. He'd managed to grab a condom out of his wallet before all the articles of clothing hit the ground. Vowing to make it to the bedroom this time, Connor lifted her up and had her straddle his waist.

He'd managed to get them to where the island was, but instead of turning to the left and continuing to her bedroom, he decided the center island would have to do. He needed to taste her again. Placing her on the hard faux stone surface, Connor tangled his hands in her hair and continued to kiss her. He loved her curls, but it was the other ones that garnered his attention.

"I want to take my time," Connor whispered, releasing her now swollen lips.

Running his tongue along her jawline, he continued down her neck and over the ample swell of her breast. He sucked her nipples into his mouth, separately in turn, loving the small cry that crossed her lips with each surrender. She was so sensitive, and with each pleading cry his dick hardened. Lauren tried to pull away, but he held her to him, nibbling and biting on her nipple until she said his name in a way that caused him to look up.

Desire was mixed with some unidentifiable emotion he couldn't quite place. There was something in her eyes made him realize that when he'd not let her move away, it made her uneasy. That was the last thing he wanted. Palming her face, he kissed her gently.

"Let me taste you," Connor murmured after releasing her lips. He studied her, waiting for her consent. It wasn't something he was used to, but if it would erase the doubts that had crept into her green eyes, then he would give her the leeway she needed. Again, Connor felt like he was missing a piece of the puzzle when it came to figuring her out. "I want more than a few seconds this time."

Lauren nodded. Instead of leaning down immediately, Connor gently pushed her back until she was lying on the counter. Slowly, he situated her hands up by her head, turning her palms downward. He wrapped her fingers under the stone counter and indicated with a squeeze that he wanted her to keep them there. He did nothing at first, wanting her to see that although that was where he wanted her, she still had the choice. Lauren watched him, but didn't move. Arousal started to darken her eyes once more.

Using his hands, he brushed his fingers over her skin, breasts, nipples, and abdomen, wondering if he'd ever be able to count the freckles that decorated her skin. Connor would love to try, though now wasn't the time. Taking her ankles in his hands, he planted her heels on the countertop as well, separating them enough so that he would be able to gain uninhibited access.

Her curls were wet. Lauren's clit was slightly engorged and glistening from her juices. Her labia were spread open like the petals of a flower, revealing her waiting entrance. Her pussy reminded him of a red rose that was in bloom. Her nectar was his for the taking and his mouth watered. Connor brought his eyes back up over her body, gauging her reaction of his scrutiny. He'd always admired a woman's body, and hers was exquisite. Curvy, sensuous, and just plain beautiful.

Not able to wait anymore and seeing that the longer he delayed, the deeper green her eyes became, Connor used his fingers to spread her silky folds. He flattened his tongue and stroked it across her tiny pearl. Instantly he felt her fingers in his hair, as if she could control her pleasure. This is why he enjoyed binding a woman. He drew away.

"Put your hands back, Red." Connor gathered her hands, careful not to touch her wrist for fear of triggering something he was still unaware of. "I just want to give you pleasure without interference. If you want me to stop, all you have to do is say so."

Lauren struggled for air. Her body felt like it was overheating and she knew the only way to cool herself off was by having that sought after release. Connor could give it to her, but there were moments that the intensity seemed almost a little too much for her. He was now standing between her legs, his eyes taking in every movement and expression she revealed. He hovered over her fiery landing strip and focused on her every reaction with those twin blue pools of freshly melted ice. It wasn't as if he were tying her down with rope, or blindfolding her to where she couldn't see. He was just asking that she keep her hands up. She could do that, right?

"Give me pleasure, you blue-eyed devil," Lauren said, hoping her interjection of lightness prevented this from getting too serious.

Connor smiled and she felt like she was melting all over again. His head dipped down and the last thing she saw were his pools of blue before his dark lashes covered them. Again, his tongue rasped against her clit, causing her to feel as if she were floating. Electrical impulses shot through her. She gripped the granite and bit her lip. How could he incite this much pleasure in her body from a quick swipe of his tongue?

"Ohhhh," Lauren cried out, lifting her hips. He'd closed his lips around her clit and sucked. He did place one hand on her abdomen, but not in a way that would cause her to panic. He'd used his fingers to pull her skin taut and her hood back, causing her clit to rise and reveal itself. It was a unique feeling and one she didn't mind. In fact, she loved it. "More."

He hummed his agreement. Connor continued to suckle, while his other hand joined in. As his finger entered her pussy, Lauren wondered if it was possible to break granite. Her grip tightened as she felt him doing something different. It took her a moment to realize that his palm was face up. He'd used his index finger to enter her, while his thumb and middle finger pressed on either side of her labia. Her engorged clit was still being suckled. The combination of sensations carried her toward a cliff.

"Please," Lauren whispered, not even knowing what she was begging for. Did she want him to stop or continue? If he stopped, she might die...but if he continued, the same outcome was foreseeable. "Please."

He didn't increase his speed. Connor maintained the same pressure, pace, and suction. That seemed to fuel her even more, triggering her body to go past a pleasure point she wasn't even aware she had. It was when his finger curled up, stroking that sweet spot within her that she saw stars.

"Connor!"

Contraction after contraction took over, but he still didn't falter. His right hand helped her stay in place, while his mouth and the fingers of his left held her in her release. It was the longest orgasm she'd ever experienced and by the time she caught her breath, Connor had made his way up her body to place a kiss on her mouth. She opened her eyes and tasted herself on his lips.

"Ready for another?"

Connor watched her sleep from his stance by the bedroom window. Lauren was lying on her side, her hand tucked underneath her cheek. Her red curls seemed to be everywhere, almost making the picture of her in bed surreal. They had used the two remaining condoms that he'd had in his wallet, but it still wasn't enough. What the hell was it about this woman that he couldn't seem to get enough of?

Turning back to the window, he leaned up against the cold frame. The snow had stopped sometime in the middle of the night, but the plows were still working their way through the city. Connor watched one as it turned right on a cross-street, heading toward the warehouse district reminding him that he should be getting dressed and heading out for his seven o'clock meeting with the team.

In between their sex sessions, Lauren had printed him out a list of clients who requested rubies as their accents to whatever items they'd ordered. He had yet to look at it, having other things on his mind. Connor would take the names with him to this morning's meeting. The question he still couldn't answer was if he would be back to see Lauren on a personal level.

The phone call from his father yesterday had brought back all the reasons why it was a bad idea to get involved with someone like Lauren. Regardless of what she said about a casual relationship, she would eventually want more. Which led straight into the situation that he knew would happen. She was the type of woman who wouldn't intentionally hurt someone, but he wasn't naïve enough to think that when someone wealthier and with a better social standing came along, that she wouldn't jump on that bandwagon.

The city scene below faded, taking him back to when he was six years old. His father's face void of the aging it had now. The vision never failed to tighten his chest with anguish, as that was when his innocence had been taken away.

"Where's Mom?" Connor said, his little fingers holding his spoon.

"She had to leave, son," Alberto Ortega replied, taking a seat next to him at the kitchen table. His father was a busy man and rarely sat with him for breakfast, so Connor knew something was terribly wrong.

"Who's going to take me to school?" Connor put his spoon back in his cereal bowl, no longer hungry. "When will she be back?"

"Connor, she won't be coming back." Alberto laced his hands together and placed them in front of him. He studied them like Connor did his spelling words. "It's important for you to understand that she does love you."

"Why isn't she coming back?" Connor asked, his eyes filling with tears. "If she loves me, then she wouldn't leave."

For the first time in his life, Connor saw his father's eyes fill with tears. His dad was strong. Strong men didn't cry, did they? He panicked and shot up from his seat. His mother had made his father cry.

"Dad?"

"I know you won't understand this, but your mother needed something that I couldn't give her." Alberto looked around the small kitchen that Connor had always felt safe in. His heart started to beat too fast. It was a

room he was coming to hate. "It has nothing to do with her love for you, son."

Connor shook his head back and forth. His grandmother told him all the time that love was strong. "Abuelita says love is stronger than anything. If that's true, then Mama wouldn't have left. That means she didn't love us."

"Your intelligence is getting the best of you, mi hijo," Alberto said, shaking his head. "Life is not always as simple as your grandmother makes it out to be. One can love and not be happy. That is your mother, who is seeking something that I cannot give her."

Connor watched as his father struggled for more words, but he didn't need to hear anything else. He wrapped his arms around his father's wide shoulders, promising to himself that he would go find his mother and bring her back. He would prove to her that he and his father loved her. Once she knew that, she would never leave them again.

"Connor?"

He jerked away from the window. Running a hand over his face, Connor tried like hell to dispel the memory as well. Turning to face her, he saw that Lauren was still lying in bed and snuggled under the covers. Not wanting her to think that anything was amiss, he made his way over to the bed.

"Go back to sleep," Connor whispered, reaching for his jeans. "I was checking the weather."

"M-kay," Lauren murmured, adjusting her pillow.

Connor waited until he was sure that she'd dozed off again before dressing. Quietly opening her bedside table drawer, he found a pen but not paper. Looking around, he saw the list she'd printed lying on the dresser. Tearing off the portion that was blank, he quickly scribbled a note and laid it down on the pillow for her to find when she awakened. It would at least give him time to figure out what he was going to do.

Chapter Thirteen

"Terry, you already know a few of my team members. But I'll make the introductions anyway. In order around the table are Jax, Connor, Taryn, Keith, and Ethan," Crest said, standing with Terry on one side of the table. He indicated each team member as they nodded according to his roll call.

"I truly appreciate all the time that you have invested in my case," Terry said, taking the seat next to Crest as everyone took their place at the table.

Connor studied him. They'd met several times—once or twice when he'd stopped in to see Crest at the office, once this past week to discuss the case, but more so at the clubs. Terry hadn't been much for the club scene, not so much as his wife had been. He was in his mid-forties but looked older. Connor knew that wasn't just due to losing his wife. He just wasn't a man who aged well. Probably around five feet, ten inches tall, Terry's hair was receding and he opted for small, round wire-rimmed glasses over contacts, giving him a bug-eyed look. He appeared to be what he was...a surgeon. Connor knew that

Crest and Terry had been childhood friends, but he failed to see what kept that friendship alive.

"They know you do," Crest said, gesturing with his hand that he wanted everyone's reports.

Each team member handed over two copies, and while Crest gave Terry a set, Connor jotted down a series of questions that he wanted answers to. He'd spoken to Terry before, but now that the investigation had gotten under way the more he realized they didn't know enough about Marilyn to even comprehend which direction the case should take them.

"I appreciate the time that you've given me to be able to grieve," Terry said, taking his glasses by the rim and moving them up the bridge of his nose. "The funeral went as well as could be expected. Marilyn's parents…"

Connor and the rest of the team allowed Terry to have a moment while he struggled with his composure. Crest knew that it was vital they have full access to Terry, but he had wanted to give his friend a time of mourning. That period was over and they needed answers to the questions that seemed to be building by the day.

"We'll do everything we can to catch who did this," Connor said. "Unfortunately, the questions we need to go over are going to be difficult for you. I know that Crest debriefed you the night you were arrested, but information has come to light that we need verified for us to continue."

"Kevin, you start," Crest ordered, leaning back in his seat and picking up Kevin's report.

Jessie had set up carafes of coffee before everyone congregated in the conference room. The only person not drinking any was Ethan and that was because he preferred those high-energy drinks with a ton of caffeine. Ethan hadn't had to turn in a SITREP due to the fact that he was on the outskirts of the investigation. He was still wrapping up old assignments, but Crest wanted him aware of the facts in case he needed to pull him in.

"I've hit up every snitch I know and nothing panned out until I came across a low-level dealer," Kevin said, not taking his eyes off of Terry. Connor's eyes and ears perked up. "He became antsy when I mentioned Marilyn's name and then clammed up. I didn't think it was a good idea to push him at the time. Before I head back out on the street to question him more, is there something I should know?"

All eyes went to Terry, who looked a little lost. Connor felt sympathy for him. The person sharing your life and who you should know better than anyone else was turning out to be a complete stranger. Now, here the team was picking apart his life. Terry's glasses had slipped again and he pushed up them up with his middle finger.

"Marilyn didn't do drugs," Terry replied, shaking his head most vehemently. He placed his elbows on the table and clasped his hands in front of him. Although his next words were muffled, they were still audible. "If you're referring to a man named Hash, it was me who bought some stuff off of him, although it's been a while. But I never gave him my name."

Connor could tell that Crest didn't know that piece of information by the way his facial expression froze. He hid it well, but Connor had to wonder what other information was being kept from them. He still had that gut instinct that they were missing a simple piece of the puzzle.

"Think Hash recognized Terry's picture on the eleven o'clock news?" Jax asked.

"Maybe," Kevin responded, not taking his eyes off of Terry. He kept the interview moving forward by inquiring what everyone else was wondering. "What were you buying from Hash that you didn't have available to you at the hospital?"

Terry swallowed and Connor noticed his knuckles turning white. Shame was written all over his face, his actions backing up that judgment. His face was flushed and his shoulders were slumped a little.

"Amyl Nitrate," Terry said, lowering his gaze to his hands. "Please understand that I work long hours. When I wasn't on call, Marilyn and I played at home and I needed...I just needed something to help enhance the experience and be able to sustain the level of passion she needed."

Kevin nodded and wrote something down on the paper situated in front of him. He asked a few more questions about his dealings with Hash, but nothing of surprise came after that. Connor glanced at Crest, seeing that he was studying Terry. Nothing fazed Crest as he'd seen it all, but he appeared to expect better of his friend.

Crest indicated that Taryn should go next. Connor was always amazed that she could look refreshed no matter how little sleep she got or how many hours on the job she put in. Her spiky blonde hair was tousled as usual and she pulled her glasses down to the bridge of her nose to look at her report. Connor leaned forward, knowing that she was a whiz with her computer. She amazed him by being able to find the smallest piece of information.

"As everyone is aware, I was able to obtain the member lists from both clubs. Joel Summit turned in his and it matches with what was in his computer. The glitch came when Gerry Mason handed his over. He deleted Marilyn's name as a member and placed her as a guest of his." Taryn looked up and over the bridge of her glasses. "Do you know of any reason why he would do that?"

CAPTURED INNOCENCE   ❖   133

Terry shook his head and sat back in his chair as if exhausted. "This is what I know and told all of you a week ago. A year ago Marilyn felt like she wasn't getting what she needed out of our scenes. She was a masochist and I had a hard time with that. I wasn't comfortable with the amount of pain she needed. She asked permission to go to the clubs more often and we chose Greg Winters as a Dom who could possibly scene with her. He agreed, but a few months ago he told us of his decision to stop."

"Do you know why?" Connor asked.

"He felt that she was pushing the envelope, wanting and requiring more."

"And Greg wasn't willing to cross that line?"

"No," Terry replied. He looked up, connecting their stares. Connor could see the level of emotion swimming in his eyes and his need to make them understand. "Marilyn was a good woman. You, of all people should know that submissives need certain things. I couldn't give her that. But at Christmas, one of her presents was a cane and I promised her I would practice with it and push my limits."

"Greg opting out confirms what I heard over at Masters," Connor said, verifying to everyone that piece of information. "Did you know that she was going over to Whip?"

"I knew she had tried it out. But as I said, we started to connect around Christmastime. Marilyn gave me an unusual gift. It was a collar, with matching nipple and clit clamps." Terry took a deep breath, as if that memory was a special one for him. "She said that it was her way of recommitting herself to me. See, I never really collared her. She was my wife, for Christ's sake. I just didn't see the need."

"And she *wanted* to be collared?" Jax asked, rolling a pen around his knuckles.

"I didn't know it until then, but yes," Terry answered. "I assumed from that night on that she was only attending the clubs on a social setting—not a play one. I work long hours and there are times I have to travel to conferences. I understood her need to be around other people in the lifestyle. When I spoke with her on the phone earlier…that day…she said she was going to stop by Masters and I mentioned that I'd meet her there when my plane landed. That was the first time that I'd been to the club in months."

"Were you aware of her attending any private parties?" Connor asked, urging Terry to keep on talking and not allow his emotions to interfere.

"What?"

"Gerry and Joel have apparently been hosting some private parties. It's my understanding that she attended at least one."

"No, she didn't say anything to me," Terry replied, his brow furrowed. "I don't understand why she would have kept it secret. We were fixing things, making them right…"

"I'm sure the two of you were," Connor said, trying to soften his tone. He shared a knowing look with Jax. "Did she ever mention Gerry to you?"

"No," Terry said. "I know about the bad blood that runs between Joel and Gerry though. Everyone does. I still can't believe…do you know if she played with anyone?"

Connor could almost see the plea in Terry's eyes for him to say that she hadn't played. The truth of the matter was, he didn't know. He and Jax still had a lot of ground to cover when it came to finding out the details of these gatherings.

"We're not sure yet," Connor replied.

"I found nothing in my investigation and research that would conclude this was the work of a serial killer," Taryn said, continuing on with her report. "We are still waiting for forensics in regards to DNA, and as far as Marilyn's computer goes, there was nothing there to indicate she'd met someone online. The police *are* searching for any type of online order or receipt for the rope that was used to tie her up, but I've come up with nothing."

Crest followed up with some questions of his own, so Connor leaned closer to Taryn. There was an angle he wanted to her to check into.

"When you said there were no related murders within the last ten years, did you look into unsolved murders *not* in the lifestyle?" Connor asked, keeping his voice low.

Taryn turned her golden-brown eyes on him, giving him a cat stare. She raised one eyebrow, as if to question his sanity. Connor realized his choice of words were poor and seeing how he'd just pissed her off, started to back away. He'd talk to her about it later.

"I love your faith in me," Taryn murmured sarcastically, taking ahold of her glasses on the side and putting them back in place. "Yes, I did. I've expanded the search, but there are small town areas that aren't so keen on electronic files. The results will take awhile, but you'll notice that I'm usually here until the wee hours of the night as well."

Connor knew that if he were to comment again, she'd probably hand him his head, but that wasn't going to stop him. He was thinking, regardless of the evidence, that they might be taking this way too personally. What if the killer didn't know Marilyn at all?

"What about redheads?" Connor whispered.

"You're really pushing me this morning and I haven't had enough caffeine," Taryn replied, looking over the table at Crest. "I'm checking every angle and that includes personal characteristics. So far, my conclusion would be that it was a personal attack against Marilyn or Terry."

Connor finally leaned back in his chair, satisfied that Taryn was cross-referencing everything. He admitted he was a control freak, but he kept replaying his conversation with Lauren from yesterday morning. She never did answer him on why she'd returned to her apartment. Her behavior indicated she was nervous about something, but then other things had intruded—mainly his need to have her. He couldn't erase the unease over her attempted mugging though. Could there really be a connection?

"The next private party is set for next month," Jax said, his voice cutting in on Connor's thoughts. "Connor was the one who got the low-down on Marilyn being at one a couple of months ago. There might be some people there who don't play in public, so I'll see if I can finagle an invite. I've also narrowed down two Doms who are well versed in shibari. I don't usually talk to them, so I need some time to get close. I've given Taryn their names and she's retracing their paths on the night of the murder."

"Do you think one of them might have…" Terry didn't finish that sentence with words, but instead waved his hand in gesture. It was still evident that he was having a hard time coming to grips with the fact that his wife was murdered. Hell, who wouldn't be? "Do you think they were at the party?"

"Again, it's a lead we're checking into," Jax replied.

"Alex Snyder was the one to give me information regarding Joel and Gerry," Connor said. "He likes Whip versus Masters, because of the bodily fluid rule. He's harmless, but he has eyes and ears low to the ground. He likes to feel important, so it's easy to obtain info from him. I'm sure you met him a time or two at Masters."

"Vaguely," Terry said. A small smile crossed his lips, although sorrow seemed to have overcome him. "When Marilyn and I did go together, we liked to use the time to play instead of socialize."

"There is one thing that stood out this past weekend. When Connor and I were at Whip, I noticed similar clamps to those that Marilyn wore on a submissive. We have no idea if it means anything," Jax said, still weaving his pen, "but considering Marilyn had them on at the time of her murder, we're not discounting anything. Joel Summit was the one to order the nipple clamps for this particular sub."

"I'm sure Crest told you, Terry," Connor said, knowing that now was the time that he should bring up Lauren, "but the vendor that Marilyn purchased her collar and clamps from experienced an attempted mugging. At this time, we don't know if there's a connection, but we're obviously not ruling it out. I have a list of clients who made similar purchases—not just Joel. Between all of us, we have a lot of leads that we're following up on."

"Can't you bring Joel in for questioning?" Terry asked, sitting straighter. They'd given him hope and now he was grabbing onto it with both hands. Connor started to doubt if giving him so much information was wise, but he was technically their client. He just hoped that Terry didn't run off half-cocked and do something stupid. "I mean, Joel's name is connected with both the party and the jewelry. What are you waiting for?"

"Terry, the police are the official investigators," Crest said, rubbing his chin. "We are working for you, but the best way for us to gather information is from the inside. If we pull Joel in now, he'll only lawyer up. He doesn't have to answer any of our questions."

"What if I—"

Crest immediately shut Terry down, warning him of the dangers of doing so. Connor knew it had to be hard for Terry to sit on the sidelines and let everyone else ask the questions and do their job. If he started to go out there and ask inquiries, all he'd do is scare off the suspect and make the trails of evidence disappear.

"I get it," Terry said, a spark of anger shining through. That wasn't a bad thing. It would carry him through the hard time ahead. "I'll let you handle it."

Crest wrapped up the meeting, but Connor saw his veiled signal indicating he should stay. One by one, they all filed out of the conference room with the exception of him, Crest, and Terry.

"Terry, if you could wait for me in my office I would appreciate it," Crest said, gathering his papers.

"Sure," Terry said, reaching over the table and offering his hand. "Connor, thank you. She was…everything to me."

Connor returned his handshake and waited until he'd left the room before turning to Crest. His irritation instantly spiked, knowing what Crest was going to say before the words ever left his mouth. What irked him the most was that Crest had every right to ask.

"Is Lauren Bailey going to be an issue?"

"No," Connor replied, looking Crest in the eye and being as honest as he could. "We're involved, but I can keep things separate. It's nothing serious."

"Whether or not it's serious isn't in question." Crest put his hands in his pockets and rocked back on his heels. "Any involvement can compromise your behavior on this case."

Connor refrained from saying that this case *was* personal and that Crest's personal interests already affected the case, but knew that wouldn't get him anywhere. He just needed to work Lauren out of his system. Once he got his fill, he'd be able to walk away.

"I'll keep things separate, Top."

"See that you do," Crest said, turning to walk away.

"Question for you, though," Connor said, waiting for his superior to turn around. "Did you know that Terry was into drugs?"

"Does it make a difference to this case?"

Connor studied him, seeing his jaw had squared with tension. Did it alter their investigation? No, he thought, it didn't. His gut instinct still told him that Terry Sweeney was innocent. However, he wouldn't want Terry operating on him in a surgery room.

"If he wants us to solve this case, he needs to come clean with us with regards to every aspect of his life," Connor said, knowing he wasn't saying anything that Crest didn't know. He still needed to say it. They were a team and had each other's back. "Let me know what else creeps up."

Crest nodded and walked out the door. Connor remained behind, gathering up his pen and notepad that he'd review in detail. His day was cut out for him, reading and examining everything he'd been given. Thoughts of a certain ginger wouldn't leave him though, and as he stared at the list she'd given him, he knew the day was going to be a long one.

Chapter Fourteen

Lauren knew that she should head to the shop to cut some stones, but after everything that had happened over the weekend, couldn't bring herself to do it. She was mentally and physically tired. She'd stayed in her apartment instead, pondering the note Connor had left. He mentioned that he'd be stopping by around six o'clock this evening and that he'd love to take her to dinner. Technically, they hadn't even had a date before they'd had sex, so he did have a point. Though, that point would be invalid if she chose not to see him again. She wondered if the dull ache in her head was due to her recent concussion or the seesaw that her mind was obviously on.

"The sex is great."

There. She said that out loud to her empty kitchen and nothing burned to the ground. Her gaze flicked to the chicken in the oven to confirm that fact before returning to her problem at hand. Connor had shown restraint in his dominant tendencies, although the underlying assertiveness was there. She'd handled it and found that her body responded to him.

"That's because you know that if you could get past your phobia, you'd be living the lifestyle." *Oh, my God.* "I'm having a conversation with myself."

She needed wine. She needed fortitude. What happened to the strong-willed businesswoman who showed no weakness?

Lauren made her way to the refrigerator and opened the door. Her wine preferences ran toward the sweet and sparkling, so she only bought red Moscato. Pulling out a bottle, she then grabbed a wine glass on her way to where she kept her corkscrew in one of the middle drawers.

If she were to categorize the issues at hand, similar to that of making decisions regarding her business, then maybe she'd come to a conclusion. She slipped the cork out of the bottle. In the plus category, she filed the following—she felt attracted to Connor, all he wanted was something casual, and he was willing to keep it vanilla. In the negative column—would he be able to conceal his dominant tendencies until their affair was over, would it stay casual, and most importantly, would she be able to keep herself from wanting more and eventually ruining whatever relationship they had, similar to what she had done with Phil? Lauren poured a healthy amount of wine, not even close to figuring out what she should do.

A knock sounded throughout the apartment. She made her way to the door, wine glass in hand, and looked through the peephole. Connor's blue eyes stared back at her in approval. Okay, so maybe she'd just let things go and see what happened. That's what nature did. Lauren swung open the door.

"Hi."

"Hi, yourself." Connor smiled and when she backed up, he entered. "I'm glad that you're checking to see who's at the door before you answer it."

CAPTURED INNOCENCE ❖ 143

Lauren realized then that she'd forgotten to tell him about the SUV that had been sitting across from the shop yesterday, but didn't want to start off their evening on such a disturbing note. She'd tell him a little later. Closing the door, she faced him.

"Instead of going out, I marinated some chicken and roasted potatoes. I thought—"

Lauren had been about to cross the room to the kitchen when his hand wrapped around her upper body. She gasped and instinctively held up her glass to prevent her wine from spilling. Within seconds, she forgot about the wine as his lips met hers with hunger. While his right hand remained on her arm, his left came up and his fingers tangled in her curls. He grabbed hold and tilted her head for a better angle. He consumed her, tasting every crevice of her mouth. By the time he was done, her lips were swollen and she was gasping for breath.

"Wine lips," Connor murmured, releasing her. "You taste good."

Lauren didn't know what to say to that, so she remained silent and turned to head back into the kitchen. She didn't have anything for him to drink, other than the wine, so she busied herself with pouring another glass while he removed his jacket and hung it on her coat rack near the door.

Connor must have gone home to change at some point. He was wearing darker jeans and a dark blue pullover shirt with long sleeves. She noted the absence of a bag and wondered if he was planning on leaving after dinner.

"You're awfully quiet," Connor said, walking up to the island and taking a seat on one of the stools.

"I'll be honest here," Lauren replied, sliding the wine glass his way, "I'm not sure how to proceed right now. I hadn't exactly planned this. I'm not even sure we should continue what we've started."

Connor didn't say anything as he picked up his glass and took a drink. She couldn't help but notice the way his lips formed over the rim. As the liquid slipped past and into his mouth, the visual caused heat to flash over her body. She lifted her eyes to his and wondered what he was thinking.

"Tell me about yourself," Connor finally said, breaking the silence. He softly placed the glass back on the counter. "Are you from the city?"

Lauren took a deep breath. She could make small talk. Leaning over the counter, she rested herself on her elbows while keeping her glass between her fingers.

"My sister and I grew up in Woodbury," Lauren said. "When she married and moved to Florida, I stayed here and decided it would be easier to live in the city. My business grew at a rapid pace, so I thought it best."

"Do your parents still live there?"

"No," Lauren said, shaking her head. She did smile, childhood memories resurfacing. "They were older when they had us and both passed away years ago. Dad had a heart attack and Mom became aimless after that. She suffered a stroke a year after he died and was never quite the same. Sue flew back home when it was mom's time to go."

"I'm sorry," Connor said, reaching out and brushing his fingers against hers. She could hear the sincerity in his voice and it made her want to ask about his family, but he continued. "Are you and your sister close? I know that Ms. Finch pops in once in a while, but you don't seem to have many friends…and I don't mean that as an insult, just an inquiry."

"Yes, my sister and I are very close." Lauren liked that he kept his hand on hers, so she didn't move. "As for friends, a few are still around from high school and college, but I don't see them often. I video conference with my sister all the time. She's my best friend, so seeing and talking to her over the computer makes it seem likes she's actually here. She's constantly trying to get me to move down with her, but it just never seems like the right time. I have a solid business here, although my online sales have tripled. I might just end up closing the shop."

"What made you get into specializing in BDSM equipment?"

"Before I answer that, I think it's only fair I get to ask you some questions," Lauren said, aware of the fact that once talk turned to the lifestyle, he might have more personal questions for her than she was willing to answer at the moment. "Your father called yesterday. Does he live in town?"

"No. He lives in New Jersey," Connor said, his finger making designs on the back of her hand. She found it hard to concentrate, but all of a sudden felt the need to know more about him. "He emigrated from Cuba when he was a teenager. He worked through high school and found that he was good with his hands. He owns a garage and has such a loyal customer base he was able to survive the economic crisis we've been having."

"Do you see him often?" Lauren found herself fascinated by his facial expressions as he spoke of his dad. He radiated affection.

"Not as much as I'd like to," Connor replied with a soft smile. "I get out to the east coast maybe three times a year and in between cases or government contracts."

"What about your mother?" Lauren asked and then wished she hadn't. His smile disappeared and his face became like stone. Connor withdrew his hand and sat up straighter, taking a drink of wine. Her skin now felt chilled. "I'm sorry. If that's a bad topic, I—"

"She left," Connor replied, his tone short. "Marinated chicken? That sounds good."

He removed himself from the stool and walked around the island. Opening the oven a crack, Connor inhaled deeply and moaned in appreciation. It was obvious that he was dramatizing his reaction, but Lauren went along with it.

"It should be done, if you want to take it out of the oven," Lauren said, moving to the cabinet where her dishes were. "I'll set the table."

"Do you like to cook?"

Lauren permitted the change of subject, wanting the playful Connor back. While they each did their duties, they kept the conversation light. It wasn't until she'd refilled their glasses and they had situated themselves at her small table that the topic turned to his case.

"You were right about the list," Connor said, using his knife to cut into the chicken. "I looked at the items ordered and a lot of your clientele like rubies cut in different styles to accentuate the leather, clamps, or chains they choose."

"It's a pretty gem," Lauren said, pulling a small potato off of her fork. She chewed and swallowed before continuing. "As I said before, there is nothing out of the ordinary with any of my orders. Joel is a nice guy, along with most of my clients."

"Are there some customers that make you uncomfortable?" Connor studied her, but she had to smile when he took a bite of her chicken and moaned in appreciation. "This is damn good."

"Thank you," Lauren said with a laugh, liking the fact that he was relaxed again. She made a mental note to never bring up his mother, although that didn't diminish her curiosity about a woman who could leave a family. Were there extenuating circumstances? "Um, customers. Let's see. There is a man who doesn't play at the clubs that comes in at least once a quarter and orders various implements. He's obsessed with butt plugs."

"Really?" Connor said, smiling. Lauren rolled her eyes. "In what way?"

"The base of certain plugs can be adorned with jewels. He happens to like that design and has a huge collection." Lauren started in on her chicken. "I'm assuming he allows the subs to keep them since he continually places orders."

"Why don't you think it's for one particular sub?" Connor asked with a raised eyebrow.

"I... well, that's a lot of plugs for one person," Lauren said, returning his look.

Connor laughed and shook his head, as if she were missing part of the picture. She mentally shrugged. They continued talking until something he said sparked a memory.

"Say that again," Lauren said, tilting her head. Why had his comment given her pause? "About color."

"Which part?" Connor asked, a sly grin on his face. "The part where I think emeralds complement your eyes or that fact that certain shades of stones can bring out the radiance in a woman?"

"A Domme said the same thing to me around a month ago," Lauren replied, trying to think back. She waved her fork, as if by doing so she could conjure the image. "She was gliding her hands over a chain inlaid with various stones and said those words."

"Do you remember who?" Connor asked, placing his fork on the plate and reaching for his wine. "At your shop or at one of your booths?"

"I was at Masters and it was a larger woman who had a penchant for black latex." Lauren could picture the woman in her head but was coming up blank with a name.

"Mistress Beverly?"

✧   ✧   ✧   ✧

Connor tensed, waiting for Lauren's answer. He thought back to his conversation with Russell, Kyle, and Bev. She exhibited her normal behavior and he couldn't think of anything said or done that would indicate otherwise.

"No," Lauren said, shaking her head. She placed her fork down as well. "This woman was thinner and had shorter hair, although similar in color."

Connor went back to eating, looking at his plate as if it would summon up a picture. Three women came to mind, but two of them were into men. Only one was into both women and men who might say something along those lines. In which case, it shouldn't concern the case.

"Mistress Vivien?"

"No," Lauren said, taking up his cue and finishing what was left of her potatoes. "Wait! I remember her name. It was Donna."

Connor stopped chewing. He couldn't picture Mistress Donna saying something like that. She wasn't into women and certainly wasn't the poetic type to speak of shades and radiance. It was probably nothing, but he'd still look into it.

"You know, I keep meaning to ask you," Connor said, finishing the last bite on his plate. Pushing the dish aside, he realized that it was the first home cooked meal he'd had in months. She was a damned good cook. "Why did you come home early yesterday?"

"I had wanted to mail those packages and had left without them," Lauren replied, toying with what was left of her chicken. Connor waited for her to look up at him. There was something she wasn't telling him. "I will admit that when I left the store, there was a black SUV sitting across the street that made me slightly uneasy. I think there was someone sitting inside, but I couldn't be sure. It drove off. When I arrived and saw my door unlocked…"

"I'm sorry about that," Connor said, and he truly meant that. Jax had no right to do what he did. "Getting back to this SUV, had you seen it before?"

The slight hesitation of Lauren's shaking head clued him right in. He finished his wine and set the glass on the table, not taking his eyes off of hers. She shifted uncomfortably, but eventually spoke.

"No, but when I was talking to my sister on the phone yesterday, I looked out the window of the building and thought I saw a similar vehicle." Lauren pushed her chair back and started gathering plates. "It pulled away. I think it was a coincidence. Being around you seems to make me paranoid."

"I don't believe in coincidences," Connor said, standing as well. He helped clear the table, all the while trying to formulate his thoughts. His gut was telling him she was a central key to this case and he didn't like that one bit. He'd told Crest that his relationship wouldn't interfere with the investigation, but if push came to shove, he knew that protecting her would come first. *Fuck.* "Has anything else out of the ordinary happened?"

"No." Lauren stacked the dishes in the sink and although he tried to rinse them off, she shooed him away. "I'll take care of them later. Would you like some coffee?"

Connor couldn't tell if she was nervous and trying to delay the inevitable or if she truly wanted coffee, so he chose the second route. He fully intended to end this evening in her bed. His cock had been semi-hard since he'd walked in and kissed her, but there was something said for getting to know her a little better. He found he wanted to, although he knew the signs of when things became too serious. It was then that he would walk away.

"Sure," Connor said, "coffee sounds great."

Lauren busied herself with preparing the pot and getting out two coffee mugs. Connor didn't immediately go into the living room, but instead leaned against the island to watch her move about. The way her hips flared and how her ass was perfectly shaped in those jeans, Connor had a hard time allowing her to finish. She'd kept her hair down, so her curls hung naturally low to the middle of her back. She wore a cream sweater where the material ruffled at the wrist, giving it a feminine appearance.

"Why shy away from a lifestyle that you obviously desire?"

Lauren's hands stilled mid-reach for the sugar. He knew he'd taken her unaware, but that wasn't such a bad thing. People tended to answer honestly when taken by surprise.

"Why would you think I *want* to be involved with BDSM? Because I enhance the implements and toys that go along with the lifestyle?"

Well, that shot his theory down. She'd made a quick recovery and placed the conversation back into his hands. He could work with that.

"I guess you could say that," Connor responded. She still had her back to him, waiting for the coffee to stop brewing. "You have to admit, the field that you're in is vast. Why choose the items you do?"

"My sister got her degree in art," Lauren said, turning around and leaning against the opposite counter. She brought her elbows up behind her, resting her palms on the granite. "We're both creative and one weekend... I think I was twenty-one... she took me to an art gallery. The artist had the most sensuous pictures I'd ever seen, and with each of his models had these simplistic yet elegant jewels incorporated within the implements."

"And just like that, you decided you wanted to make them?" Connor asked, not understanding her thought process. "I mean, I assume a twenty-one year old girl would be wary of such a lifestyle, even on the outskirts."

"Let's just say my business mind went into a tailspin." Lauren shrugged and then smiled. "Sex sells. Jewelry sells. They always will. Blend them together, and chances are a person will be successful."

"And there is the calculating mind I knew to be in there," Connor said, smiling back at her. "So now I understand the business aspect of it. But you can't stand there and tell me that the nature of the lifestyle doesn't draw you in. You've never been curious?"

Connor knew he'd lost her the minute he'd asked the question. *Fuck.* She turned, and since the coffee pot had beeped while she was relaying her story, Lauren poured each of them a mug. She doctored hers while leaving his black. Turning, she surprised the hell out of him when she handed him his coffee and answered.

"Yes, but it didn't work out."

Although she'd actually replied, she didn't look him in the eye. Connor couldn't stand to see her brows furrowed so deep, knowing that he was the one to obviously bring up something painful, so he stopped her by taking her cup from her and placing both on the counter.

"Look at me," Connor murmured, moving in close to her. She lifted her head, giving him access to her beautiful green eyes so clouded over with torment. "I'm sorry. I seem to be saying that a lot tonight. It's obviously too much of a personal issue to share with someone you just met."

"We've had sex," Lauren said, tentatively resting her hands on his chest. "I think that's as personal as it gets."

"Sex is superficial," Connor said, in total disagreement. He slowly shook his head. "It's the underlying emotions that we keep hidden when we are at our most vulnerable. Sharing them just makes it more so."

"Do you share?"

Connor slowly shook his head again, realizing that he'd just gotten caught in his own trap. He leaned down and captured her lips, still tinted from the wine and tasting just as sweet as before. Wanting to learn more about her, he'd inadvertently opened himself up. He needed to tip the scales again, but Lauren pulled away before he could do so. When she bit her lip, he would have brought her back against his body so that he could take over, but she leaned around him for her coffee and headed into the living room.

"I suffer from claustrophobia. It stems after an event that happened when I was younger," Lauren stated matter-of-factly. "Being bound in any way isn't good for my mental health."

Connor grabbed his coffee, needing to see her face and wanting to know more. He was just about to join her on the couch when his cell phone rang. The sound did get her to look up at him, giving him full view of her beautiful face. He studied her for a few seconds, before giving in and placing his mug on the coffee table. She gave him little clue as to what she was truly feeling and that in itself said a lot. Lauren was expressive in every subject, except this one. There was something more to it, but unfortunately he couldn't ignore his call.

"I have to take this," Connor said regretfully, digging his cell out of his front pocket.

"Please, go right ahead," Lauren said, her words coming out a little too formal for his liking.

"Yeah, speak to me," Connor said, seeing that it was Kevin.

"Need your help down on Park near the Metrodome." Sounds from the passing traffic and honking horns could be heard over the phone. "How far away are you?"

"Close." Connor rubbed the back of his neck, knowing he had no choice. If Kevin called, it was for a damn good reason. "I'll be there in ten."

It fucking killed him to see the obvious relief cross Lauren's face. They'd both learned a little about each other this evening, and though he would have given anything to know more about her, maybe leaving this as is for a while was a good idea.

"Thanks for staying in for dinner this evening," Lauren said, leaning forward to place her coffee next to his. She stood and faced him, crossing her arms as if she didn't know what to do with them. "If I remember anything else, I'll give you a call."

Connor closed the distance, but instead of claiming her lips like he wanted to, he tilted her chin and gently kissed her forehead. Looking down at her, he wanted nothing more than to stay and hear those inner emotions he spoke of earlier, but knew that now wasn't the time. He hoped like hell that it was in the foreseeable future. She was becoming an enigma that he'd like to solve before things ended.

"Thank you for a wonderful dinner, Red." Connor released her and stepped back. "I'll be in touch, but if something *coincidental* happens that makes you feel uneasy, I want to know about it ASAP."

Lauren's lips curved into the smile she'd obviously been fighting at his attempt at humor and it alleviated his frustration at having to leave. However, he was dead serious about his request. Connor didn't believe in coincidences, which was why he was going to have Taryn check the traffic cameras in the area first thing in the morning once again. The angle into the alleyway hadn't been good for what they'd needed, but if the SUV was on the main street, they should hit paydirt. If someone was watching and keeping tabs on Lauren, he wanted to know who.

Chapter Fifteen

Connor instantly awoke at the sound of his front door opening. Leaning over and putting his hand on the biometric gun safe he kept on his nightstand, the cover popped open to reveal his Sig P220. In under three seconds he had his weapon in his hand. What kind of suicidal moron would break into a former Marine's house on a Wednesday night?

"Connor, let's ride," Jax yelled from the bottom of the stairs. "There's been a break in the case."

"Fuck," Connor murmured, having his answer on who was in the house. His heart still pounded in his chest at the rush of adrenaline. Louder, he called out, "Give me five."

He walked over to his dresser and pulled out a fresh pair of jeans. Gathering the rest of his clothes, he went into the bathroom. After having used the toilet, washed his hands and threw some water on his face, he dressed and slung his shoulder harness on and holstered his weapon. Collecting two spare magazines, he was reminded of what an old grizzled marksmanship instructor had once told him. Always carry more ammo than you think you'll need. You don't want to die in a gunfight for lack of shooting back. He was downstairs in four.

"Took you long enough," Jax said, waiting by the front door.

"What the hell time is it anyway?" Connor asked, grabbing his keys off of the side table in the entryway. He could really use a cup of coffee, but he knew that it would have to wait. "And where are we headed? A break could mean anything from a witness statement to an all out confession."

"It's two-thirty in the morning and we're headed to the suspect's residence."

Connor had already snagged his jacket and was halfway out the door when Jax's words hit home. He looked over his shoulder. "No shit. Who?"

"You know those two names I gave Taryn to run through the database in connection with shibari?" Jax asked, closing the door behind him and following Connor to the curb where the Jeep was parked. Damn, it was cold. It had to only be in the mid-twenties out here. "One of the men came up as a hit for a convicted rapist."

"We know 'em?" Connor used the key fob to open the doors.

"Not really," Jax replied. He opened his door as Connor walked around to the driver's side. "His name is Gabriel Lucas. He's got a house in Edina, which is where we're meeting Crest and Kevin, along with Detective Morrison, who's in charge of Terry's case."

"I bet Morrison is shitting bricks," Connor said. Once they were both inside with the engine started, he turned the heat on full blast. The front window had yet to ice over due to the fact that he'd only been home from the club for an hour. Just enough time to fall asleep. "How did Crest even pull that off? Detective Morrison is convinced Terry did it."

"We both know that Crest always gets what he wants. It doesn't hurt that Taryn pulled in evidence from traffic cams the night of Marilyn's murder. Our resident squid was smart enough to get video footage on Marilyn's vehicle and the surrounding traffic as she headed home that night." Jax pulled his cell phone out of his pocket. Looking at the screen, he gathered the information they needed and cut into his debriefing with directions. "Take I-394 W to MN100. It'll get us there faster since no one is out at this fucking hour."

"Are you telling me that Gabriel Lucas followed Marilyn home?" Connor asked, shifting in gear and pulling away from the curb. "I'll be honest with you. I don't know the guy. Did he play at Masters?"

"He came in a few times here and there, but mostly on weeknights. Taryn was able to follow the traffic cams all the way through until the exit for Maplewood. Want to take a guess as to the make of his vehicle?"

Connor felt his blood turn as cold as the wind that was hitting the Jeep. He glanced over at his friend, who was looking his way. Had Gabriel Lucas been targeting Lauren next?

"Black SUV?"

"More like dark blue, but Lauren could have easily mistaken the color if she hadn't been too focused on it."

"Maybe," Connor said, forcing his attention back on the road. "Saying it's true…a convicted rapist, who's well versed in shibari, follows Marilyn Sweeney home from the club and kills her. Why? The autopsy showed she wasn't raped."

"No, but his previous victim had red hair."

Connor tightened his grip on his steering wheel. Is that why he'd been going after Lauren? Because her features resembled those of past targets? He resisted the urge to call her, knowing full well that Crest would have verified that Lucas was at home if they were apprehending him.

During the short ten-minute drive, they played devil's advocate, going through the evidence piece by piece. After Connor got off of on the exit, Jax steered him to the correct address and they parked down the street. Exiting the Jeep, they made their way to where Crest and Kevin were situated behind an unmarked police car. Morrison was with them, along with four uniformed officers.

"Glad you could join us," Crest said, shooting them a look. That just meant that he'd been here for a while and didn't like freezing his ass off. Connor didn't bother to remind him that he'd had to drive from downtown, because he knew excuses didn't matter. "SITREP is this…suspect is inside with his wife, presumably in bed. No children involved. Morrison will take two uniformed officers and try to take him into custody in a civilized manner. The other two will cover the sides and you two will take the back. He doesn't know we're coming for him, so we have no idea how he'll react."

Connor and Jax nodded their agreement. It was obvious that Crest didn't think this would go down easy, as he had shed his suit in favor of denim and a suede jacket, which he had left unzipped for easy access to his holster. He'd met Detective Morrison before and his sour disposition hadn't changed.

"Take these," Crest said, giving them radios. Connor took his and attached it to the waistband of his jeans, letting his jacket lay behind it. He intuitively turned on the power setting to the lowest volume level and adjusted the squelch. "If Lucas comes out willingly, we'll signal Code Four."

"Anything else?" Morrison asked wryly. "This is still my investigation, regardless that the Lieutenant signed off on this.

Lucas served his time and was probably just heading home that night."

"In the opposite direction?" Crest asked. "I'm doing my best to remain cordial, Morrison. Don't give me reason to believe you're that ill-advised."

"Let's just get this over with," Morrison said, his face red. Whether or not it was from the cold or Crest's rebuke was anyone's guess.

"I'll cover the garage, in case he decides to exit that way," Crest said, pulling his gloves off and slipping them into his coat pocket. Connor did the same, ensuring his hands were free and drew his pistol. He checked to ensure he had chambered a round. "Positions, gentlemen."

Each headed to their assigned post. Connor and Jax had to use the back gate, although they took their time confirming there wasn't a dog behind the privacy fence. He glanced down at his watch, knowing that Morrison would be ringing the doorbell at any moment.

Connor made an oblique movement with his hand, alerting Jax that he should cover the back door near the side of the house. The square footage was above average and Lucas's residence also had patio doors. It was dark enough that Connor used the coverage afforded by the table on the deck.

He was still studying the exterior when a dog's barking alerted them that Morrison had indeed rung the doorbell. A few minutes passed and there was still nothing but silence. Connor didn't take his eyes off of the patio door.

"Movement," Jax whispered, his voice carrying enough to inform Connor of the potential flight of their suspect. "To your right."

Connor squinted, trying to see through the window and the drape that covered it. He was guessing it was the kitchen, but he was finally able to vaguely make out the shadow that passed by. Within seconds, the patio door swung open and presumably, Gabriel Lucas tried to make a run for it. The idiot was wearing pajama pants. How far did he really think he would get?

"Stop!" Connor stepped up and aimed his weapon at his chest. Lucas froze midstride. He was average height and weight and not what one would think looked like a rapist. "You're wanted for questioning in the murder of Marilyn Sweeney. Turn around slowly and place your hands on the back of your head."

"You won't shoot an unarmed man," Lucas said, clearly panicked.

Connor gritted his teeth, knowing people like Lucas always chose the wrong path. He instinctively knew that Jax was making his way to the patio. Sure enough, Lucas decided to try and run for it. The patio had two sides that were open and he opted for the one on the left.

"Got 'em," Connor yelled, forewarning Jax that he would physically subdue the subject and for Jax to shoot only if necessary.

They'd been by each other's side in combat too many times to count, but that gave them the advantage of knowing how each other operated. It took him two seconds to holster his weapon and follow Lucas's lead. Connor calculated his options and knew that he'd have easier access by jumping over the rail.

Lucas had gotten down the two wooden steps. Connor placed his hand on the wooden rail and jumped over the bannister. He'd timed it just right and landed directly behind Lucas. Before their subject had a chance to really gather momentum, Connor had him collared within seconds.

"Wrong choice, Lucas," Connor said, pushing his knee into Lucas's lower back. A zip restraint appeared over his shoulder and he took it from Jax. Placing Lucas's hands through the loops, he yanked it tight. "On your feet."

"Listen to me," Lucas pleaded, finding his balance and trying to look over his shoulder. "I don't know anything about any murder."

"Then why run?" Jax asked dryly, going around them and leading their way out of the backyard. He reached for his radio and brought it to his lips. "Echo Eight Charlie, Echo Five Oscar, Code Four."

"I'm heading home for a couple hours shut eye," Connor said, walking out of the precinct. It was only six-fifteen in the morning and the sun had yet to fully rise. "You doing the same or do you want me to drop you off at the office?"

"I'll ride home with you," Jax replied, adjusting his skull-cap. "If we're hitting the clubs tonight, we need sleep."

Connor was exhausted, but what he would have really liked to do was head over to Lauren's apartment. She probably wasn't even up for the day yet, and it wasn't like anything had changed with the case. Nah, it was best if he went home and slept.

"That was a bust," Jax said as they walked around the corner of the police station to where Connor had parked the Jeep. "By the time Lucas's lawyer got there, I think he'd ended up spilling his whereabouts for the entire last year. His attorney certainly has his work cut out for him."

"How the hell did he get a membership at Masters?" Connor asked, wondering exactly how good of a job Joel had been doing on the background checks he'd promised the members.

"Lucas is a convicted rapist. He doesn't even dispute that, and yet Joel allows him into what is supposedly an exclusive club?"

"If that leaks out, there are going to be some pissed off people," Jax said, shoving his hands in his jeans as they walked. Connor slid his gloves on, and then reached into his coat pocket for the keys. "Lucas is lucky that the waitress at the restaurant where he picked his wife up that night confirmed his whereabouts."

"Everything fit, though, didn't it?" Connor pressed the button to unlock the doors. Unfortunately, ice had accumulated on his windshield this time and he reached into the back seat for the scraper. He threw the keys to Jax so that he could turn over the engine, but kept the door open so they could still talk. "Lucas raping that redhead three years ago in St. Paul, him knowing shibari and leaving the club the exact time that Marilyn did, and he even owned a fucking SUV. Shit, he even tried to run. If that doesn't smack of guilt, I don't know what does."

Jax rubbed his hands together, blowing on them. "Coincidence. His wife was at the Applebee's in Maplewood. Her car broke down and she called him to get her. That lead is now bust and we're back to square one."

"Lauren's big on coincidence, too, but you don't see me buying into it," Connor said. He finished scraping the windshield, figuring the amount he'd gotten off was enough. Tossing it into the backseat, he climbed into the driver's seat and closed the door. Cranking up the heat, he then clicked his seatbelt into place. "Not that I can find a hole in his alibi. Taryn was able to confirm it, too, once she had his destination. Can't argue with the squid."

"At least Crest was able to make an agreement with Lucas through his lawyer to remain quiet regarding our interest in the case. Although, did you see the way Crest looked at Morrison? Nothing ever seems to get under Crest's skin, but I swear if he'd been able to legally take Morrison out, he would have." Jax moved a vent his way, leaving his fingers in front of the lukewarm air. "At least Lucas agreed to stay away from the clubs."

"I think Crest believes in karma…although he'd probably like to help her along. As for the clubs, it's a good thing Taryn is conducting a background check on every member. God knows what she'll find." Connor maneuvered through the traffic that was still light, considering it wasn't the morning rush hour yet. "Besides Joel, Gerry, and their private parties, we're grasping at straws."

Chapter Sixteen

"*H*eavy snow, fierce wind gusts, and ice are expected to shut down the Twin Cities throughout the weekend. City officials are requesting that everyone stay in their residences and only venture out in the event of an emergency. The Metro Transit System will shut down at three o'clock this afternoon, giving travelers five more hours to schedule their way home as well as giving them time to gather supplies."

Lauren looked at her watch, confirming that it was ten o'clock on Friday morning. She'd had the television on all morning, trying to decide if she was going to finish cutting those stones that were needed for the next few specialized orders. Now she knew it was pointless. As for their suggestion to gather supplies, she wasn't so sure it was a good thing she'd gone to the grocery store yesterday. On one hand, she had an abundance of supplies, but on the other, if her power went out, most of her refrigerated items would spoil. At least she'd had the wherewithal to grab a couple cases of bottled water.

"Seventeen to twenty-two inches are expected from this afternoon through Sunday night. This is the biggest storm to hit the Twin Cities in years. Stay tuned for more updates."

Lauren's phone rang and she reached for it, her heart suddenly palpitating at the thought it would be Connor. She'd heard from him twice since Monday, both courtesy calls to ensure that she was all right. She wasn't so sure what she was, considering what she'd shared with him after their dinner on Monday night. What the hell had she been thinking? It was a question she was asking herself a lot lately. She'd done her best to limit the conversations, but somehow they'd ended up talking for a good thirty minutes each time. Looking at the screen, she saw a familiar number but knew it wasn't Connor's.

"Hi, Joel." Lauren leaned toward the coffee table, setting her mug on the dark surface. "I take it you're canceling tonight's activities?"

"Yeah, sorry about that. That's one big storm headed our way," Joel said, his voice coming through the speaker louder than needed. Lauren fiddled with the volume on the side of her phone. "First the mugging, now the storm. We'll get you back on the docket soon."

"I appreciate that," Lauren replied, picking up the remote and muting the news anchor.

"Speaking of what happened… have they caught the guy who tried to mug you?"

Lauren thought back to Connor's inquiry into Joel's specialized order and his belief in no coincidences. A shiver of unease ran up her spine, but she tried to shake it away. This was Joel. He'd been a business acquaintance for years. He was only asking because it was the nice thing to do.

"No, not yet," Lauren responded. She wanted to change the subject. "How's business?"

"Honestly, since Marilyn Sweeney's murder, it's been down." There was a pause and for a brief moment, Lauren thought the call had been disconnected. "Don't get me wrong, my regulars are still coming in, but the newer members are keeping their distance. With the media splashing it all over the news, regardless that it was Terry who did it, they're making the lifestyle out like it's an evil pastime."

"Do you really think he's guilty?" Lauren asked, immediately wishing she hadn't. This was a subject she should stay far away from. She didn't want to inadvertently slip up in some way and compromise Connor's case. "Forget I asked. It's none of my business. I didn't really know them anyway."

"You don't think Terry did it?" This time, the silence was extended and Lauren threw her head back on the couch, mentally cursing herself out.

"As I said, I really didn't know them," Lauren replied. "The whole thing is just a travesty."

"Did the police ever stop by to question you? They seemed rather interested in my list of vendors."

"Yes, but I haven't heard from them since." Lauren breathed a sigh of relief when a knock came at the door. "Joel, someone's at the door. Just give me a call when you have the next open social."

"Yeah, will do. Take care."

"Bye." Lauren quickly hung up, grateful for whoever had interrupted. She hadn't taken two steps when her phone rang again. Looking at the display, her heart skipped a beat. It was Connor. "Hello?"

"Red, did you hear about the storm? Are you at home?"

"Yes," Lauren replied. "I decided not to go to the shop."

She'd finally reached the door. She swung it open, fully expecting it to be Ms. Finch. Rick Hastlen stood in front of her.

"Hi," Rick said, looking a little awkward. He ran a hand over his thinning hair. "I just wanted to see if you needed anything from the store."

"Lauren, who is that?"

"Um, I gotta go. I'll call you later." Lauren disconnected the call, knowing full well Connor would be left wondering who was in her apartment. For a brief moment, it made her smile. "Hi, Rick. I appreciate you asking, but I went yesterday. I'm all stocked up."

"Okay. I was just checking," Rick said, shifting on his feet. She could tell he'd come home after work, considering he was still in his suit and tie. It hung a little loose on him and his tie was crooked. "My office closed down for the weekend."

Lauren hated when that uncomfortable moment came when a person prolonged a conversation. She knew Rick expected her to invite him in, but she wasn't going to. A part of her felt bad for him because he really was a nice man…just not for her. An image of Connor in bed above her while holding her wrists down flashed through her mind. She instantly touched her wrist, wondering what the hell had just happened.

"I'm sure your company is just taking precautions," Lauren said, mentally shaking her head so that the disturbing picture would go away. Her cell phone rang. The vision might have dissipated, but Connor was certainly persistent. She didn't immediately answer. "I'm doing the same and not even going into the shop today. Have you checked with Ms. Finch?"

The sliding of a deadbolt could be heard and Lauren couldn't prevent a smile. Ms. Finch stuck her head out regardless that she was still wearing her old-fashioned curlers.

"Are you going somewhere, Rick?" Ms. Finch asked.

"I, uh, was just asking Lauren if she needed anything from the store. It sounds like we're going to be cooped up for awhile. Do you need anything?"

"No, thank you. I had that young delivery boy from around the corner bring me a couple bags of groceries yesterday." Ms. Finch widened her door and stepped into the hallway. "I love that new convenience store. Lauren, aren't you going to answer your phone? It might be your young man calling."

"Man?" Rick asked, looking back and forth between them.

"I said I'd call you back," Lauren replied into the phone the instant she brought it to her ear, while at the same time smothering a groan when Ms. Finch launched into how nice Connor was.

"I'm not sure the term you young people use today, but in my day he'd be considered her boyfriend," Ms. Finch said with a fond smile. "With the amount of times he's been by, I would say that title would constitute their relationship. However, I haven't seen him in a few days. It's nice to know he's calling her now."

"Did Ms. Finch just call me your boyfriend?" Connor replied, his tone lighter than before and definitely laced with humor. Lauren was losing control of the situation and it didn't help that Rick obviously wished he hadn't stopped by. "And I know you said you'd call back, but you sounded stressed and when I heard a man's voice, I thought I'd better check in again."

"I'm going to go now," Rick said, looking more uncomfortable with every passing moment. Lauren felt bad for him. Just because she wasn't attracted to him, didn't mean she wanted her personal life rubbed in his face. He took a step away from them. "If you need anything, though, just let me know. I'm just down the hallway."

"Did you decide to throw a party and not invite me?" Connor asked, making Lauren realize she still held the phone to her ear.

"Damn it, Connor," Lauren whispered, although she'd turned her head away from the two people staring at her. It wasn't like they couldn't hear her, which only added to her frustration. "Is there a reason you called?"

"From the sound of it, the same reason as the man just said." There was a slight pause, giving Lauren a chance to look back into the hallway. They were both standing there, staring at her. "I take that's the infamous Rick that Ms. Finch keeps talking about?"

"Hold on," Lauren murmured in agitation, cradling the phone into her shoulder. "Rick, I appreciate you stopping by. I really do. Ms. Finch, just knock on my door should you need anything. I've got to take this call."

Lauren flashed a quick smile and then ducked back into her apartment. Shutting the door, she took a deep breath and wondered how she'd ended up in that predicament anyway. Pulling the phone away from her body, she knew why.

"Connor, I appreciate the call," Lauren said, as she continued to walk into her living room. "But I went to the store yesterday."

"That's good. Our investigation has come to a stand still for a few days, considering the clubs will be closed. I was thinking of stopping by."

Lauren held her breath at the implication of his words. He wanted to ride out the storm with her and this must be his way of testing the waters. Is this what she wanted? Had he stayed away all week to give her space? She slowly let the air out of her lungs, knowing full well he was far from out of her system. He'd not brought up the fact that she'd confessed her phobia to him, so maybe—just maybe—things could be kept at an arm's length while still enjoying the benefits of whatever this was between them.

"I'd like that," Lauren said. "How are you planning to get here? Do you own a sleigh?"

"My sleigh is in the shop," Connor responded with what sounded like a smile. Lauren heard people in the background. "I do have my Jeep, but since my office is close by, I'll leave it in the underground garage and just walk. Say around three?"

"At around two o'clock, I'll see if we can get a pizza delivered before the local joint closes." Lauren reached for her coffee, but seeing her fingers trembling, she decided against more caffeine. "Anything you don't like?"

"Just anchovies. Nasty little suckers."

Lauren smiled. From the tone of his voice, he'd just shuddered. She knew that once he arrived, he'd be here for the length of the storm. Three days of sex...vanilla sex. Every other worry would go out the window for that brief time. Maybe she'd call her sister to rub it in. It wasn't everyday that she could claim a sex romp.

"Got it. See you at three."

It was after two-thirty and the majority of the team had gone home. When Connor had told Jax that he was heading over to Lauren's, his best friend just smiled and held a hand up in a goodbye gesture. Taryn had followed suit, along with Kevin. Unfortunately, she hadn't been able to get a good angle on the license plate of the SUV that had been parked in front of Lauren's shop. Ethan hadn't even been into the office, as he'd been taking care of one of those open cases. That left Crest and Jessie, although the two seemed to stay far away from each other the majority of the morning. Her being Crest's personal assistant didn't seem to be working out too well, but she was damned good at her job. It looked like Crest was between a rock and a hard place.

Connor shrugged into his jacket, grabbed Jax's skullcap that he'd left on the desk knowing his friend wouldn't mind, and started walking toward the front of the office. Jessie was sitting at her desk, her fingers flying over her keyboard.

"I'm heading out for the weekend," Connor said, stopping before passing her area. He pulled the cap down over his hair and then reached inside his pocket for his gloves. "You should get going too. The storm has already started."

"I have a few more reports to type up for Gavin," Jessie replied, looking up from her computer with a smile. Her eyes sparkled and for some reason, Connor had a feeling she was glad he was leaving. He'd love to be a fly on the wall after he left. Jessie reached over and grabbed something from the printer, handing it to him. "That's a supplemental report from the detective in charge of Terry's case."

"Thanks," Connor replied, folding it and putting it in his pocket. He then started to put on his gloves. "I'll read over it later. You have a good weekend."

"I fully intend to," Jessie said, sitting back down in her chair. "You, too."

Connor smiled at her enthusiasm and figured Crest had his work cut out for him. Jessie obviously had something up her sleeve and he just hoped Crest knew what was coming. She was unlike any of the women Crest usually got involved with, which were older, sophisticated, and used to a particular lifestyle. Jessie was young, spirited, and naïve. Plus, if those two ever got together, it would make for an ugly workplace and Connor, for one, liked things just the way they were.

Chapter Seventeen

*C*onnor *knocked on Lauren's door, pretending not to notice the shadow that blocked Ms. Finch's peep hole. He was tempted to look over and wink, but the sound of Lauren sliding her deadbolt grabbed his attention. Lauren swung it open, which prompted him to want to chastise her for not checking to see who it was, but she looked so damned good that he kept his mouth closed. What the hell had caused him to wait four days before seeing her again?*

Stepping inside without a word, Connor pulled her to him and claimed her lush lips, which were covered in gloss. He didn't miss the black wrap-around sweater that molded over her breasts or the cream corduroys that ran down her legs, but they weren't where he wanted his attention.

He kicked the door shut behind him, spinning her so that her back was against the wood. Lauren responded in kind, taking his face in her warm hands. He unzipped his jacket as her fingers ran up the back of his head and sliding under his cap and making it fall to the floor. He had every intention of taking her up against the door when a knock vibrated against them. Connor dragged his lips away from hers, opening his eyes to see her stunning green ones staring back at him, sparkling in amusement.

"Pizza, right on time."

"*Your timing sucks,*" Connor murmured, leaning in to steal one more kiss. "*But since I'm starving, I'll let you off the hook.*"

Lauren gave his chest a little push, giving her room to spin around and open the door. Again, Connor felt irritation over the fact that she hadn't verified who was at the door. Standing behind her, he made sure that it was the pizza delivery person, not caring that the man kept looking over her shoulder at him. The delivery guy handed over the box, took the money, murmured his thanks, and scurried on down the hallway.

"*Did you have to make him so nervous?*" Lauren asked, stepping back and bumping into him. She slammed the door shut and turned around. She looked exasperated. "*He was just doing his job.*"

"*You've not been checking to see who's at the door lately,*" Connor said, making his irritation known. He pulled his jacket down his sleeves, hanging it up on her coat rack. "*Last Monday, and twice today in a matter of minutes.*"

"*Did you ever think it's because the guard downstairs called to let me know?*"

"*Did he?*" Connor asked, following her to the kitchen.

"*No, but that's beside the point,*" Lauren said, setting the large box down on the counter. "*It's my apartment, and besides, Ms. Finch is constantly monitoring the hallway. She's better than any security guard.*"

Connor felt his frustration mount, but knew that there were limitations within their newfound liaison. Although temporary, he was still used to having a certain amount of control over the submissives he partnered with. As a matter of fact, it had probably been over a year since he'd been with someone not in the lifestyle.

"*I'm asking,*" Connor said, although he couldn't prevent grinding his teeth together, "*that you check to see who's at your door before answering it. Especially with the events that have occurred.*"

Lauren was grabbing some plates and napkins when she stopped and looked up at him. He wasn't sure that she knew how much control it took him not to just order her to do it, but her face softened and nodded.

"I know it doesn't seem like it, but I usually do." Lauren walked over and handed him a plate with the napkin underneath. *"Why don't we eat and watch the news. See how bad things are about to get. It's been years since we've had a storm of this nature."*

Connor nodded, knowing they didn't need to rush although his cock was telling him something different. He reached for a couple slices of pizza, hoping like hell she had an extra toothbrush handy. He hadn't exactly planned this, but didn't want to take the time to head to his place for an overnight bag. Plus, he planned to be in bed for the majority of his time here, so why bother with clothes?

A thought slammed into him that caused him a momentary panic, but he immediately remembered seeing a box in her nightstand when he'd been looking for a piece of paper to write on. She had a dozen unopened condoms stashed in there. As they walked over to the couch with their food, he had a feeling she would be out of them by the time Sunday rolled around.

They'd managed to eat half the pizza before ending up in bed. The wind rattled the windows and the blinds had been left open, giving them a glimpse of the snow that was falling at an enormous rate. The flakes seemed to dance underneath the streetlight, as if fighting gravity. They were losing.

Lauren was tucked in close to his side, her cheek against his warm chest. She snuggled closer, closing her eyes and willing sleep to come. She could tell that Connor wanted to talk and had no doubt what it was about. Why did men inherently need to fix something they thought was broken? She tried to look upon this like her sister did in every facet of life…with humor.

"I was thinking about what you said in the beginning of the week…about your phobia," Connor said, his chest vibrating.

Her eyes grudgingly opened. Okay, maybe humor was a little overboard. Her sister always had been the optimist, while she was a realist. She'd known he wouldn't be able to leave it alone. He ran his hand up her forearm, coming to stop only when he reached her wrist, which was lying next to her cheek.

"Have you tried—"

"I really don't want to talk about this," Lauren said, hoping that he'd leave well enough alone. She felt his finger envelope her wrist.

"A lot of people within the life—"

"Have claustrophobia?" Lauren asked, sliding her wrist from his hold. She turned over and sat up on the edge of the bed. Grabbing a hair band off of the nightstand, she went about pulling her curls back. "Have worked their way through their fear?"

Lauren didn't give him time to answer, as she stood and reached for her robe draped over the chair. She purposefully put it on slowly, not wanting him to get the idea that she was angry. She wasn't. But that didn't mean she would allow him to control the conversation. He knew that wasn't the type of relationship they'd entered.

"I'm sure they have," Lauren said, responding to her own question. "That doesn't mean I can or will. Would you like something to drink? I'm going to go into the kitchen for some water."

Lauren had finally turned back to the bed to see that he was sitting up. The blanket had fallen to his waist, covering up the one part she wouldn't mind seeing at this point. It was a good thing this was casual, because it looked like the only thing they had in common was the physical chemistry.

When he didn't answer, but only continued to stare at her with those blue eyes of his, Lauren opted not to ask again.

She'd get her water and give herself some breathing space. If he didn't let the conversation go, she didn't know what she'd do. It wasn't like she could kick him out in the snowstorm.

Lauren turned and walked through the bedroom door. They'd left the lights on in the living room and kitchen, so she had no trouble navigating. A look at the clock on the stove told her it was still early…only seven o'clock at night. She decided to box up the rest of the pizza and put it into the refrigerator. They could have it for lunch tomorrow.

"You're awfully defensive," Connor said, startling her. "Is it so bad to want to get to know the person I'm sleeping with?"

Lauren looked up to see him walk out into the living with nothing on. The sight of his masculine, firm body had her thoughts jumbled, and for a moment she forgot what he was talking about. His cock was semi-hard and a thought struck her that she hadn't tasted him yet. Would he taste musky or salty? Would his flavor be rich?

"I truly didn't mean to upset you."

Connor continued to walk across the floor. She looked up into his face, noticing a light five o'clock shadow forming. It made him all the more attractive, but now that his eyes held a hint of sympathy, it ground her the wrong way.

"You didn't upset me," Lauren replied, taking the box and turning away from the sight of him. She opened the refrigerator door and made room for the big box. "I shouldn't have brought it up before. It has no bearing on our…well, whatever this is."

Lauren grabbed a bottle of water, almost afraid to turn around, but not wanting him to know that. She shut the door and took a deep breath. Spinning around in her bare feet, she was surprised to see him sitting at the island. Naked. She had a feeling she'd never look at that area the same again.

"Even with a casual relationship, I like to know who I'm involved with," Connor said, his eyes saying what he wasn't. "I think I will take a bottle of water, please."

Connor wanted her to tell him about her past and really, if she put it in perspective and said it the right way, there was no reason she shouldn't tell him. She had enough wherewithal to turn down what he would try to propose. Lauren handed him her bottle of water.

"Let's make a deal," Lauren said, turning to the refrigerator to grab another water. "You don't try to offer a suggestion on how to make my phobia disappear and I'll tell you all about it."

"Can't take that deal," Connor said, after taking a swig of the cool liquid. "I learned the hard way not to make promises I couldn't keep. But, if I make any suggestions, you have every right to turn them down."

Lauren laughed, just like he probably knew she would. His arrogance knew no bounds. She left the kitchen and walked into the living room, taking a seat on the couch. It was surreal to look back and see him follow. He was so comfortable in his nudity.

"I think I'm being generous," Connor said, getting the smile to remain on her face. He sat down next to her, his warm thigh against hers. "How old were you when this *event* happened?"

"I was eight years old and my parents had taken my sister and me on vacation." Lauren took a shaky breath. However, it wasn't from fear of remembering so much as it was opening herself up to another, regardless of the nature of their relationship. "We went horseback riding and when everyone stopped to take a break, I wandered off. There was this windmill with a couple vanes missing and a bunch of old rotten boards covering an old well. I decided to climb on the windmill. I wanted to see the farm from a little higher up."

Connor surprised her by taking her water and placing both bottles on the floor. Leaning back against the armrest, he pulled her down beside him. On one hand, it was easier to recall that time when she wasn't looking at him, but on the other, she was afraid to take his comfort for fear of what it would mean. She didn't resist, wanting his warmth to soak into her skin.

"I take it something went wrong?"

"I fell through the boards covering the well," Lauren said, and then chuckled as fonder memories surfaced from when she was younger. "I wasn't the most coordinated child. And just so you know, I anticipate a story in return."

"I wouldn't have expected it any other way, Red," Connor replied, snickering at her attempt to finagle a childhood memory from him. He turned his head, placing a kiss on her forehead. "How bad were you hurt?"

"Believe it or not, I wasn't. I was wearing my riding gloves and had grabbed ahold of the cable. Since I didn't weigh much, the speed at which I fell wasn't as fast as it would have been otherwise. The cable hanging down from the windmill was old and rusted…caked with dirt."

"Did someone see you fall?"

"Yes, and my parents ran over immediately," Lauren said, hearing her mother calling her name as if it were yesterday. She kept her eyes open, not wanting to get drawn back in time. "I remember being so scared. It was dark, the water was cold, and there really wasn't as much room as one would think down in that hole. I didn't know if I would drown or not. I just knew I had to get back up to the top."

"You said you had grabbed the cable…were you able to pull yourself up enough to keep your head above the water?" Connor asked, his voice soft and his touch gentle. He was lightly caressing her arm.

"Yes," Lauren whispered, watching his bicep move with each stroke. She knew that he had the same innate gene that most men had when it came to protection. "But it didn't matter. I panicked and started to push against the walls of the well. I didn't realize there were cracks and holes in the cement. My left hand broke through a crevice and when I tried to pull free, I was trapped."

Connor could hear the fear and desperation of a little girl as if he'd been sucked back in time. He tightened his hold on her, and for a brief moment thought of telling her to stop. This was beyond sharing details of their lives to get a general knowledge of the person they were sleeping with. Yet, he wanted to hear what she'd gone through. The way she held her left wrist gave away that she never truly got over being trapped in that well.

"How long were you down there?" Connor asked, fearing the answer.

"Eight or nine hours," Lauren replied, her warm breath brushing his chest. Connor cringed at her answer. That was a long time for a little girl to be confined. "My father wanted to climb down the well, but the owner of the horse farm wouldn't allow it. They called 911 and requested help, but the nearest town was a good thirty-minute drive. My parents and sister never left, continuously talking to me."

"What took the firemen so long to get you out?"

"The crevice contained jagged edges and every time I tried to pull my hand out, the rocks would tear my skin." Connor had tucked her in on his left side, so her left wrist was visible. He lifted it up and kissed it gently, finally seeing the almost invisible white scars. "When the firemen arrived, one of them was able to be lowered into the well, but needed special equipment to get my wrist released. It took a couple of hours to locate what they needed and then they were afraid the well would crumble in if they took too much rock out of the side."

"I can just imagine how terrified you were," Connor murmured, slipping his fingers through hers and resting their hands on his chest. "And what your parents and sister must have gone through."

"Anytime something closes around my wrist, it's as if I'm eight years old again, trapped in that well," Lauren said, tightening her fingers against his. "So, I avoid all situations that would put me back in that place and time."

They both fell silent and Connor continued to hold her, wishing they were at his house. He had a fireplace that he loved to use in the wintertime, but it was useless dwelling on things that couldn't be changed. Her fear could be altered though, given the right circumstances. From their earlier exchange and Lauren's wariness that he would make suggestions regarding her phobia, it was obvious other people had made recommendations.

Questions ran amok in his mind, but Connor was logical, if not methodical. He wouldn't broach the subject unless he had more answers first. One being, did she want to be in the lifestyle? She had submissive tendencies, which coincided with his dominant ones. That he was sure of. She surrounded herself with the lifestyle almost every hour of the day. Although they agreed on casual, it would be nice to walk away knowing he'd given her something other than good sex.

Chapter Eighteen

"We haven't lost power yet," Connor said, coming up behind her the following morning and kissing her neck. "Have you checked the news to see how much snow has fallen?"

Lauren turned her head to see that he was shirtless. He wore his jeans low to the hip and unbuttoned on top. How did he expect her to make them pancakes without burning herself if he walked around her apartment like that? She glanced down, knowing that she was naked underneath her robe. At least she was technically covered.

"No, not yet. But from the looks of it, "Lauren said, gesturing toward the window with her head, "the winds have definitely picked up."

"Can I help?" Connor asked, edging his way to the coffee machine. He snagged a piece of bacon before reaching into the cabinet for a mug. "Do you need a refill?"

"No thanks." Lauren finished stirring the pancake batter and turned to the island, where she had the electric skillet set up. "How has work been? Any closer to finding out who murdered Marilyn Sweeney?"

"We have a few leads," Connor replied, walking around to where the stools were. He sat facing her with another strip of bacon, a big smile on his face. "What about you? Anything jog your memory about an order or a conversation? No more SUVs?"

"No more suspicious vehicles and trust me, there's nothing to remember." Lauren used a ladle and scooped the batter, pouring a nice circle onto the hot skillet. "I haven't been to the club to use the vendor table in a while. I was supposed to go last night to the social hour, but with the storm, Joel called and cancelled."

Lauren frowned, remembering their conversation and the weird vibe she got from it. She went to work, pouring a second pancake and watching the batter bubble.

"Why the frown?" Connor asked, taking a drink of his coffee.

"Joel just sounded a little tense, I guess," Lauren said, grabbing the spatula. "Tense isn't the right word, though. I don't know. I brought up that Terry seemed like such a nice guy and then Joel asked if I thought someone else murdered Marilyn and if the police had stopped by. It was nothing, really."

They fell into silence and Lauren flipped the pancakes, waiting for the other side to brown to a golden hue. It wasn't an uncomfortable stillness and she found she rather enjoyed Connor's company. After sharing with him what had happened to her as a child, they talked about mundane things. He'd yet to share with her something from his past.

"You know, I think you purposefully started talking about the Minnesota Vikings last night instead of telling me something about yourself." Lauren pointed the spatula his way, garnering her another smile. "You said a story for a story."

"I think it was you who said that, but I'll fulfill my end of the bargain." Connor said, placing his mug on the counter. It was hard not to stare at his chest when he was sitting right in front of her, but she tried to concentrate and look into his eyes. There was amusement lurking in those blue eyes of his. "What would you like to know?"

"You mentioned you're an ex-Marine."

"There is no such thing as an ex-Marine," Connor said, his brow furrowed. She laughed, seeing how the term agitated him. "Once a Marine, always a Marine."

"My apologies, Mr. Marine," Lauren said, taking a little bow. "So tell me what made you want to be one?"

The two pancakes were done, so she dished them out onto his plate and pushed it toward him. The syrup and bacon were already to his right, so Connor was set. She went about ladling more batter into the skillet.

"I was raised in Jersey and we were blue collar," Connor said, not touching the food on his plate. Before she could ask him why, he continued, "There weren't a ton of options for me and I knew I could never afford college. My father does well, and it was enough to support us, but college was too much."

"Are you not hungry?" Lauren asked, breaking into the conversation. "Or do you think I'm that bad of a cook?"

"I'm waiting for you," Connor said, as if it was the most natural thing in the world. "My father would tan my hide if I ate while you were still cooking."

"It sounds like your father raised you right." Lauren smiled and flipped her pancakes. "So, college was out and you chose the military. Why the Marines?"

"Why not?" Connor countered. He picked up his coffee and took another drink. "I'm not one to do things half-assed. I wanted to be the best and I was willing to work for it. Being a

Marine isn't a bed of roses. We get the shit jobs that nobody else wants, but we do it with honor and integrity with little thanks or appreciation. But we're not there for anything other than the mission. It's our duty."

When Connor was done speaking and tilted his head toward her pancakes, Lauren realized that she got so caught up in hearing his story that she was burning them. Quickly flipping them again, she sighed in relief that they were still edible. Looking up at him through her lashes, she saw him fighting a grin.

"Anyway, I went to boot camp, and for twelve years I served our country."

"Retired?"

Connor shook his head. "You have to have twenty years to retire."

"But you only had eight left." Lauren scooped the pancakes out and placed them on her plate. There was still batter left, but once they ate and wanted a second round, she would make more. "Why not finish?"

"Because Crest made me and Jax offers we couldn't refuse."

Connor grabbed a couple pieces of bacon and put them on her plate. He pulled it to the setting next to his and waited for her to walk around the island. Lauren snagged her coffee and joined him, really liking the fact that he'd waited on her. She wasn't sure why it made such a big impact, but it did nonetheless.

"Jax, the one who staged the break-in on my apartment?" Lauren said, giving him a wry look.

"Yes," Connor said, laughing, "that Jax. But he's a good guy. Like I said, neither one of us could turn down Crest's proposal."

"What offer was that?" Lauren asked, reaching for the syrup.

"A chance at a normal life." Connor waited for her to finish and then added the sugary maple liquid to his pancakes. "Jax and I were in the same unit and had already been on two combat tours. A third was likely and it's tiring...not just on the body."

They both ate while Connor shared stories of his time in the Marines and she realized just how close he and Jax were upon finding out they'd purchased an old Victorian house and turned it into a duplex. They sounded more like brothers than friends.

"Okay," Connor said, finishing off his last bite. "Enough about me. I have a question for you."

Lauren was still working on her breakfast, but she knew that he still had to be hungry. The pancakes weren't large and there was still quite a bit of batter left. She was about to slide off of her stool to make him more, when he put a hand on her arm and shook his head. He stood and walked around to the other side, picking up the bowl.

"You're my guest," Lauren said, shaking her head and feeling bad that he was going to cook. "I'll make us more."

"I can do it while you finish what's on your plate," Connor said.

It was one thing to sit next to him and eat, while having such a carnal view of his body, but seeing Connor cooking was in an entirely different spectrum. Lauren put down her fork to enjoy the sight and sip her coffee. She knew what topic he was going to hit and though she was ready to rebuff any suggestions he made, she knew it was the Dominant in him that needed to make them.

"Hit me. What question do you have?" Lauren said, leaning back in her chair.

"You make it sound like you already know what I'm going to ask, Red." Connor cocked an eyebrow, but he didn't stop pouring the batter into the skillet. "Give the woman a little sex, and now she can read my mind."

Lauren laughed, choking down a little bit of coffee. From the gleam in his eye, Connor seemed to have made that comment on purpose. She grabbed a napkin and wiped away the tiny spills. He was still grinning like a madman.

"You're bad," Lauren said, shaking her head and standing up to get another refill.

"Not as bad as I could be," Connor replied with a smirk. "Okay, Miss Know It All, what is my question?"

"Your question," Lauren said as she brought the pot over to the counter and refilled their cups, "is have I ever tried to overcome my phobia. My response is yes and I can already answer your second question. No, I don't want to try again."

Lauren walked back over to the burner and placed the pot back in its rightful place. She picked up her sugar cubes and turned to the refrigerator for her creamer, but Connor beat her to it.

"You're wrong." Connor kissed her and seemed pleased that she hadn't guessed right. He handed her the carton and then shut the door, before going back to watch his pancakes. "Those might have been my second and third questions, but not my first."

Lauren couldn't suppress a smile as she walked back to her stool. She liked this playful side to him. She dumped her sugar cubes in the coffee and then poured in the right amount of creamer. He handed her a spoon before she even realized she'd forgotten it.

"Then what is this much anticipated question?" Lauren asked, clanking the metal spoon against the cup before shaking it off and placing it on a napkin.

"If you didn't have claustrophobia, would you be in the lifestyle?"

Connor had just flipped the pancakes once more before zeroing his gaze on her, seemingly watching for whatever subtle signs she might give. Not having expected his question to be worded quite that way, Lauren was sure he could see a lot. She took a sip of her coffee, not caring that it scalded her mouth. She just needed the extra time to formulate her answer.

"Maybe."

Connor cocked his eyebrow again and gave her a disbelieving look. Yeah, yeah, she knew it was a cop-out answer, but responding any other way was bound to lead them down a path she wanted to avoid.

"Fine," Lauren exclaimed, putting her mug down on the counter. She pushed her plate away and leaned forward. "Yes, I probably would. And yes, I have already tried with a man I trusted and it ruined our friendship. He was a good man and although this was years ago, he still felt uncomfortable with the way things went down. It's a case of been there and done that...have the T-shirt. Why is it that every dominant male I run into thinks he can fix what's wrong with any woman?"

Connor scooped the pancakes out with the spatula and put them on his plate when she shook her head that she didn't want anymore. Lauren tried to wait patiently for his answer, but couldn't remain still. She picked up her mug to have something to hold onto. She knew having this conversation would make her antsy. It always did.

"I take it you tried more than once?" Connor came back around the island and took his seat. He immediately reached for the syrup as if they were having a normal serious conversation. "Your question to me makes it sound like more than your friend thought they could help you."

"Considering my business," Lauren said, turning her stool slightly so that she faced him, "I've been out a few times here and there with men in the lifestyle who felt they could *help* me in conquering my fear. It wasn't that much of a stretch of the imagination to think you'd offer the same."

Lauren inwardly cringed at how bitchy that sounded. She didn't mean to have it come across that way, but she wasn't going to sugarcoat it either. In her experience, men like him felt they were saviors.

"Ahhh," Connor replied around a bite of bacon. He swallowed and then pointed the rest of the strip at her. "You're lumping me with all of those men. And here I thought I was different."

Lauren's lip turned up, unable to prevent another grin from appearing. Okay, so she really liked that he poked fun at himself. That didn't mean he would get a shot at helping her with her phobia.

"I know firsthand how it can destroy a friendship." Lauren took another sip of coffee, trying to word her next sentence carefully. "We're in a casual relationship, but I would still like to retain some type of friendship when we go our separate ways."

"Like me that much, do you?" Connor said, popping the rest of the bacon in his mouth.

She stared at his lips a little too long, but found that her body was ready for another tumble in the sheets…even though she couldn't remember what round of sex they were on. She was coming to really appreciate this snowstorm.

"Maybe," Lauren replied, keeping the coffee cup in front of her mouth so that he didn't see her smile.

She watched as he finished eating, another comfortable silence settling over them. He seemed to be pondering something and she wondered if maybe she'd been wrong about assuming his need to *fix* her. Connor might have just wanted to offer a non-sexual suggestion in regards to claustrophobia.

"Are you saying that you are different than every other Dom out there?"

Chapter Nineteen

Connor didn't answer her question immediately and instead pushed his plate away. He reached for his coffee, acquiring him more time before he had to answer. Lauren was wrong in her assumption that men wanted to *fix* women. Dominant men protected their women, even from their own fears. She'd know that if she'd given someone in the lifestyle who truly knew what they were doing a chance to help her overcome her anxieties.

"Did you ride a bicycle when you were young?" Connor asked. He drained the rest of his coffee and stood. Again, he waved her off when he reached for the plates. "You made the majority of breakfast, so I'll clean up. Back to my question—did you?"

"Yes." Lauren appeared slightly cautious as to where he was leading this, but Connor felt she'd see his point of view in the end. "I did."

"Did you start with training wheels?" Connor went to the sink on the far side of the kitchen and busied himself with rinsing them off before placing them in the dishwasher. "Or did you learn straight from the get-go?"

"Training wheels," Lauren replied. He could hear the resignation in her voice. "I can see where you're going with this, but using training wheels is totally different than using a person who has feelings."

"Did you try once and then give up?" Connor asked, remaining on topic and not allowing her to steer the conversation.

He'd let her take the lead up to this point in their relationship, because he'd truly thought she didn't *want* to be part of the lifestyle. But now that he knew different and that it was a fear she didn't want to confront, he sought to see how far he could push her before she realized she could have everything she desired.

"Of course I tried more than once." Lauren's voice was closer, but he didn't turn around. Connor kept his focus on the dishes. She finally sidled closer and into his peripheral vision. "But like I said—"

"And different ways? You know, on grass or the sidewalk. Maybe a slight incline or a straightaway?"

"Yes," Lauren answered, her tone becoming clipped.

"Will you tell me what happened with your friend?"

"And what if I tell you that I want to end this conversation and continue with what we've been doing?"

Connor loaded the last dish and then reached for the towel on the counter. Taking his time, he dried his hands before tossing it back on the granite and turning to her. Within seconds, he had his arms placed on either side of her. A tiny gasp escaped her lips and she tilted her head up so that their eyes connected. Her pupils dilated and her gaze dropped to his lips.

"Do you really want it to be like that?" Connor murmured. The green of her eyes deepened and he wouldn't have continued to push if he didn't think she was willing. "If you truly want to continue the way we are, we will. I'm enjoying myself. You're enjoying yourself. But I can offer you so much more and maybe, just maybe, when this ends...you can take more out of this than what you had coming in."

"And what do you get out of this?" Lauren whispered, her eyes searching his.

"The satisfaction that I helped you grow," Connor answered honestly. "It's like those training wheels. If you tried the sidewalk and it didn't work, then let's try the grass."

"You seem a little harder than grass," Lauren murmured, dropping her gaze when he didn't smile. This was too important to make light of right now. "The minute Phil had my wrists confined, I panicked. It'll be no different with you."

"Then I won't bind them," Connor said bluntly, pushing away from her. He held out his hand and waited. "Give me one hour to show you what submission really is and whether or not it's truly for you. If at the end of that hour you find that it does nothing for you, we continue on with the way we were."

Connor could see the temptation in her eyes. She looked down at his outstretched hand and then back up to his face. He would love to know exactly what she was thinking and feeling, but all he saw was trepidation. Lauren was so independent and strong-willed, but that didn't mean she wasn't a submissive at heart.

She slowly nodded and Connor released his pent-up breath. He wasn't so sure why it was important for him to have her accept this. He didn't think it had so much to do with her phobia as it did for a need within him to show her what the lifestyle was really about.

He waited until her hand was within his and led her through the kitchen and living room area, not stopping until they reached the bedroom. Connor turned her to him once they reached the bed and slipped his hands underneath her robe, pushing the material off of her shoulders. Lauren didn't move to help him, so he stopped before untying her lash.

"Let's try something," Connor said, cradling her face. "Have you ever been spanked?"

"I'm more worried about panicking while tied up than I am about being spanked." Lauren rested her hands on his forearms, though he could see the word alone caused her nipples to harden.

"That's your problem," Connor murmured, leaning in to capture her lips. Once he had his fill, he pulled back. "You seem to think that BDSM is all about bondage when that is far from the truth. I think those implements you work with have tainted your thoughts. Can it add to a scene? Yes, but it's where your mind is that is vital."

Connor let her hands fall when he moved his arms. Taking his fingers, he trailed them around the mounds of her breasts, circling and circling until he came to her areolas. Her nipples were now aching, waiting to be touched. He then started making larger motions outward. She didn't quite smother her groan.

He trailed one finger down her abdomen and through her curls. One day, he would love to be the one to shave them off. Connor brushed his knuckle across her clit, but he was more interested in her pussy. She was damp, but not as wet as he knew she could be.

"See, submission is a mental state." Connor reached for her belt and untied the material, allowing it to fall around her feet. "I want you to walk around to the end of the bed, a few feet away, and stand there with your feet spread shoulder width apart."

He saw her hesitate, but didn't comment. Connor never broke his stare, wanting her to know that his patience knew no bounds. This was different than working with the subs at the clubs…they knew protocol and they were aware of most aspects when it came to scenes. Regardless of what she did for a living, Lauren was basically an innocent.

She moved slowly, but she eventually did as he asked. Connor rolled his shoulder, loosening the strained muscle. It had been a while since he'd had a scene and this was too important to take lightly. He walked through in his mind the way he wanted this to play out, needing her to crave more of what he was giving her when the scene was done. That was how he would know it went well.

Taking his time and believing that it would only further arouse her by letting her thoughts get carried away of what might happen, Connor removed his jeans and underwear. He didn't need a condom just yet, so he opted to leave the box in the drawer. Walking around to where she was, he sat on the edge of the bed in front of her. Leisurely, he looked her up and down. Her curves were sensual and perfectly shaped into an hourglass. Was Lauren even aware of what she did to him on a physical level?

"A couple ground rules," Connor said, his voice deepening. It always did when he was running a scene. "You are not to speak unless asked a direct question. You are to follow my orders. It is that simple. Do you have any questions?"

"Don't I need a safe word?"

"We won't be doing anything that would require you to use one," Connor answered. "We will discuss safewords at a later time. For now, all you have to do is say no."

"Okay." Lauren gave him a pointed stare. "How is this helping with my fear of bondage?"

Connor didn't answer right away, because he wasn't sure it would help alleviate her phobia. But if Lauren understood that the lifestyle wasn't all about being tied up and whipped, maybe she would see it for what it truly was…freedom. She didn't need to be bound to achieve freedom.

"Save that question for later," Connor said. "But remember this, for every order you do not follow, you'll receive a spanking—and that is when we will cover safewords."

Lauren's breath hitched, but she still stood in front of him without moving. He knew he was pushing with that last sentence, but she wasn't unaware of what took place in the clubs. She just seemed to have a misconception about bondage.

Her eyes searched his and Connor knew he wouldn't address the normal submissive etiquette unless this went well. Usually a submissive would avert her or his gaze. They could always expand their scenes if she was willing.

"Lace your fingers behind your neck and take a step forward," Connor ordered, keeping his voice low. It took her a moment, but she did as he asked. "Closer."

Connor waited until her breasts were right in front of his face. He then looked up, finding her heated gaze locked in on his. He smiled, and not breaking their connection, flattened his tongue and licked her nipple. Lauren sucked in air but didn't move. Did she realize that although nothing was holding her hands behind her head, she'd kept them there at his request? That was a form of bondage, but he would continue to test her limits.

"Do you like a little bit of pain with your sex, Red?"

"Um, no," Lauren answered, her voice shaky. "At least, I don't think so."

Connor had to resist the urge to chastise her for not using a title. He reminded himself that this was just a test and not a true scene that would require the use of *Master* or *Sir*...although, he'd love to hear either word pass her lips. It had been quite a few months since he'd played and he was coming to think that was a little too long to go without fulfilling his basic need to dominate.

Connor sealed his lips around her nipple and sucked slightly, bringing the hardened nub deeper into his mouth. He gently rubbed his tongue over and over her nipple. When he felt her push against him he lightly bit down, letting her feel what a nip could do after an onslaught of pleasure.

Lauren gasped and she went to jerk away, but he gripped her hips. Using his tongue once more, he soothed the sting. Gradually he pulled away and looked up into her beautiful face. Her eyes were as dark as the sea and as in just as much turmoil.

"Feel good?" Connor asked, knowing what her answer would be. She nodded, as if afraid speaking might ruin the moment. "Let's find out, shall we?"

Connor let one hand brush down over her skin and using one finger, ran it through her folds. She was dripping wet. He hadn't taken his eyes off of her face and literally saw the flush rise up in her cheeks. It made her all the more beautiful. How far would she allow him to go before moving her hands?

"Your pussy is very wet, Red," Connor murmured, loving how his words seemed to spark something within her. He could swear he felt another dollop of cream leak out of her. "That pleases me."

Lauren had never experienced anything like this in her life. Her entire body felt like it was on fire and all he'd done was suck on her nipple and run his finger through her folds. Was she wet?

Hell, yes. She was drenched. She was ready to come and wanted him to touch her clit.

This had nothing to do with bondage, but it felt good all the same. A few commands and she was like putty in his hands. Was she aroused enough not to panic if he tied her up? No. But she'd tell him later that his little scene didn't work the way he thought since she could still move her hands. Right now, she wanted to come.

Lauren knew that his words made all the difference in this little play act he had going and something washed over her with his approval of her arousal. She felt elated that he was pleased, but didn't stop to analyze it.

"Connor, please touch my clit," Lauren pleaded, knowing she wasn't supposed to talk, but not able to help herself.

"One," Connor said. He inserted his middle finger into her pussy and Lauren's vision darkened. God, that felt good. She leaned her hips forward, hoping he'd go deeper. He pulled out. "We'll see how many spankings you have earned by this evening, and then, only at the time of my choosing will you take your punishment."

Lauren opened her mouth to protest, but remembered at the last minute that he hadn't asked her a question. She wasn't sure what she would have said, seeing as his words had affected her body in a way that she was just beginning to realize was beyond anything she had ever felt. Her knees were beginning to shake and her heart rate was faster than normal. Every time he spoke in that wicked way, her body responded. Lauren wanted more.

Connor pushed his finger back inside of her and then started to thrust it slowly in and out. It was enough to keep building her impending orgasm, but not fast enough, and sure as hell not enough for her to achieve release. It was only when he slowly pulled his finger out of her pussy and nothing else happened that Lauren realized she'd closed her eyes. Opening them, she looked down into an ocean of blue.

"Where are your hands?"

He was asking her something that trivial when all she wanted was an orgasm? Lauren figured her face showed her confusion, but he still waited patiently for her answer. She snuck a glance down to his cock, which was hard and from this angle, pulsing with his heartbeat. Didn't he want to do something about that as well?

"Behind my head," Lauren responded, looking back up to his face. He didn't seem happy about something, but unless he told her what was wrong, she couldn't figure it out and do whatever he wanted. "That's where you told me to put them."

"Why didn't you move them? It's obvious from the way you're gyrating your hips that you want me to do more than fuck you with my finger."

His coarse language sent shivers through her core. Her pussy responded and the spasms were almost painful. Connor had removed his finger, and now there was nothing to grab onto. His question reverberated through her mind though. It seemed idiotic.

"Again, because that's where you told me to put them," Lauren responded, not caring that her tone indicated she was getting agitated.

"We need to work on your respect," Connor murmured, sliding his hands back up to her breasts. He took each nipple in between his fingers. "You should know enough about the lifestyle that a submissive shows respect to her Master."

If Lauren hadn't been so worked up and sexually frustrated she would have laughed. She'd honestly never pictured herself in this situation due to her past experience. Had she yearned for it? Yes. And considering the way her body was responding to his tone, his words, and his actions…she'd been right about her submissive tendencies. That didn't mean she would automatically fall to her knees.

"Are we in a true scene?" Lauren asked, a little confused. Wasn't he just showing her something? And whatever it might be was lost on her, because they weren't addressing her phobia. It was hard for her to concentrate on anything other than the fact that she needed to come. "Is this what you do at the club?"

"A scene is whatever I choose to make it," Connor said, rolling her nipples in between his fingers. Jolts of electricity shot through her, traveling straight to her clit. "Now answer my question. Why are your hands still behind your neck?"

Lauren would have responded the same way she had earlier but he pinched her nipples and caused her to gasp. Her fingers slipped, but she tightened her grip at the last second. When he smiled up at her was when she realized that although she wasn't bound by cuffs, ropes, or ties…it was his order that kept her hands in place. He'd effectively restricted her by his command.

"But—"

"Would you like to come, Red?" Connor asked, releasing her throbbing nipples.

"Yes, please," Lauren responded quickly. She had no idea why she added on the *please*, but her mind was running a thousand miles an hour now that she grasped what he'd done. She needed to tell him it wasn't the same as true bondage. It wasn't, but as his fingers slipped back into her folds and gathered her cream, all thought left as the pad of his digit connected with her clit and moved in a circular motion. "Please, please, please."

Lauren was grateful that his left hand held her hip. His grip kept her grounded, for she knew that if he hadn't had ahold of her, she would have buckled. The room seemed to spin as blood rushed through her ears. Her body felt suspended as he applied more pressure to her clit. Finally, her pussy exploded and spasms rocked her to the point of crying out.

Connor brought her down gradually and when Lauren finally opened her eyes, she found him staring up at her. She was relatively sure that he'd been watching her the entire time…her face, that is. He slowly reached up and took hold of her wrists, steadily bringing them down to her sides. Lauren hadn't realized how stiff her muscles were until he took each arm and rubbed it down. She moaned in relief and gratitude.

"I think I need to lie down," Lauren whispered. "You've zapped my energy."

He stood and kissed her. It dawned on Lauren that what just happened hadn't been as intimate as it felt. What they had just done made her feel closer to him, yet they had touched less. It didn't make sense, along with the fact that he thought this might help her deal with her phobia. Connor might have told her to keep them there, and in a way, she respected his request…but that had nothing to do with having her wrists bound by leather.

"Climb back into bed," Connor said. "I'll go grab us more coffee and then we can talk. I want you to think about what just happened and then tell me your feelings on it."

He moved toward the doorway, leaving her standing at the end of the bed. Although confusion was starting to set in over the entire scene they'd just shared and she had no idea how she was going to form the words to explain what she felt, Lauren did take time to stare at his naked backside as he walked away.

His ass was lean and his muscles moved with each step. She very much appreciated his parents' genes.

"That was an order," Connor called out, not even bothering to look back as he left her sight. Lauren smiled. Maybe a spanking wouldn't be so bad after all.

Chapter Twenty

Connor paused outside the bedroom door, holding both coffee cups. He needed another moment before facing her again. Did he really want to take her down this road? He hadn't been lying when he said that a Dominant's need and responsibility was to protect his or her submissive. But Lauren was just a casual affair that would eventually end, right? Was pulling her into the lifestyle really for her benefit? Some submissives became too attached to their temporary Masters. Was he playing games with her emotional state at her expense?

An image of Lauren standing with her legs spread open, her juices glistening on her inner thighs, her curls damp from her cream, and her eyes deep with arousal appeared in his mind. There was no doubt she was turned on by the lifestyle. She responded to each command he gave. Connor even understood why she had chosen her profession as it kept her on the outskirts of what she truly desired but never had the courage to really obtain it. But was he the one who should be helping her? Would she understand the difference between a temporary and a permanent Master?

Taking a deep breath and knowing he would continue with their chosen path anyway, Connor stepped into the bedroom. Lauren was sitting up on the far side of the bed, the top sheet covering her. He resisted the urge to smile, wanting her to know that his next command was to be followed.

"Drop the sheet," Connor ordered, holding up her coffee and waiting patiently as she slowly complied. He didn't miss that the pulse in her neck started to beat faster. "I want access to you at all times."

Connor had enough experience with submissives to know that Lauren would follow in the beginning and then want to test his limits. She hadn't reached that point yet, trying to figure out this new rush of feelings that were overwhelming her. When she did, things were bound to become fun.

"Good girl," Connor said as she kicked the sheet to the bottom of the bed. Those red curls still needed to go and he debated on doing it now. Nah, it could wait. They truly needed to go over how she felt right now. "Here's your coffee, just the way you like it."

"Thank you," Lauren said, a smile breaking across her face. He didn't say anything about the fact that she brought the cup in front of her, thus using her arms to cover her breasts. They technically had two days of nothing but being able to scene and for him to take her to new heights. She took a tentative sip, obviously testing the temperature of the creamy liquid. "Hmmm… you make it better than I do."

"That's just so you don't kick me out into the snowstorm." Connor plumped his pillow and set it up against the head-board, before making himself comfortable.

"After what I just experienced?" Lauren said, sending him a sideways glance. "I think I'd like to taste a little more of what you have to offer."

Needing to be facing her so he could see her expressions, Connor took a drink of his coffee before setting his cup on the nightstand. Turning on his side, he used his elbow to rest himself on by placing his head in his palm. Now he could see her clearly. Was she still flushing?

"What did you like about the scene?"

"You keep calling it that," Lauren said, not lowering her arms. He let that go for now. It was a vulnerable thing to do, being honest about one's feelings. "That's not exactly how I picture a scene at a club. You said a scene is what you make it, but that was technically vanilla in nature."

"Really?" Connor asked. "You followed my instructions. You kept your hands where they should be and only answered me when I specifically asked you a question. Yes, you messed up once...but there are times our feelings overwhelm us. It happens and will continue to happen. But the bottom line is that I controlled you."

"But I chose to do that. I wasn't tied up. My wrists weren't encased by material. I was free to move them."

"We already went over this. I told you to keep them there, so you did. That is essentially binding them there with my words. You just can't physically see the tethers. As for you choosing to do so, that's the gift that a submissive gives her Master."

Connor watched Lauren drink her coffee, her eyes lowering to his cock every now and then, and knew that the scene she just experienced was light enough that he could start another. Maybe the scene had been too light. Pushing that thought away for now, he pushed her a little further with regards to her emotional state.

"How did you feel when you followed my orders?"

"Hot." Lauren rolled her eyes when he laughed. "Not hot, as in *hot*…but hot as in I felt as if I was on fire."

She paused, as if trying to figure out how to express her words correctly. Before Connor could tell her that he wouldn't judge her and that there were no right or wrong answers, Lauren took a deep breath and continued.

"My heart raced like I'd never felt before. My knees felt like they were going to buckle from the first moment you touched me. My blood was rushing through my body with every word that came out of your mouth." Lauren finally lowered her hands, although she didn't take her eyes off of the cup in front of her. Connor noticed that her breasts seemed fuller and that her nipples were hardened. Since it was relatively warm in her bedroom, he highly doubted her body's reaction was from the temperature. "I always knew that I had an interest in the lifestyle, but all the same, what we just did still felt vanilla to me. My reaction was stronger, yet we really did nothing that would imply…well, BDSM."

"Why?" Connor asked, honestly curious as to why she would say that. "Because there were no whips or chains? Your business clientele lives and breathes this lifestyle. I would think you wouldn't have such a black and white outlook of the definition. You, yourself, said that your friend who tried to help you was into BDSM. Did you discuss things in detail?"

"I've read books," Lauren said, defensively. "When Phil tried to help me, I was in my early twenties. I'm not sure how much he knew. We were young. And it's not like I strike up a random conversation about people's lives. What you and I did just seemed…vanilla."

"Physically or mentally?"

Connor finally saw recognition dawn and felt a stirring in his cock. It was now only semi-hard, but seeing as he hadn't had a release since last night, it was a wonder he didn't have a case of blue balls. He'd always prided himself on making the scenes benefit his submissives and now would be no different. He doubted he would see relief until this evening.

"I admit there was a different ambiance this time. It seemed deeper, more intimate. Yet, I didn't really physically engage and you didn't—you know."

"Come?" Connor asked. "The scene was not meant for me. It was more of a mental exercise for you, but I can see that maybe I need to broaden your horizons."

"As a Dom, do you ever do scenes for you?" Lauren asked, seemingly becoming more comfortable with her nudity. She shifted to face him, soaking in every word that he was saying. Her green eyes were now sparkling like those emeralds he first saw in her shop. She was like a kid in a candy store. "You know, so that you can—"

"There are times that Doms play out scenes for their pleasure, but I get my enjoyment out of my submissive's gratification…when she earns it."

Connor watched her pupils dilate and her lips part. He knew Lauren might enjoy the aspects of the life he led, but even he was taken aback at her immediate response. It made the Dom inside of him wonder just how far he could take things.

"Okay," Connor said, thinking of different scenarios of which to attempt to sincerely show her the mental aspects of the lifestyle. "So I take it we're in agreement that you want to lightly explore the lifestyle and allow me to guide you through exercises that might help with your phobia, correct?"

"Yes," Lauren answered, the word a little breathless.

"Then let's concentrate on some preliminary items." Connor let his eyes roam her body, letting Lauren know that he was inspecting her. Could she feel the heat of his gaze? "One, I want you to write down what your soft and hard limits are. Soft limits are those things that you would be willing to try and hard limits are things that you will absolutely, unequivocally not do—whether it goes against your morals, something that might affect your health, or you simply won't do. Once you do that, I'd like time to look it over. During that period, you will then go into the bathroom and take a nice, long hot bubble bath. When you emerge, I want your pussy bare…every piece of hair gone. Then you will stand in the middle of the room as you did before and wait for further instructions. Do you understand?"

✧   ✧   ✧   ✧

"I understand that I'm getting in way over my head," Lauren muttered, sinking into the vast amounts of bubbles that lay on the surface on the hot water.

She knew that having him here during the snowstorm had the potential of leading to more than a vanilla affair. Maybe subconsciously that's what she'd been hoping for. That small scene he'd demonstrated had certainly awakened her body in a way that doing it missionary style never did. But were things moving too fast?

Knowing she needed to talk to her sister, Lauren wiped her right hand on a towel. Picking up her phone that she'd placed on the tile next to the razor and gel shaving cream she used, she hit the speed dial button. After three rings, Sue picked up.

"How much snow have you gotten?" Sue asked, without the standard *hello*. "Dave and I have been watching the news. You should have come down to visit before it hit. We could be at the beach right now."

"I'm thinking I like where I'm at now." Lauren popped one of the bubbles with her finger. "Connor's here."

"Stuck in a snowstorm with only sex to pass the time," Sue said, humor coming through the phone line loud and clear. "Dave will be jealous."

"Connor knows what happened to cause my phobia," Lauren stated, wanting to get to the point so that Sue could help her figure out if she'd lost her mind or not. "I told him last night."

"Let me guess," Sue said in a wry tone, "he thinks he can *fix* you."

"He thinks he can *help* me," Lauren said, getting a little defensive. "I basically said the same thing you did, but Connor explained things in a tad bit different way."

"Did you tell him you already tried with Phil, a friend you trusted?" Sue covered the phone and some muffled words came out. Lauren wasn't sure if her sister was speaking with Dave or the kids.

"Yes." Lauren thought back to her and Connor's earlier conversation. "Connor gave an analogy that made me see things differently. I'm thinking of seeing if it works."

"Translation," Sue said, laughing, "you already tried something and it peaked your interest. Do I get the juicy details?"

"No," Lauren replied, smiling.

"Let me get this straight. You're in the middle of the worst snowstorm Minneapolis has seen in years, with a hot man who has dominant tendencies and wants to screw your brains out and you're on the phone with me?" Sue made that tsking sound she always did when Lauren wasn't doing the right thing. "What is wrong with this picture?"

"I guess I wanted to hear that this isn't a mistake," Lauren said, popping some more bubbles. "You know, my older sister telling me I should be careful. That I technically just met this man and I shouldn't rush things. Maybe even throw in there that I wanted this to be casual and things might be getting too deep."

"Anything else you want me to say?" Sue asked, her tone still light.

"Yes, that tomorrow will arrive and he will leave. Well, maybe by Monday morning, after the roads have been cleared." Lauren looked over at the razor. "You should say that things will go back to normal, except maybe a booty call here and there because that's the way I wanted it. It's the way Connor wants it."

"I'm pretty good at this advice thing," Sue said, a tenderness entering her voice. "Before I continue giving you more counsel, did he give you a reason why *he* wanted things casual?"

Lauren thought back over past conversations and realized that Connor never did give her a specific reason. "No. But maybe he's not looking for anything permanent right now. Does there have to be a reason?"

"You're getting defensive," Sue said. "Which could only mean that you're falling a little faster than you'd intended. Carrot Top, you always hold yourself back from a man because deep down, you want to be part of that lifestyle in which you work. Unfortunately, the men you choose to date are as boring as watching golf on television. Connor is the first one giving you what you need and you're afraid you'll fall too deep. I get that. But what do we always say?"

"YOLO," Lauren answered, reiterating their *"you only live once"* motto.

"That's right. Not that you've been living your life like that. It's been me and although I have Dave, sometimes it gets lonely being the only daring one. I have two kids! How much more daring can a woman get? So, just make sure you don't fall too deep. Enjoy this weekend and take it for what it is...a fun time. YOLO."

"Love you," Lauren murmured, sneaking another glance at the razor.

"You, too. Now go burn up those sheets," Sue ordered. "All this talk of hot sex is going to make Dave a happy man. If you do start living the YOLO life, maybe I'll finally get you down to Florida. Hey, call me after the storm lifts and we'll compare notes. Ta-ta!"

Lauren was still smiling as she disconnected the call. Shaking her head, she set her phone down beside the shaving gel. Technically, her sister was right. Why *not* enjoy what she was being offered? What had made her suddenly fearful of continuing and why was she hesitating now? Was it that the more time they spent together, the more she was falling for him? Those emotions that he'd generated this morning had been intense and she knew that had something to do with it.

Picking up the can of shaving gel, Lauren could feel her heart rate accelerate at doing something so illicit. She'd always had curls down below but had kept them trimmed in a neat, tidy line. If she didn't remove her hair, would Connor spank her immediately? Knowing that she'd accumulated one already had her anticipating what it would feel like to have the palm of his hand land on her ass. Would it sting? A shiver ran down her lower spine and into her crevice.

Lauren started with her right leg, pressing the top of the can and producing a line of turquoise gel that she ran up to her knee. The color reminded her of Connor's eyes and she suddenly wanted to rush through this and see what his reaction would be once he saw her newly shaved body. Using her hands, she smoothed the cream around and quickly got to work.

Minutes later, she was ready to shave her pussy, but wasn't sure exactly how to go about it. Going through her options, Lauren hopped out of the hot bath water and sat herself on the edge of the tub, keeping her feet in the water. Lifting one foot, she placed it on the opposite side and spread her legs wide. Her pussy produced a spasm at the position and Lauren felt the blood start to pool in her clit. How was she going to do this without nicking anything important?

Again, Lauren picked up the can and pressed the top, producing a big swirl of cream in the middle of her palm. She rubbed the gel all over her pussy and the coolness had her sucking in her breath. Her clit now throbbed, wanting to be touched and given another orgasm. Really? Since when had she turned into such a nymphomaniac?

Lauren picked up her razor and swiped the first row of hair away. The feel of the sharp blade coming so close to her clit raised the hairs on the back of her neck. She closed her eyes and inhaled deeply, wondering how she was going to get through this without touching herself. This simple act was downright erotic and Connor damn right knew that it would get her hot and needy before their next scene.

Dipping the razor into the water and washing away the tiny curls, Lauren bit her lip and got to work. Connor was waiting on her, and for once she wasn't focused on her phobia. She wanted more of what he'd given her this morning. YOLO.

Chapter Twenty-One

"What are we doing out here?" Lauren said, her teeth chattering with every word. The gloves she wore weren't doing a damn thing to keep her fingers warm. At least the scarf and her hat, which she had on low over her forehead, were keeping the wind from stinging her cheeks. "It probably would have been wise to shave down below *after* this bright idea of yours to go trekking in the snow. Every little piece of hair helps, you know."

Connor laughed but still continued forward. His military jacket was zipped up and he had a skullcap on, which only managed to emphasize his cheekbones. His cheeks were already red and they still had a couple blocks before making it to the park. She was grateful that the snow had lightened somewhat and knew that the grace period wouldn't last for long. The worst of the storm had yet to hit.

"Things were becoming too intense and I thought a walk to the park might cool us down." Connor looked her way. His blue eyes were back to studying her intently. "I want to make sure that you're not going to regret this come Monday morning."

"*This* meaning allowing you to show me facets of the life-style?" Lauren asked, meeting his gaze head on. "Isn't that what you offered me?"

"Yeah, I did," Connor murmured, looking away from her.

They fell into silence as they walked the rest of the way, giving Lauren time to contemplate what he was saying. It wasn't her that he was giving time to, but himself. Something her sister said resurfaced, and now it was making sense. Did Connor feel that by taking things a step further than just a vanilla relationship that she would become too attached to him? Or was it the other way around? Maybe it was a good thing he was giving them time to chill…and not just in the literal sense.

The park came into view and Lauren was surprised to see quite a lot of people milling about. Some were couples, walking hand in hand through the snow. Others were parents, watching their children have snowball fights and build snowmen. There were even a few people with their dogs on leashes, allowing them to play in the snow.

"Come on, let's show these kids how it's done," Connor said, releasing her hand. He leaned down and started to make a snowball. "You make the body and I'll start on the base."

"I haven't made a snowman in years," Lauren said, laughing and allowing the afternoon to be what Connor intended—a fun-filled time. A boy around the age of twelve had heard what Connor said and shouted for his friends to come help. "Connor, I think we have competition."

"Then what are you waiting for, Red?" Connor asked, exerting what must be some pent-up energy. He'd already expanded the snow in his hand to a basketball. "You'll be sweating in no time and those chattering teeth will stop. I wouldn't want to be the cause of you getting a chipped tooth."

"Such a gentleman," Lauren said, laughing. She saw the boys and girls going to work, side by side. This was starting to be fun. "Okay, Marine. Let's see you do your best."

For over an hour, she and Connor worked on building their snowman. Seeing him interact with the boys and girls was eye-opening, because she would have bet her inventory of gemstones that he would have won the battle hands down. As it was, once the bodies were made, Connor and the kids made a pact. Whoever decorated their snowman with whatever could be found and finished first, won. It was a fair fight up until the end.

"All we need is a nose," Matthew, the leader of the other team said. He was a cute blonde boy with brown eyes and a smattering of freckles. Lauren caught him a few times looking over at a girl his age who kept smiling his way. He was smitten. "Everyone, look around for a stick!"

Lauren noticed that Connor had slowed down in his search of items. They found pieces of mulch buried underneath the snow for the eyes. Using rocks for the mouth and the buttons down the body, they also needed a nose. Everyone turned to the closest tree and made a beeline for the branches. Lauren could hear the parents' laughter as Connor made a dive for a perfect stick but came up short. She knew he did it on purpose, but Matthew was too busy screaming for joy that he'd found the nose.

Lauren leaned down, picking up a stick and waving it at Connor. She knew that he'd want to at least give a show of effort in his attempt. It wouldn't do for the kids to think they won because they'd allowed it. Connor gave a Semper Fi shout and bolted after Matthew, who was now running as fast as his little feet could carry him.

Matthew ran toward his snowman, holding his stick like a javelin. He looked behind him, seeing Connor three steps behind. He stabbed the stick into the snow, seconds before Connor did. A round of cheers went around the children and their parents, Connor falling in the snow and holding his chest. Before she knew it, he'd grabbed her ankle and cushioned her fall.

"That was fun," Connor murmured, nudging his cold nose against her neck until she was laughing. "We'll have to come out tomorrow."

"And get our asses kicked again?" Lauren asked, seeing Matthew walking toward them. She maneuvered herself off of Connor until she was sitting next to him. "You make a mean snowman, Mr. Matthew."

"Will you guys be out tomorrow?" Matthew wiped snow from his eye.

"And miss another battle?" Connor replied, hoisting himself up on his elbow. "We wouldn't miss it, buddy."

"Cool," Matthew exclaimed and then ran off, yelling to his friends that the war continued.

"That was nice of you," Lauren said softly, leaning back on her elbows as well. The two snowmen stood side by side. It *had* been nice to get out of the apartment for a bit. Connor had been right; although sneaking a look at him, it had done nothing to appease her attraction to him. In fact, if anything, their time at the park had made him all the more likeable. "You're a sweet man."

"Sweet?" Connor's mouth twitched. "I don't think I've ever been called that. As for being nice...I manage it every now and then. This was fun. We exerted some energy and you'll be hungry for dinner."

Lauren could have mentioned that there were other ways to exert energy, but figured she'd maintain some sort of discipline. They still had today and tomorrow before reality returned. Instead, she focused on two things.

"I know you let Matthew win. And what *are* you making for dinner?"

"It's a surprise," Connor said, snagging her jacket sleeve and pulling her back over top of him. "Do you like Cuban food?"

"I like most food," Lauren said, noticing the snow had started to come down a little harder. The second wave of the storm was hitting. Flakes were starting to land on his red cheeks. "I like it even better when someone else cooks."

"That's good. Because you'll be busy. As for why I let Matthew win…the boy has passion and a competitive nature. He worked like hell, right alongside of us. The other ones only gave a half-hearted effort, but him—well, let's just say he reminded me of me."

Lauren's mind was being pulled into two different directions. What was she going to be doing while he cooked? And had he even checked to see what she had in the freezer and refrigerator? It wasn't like she cooked Cuban food every day. But it was his comment that Matthew reminded him of himself that grabbed her attention the most.

"Why does Matthew remind you of yourself?"

"Did you notice that he was by himself out here?" Connor nodded toward an apartment building across the road. "He lives there. Not the greatest apartment complex. I saw him coming out when we were still a block away. One of the mothers asked how his father was doing, but there was no mention of a mother. The look on his face…let's just say I remember feeling that way. He needed to prove himself and I gave him a helping hand."

Lauren was afraid to speak or move for fear that he would stop talking. He'd shared stories about his time in the military as well as his shenanigans with Jax, but never much about his childhood. Connor was still looking across the street to where Matthew had gone.

"Do you feel the need to prove yourself?" Lauren whispered, hoping that she hadn't made a mistake.

"I did," Connor confessed, a faraway look on his face. "But not anymore. Kind of like my father when he immigrated here. Once he'd accomplished what he'd wanted, he took pride in his work and cultivated it into a living. I did the same."

"Do you look like him?" Lauren asked, wondering if she were stepping into a minefield by the roundabout way she'd asked about his mother. "I find it hard to believe he has blue eyes."

"My mother was a Jersey girl, through and through," Connor replied, his blue eyes focusing again and coming to rest on her face. His voice didn't give much away, but his statement confirmed her belief that his mother was American. "I don't even remember what she looks like. Have no desire to either."

Some bitterness leaked through his voice and she could hear the white lie within his words. Connor did remember what she looked like, but Lauren assumed this was his way to state that his mother held no importance in his life.

"I still have my father, so I can only imagine what it's like not to have your parents around anymore. For that I'm sorry, Red."

Lauren smiled tenderly, having come to terms with the loss of her parents a long time ago. She still missed them immensely, but it gave her and her sister comfort to know that wherever they were, they were together. Connor had his father and she knew from the tenor in his voice that he loved the man very much.

Snow had made the bottom of her jeans wet and the cold against her skin sent a shiver up her spine. The storm had picked up and now the wind was starting to gust. Being so observant, Connor didn't miss her slight shudder.

"Let's get you home." Connor claimed her lips once more and she relished the heat he radiated. Pulling away, he slid out from underneath her and helped her stand up. "We don't want you catching pneumonia. I have big plans for you, Red."

Chapter Twenty-Two

Connor stood at the sink and rested his hands on the countertop. He took a deep breath and hung his head, trying to collect his thoughts. They'd made it back to the apartment and he'd changed their plans again, sending her into a hot shower as he made dinner. Cooking the meal gave him extra time to think. It had been a simple Cuban pork adobo recipe that he'd learned from his father and she'd had all the ingredients.

They'd enjoyed some light conversation throughout the meal, which was much needed with how intense this weekend had become. Now Connor knew why he and Jax kept their play to the club scene...it was brief and no one got attached. Even with Ashley, he'd only ever played within the club. They'd fuck like rabbits when they got to her apartment, but at least he'd been able to maintain his distance when he'd left to go back to his own place afterward. So why when Ashley had upgraded to a wealthier target did it take him by surprise?

Shaking his head, Connor ignored that thought and reached for the dishtowel. Maybe he was having a mid-life crisis a little early. It was known to happen with men in their thirties. He hadn't lied when he told Lauren that giving her this experience was something he wanted, but even that brief scene this morning seemed too intimate. They'd agreed on a casual relationship, but that didn't mean he could end it without some sort of explanation. Who knew how long it would take him to get Lauren out of his system, but by teaching her the ways of the lifestyle it might speed it up. She was hell on his psyche.

Wiping his hands dry, he threw the towel back on the counter and turned to face the living room. He'd sent her into the bedroom to give her time to get into position. Connor had asked beforehand if it was all right for him to check her non-designed inventory. The flush on her face was evident, but he didn't give away what he was looking for. Upon her consent, he'd gone into her spare bedroom and found the items he needed. To his surprise, he even found a tube of lubricant and figured she used the stuff on the zippers of some leather corsets that she ornamented.

The objects Connor had chosen were now waiting for him on the counter. As he gathered them up and walked toward the bedroom door, he felt more and more like himself. He just needed to treat this as if they were in a club. What was about to happen was no more intimate than anything else he'd ever participated in. Lauren wanted to be given the freedom to enjoy the lifestyle and he was able to give that to her.

Crossing the threshold, he was careful to keep the items out of Lauren's line of vision. He didn't look at her right away, but instead walked around the other side of the bed and placed the objects in the chair by the second nightstand. Connor reached for the edge of his shirt and pulled it over his head. Letting it fall to the floor, he listened carefully and could hear her shallow breathing. Rolling his shoulder to ease the tension, he felt the atmosphere envelope them and knew it was time to push her boundaries.

Turning around to face her, Connor saw that she stood in the middle of the room, feet shoulder width apart and her hands clasped behind her head. He walked toward her, noticing her nipples grow harder in direct relation to the nearness of his body. Her freshly shaved pussy was a sight to see. He was relatively sure the warm air was lightly brushing against her clit as he could feel the movement of air against his chest. Her clit was enlarged, although not as swollen as he intended it to be before she gained relief.

"Your hard limits include blood, edge play, watersports, and scat."

Connor saw her startle at his words as they broke through the ambiance. He raised his gaze to look at her face. Her plush lips were parted and her eyes were set on him. He'd correct that later, but for now he wanted to make sure she understood the basics. And he really enjoyed seeing the way her eyes changed color when her arousal spiked. She should be aroused, considering she was practically surrounded by the lifestyle day in and day out, but there was a naiveté about her that was exquisite.

"Those are good to start with, although I'm sure as I bring up other limits you'll find that you'll want additional ones included. As for your soft limits, I see anal play was written down. I like that."

He walked behind her and ran a finger down her spine. Goosebumps followed and she couldn't prevent the shudder that shot through her. Connor was captivated with her responses. It was almost as if she were truly innocent.

"I'm going to ask you questions and I want truthful answers." Connor walked back around to stand in front of her.

Placing a finger underneath her chin, he angled her face up toward his. "Have you heard of a safeword?"

"Yes, of course I have." The irritation of her tone almost made him smile. "We talked about them earlier."

"Then I'd like for you to choose one." Connor's thumb caressed her lower lip. "If at any point through the rest of our seclusion you feel uncomfortable with what I'm doing, all you have to do is say that word and our play will stop."

"As in…finite?" Lauren asked, her brows furrowing.

He liked that she wanted clearer answers. It meant she was paying attention. Connor needed to assure himself that there were no misconceptions.

"No, I mean the scene stops and then we will talk about what is making you uncomfortable." Connor dropped his hand. "What is your safeword?"

"Tourmaline," Lauren murmured. "It's a type of gem."

"And my title?"

He'd noticed that her gaze had snuck over to where he'd placed the items that he'd brought into the bedroom with him, but his question had her green eyes snapping back his way. They'd darkened to the emerald color he loved so much. Her quick inhalation gave him the indication that she liked the idea of calling him Master, although she remained quiet.

"It seems we have to go over a few more ground rules," Connor said, deepening his tone to make her aware that they were within a scene. From the tremor that shot through her, she was well aware of it. "You will call me Master or Sir during a scene. You will not speak unless asked a direct question. You are to follow my orders. It's that simple. Do you understand?"

"Yes," Lauren replied, her voice soft and low. "Master."

Hearing his title come off of her tongue made his cock harden. Connor saw the pulse in her neck flutter and knew that calling him by that word gave this entire scene the significance it needed. She'd just hammered the nail into his coffin.

"Good girl," Connor murmured, closing the distance between them.

Lauren's hands were still clasped behind her neck, so he took ahold of her wrists and lowered them. He kept pulling until he'd connected them together at her lower back. Reaching up, he gathered her curls up and away from her face. Taking her hair tie that he'd swiped from the nightstand, he cinched her hair up into a ponytail. Seeing more of her hair ties on the dresser, he moved away to grab them. In one swipe, he had two in his grip.

"Hold out your wrists," Connor ordered, making sure he was looking directly at her when he issued the command.

Her hesitation was obvious, but he waited patiently. Lauren would either comply with this simple request or use her safeword. He was betting that her comfort and trust in him at this point would win out over her apprehension. He'd done nothing to cause misgivings. She slowly brought her hands out in front.

Without a word, he placed both ties around each of her wrists, but did not connect them in any way. Lauren wasn't aware of it, but that was all he'd do for now in regards to restraint. Connor looked upon her phobia as that of assembling a gun...with care and precision. Each piece had a place, and if put together properly, functioned to the best of its ability. Her first scene, he'd asked that she keep her hands in place. For this, the feel of something wrapped around her wrists would give the sense of bondage, but no more so than when he'd required it of her this morning.

"To reiterate what I feel should be your discipline...for every command you do not follow, for every word uttered that

I have not asked for…will be added to your spanking before bed. Now, I want to inspect what you are so freely giving me. Bend over and grab your ankles."

✧   ✧   ✧   ✧

Lauren felt lightheaded at his command, and for a brief moment believed she'd faint if she followed it. The butterflies flying in her stomach wanted an escape and she was afraid she'd give them one. Slowly, she bent over to where she could grab her ankles. How was it that he hadn't even touched her, yet she felt as if they'd just had sex for an hour? A light sheen of perspiration had already broken out over her body and her knees felt like jelly. Lauren forced herself to lock her knees in place.

"You have a beautiful body," Connor said, slowly walking around her. His bare feet came into her line of view and it struck her that they appeared masculine. The thought made her want to giggle, which was so unlike her. She wasn't that type of woman, yet her emotions were running rampant. "Your crevice is curved with precision, while your rosebud is perfectly centered and lightly dusted with your red hair. The things I will show you will fulfill every dark fantasy you've ever had, Red."

Heat infused her body as wicked images flashed through her mind. Why wasn't he touching her if he wanted to show her all of these things? Lauren could feel his heat from inches away and her anus throbbed with the need for contact. She'd never been introduced to anal play, mostly due to the fact the men she'd been with were vanilla in nature, but that didn't mean she didn't want to experience it. Again, why was he not touching her?

"Palms flat on the floor and spread your legs wider," Connor ordered, not moving from his position. "I want to see how well you shaved your pussy. I warn you now, should it not meet my satisfaction, that will only add to your count."

She was relatively sure that Connor knew his words would produce her pussy to cream. Lauren felt the moisture seep through her folds as her hands touched the hardwood floor in front of her. Shifting her feet farther apart, her juices slipped past and coated her inner thighs.

"It pleases me to know that my voice alone can make you aroused," Connor murmured, surprised her when he slid a finger through her lips. Spasms rocked her pussy, but he did nothing more. She heard him hum and knew that he'd tasted her. "Your flavor is unmistakable. I can't seem to get enough, but right now we have other things to do. I want you to stand, walk over to the bed and situate yourself on the end of the mattress. You are to place your knees on the edge and keep them separated as wide as you can while your shoulders rest against the comforter. Your ass will be up in the air and exposed to me, while your arms are to either side of you."

Lauren took her time to stand, the lightheaded feeling have never fully gone away. She was having trouble slowing her heart rate and her mouth had gone completely dry. Did he plan to bind her arms to the mattress? Was that even possible? She didn't have any type of contraption to do that, but then again, she wasn't sure what the hair ties were to be used for. They felt no different to her than when she wore her watch on her left wrist. He'd placed them on her, so she assumed he had a reason for doing so.

Making her way to the edge of the bed, Lauren tried to see what he'd placed on the chair. Was that her tube of lubricant that she kept in the spare bedroom for work? Zippers tended to get stuck and chains managed to become tangled…KY Jelly was a simple solution. But she knew his intentions would be

230 ✧ KENNEDY LAYNE

totally different. She should be focused on what he had planned for the wrist ties, but her anus was pulsing with what he intended for the lube.

"What were my instructions?" Connor asked, his voice in her right ear. The warmth of his breath caused her to tilt her head as shivers rolled through her. "At this rate, we'll have to toss out counting how many spankings you obtain. Maybe I *should* integrate them within this scene. It might help you focus on me instead of what is on that chair."

Lauren wasn't sure if she should answer or not, considering Connor had spoken after his initial question. Instead, she quickly climbed onto the bed and situated herself the way he required. The vulnerability of the position wasn't lost on her. She gathered up the comforter in her fists for something to hold on to and wished her mental state had something similar. As it was, she felt as if she were in free-fall.

"I think that is what we shall do, so that after our scene I can hold you and fall asleep peacefully. Knowing how we'll both be satiated, mentally and physically, can be rather exhausting." Connor walked over to the chair, but since her cheek was resting on the blanket, she couldn't see what he'd grabbed. He walked back and continued until he was behind her. She resisted the urge to move her hips. "Have you experienced the pleasure of a butt plug, Red?"

"No," Lauren whispered. The sound of her voice seemed far away as blood rushed through her ears. She tried to attach his title to the word, but her long pause was evident. It seemed to give him so much power, yet that was what she wanted. "Sir."

"By the time this scene ends, your words will flow together nicely," Connor said, his promise ringing through the air.

"Now, I'll ask once again to give you more practice. Have you ever experienced the pleasure of a plug?"

Lauren's breath caught as she felt his finger brush over her tight ring. In a whoosh of air, her words came rushing out. She'd never been touched there by a man.

"No, Sir, I haven't."

"Now, see, wasn't that easier?" Connor asked. She heard the familiar click of the tube, knowing he'd flicked it open with his thumb. "Ask me to place the lube onto your tight hole."

It was one thing to answer him, but something else entirely to ask for something so wanton. Lauren knew before the words ever flowed out of her mouth that this was another turning point in her journey. With each command that fell from his lips, it was as if a section of her mind and soul were expanding. She licked her lips.

"W-would you please put some lube on my h-hole, Sir?" Lauren whispered, sparking something inside of her that was close to irritation. She was a strong-willed woman who never stuttered in her entire life. She wasn't about to start now. In a louder voice, she repeated, "Please put lube on my anus, Master."

Connor chuckled, as if knowing she was gritting her teeth. As the cool gel touched such an intimate area, Lauren lost her frustration in exchange for her arousal being reignited. Not that she ever lost it, but it spiked at an amazing rate. She couldn't suppress a moan, especially when she felt his thumb rub it around her ring. He didn't utter a word, just repeatedly brushed over and over her sphincter until she was pushing back.

"Would you like something, Red?"

He was reducing her into a massive puddle of need. Lauren's hips were undulating on their own and her brain refused to function. He didn't let up, eventually causing her to cry out in desperation to know what it would feel like if he were to breach her there. She needed to know.

"Please, Sir, I want you to put the plug in my ass."

"Your words are flowing now, Red," Connor said, approval lacing his tone and making her feel a warmth spread out inside of her. The outside of her body was ready to catch fire. "My pleasure."

With those two words, he removed his finger and she held her breath. This was it. Would it feel good? Would she feel full, like she did when her pussy was filled? Would it hurt? Lauren felt the tip of the plug and as it parted her sphincter, her mouth mimicked the action. The second the stinging sensation electrified throughout her ring, she moved her hands and tried to lean up.

Smack!

"Did I say you could move?"

"No, Sir, but—" Lauren felt the air whoosh out of her once more as he smacked her other cheek. Heat blossomed once more. "It stings."

Lauren felt him lean over her, his chest to her back. A different warmth effused her. She felt Connor's fingers entangle in her ponytail and bring her head back. His lips touched her ear.

"You moved your hands, Red," Connor whispered, his disapproval evident. "Now, I want them back where I told you to place them. Those ties around your wrist are to signify bonds. Do you feel them, Lauren? Do you feel them wrapped around your skin and holding them where I desire? I won't tell you again. You are not the only one who can halt a scene. It would do you well to remember that."

Connor slowly released his hold on her, but it took a moment for her to move. Had he just threatened to stop what they were doing should she not listen to him? Were Dominants allowed to do that? She guessed it didn't matter. He said he would and she believed him. The question Lauren had to ask herself was how badly did she want this scene to continue?

Lauren slowly eased her shoulders back down onto the mattress and stretched out her arms. The ties around her wrists seemed to make their presence known now that he brought attention to them and a sliver of unease went through her. The kind she got when she felt like she was being closed in. Closing her eyes, she took a deep breath and tried to alleviate her anxiety.

"Good girl, but keep your eyes open," Connor said, but it was those two words that had more of an affect on her than she would have ever imagined. "Now, where were we?"

With that question, Lauren felt the tip being replaced on her tight ring. She inhaled and waited for that initial sting, knowing it was coming. She waited, but nothing happened.

"I want you to count your breathing. One."

Lauren inhaled and then exhaled.

"Two."

She did it again and slowly felt him insert the plug.

"Three."

Repeating the action, the sting made itself known and the air shuddered out of her lungs. Her fingers tightened in the blanket.

"Do you know the amazing thing about the human body?" Connor asked. The plug held her in place, though she was certain it wasn't too far inside of her. Why was he asking her questions now? Lauren was to the point where she wished he would just shove it in or take it out. "It knows better of what we enjoy and desire than our mind."

She felt his finger travel through her folds and felt the unmistakable moisture trail behind him. She was drenched and knew that Connor was right. He had stopped when the sting had truly begun, but now that he'd allowed her time to adjust, Lauren felt pleasure and pain mix. Her body truly enjoyed it, while it took her mind a moment to catch up. The ties around her wrist felt as if they no longer existed.

"Shall we continue?"

"Yes, Sir," Lauren murmured, snuggling into the softness of the blanket beneath her. She would do this for him. He had earned her trust and she wouldn't let him down. "Please."

"Breathe," Connor ordered, at the precise moment he pushed the plug in farther.

A deep-seated burn set in as her sphincter opened further and allowed the plug entrance. As it sank deeper inside of her, Lauren heard a guttural groan and knew it was her. Her ring finally closed around the ridge. She was afraid to shift, not knowing if the slightest movement would make it hurt worse. Burning embers seemed to engulf that area.

"Let it morph with the pleasure," Connor murmured.

She heard his words over the rush of blood in her ears and knew instantly what he meant when she felt his finger slide into her pussy. Lauren would have thought it impossible. It was as if it were the first time anything had been inserted inside her pussy, for the nerves had been awakened in a different sense. If Connor had pulled out his finger, she had no doubt she would have come instantly. Instead, she felt him massage the inside of her sheath and keep her hanging on the edge.

"Are you to move your hands from where I tell you to place them?" Connor asked, as if this were a normal situation.

She knew what was coming and it ratcheted up her arousal, if that was even possible.

"No, Sir," Lauren exclaimed.

Smack!

"Ah!" Lauren cried, fisting the comforter even tighter within her grip. He'd delivered his slap with his other hand, keeping his finger inside of her. She wanted to come. She needed to come. The necessity to come was overwhelming. "Please."

"You mark beautifully." Connor lightly rubbed the area that was throbbing. "The pink contrasts with your skin to show exactly who you belong to. Which begs another question. Are you my submissive now?"

"Yes, Sir," Lauren replied, figuring out she would have said anything at this point to have him continue.

Smack! Smack! Smack! Smack!

"Now there's the shade of pink I like to see," Connor murmured, using his hand to brush over her heated skin. He pulled his finger out so slowly that she whimpered. Having lost all contact with him seemed unbearable. She'd rather be spanked than have him do nothing. She heard the tear of a wrapper and held her breath. "Would you like to come?"

"Yes, Sir," Lauren replied softly, when what she really wanted to do was scream her answer.

"Keeping position with your shoulders on the bed, give me your right hand," Connor ordered. His tone brooked no argument, and when she felt the tip of his cock at her entrance, the thought of disobeying him never crossed her mind. She forced herself to release the blanket and pulled her arm back. His fingers enclosed around her wrist and settled their connection on her lower back, setting her heart racing faster. She jerked to get it back. "It's just for me to hold on to for leverage."

Lauren's mind was in a war with her body. She knew that his grip on her wrist wasn't for leverage, yet she didn't have time to dwell on it when he started to enter her slowly. The feel of his cock sliding inside of her was unlike anything she'd felt before. It was as if he was contending for room in her body and didn't intend to lose. His fingers tightened, but before she could pull away, he jerked her toward him. Connor's cock sunk balls deep into her pussy, causing her to cry out. It felt euphoric.

"Sir."

"I'm leaving the choice up to you, Red," Connor said, his voice coming across hoarse. It gave her little satisfaction to know he was just as affected as her. Lauren was too caught up hanging from the proverbial cliff to understand what he meant. He made it clearer for her in the next sentence. "Hand me your other wrist and I'll fuck you so hard you'll see stars. If you choose not to, I'll fuck you slowly until I obtain release…"

His meaning was clear. Connor wouldn't allow her to orgasm unless she gave him her wrist. She knew that he would grip her as if she was bound, but he was leaving the choice up to her. It wasn't really an option though, was it? She *needed* to come. All of her senses were in overdrive, and as she pulled her left arm back, essentially making her defenseless against the bed, Lauren mentally prepared herself for the panic attack that was about to take place and ruin this entire scene. It never came.

Lauren cried out as he wrapped his fingers around both wrists and used them as his anchor. Over and over Connor drove his cock into her, shoving all thought aside. All she could do was feel and experience exactly what he said she would. Pinpricks of light flashed in her vision as the first spasm tore through her.

"Sir…"

The orgasm rocked her hard. Lauren's ass clamped down on the plug and his cock felt enormous. Her toes curled and she dug her fingernails into the palms of her hands, riding wave after wave of pleasure. She felt his shaft swell, mostly due to the fact that the plug had made for tighter space, and heard him shout his release. It still didn't stop his onslaught as he continued to thrust in and out of her.

Finally, although her pussy was still experiencing small spasms, Connor gently released her. Not caring if she had no grace, Lauren stretched herself out on the comforter, but moaned as the action caused his cock to slip from her pussy. All she could hear echo throughout the room was their breathing.

"Stay where you are," Connor ordered in a low voice.

Did he think she was going anywhere? Lauren broke into a smile as she lay there, listening to him enter the bathroom. She heard the sounds of the toilet flushing and running water. Within minutes, he'd returned and placed a warm cloth on her pussy. The heat took her by surprise and she inhaled sharply.

"Push out," Connor said, as she felt him take ahold of the base of the plug.

"What?" Lauren said, starting to pull her legs up so that she could crawl up to where her pillow was. "That's okay. I'll get it."

"Lauren, that wasn't a suggestion." Connor didn't release his hold on the plug. She could still hear the tone that he used when in a scene and realized that this was still a part of it. "If you're worried about the cleanup, don't be. After everything we've done, you have nothing to be embarrassed about. It's my responsibility to see to your aftercare. You won't deprive me of that."

"Yes, Sir," Lauren whispered, immediately finding herself falling somewhat into that zone. She pushed out, and as he pulled felt the plug slip from her body. Instantly the warm cloth was drawn through her crevice. Since one leg was bent slightly, Connor was able to clean her thoroughly. She buried her face in the covers, unable to get over this type of discomfort. She wasn't quite sure what to say, so she resorted to the standard, "Thank you, Sir."

"You're most welcome, Red," Connor replied, although she could tell that he was smiling. "Trust me, you'll sleep better without the plug. However, there might be times I will order you to have it inside of you just so that I can claim your ass in the morning. There's nothing like a tight ass on my cock first thing at dawn."

Lauren moaned at the thought of his dick in her ass. The plug had felt as if it was going to split her in two. She couldn't imagine what his cock would feel like there. Connor gave a small tap of her ass, indicating she was free to scoot up on the mattress. She took advantage and crawled to where her pillow was situated. The coolness of the pillowcase felt wonderful against her cheek.

"I'll be right back," Connor said, his voice fading as he went back into the bathroom. She wasn't sure if she dozed or not, for the next moment he was back and wrapping his arms around her. "Feeling good?"

"Yes, Sir," Lauren murmured, keeping her eyes closed.

"I think it's safe to say we're making progress and having fun doing so, wouldn't you say?" Connor asked, his lips brushing against her neck.

Lauren heard something in his voice that she couldn't put a finger on, but sleep was pulling her under. His warmth only added to her comfort and she snuggled in closer to him. The only thought she had as she drifted to sleep was that he'd wrapped his fingers around her wrists and she hadn't panicked. She knew it was due to the fact that he'd strung her arousal to the point where nothing else mattered except that elusive orgasm he'd so willingly gave her. Regardless of how, it had been done.

Could he take it further by actually using wrist cuffs? Lauren wasn't so sure, but then again, she never would have imagined herself coming this far. The lifestyle, if this was a taste of it, had exceeded her wildest dreams. If this happened to be as far as he could take her, Lauren was satisfied.

Chapter Twenty-Three

Connor looked at the clock on the nightstand, seeing that it read four thirty-seven in the morning—Monday morning. He turned his head to see that Lauren was still sound asleep. Last night's flogging scene had been rather intense, although he'd yet to truly bind her wrists. She'd taken to the role of submissive like a queen bee to honey, although she still maintained her feisty attitude outside of the bedroom. Their second battle with the children had been fun. Unfortunately, the snow had been falling at too fast a rate to make a good snowman. They'd opted for a snowball fight. The weekend had passed by faster than he'd intended and a part of him didn't want it to end. The other couldn't wait until sunrise.

Knowing he wouldn't be able to get back to sleep, Connor removed himself from under the sheet and padded across the hardwood floor. Entering the bathroom, he closed the door before switching on the lights. He looked at his reflection and saw the same man who'd arrived here Friday afternoon. He didn't feel like it though. Something wasn't sitting right and he couldn't put a name on it…or refused to. It didn't matter either way.

His six o'clock shadow had turned into more than that and he ran a hand down his jawline. Connor figured he'd take a shower here and then stop by his place on the way to the office to make himself presentable. The last thing he needed was to have the team up in his grill about where he spent the snowstorm. At least the worst part had passed last night, allowing the transportation crew to do their job.

Turning, Connor reached into the shower and spun the handle. Waiting for the water to warm, his thoughts turned to how he was going to handle this morning. Did he want to just walk away now? Hell, no. That answer was easy to come by. He still had a vast amount to teach Lauren that he felt she should experience, but at what cost? She'd placed her trust in him and the more they traveled her journey together, the more intimate the scenes became. Could she still maintain a casual relationship?

Steam started to rise up into the air, indicating that he'd been standing outside the shower for way too long. Connor stepped inside the stall and closed the door. He leaned his hands up against the tile and hung his head, allowing the hot water to soak into his muscles. It had been a couple of months since he'd worked his wrist and shoulder with a flogger, and though the scene was light he could feel it. Those were definitely different muscles than most people used.

Connor heard the click of the bathroom door way before he felt the draft of air waft across the one-foot opening above the shower door. He smirked when he heard her discreetly use the toilet. His own question reverberated through his mind regarding Lauren having issues with this being casual. He'd see to it, because he wasn't ready to let this go. Not by a long shot.

He turned his head, ignoring that water now running down his cheek. There she was, her red curls taken out of the tie and now draped across her shoulders. It didn't quite reach her nipples, which were now pointing in his direction. He still couldn't get enough of her and his cock hardened. Looking up into Lauren's face, he saw that her emerald eyes were darkening as she took in the sight of him. Connor was glad to see that the feeling was mutual. Maybe this morning wouldn't be so bad after all.

"If you don't close that shower door in two seconds, your ass is going to feel the sting of my palm," Connor said, making sure his promise was stressed through his tone. It worked, for she quickly complied. He turned to face her. "On your knees."

Surprise flashed through Lauren's eyes and he knew he'd startled her with his request. Connor had pretty much kept every scene focused on her. As he said to himself earlier, this was her journey. He was just the teacher. Right now, the student needed to see to the instructor's needs.

Lauren slowly lowered herself and without hesitation reached for him. Connor didn't dissuade her, for the feel of her fingers felt exceedingly pleasing on his sac. The hot water had nothing on her mouth in terms of temperature. When her lips closed around his cock, Connor had to grab her hair for something to hold on to. Damn, she had perfect suction.

She took him back to her throat and then let her tongue glide back on the underside. Lauren's fingers fondled his testicles, causing them to rise with pleasure. When she drew him back into her mouth, her lips pressed into his tip, triggering his involuntary forward motion. Shit. He was going to blow his load before this even got started. Over and over, she fucked him with her mouth until his sac clinched his balls.

Connor tightened his fingers in her curls and looked down at the sight in front of him. She was fucking beautiful. To hell with it. He let out a shout and threw his head back when his cum shot out of his cock and down her throat. He felt her swallowing and her actions elicited more jizz. Feeling Lauren rest her cheek against his leg, Connor figured the office could wait for a couple more hours.

✧   ✧   ✧   ✧

"Well, look who it is," Jax said, stepping inside Connor's kitchen. "I was heading into the office when I saw your Jeep outside. You're lucky the plows came through before you got home. Glad to know you survived the weekend. Did Lauren?"

Connor had just finished shaving and changing into jeans and a black pullover shirt when he'd detoured to make himself some coffee. The Victorian house that they had converted into a duplex suited both of their needs. They each came and went from each other's residence, especially since Jax never bought any food.

"She's just fine, thank you," Connor said, not about to discuss his weekend with Lauren. He glanced at the clock above his stove and saw that they weren't expected in the office for another half hour. He opened the cabinet above the coffee machine and grabbed the filters. "It was nice to take a break from the case. It gave me a new perspective. I have some new thoughts regarding Joel, Gerry and this private party shit they've been having."

"Don't schedule anything this evening," Jax said, shrugging out of his jacket and slinging it over one of the kitchen chairs. "You need a session at the gym. I'll call and request a ring."

Connor was about to tell him to fuck off when he thought better of it. It probably was a good idea to let off some steam. These past few weeks, they'd been so caught up in the case that they hadn't had time to hit the gym together. Finally hitting the brew button, he turned around and leaned against the counter. It was the first time that he'd gotten a good look at Jax.

"You look like shit."

"I'll still be able to kick your ass," Jax replied, running a hand through his blonde hair. It was longer than he usually wore it and looked a mess. His eyes were bloodshot and he yawned, not bothering to cover his mouth. "Have you seen my skullcap?"

"On the front table," Connor replied with a smile. "I borrowed it."

"Fucker. Seriously, what's going on with Lauren? You're usually not so tight-lipped."

"It's a casual thing," Connor answered, knowing that Jax just wanted to make sure his head was screwed on straight. With the way his friend looked this morning, maybe it was Connor that needed to find out what was eating Jax. "I made sure of that going in. She wants a taste of the lifestyle, so I'm providing that. We're benefiting each other for now."

Jax studied him and Connor met his stare head-on. He had things under control. Lauren was satisfied and content when he'd left. She was well aware that he was working a case, so she wouldn't expect to hear from him for a few days. He'd call her mid-week; see if she wanted to get together. Next weekend would be shot, since he and Jax would be hitting the clubs.

"You usually don't play at home," Jax said, leaning back in his chair. "If you're playing with her, is she going to be able to keep things separate?"

"I said I have it covered," Connor replied. He pushed himself off of the counter and grabbed the to-go cups that he kept on hand. He turned back, catching Jax checking his cell phone. He was acting strange. "Something going on with you that I should be aware of?"

Jax didn't reply right away. Instead, he leaned forward and placed his elbows on his knees. Connor remained silent, knowing that his friend would talk when he was ready. He'd sensed a change in Jax before their last combat tour, but couldn't put his finger on it. That was a long time ago, but his mannerisms now matched how Jax was back then. He just seemed distant.

Both of their phones beeped at the same time, indicating a text. Connor dug his cell out of his pocket and looked at the screen. Crest was asking the team to meet him at Terry's residence. He'd been shot.

"Fuck."

The suburb of Maplewood was still digging out from the storm. Connor drove and Jax rode shotgun. They never did finish their conversation and he made a mental note to pick it up later today at the gym. Maneuvering around and sometimes going over the mounds of snow the plows had left behind, he pulled up to Terry's residence. Police cars were still parked out front, but no bystanders were out in this cold.

"This can't be good," Jax said, looking straight ahead and seeing Crest walk out the front door. Connor knew by the way he was walking that he wasn't happy. "Isn't that Detective Morrison?"

"Yep," Connor said. He pulled in behind one of the squad cars and shoved the gear into park. "Five bucks says Crest gave enough pressure to the higher ups that they're forcing Morrison to use us as consultants."

"You're on," Jax said, tugging his skullcap in place and then pulling on his gloves. He reached for the door handle.

"Morrison doesn't look that pissed, although for how far back his hair receded, I'd be fucking annoyed too."

They both got out of the Jeep and walked up the man-made path that the police must have created. Crest had already taken out his phone and held it to his ear. When he asked to speak with the governor, Connor thought Morrison would pull his piece. Seeing movement behind him, two detectives were walking out of Terry's front door. They stood on the front porch. It was the detective that had been in Lauren's store the first time he'd met her. What was his name again? Hagen—that was it.

Crest stepped back a few steps and had a brief conversation with whoever was on the phone. Connor had no doubt he'd get his way and held out his hand for his take of the pie. Jax shook his head.

"We're even. It technically hadn't happened before you made the bet."

"Technicalities? Really?" Connor shook his head in mock disgust. Morrison closed the remaining distance between them. He was able to shoot off one more question to Jax. "You realize that we're about to go full force with this investigation? No more undercover bullshit."

"Yeah," Jax said in a low voice, "which will be hell on my social life."

"Morrison," Connor said, taking his aviator sunglasses off. He squinted as the morning sun glared off of the snow, but still offered his hand.

"This isn't Crest's case or that of CSA's," Morrison said, his words clipped. "You're not even fucking law enforcement."

"That's a little harsh," Jax said, seemingly happier than he was this morning. He was back in his element of pissing people off. "Wasn't it Kevin who busted that drug dealer in your jurisdiction when one of your narcs was too busy powdering his nose?"

"Look, you son of a—"

"All case files are to be handed over," Crest said, cutting Morrison off. He slipped his phone inside of his dress coat. "Officially, as of now, we're hired consultants by the city to aid you in this investigation. You'll be getting a call from one of your superiors."

Morrison didn't immediately reply, but instead stood in front of them with his hands on his hips, staring at the ground. Connor appreciated his restraint. They gave him the time he needed not to have that aneurysm that was about ready to pop in his brain. Connor noticed Hagen staring in his direction and knew what was coming before the man even closed the distance and opened his mouth.

"You were that guy at Incandesce when I was interviewing Lauren Bailey," Hagen said, walking up to stand next to his supervisor.

"Was I?" Connor replied, feigning innocence.

"Hagen, head back to the office and have Cathy make copies of everything related to Sweeney's murder. See that it gets to CSA by the end of the day."

"You're with CSA?" Hagen asked, looking from Connor to Crest. "Have you been working this case all along?"

"Hagen, do as I say," Morrison commanded. He looked at Crest, not bothering to confirm that Hagen and his partner followed his order. "I want anything you find."

"And I want you to drop the arrest." Crest stood there, hands in his coat and not looking like it was only thirty-three degrees. The man was made of steel. "Terry Sweeney didn't murder his wife and you know it. Your detectives made an early arrest and fucked up. Even the prosecution is grasping at straws, figuring out how to get this to stick. You and I both know that Lou Moser will have this in front of a judge by noon today, getting the charges dropped. He'll claim his client is fighting for his life because you and your detectives were too lazy to do their job. If you hold a press conference beforehand, you and your department can save face."

Without a word, Morrison headed to his vehicle. The veins at his temples were bulging, but his silence meant that he knew Crest was right. The charges would be dropped within the hour. They remained silent as they watched him head to his unmarked vehicle parked in the road.

"That went better than expected," Jax said, looking past all of them to the house. "Self-inflicted or attempted murder?"

"He was shot point blank in the chest upon answering the door," Crest said, brushing past them to walk up the drive. "Neighbor to your left was in his garage, getting ready to shovel his driveway when he saw a black SUV pull up. Mr. Nichols thought it was odd, considering the man walked through the snow to gain access to the porch."

"Black SUV?" Connor asked, his thought directly zeroing in on the description. "Did he get a license plate number?"

"No," Crest replied. "And I already know what you're thinking. I don't believe in coincidences either. I've already put in some calls and I'll have someone on Lauren Bailey within the hour. They'll be discreet and she won't even know they are there."

Connor hammered down his immediate instinct to call Lauren and make sure she was all right, but knew he needed to focus on what was in front of him. Crest said he would have someone watch over her and he trusted that. Still, he didn't feel comfortable not being the one to watch her back. He rolled his shoulder, already tightening with tension.

"Within a minute, Nichols said he heard a shot," Crest said, continuing even though he had to know that what he said affected Connor's mental state. "He yelled out that he was calling the police when the man ran for his vehicle and drove off."

"Any description?" Jax asked, stepping onto the porch.

"None," Crest replied. "Said the suspect was too far away."

"Where do you want us to start?" Jax asked, looking behind them when an engine revved. Kevin had arrived.

"Kevin is going to take the house and search it from top to bottom. Obviously, Terry knew something that made the killer come after him. We need to know what it is. Maybe Morrison missed something the first time this house was a crime scene. I'm heading to the hospital," Crest said. Connor knew that he'd try to question Terry as soon as he came through surgery…provided he made it. "We're officially on the case, but I still want you two undercover. Make it known that since you two socialize within the community you have nothing to do with the case. Conflict of interest and all that bullshit."

"Do we have full control?" Jax asked.

"Yes. So I want everyone formally interviewed that you feel has a connection to Marilyn and Terry Sweeney. Kevin can initiate it. Get Ethan up to date, but remain in the background. I want alibies, starting with Joel Summit."

"Joel?" Connor asked, not surprised in the least, but wondering if Crest knew something that they didn't.

"Taryn pulled up Terry's last call," Crest said, waving for Kevin to get his ass up to the house. "Eleven thirty-nine last night, Terry called Joel Summit. I want to know why."

✧   ✧   ✧   ✧

Things weren't going as planned. He paced back and forth in the random parking lot, ignoring the cold. It didn't faze him. Nothing did. He took a drag on his cigarette and held it in his lungs. Fuck. He'd been impulsive and made a mistake this morning. It wouldn't happen again.

The nicotine rushed through his blood, calming him like it usually did. He needed something stronger, but that would be his reward for taking care of what needed to be done. It was time to clean up his mess. Loose ends had to be clipped and he knew just who to start with.

Chapter Twenty-Four

"Our weekend together does not constitute you telling me what to do in my business life," Lauren said, making her anger known. "I get a lot of specialized orders when I attend Masters' social hour. I missed the previous month, and I don't intend to miss tonight."

"I'm not telling you what to do with your company, Red," Connor said, his voice practically vibrating her phone. "This is about your safety, which damn well is my business. And you're the one who said you could probably make a decent living just doing online orders. What is so hard about taking my advice?"

Lauren had come home early to have a bite to eat and change before heading to Masters. Social hour began at six o'clock and she wanted to arrive a half hour early to set up. This week had passed by agonizingly slow. She'd only heard from Connor once and that was mid-week. Apparently, the case had heated up with Terry's shooting…or else he was using that as an excuse. The thought stung. She wasn't sure how he felt about their weekend, but right now didn't have the time to focus on it. She needed to leave.

"Because it's not advice if you're ordering me to do something. Connor, I have to go. I'm late as it is." Lauren walked to the side table by the door and fished her keys out of her purse. "Casual, remember? My safety is my concern and everything has been fine. No SUV sighting, no break-ins, and no attempted muggings. Go work your case and call me when it's over."

Lauren disconnected the call, ignoring the fact that her fingers were trembling. She wasn't going to deny that it stung when she didn't hear from him until Wednesday night. Some sort of depression had settled over her after he left on Monday morning and she wasn't sure what it was.

By the time he'd called, Lauren pretty much had it figured out on her own. The trust that she'd placed in him to conduct those scenes had shifted something inside of her. Connor made her realize that she could have a man in the lifestyle, regardless of her fear of bondage. She was pretty damn sure he didn't want to hear that though. He was dead set on keeping this casual. The question was, was she?

Her phone rang again, but she ignored it. Grabbing her jacket and slinging her purse over her shoulder, she headed out the door. Using the key, she ensured the deadbolt clicked into place. Lauren thought that she was free and clear when she heard the chain on Ms. Finch's door slide against the metal. Damn it.

"I thought that was you," Ms. Finch said after having opened the door. "Are you heading out with your nice young man?"

"No, Ms. Finch," Lauren answered, pasting a smile on her face. "I have a showing for my jewelry."

Her neighbor had no idea that the gems she used were for kink related items and Lauren thought it best to keep that under wraps. Ms. Finch just assumed that the stones she worked with were for necklaces, bracelets, and earrings. It was best not to give the woman a heart attack before her time.

"You be careful, dear," Ms. Finch said, looking up and down the hallway. "I keep thinking someone is roaming the hallways, but every time I look out my peephole, no one is there."

"Maybe it's Ms. Trimino sneaking her cat in and out." Lauren chuckled when Ms. Finch's face lit up at the thought. "Now you be nice. If it wasn't for Ms. Trimino, that cat wouldn't have a place to live."

"But it's against the bylaws," Ms. Finch said, her eyes twinkling. "Maybe if I can prove she's harboring an animal, she'll tell me the recipe for her peach cobbler."

"It's not nice to blackmail, either." Lauren started to walk down the hallway. "Behave while I'm gone."

She made it to the elevator and looked back. Ms. Finch had gone back into her apartment and the corridor was empty. She hit the down button, ignoring the vibration of her phone. Connor could call and text all he wanted, but it wouldn't change the fact that she was going to the social hour.

"Damn it," Connor said, tossing his cell phone on his desk.

"You should know better than to get involved with redheads," Jax said, putting his feet up on Connor's desk. He'd snagged the chair while Connor had gotten coffee earlier and had yet to leave.

"Are you shitting me?" Connor asked, tossing Jax an irritated look. "You're the one who pushed the damn issue. Don't you have work to do?"

"Yes, he does," Crest answered. Connor turned to see that he was motioning everyone to the table that was situated between the cubicles. Ethan was out, Kevin was on the phone, and Taryn was walking down the hallway with Jessie. Jax dropped his legs and rolled Connor's chair closer. Once everyone was in place, Crest leaned his hands on the surface. "Updates."

"Ethan has officially interviewed every member of Masters and Whip," Connor said, filling in for his teammate. "He also was able to reach Greg Winters by phone. There are five people at Masters who have no alibi and seven people from Whip. As we all know, Joel said that Terry had left him a message to call him back. Terry was shot before Joel could and states he has no idea why."

"Do you believe him? Does Kevin?" Crest asked, looking between Connor and Jax.

"At this point, we don't know," Connor answered. "If it weren't for his relationship with Gerry and these play parties they throw, I'd say yes. But until Jax can get in there…"

"SITREP is on your desk," Jessie said, leaning up against the back of Taryn's cubicle. "Ethan also just informed me that he's following up on an interview that marked Nick Klaus as a Dom who is well experienced in the art of shibari. He apparently moved here around four months ago."

"You two know him?" Crest asked, directing his question toward Connor and Jax.

"Never met him and never heard of him," Connor replied, looking at Jax who was shaking his head. "Did Ethan say which club he was a member of?"

"He's not," Jessie answered. There was a subtle confidence in her stance that had never been there before. Connor looked sideways at Crest, watching as his superior stood straight and crossed his arms. Apparently Crest sensed it too. "He's a regular at Gerry's private play parties."

No one said anything, as Jessie's casual use of Gerry Mason's first name rang a little too personal. She didn't even blink. Neither did Crest. The tension mounted until Kevin hung up and joined the meeting.

"So, what'd I miss?"

"Fill you in later, buddy," Connor murmured, slapping him on the back. "Taryn, did you confirm that we received everything from Detective Hagen?"

"Yes, everything is in order. From my contact at the lab, the DNA results should be in soon as well." Taryn pushed her black-rimmed glasses up on her nose and shot Crest a wry smile. "Apparently Crest has some pull there, too."

"How's Terry doing?" Kevin asked, crossing his arms. He was larger than Connor and Jax, having been a country boy before joining the Marines. His shoulders were broad from working the land and he'd kept it that way, his muscular frame having come in handy in the service. "Has he awakened?"

"No," Crest said, shaking his head. It was easy to see that the man was exhausted. "His father has pretty much camped out in the hospital room and I've been spending as much time as I can with him."

Kevin had found nothing in the house that gave them any information on who might have been responsible for shooting Terry or murdering Marilyn. Taryn had both of their phone records…legally…and there was nothing out of the ordinary before or after Marilyn's death. She had been given access to their computer but had come up with nil. They were still coming up empty.

The only solid leads they had were the private parties being hosted by Joel and Gerry and the fact that someone thought Lauren knew something. The second lead couldn't be proven.

"Connor and Jax, look over the list of members that have no alibi. Make sure you have contact with them this weekend. Taryn, I want a background check on Nick Klaus first thing Monday morning. Kevin, keep scouring Marilyn and Terry's personal life. Something has to be there. Jessie, I want to see you in my office."

Connor winced, feeling compassion for the girl. He was starting to get the feeling that Crest had been keeping his distance due to her age, but if Jessie was dabbling in the lifestyle...

"Crest, are we going to meet this new guy you hired?" Jax asked before everyone disbanded. "You said he's been keeping an eye on Lauren Bailey."

"You'll meet him soon enough," Crest said, turning and walking away.

Crest didn't stop to see if Jessie was following behind. Connor saw her roll her eyes and the action reminded him of Lauren, who was hankering for a spanking if she didn't answer his next call. All he'd asked of her was to cancel her vending table tonight at social hour. She was well aware of his ongoing case and it was a double-edged sword. One, she could let something slip that he was working undercover and blow things wide open. He and Jax wouldn't get anyone to talk then. Two, it was for her own safety.

"Have you swung by to check on her?" Jax asked, using his boots to roll himself back. "We had some late nights at the club this week."

Connor didn't answer right away. Yes, he'd gone to the club Tuesday and Thursday night. He'd even forced himself to do a light caning scene with a submissive that was a bit of a masochist, although it didn't extend beyond that. He didn't want to examine why he felt guilt over that. He was undercover, to an extent, and the members would have thought it odd had he not played. There were only so many times a Dom could go and not scene without it looking as if something was amiss. The scene he'd done hadn't even been in a sexual context, yet all he kept thinking about was Lauren.

"A couple times," Connor admitted, reaching for his jacket. He tugged and then yanked it out from underneath Jax's back. "Whoever the guy is that Crest hired, he's good. I didn't detect his presence at all."

"Either that, or he's slacking and not watching her the way he should be," Jax said, standing and walking around the side of the cubicle. Connor looked after him in disbelief. Like that's what he needed to hear. Jax returned, his coat in hand. "I take it we're heading to social hour?"

"You're an ass."

Chapter Twenty-Five

M asters' social hour turned out to be successful. Lauren glanced at her watch and saw that there was still a half hour left. The majority of the people who had stopped by were guests, checking out the club. A married couple had purchased a pair of nipple clamps that she'd outfitted with sapphires and a submissive had bought herself a corset that Lauren had adorned with amethysts. Nipple clamps were the highest seller this evening and she knew she'd have to restock within the next week or so. There were a few members milling about, wanting to see the newbies that might join, but they were well aware of her items and rarely stopped by her table.

She had set up near the entrance after the foyer, giving the newbies room to maneuver around the room and look at the equipment. The St. Andrew's cross never failed to draw her attention and it reminded her of the position Connor had her take on the bed for the flogging scene. It had been light and she appreciated that, even coming to love the sensation of having the tendrils of leather falling on her skin.

"You don't listen, do you?" Connor asked, startling her. She turned quickly to see that he was walking toward her, although his voice was low. It was obvious he didn't want to be overheard. He was clean-shaven and she was able to catch a subtle scent of his cologne as he came to a stop in front of her table. "I told you it would be safer for you to stay at home until this case was over."

"And I told you that nothing has happened to indicate I'm in danger," Lauren replied, keeping her voice just as soft. "Unless you're aware of something I'm not, I still have a life. I'm fine, really. I have a half hour and then I'm packing up and heading home."

Lauren looked around, but no one was paying attention to them except the man who had been three steps behind. He was now standing side by side with Connor. The handsome blonde flashed her a smile and it was impossible not to smile back. It was infectious.

"You must be Jax," Lauren said. "You know, breaking into my apartment wasn't such a bright idea."

"Turned out rather well, if you ask me," Jax replied, giving her a wink. She couldn't help but laugh and hoped no one noticed. Connor looked even more aggravated. "Nice to meet you, Lauren Bailey. I'll give you two a minute."

"He's nice," Lauren said, watching him walk away. Jax didn't go unnoticed, as a couple of newbies watched him walk towards the bar. She had no doubt that Joel would have two new members before the night was through. "If you stay at my table too long, Joel or one of the regulars might think it's odd. You've never shown up for social hour before."

"Exceptions can be made," Connor said, his irritation evident. He picked up a collar and feigned interest. "I can't go into it now, but new information has come to light that indicates your *coincidental* SUV might not be so accidental."

She had expected to see frustration in his eyes, but when Connor looked up at her, she thought she saw fear. Lauren felt her heart melt and almost reached out to touch him. She wanted the closeness they had last weekend. Carefully scanning the room and seeing that no one was looking their way, she leaned closer.

"Like I said, I'm done in a half hour. Why don't you meet me back at my place and you can catch me up on things." Lauren saw a brunette head their way and knew she'd better finish talking. "I know you can't talk about the case, but if something involves me, then I should know."

"Lauren, I can't—"

"If it isn't Master Connor," the brunette said, laying her hand on his arm. "I heard you had fun with Brie on Tuesday night. Are you sticking around? I'd love it if I could scene with you tonight."

Lauren tried to swallow, but her throat wasn't working. Connor had been at the club, playing? She didn't know why that created such a sharp pain in her chest, but right now it was a struggle to breathe. Looking down, she saw her invoice pad and picked it up, giving herself something to do. Lauren hoped like hell he didn't see the trembling in her fingers.

"We'll see," Connor said, his voice a little tight. Lauren wondered if the brunette caught the tension. Seeing as her hand was still on his arm, Lauren doubted it. "Jax and I were thinking of heading over to Whip. We just stopped by to see what kind of action might be taking place tonight. If I'm around later, I'll look for you, Casey."

"I heard that Gerry was doing some sort of fire play scene," Casey said, finally letting her hand fall. Lauren figured nothing would seem out of the ordinary if she were to start boxing up some of the duplicate items. She needed to leave before she embarrassed herself. Connor didn't need to witness her struggling with ground rules they'd already set in cement. "I'm not much for that kind of play, but you know that."

"Connor, a little heads up that your co-worker was going to interrogate me would have been appreciated," Joel said, walking up to them. Lauren gritted her teeth, just wanting to leave. "I just reamed Jax a new asshole. What happened to loyalty, man?"

The last thing Lauren wanted to do was stand here and listen to them talk. Casey was still standing close to Connor and Lauren refused to even look his way. She'd agreed to a casual relationship. It wasn't his fault that she wasn't cut out for it. No wonder she left the YOLO attitude up to Sue. She sure as hell wasn't cut out for it. Lauren felt a little sick to her stomach, but continued to toss random items into the boxes. She'd sort them out later.

"Hey, you know how it goes. I heard CSA was hired by the Maplewood Police Department, but since Jax and I are part of the community, Crest gave orders that we're not to be involved."

"I get it," Joel said, nodding his understanding. "He wants someone impartial. But you know that no one here is capable of murder. Can't you and Jax tell him that?"

"We're staying out of it, Joel," Connor said, setting down the collar on the table. "We have our orders. Whoever has the case will figure that out on their own. You have nothing to worry about."

"Lauren, did you get a call from one of the CSA investiga-tors?" Joel asked, dragging her into the conversation. "I heard they've pretty much questioned anyone who had contact with Marilyn Sweeney."

Lauren pasted a smile onto her face, hoping it didn't across as too fake. She'd been placing more items in one of the smaller boxes, hoping to stay out of the conversation, but it wasn't meant to be. A lot of things weren't. She turned her attention on Joel. He was wearing his usual leather outfit, reminding her more of someone out of the sixties. He had the hairstyle to go with it, along with an oval face and longer nose.

"Yes," Lauren replied, technically not lying. Connor had asked her questions, but she knew that wasn't truly what Joel meant. Apparently there had been quite a lot of happenings this week that she'd not been privy to. "Just your standard questions. Social hour seems to be thinning out, Joel. I think I'll pack up and head on out."

"I know I always ask you the same thing, but if you'd like to become a member and stay for play hours, all you have to do is say the word," Joel said.

"Kyle couldn't handle me," Lauren automatically replied, giving her standard answer and eliciting a laugh from Joel. Connor remained conspicuously silent. "I appreciate the offer, but you know that I don't play. It was a nice turnout this evening, Joel."

"Good to hear. I'll be in touch and we'll set something up for next month."

Joel's name was being called, so he excused himself. Lauren went back to packing her items, quicker now than before since she'd said she was leaving early. She paid little attention to Connor and Casey, who were still standing there. She heard him say something to the brunette, but couldn't quite make out what it was. Reaching back on the table for the larger items, she was startled when Connor's warm hand wrapped around her wrist.

"I have to work tonight," Connor murmured, blocking their connection with his body. "I'll stop by—"

"Connor," Lauren said, looking him directly in the eye. She needed to get her point across, regardless of the knot in her chest. "I get it. You have nothing to worry about. We're not exclusive and you're free to play with whomever you want. I'm not going to cause some dramatic scene and blow your cover."

"I didn't touch Brie in a sexual way," Connor stated, his jaw tightening. "If I hadn't done something, Joel and the other members would have automatically known something was wrong."

"You're the one who said there are different types of submissives," Lauren murmured, trying to remain hidden behind his body while keeping her composure. "I guess I'm not one who shares."

"Everything good here?" Jax asked, interrupting the moment.

Lauren pulled her wrist back, immediately wrapping her own hand around it. The deceptive feeling of pressure that she'd always felt had returned. Had it ever really gone away? She didn't miss Connor glancing down at her movement.

"No."

"Yes." Lauren ignored Connor's negative answer and turned her attention on Jax. "I just need to finish packing up. It was very nice to meet you."

"You, too," Jax replied, looking toward Connor for some cue. He could look all he wanted. She was done for this evening. She needed to go home and have a glass of wine. The bottle was sounding pretty good though. "Does Joel have someone help you to your van?"

Lauren almost asked how Jax knew she drove a van instead of a car, but then thought better of it. Of course he knew. She would have wondered what else he was privy too, but realized that Connor wasn't that type of man. Regardless of what she was feeling right now, he was an honorable man. That almost made it worse.

"I have a dolly, so I'm fine." Lauren glanced over his shoulder to see Joel looking their way. She lowered her voice. "We're starting to attract attention."

"Since we never come to social hour, they'll think we're just browsing your table," Connor said, his voice tight. "We need to talk."

"Right now, you have two submissives headed your way," Lauren said, tilting her head to the women behind him. "Enjoy your evening."

She'd sounded like a total bitch. Lauren loaded up the dolly and closed the back of her van. Making sure it was locked, she started around the driver's side but came to a halt when she saw two men arguing on the other side of the parking garage. One of them was Joel and she stifled a gasp when the other man shoved him in the chest.

Not wanting the two men to think she was spying on them, Lauren took a step back behind the van. She crossed her arms, her white sweater not enough to ward off the cold. When she'd started loading the boxes, she'd thrown her coat into the front seat. Connor's ire over her penchant for doing so sprang to mind, but raised voices brought her back to the present.

"I won't go down for this," Joel said, his voice rising and carrying through the evening air.

Lauren couldn't distinguish what the other man said, but she could have sworn he mentioned Connor and Jax's names. She edged closer to the side of the van, her heart beating fast. Were these two responsible for Marilyn's murder? Is that what they were fighting about?

"…can't back out now," the man said. "…make sure…aren't…next weekend."

Lauren heard footsteps headed her way. She pulled back, flattening herself against the back door of the van. She squeezed her eyes tight, hoping like hell they didn't see her.

"They're headed over to Whip tonight," Joel said, his voice near the front of her van. "Take care of it or I'm backing out."

Lauren heard the metal door to the exit open and then slam as it closed. She held her breath, not hearing the other man. Where had he gone? Silence seemed to descend over the parking garage. She slowly exhaled, hearing nothing but her breath along with the blood rushing in her ears. Should she chance looking around the side of the van?

A car door slammed, causing Lauren to jump. An ignition turned over and she heard the engine rev. Within seconds, the vehicle pulled out and the sound faded as it drove down the ramp. She waited, wanting to make sure that the coast was clear before getting inside the van. Counting to one hundred, Lauren finally peeked around the side and saw nothing. No one was there.

Quickly, she jumped inside of the van and locked her doors. Lauren reached over to the passenger seat and moved her coat, looking for her purse. Finding it, she fished out her cell phone out and then stared at it, wondering what she should do. The last thing she wanted was to talk to Connor when her emotions were in such a turmoil, but knew she had no other choice. She threw her head back onto the headrest. So much for her self-pity party.

Chapter Twenty-Six

"Who is that?" Lauren whispered, turning to face Connor. She peeked over his shoulder at the large man dressed in black, leaning against the wall near her front door. "He's huge."

"Crest hired him. I just met the man myself. He goes by Lach. Red, I need you to listen to me," Connor said, catching her attention. She'd wanted this to remain professional, but having him back in her apartment made it anything but. He hadn't left her side since she called him from the parking garage. "When Terry Sweeney was shot, his neighbor saw the person who carried it out. He was driving a black SUV."

Lauren felt her breath catch in her throat. She searched his gaze, knowing there was more to the story. She looked back over his shoulder and finally figured it out.

"Lach's been following me?"

"Keeping an eye on you," Connor said, as if that made a difference. To her, it was the same thing. "Crest ordered it after Monday morning. After the shooting, we officially got the case. I wasn't lying to you that I've had a hell of a week."

"I didn't say you were," Lauren replied, not liking where he was leading this. "There's no reason to bring up our personal relationship right now. Crest looks like he's finishing up his phone call and Lach looks like he's getting antsy."

"This is real, Red. I can't give you a reason why the killer may have targeted you to begin with, other than he thinks you know something. I also can't give you a reason as to why he's left you alone, after having followed you in the beginning."

"I don't need reasons," Lauren said, brushing past him. "I just need a little sanity back in my life."

❖   ❖   ❖   ❖

Lauren's last comment made Connor want break something. Damn it, but she was a stubborn woman. There was no mistaking the pain in her eyes when Casey had come over and mentioned his scene with Brie. He'd never intended to hurt her like that. Connor could tell himself that he'd been working undercover, but the bottom line was he'd wanted to prove that Lauren didn't have any kind of hold over him.

Connor looked at Lach, not sure what he thought of the new team member. He didn't talk much, but that wasn't a prerequisite. Within seconds of Lauren's call, which he'd managed to get as he and Jax had left through the main entrance to walk over to Whip, Connor had received one from an unknown number. It was Lach, telling him what had transpired in the parking garage and that he would wait until Connor arrived. Apparently Lach knew quite a bit about their relationship. He had no doubt Lach had gained that information from Crest, along with the rest of the case details.

"Connor," Crest said. Lauren was already in the living room, standing next to him. "Jax is entering Whip now and will take over this evening. What are you thoughts?"

"Lach positively identified the man as Gerry Mason. Jax knows this and will work that angle. The two men have always had a love/hate relationship. Something prompted them to have these private parties, but it's obvious from the conversation Lauren overheard that there's tension." Connor kept his eyes on Lauren, wanting to stay with her but knowing he should go back out into the field. "According to Lach, neither man saw Lauren. She should be safe, although I still feel she needs protection."

"Agreed," Crest said, before turning to Lauren. "I won't apologize for having put a protection detail on you, Ms. Bailey. Whether or not the SUV you saw is the same one that Terry's neighbor witnessed at the time of his shooting, I don't know. I don't want to take a chance that you could be hurt."

"I understand," Lauren said, her focus on Crest. Connor had to wonder if she really did comprehend the danger she was in. "I would appreciate to be kept up to date though, when it comes to me. I still have no idea what, if anything, this person feels I know. But if you feel that Mr. Lach needs to keep an eye on things, that's fine."

"You are to carry on as if you know nothing of what you saw this evening," Crest ordered, picking up his dress coat that he'd placed on the couch. "I have an appointment that I cannot miss, so if you'll excuse me, I'll leave you in capable hands. Connor, could I have a word with you before I go?"

"Yes," Connor replied, walking toward the door where Lach was still waiting. Crest came up to both of them, his cell phone back in hand.

"Lach, take your position back up and call if you think anything is amiss. I'm heading back to the hospital. Mr. Sweeney called and said there's been a change in Terry's condition. It was a message, so I'm not certain if it's good or bad. Connor, get ahold of Kevin and give him the run down on the events that just took place. Maybe it's time for Kevin to lay the pressure on Joel and Gerry. If there is tension between them, maybe we can get one of them to crack."

"Already done," Connor replied, crossing his arms. "I also gave Jax a heads up that Kevin might stop into Whip tonight. With his presence in front of the members, Gerry will immediately take him into the back office, but the damage will be done. The guests will see that the clubs are being scrutinized."

"We can only hope someone panics and makes a mistake," Crest said, looking down at his phone when another text came through. "I need to go. I want SITREPs on my desk by morning."

With that last order, Crest left. Connor looked back at Lauren who was now in the kitchen. She was pretending to clean the counters, but he could tell from her body language she was eavesdropping. Would she still be willing to listen after Lach left?

"I appreciate that you've kept such a close eye on Lauren," Connor said, turning back to face the large man.

Lauren had been right. He was big and stood at least a good four inches taller than Connor. He had dark brown hair that was cropped close and there wasn't a strand out of place. The way he carried his shoulders, it was easy to tell that Lach was military.

"It's an assignment, like any other," Lach replied, his voice deep. "I'll take up my post and let you know if I see anything out of the ordinary. It's obvious that you're personally involved with her."

Since his tone hadn't changed, Connor wasn't sure if he'd just thrown a dig his way or not. He didn't give a shit what

Lach thought. Regardless of his relationship with Lauren, he would do his fucking job.

"I appreciate that," Connor said, keeping things short. "Welcome to the team."

Lach didn't reply, but did nod in acknowledgement. Turning, he followed Crest's trail and left. Connor made sure the deadbolt was turned before facing Lauren. She was leaning against the counter near the sink, her arms crossed and staring at him like she was ready to do battle.

"My orders are to blend in at the clubs and garner as much information as I can," Connor said, staying where he was. "Jax and I are part of that community and at the end of this case, we will apologize to anyone we offended by doing our duty. You and I…"

"You and I what?" Lauren asked. "I told you at the club, you have nothing to apologize to me for. We agreed this wasn't serious. You can play with whomever you want to. Just as long as you know that I can do the same."

Connor fisted his hands and took a step forward. An image of her with another man caused anger to swell in his chest. Were all redheads this goddamned stubborn?

"Lauren, if I hadn't started to play, everyone that I socialized with would think something was wrong and immediately feel I was only there to investigate them. The scene was not sexual in nature. You seeing another man, let alone a Dom, is off the table. This is the only case that has ever crossed into my personal territory and—"

"Wait a second," Lauren exclaimed, straightening and taking a few steps toward him. "You're going to stand there and tell me that you played with a submissive because it was your *duty*? Just because you introduced me to a different aspect of the lifestyle doesn't mean I have "naïve" written across my forehead. You played with her because you wanted to play with her. That's fine. But man-up about it, Connor."

Damn if her anger wasn't stirring his cock. Did she just question his manhood? Connor took another step and then stopped, knowing she wouldn't want his touch right now. How could he explain to her that the scene hadn't generated his interest in any way? Did he even want to?

"I knew what I was getting into. We both agreed to the terms," Lauren exclaimed, coming closer and pointing a finger at him. "This is not exclusive, Connor, and I have every right to either have a simple dinner with Rick across the hallway or have a scene with Kyle at the club if I so choose."

"We said casual meaning nothing serious," Connor said, wanting to correct her. He knew his voice was rising, but damn it, she was frustrating him. "That doesn't mean we are seeing other people while we fuck each other."

"So because you didn't put your cock in her pussy, that gives you a pass to flog her ass?" Lauren was now one step away from him. "If you want this *casual* relationship to continue, I don't give a rat's ass what your duty is. You can take *me* to the club until we decide we're over."

"It was a cane, not a flogger." Connor saw her eyes flare and knew that wasn't the right thing to say at the moment. "And you're nowhere near ready for that."

"Try me."

Connor shook his head, not even sure of what to say to that. It wasn't that he didn't have the words; it was just that she'd managed to short-circuit every fucking nerve in his body. He'd gone all week, making sure to keep his distance. Conduct-ing scenes and initiating the aftercare could induce intense feelings that could be misconstrued as something more serious than what they were. He'd been giving Lauren time, knowing she was intelligent enough to understand that this was nothing more than sex. Yet, here she was, standing before him saying...he didn't know what the hell she was saying.

"I'm on a case, Red," Connor murmured, trying to keep himself from reaching out to her. His anger and arousal were mixing. Right now, all he wanted to do was fuck her. "Even if I did agree to that, which Crest would never go for, you couldn't handle the club scene."

"You said it yourself," Lauren said in a low voice, as if she too were trying to control her emotions. "This case has crossed over into your personal life. What better way to blend in then by taking me to the club? You and I both know that people saw us talking tonight. Having me show up with you tomorrow night would give them something else to talk about, instead of speculating if you're really there on business or pleasure. And if the killer were after me at some point, maybe it would scare him to think I told you whatever it is he's scared of me knowing. And for your information, I can handle a club scene just fine."

"The only thing I can think of is that you're running on adrenaline from what happened this evening," Connor said, needing her to see what a dumbass idea this was. "You can't even have your wrists bound. What the hell would happen if I cuffed you to the spanking bench or the St. Andrew's cross, huh? You'd panic and then I'd be dealing with you instead of doing my job."

"If you had bothered to come back at some point throughout the week, maybe you would have realized that this weekend gave me a taste of what I really want." Lauren closed the distance between them and tilted her head up, her green eyes now emerald in color that dared him to take her in hand. Connor's cock had never been so hard. "Master."

Chapter Twenty-Seven

Lauren had lost her mind. There was no explanation for why she was taunting Connor into dominating her when she should be showing him the door. What right did he have to think he could play, even in the line of duty, and expect her to be okay with that? Something had come over her, some type of confidence she hadn't been aware she had, but she would give him a choice. Either he stayed and saw firsthand that she could do a scene at the club or he could walk away. Connor didn't need to know that she'd be crushed if he chose that latter.

"Damn you," Connor uttered, doing what she'd been hoping for. He brought his hands up to frame her face and claimed her lips. Only this wasn't like the other time and Lauren realized she'd unleashed something inside of him. There was nothing left of her that was hidden by the time he was done. "Undress."

Connor tore away from her, leaving her standing a few feet from the kitchen. He strode past the living room and opened the door to her spare bedroom. Lauren's heart palpitated, knowing that he could only be going in there for one thing.

Restraints. She'd provoked him, but was she truly ready for this?

Lauren quickly removed her clothes and waited for him to return. Her nipples were hard, but she knew it wasn't from the air as it brushed against the sensitive tissue. Her body had been responding to him since he'd walked up to her at the club. She caught sight of movement and saw Connor walking back through her apartment. What she saw in his hands had a tremor course up her spine.

He didn't stop until he was right in front of her, and even then slowly continued to walk forward. Lauren had no choice but to back up. Within five steps, her ass hit the kitchen table. She searched his eyes for reassurance and all she saw was blue fire.

"Give me your wrists, Red," Connor murmured, his dominant tone making her realize that this was it. She'd pushed and pushed until she got what she wanted. But could she handle it? "Now."

With her heart ready to beat out of her chest, Lauren slowly raised her fists in front of her. She was glad her fingers were curled into her palms, for this way he wouldn't see them trembling. Despite the intensity coming from his body, Connor gently took ahold of one wrist and wrapped one of her generic white cuffs around her skin. A light perspiration broke out over her flesh and the weight instigated immediate anxiety.

"Look at me," Connor ordered. She hadn't realized she'd been watching his hands lock the cuff into place. Dragging her eyes away, she met his gaze. "Breathe."

She saw him wait for her to do as he commanded, but it took a moment. Memories of her time in the well resurfaced, as well as when Phil had tied her hands to the bed. Lauren exhaled but had trouble dragging in air. It felt as if her lungs had been encased in cement. She might have pushed for this too soon. What the hell had she been thinking?

"Did you not hear me, Lauren?"

"Y-yes," Lauren replied, using the last of her oxygen.

"Yes what? It would seem like last weekend never happened." A spark of anger ignited and Lauren felt her lungs expand. Did he not realize how hard this was for her? Connor leaned in close, until they were eye level. "I asked you what my title was."

"Master," Lauren said, a bite to her tone.

His face was so close that she hadn't seen his right hand come up to her breast until she felt his fingers enclose around her nipple. He pinched slightly, causing her to gasp. When Connor started to roll the hardened pebble, she let out her air with a moan.

"Good girl," Connor murmured, straightening. "Other wrist."

Lauren's arm involuntarily rose, offering him her other wrist. What the hell had just happened? He'd gotten her so caught up in his spell that her anxiety had diminished. As the other cuff was placed around her wrist, her apprehension returned in full force.

"Do you see this?" Connor asked, and pulled something from behind him that must have been in his back pocket.

"What...wait," Lauren said, reaching for the paddle. A little bit of reality returned. "Put it back. This is for a client. He wanted diamonds put in around the edges for an extra bite."

"What a good idea. I might have you do that later, but whoever the client is will have to wait for another one to be ordered. This paddle will be used this evening. It seems to me that you're forgetting your place."

Lauren instantly knew what he was referring to. She'd not used his title and technically had mentally exited the scene, but couldn't he see she was dealing with a lot right now? Looking down at her wrists, she caught a glimpse of something hanging from her left one. It was a locking mechanism to latch them together. Her vision tunneled.

"Turn around and face the table."

Lauren's body acted on its own accord, but she didn't lower her hands. Instead, she kept them in front of her almost as a barrier. Only when her back was toward Connor did he close the distance until she felt his body against hers. He slowly laid the paddle on the table.

"I want you to lower your hands."

Lauren shook her head, drawing her forearms tighter against her chest. She'd been wrong. She couldn't do this. The cuffs felt like they were burning her skin. She gasped when she felt his right arm curl around her. His fingers sought her clit and she released another moan when they made contact with the sensitive nub. In a circular motion, he massaged the engorged flesh, causing her arms to lower as she gripped his hand against the pleasure he was creating. It was in too direct contrast to the panic that was setting in.

"Good girl." Connor had touched her clit on purpose, knowing the pleasure he was providing her, yet Lauren's grip didn't stop his administrations. He was making her feel so damn good that it was pushing away some of her fear. "Now place your wrists together at your lower back."

Lauren whimpered, feeling her previous confidence slip. Yet there was something inside of her that knew Connor would catch it and not leave her hanging. He would see her through this. She just had to do what he said. As his fingers drove her further and further toward an orgasm, she moved her hips with his motion.

"That's right," Connor murmured against her neck. "Such a good submissive."

As he brought her right to that brink, Lauren felt something snap into place. Her wrists were bound together at her lower back. Her pussy was starting to produce ripples and when he pulled away, Lauren cried out. Emotions and sensations mixed together, but there wasn't one that was winning out over the other. It was as if she were hovering, not knowing which direction to go. He made that decision for her.

"There is something you need to be aware of, Red," Connor said as he pulled away and placed a hand in the middle of her back. Pushing her down, Lauren found herself flattened against the table. Using his foot, he nudged her ankles until they were far apart, giving him full access to her pussy and ass. "I control these scenes, not you. The next time you want a scene, you'll ask me politely. What you just did is called topping from the bottom and I will not tolerate it. Do you understand?"

"Yes, Sir," Lauren whispered, her cheek now resting on the cold surface. It was as if he had laid her nipples on a sheet of ice. She wished it would cool the fire raging inside of her as she felt his finger slide down her crevice. Her anus puckered, which initiated an entire new wave of tremors. Her chest still felt tight, but hearing him talk kept her anxiety under control. "I understand."

"Good." Connor reached for the paddle, which was in her line of sight on the table. The heat that the cuffs had introduced to her wrists initiated all over again. All she felt was the restriction and her breathing became shallow. Lauren tugged, not able to move them. She was just about to rear back up when Connor placed his left hand on her back, trapping the cold metal of the closure between the cuffs against the small of her back. "Keep your eyes open. If I see you close them, you'll find out what orgasm denial truly is."

Lauren's pussy throbbed around nothing but air, as if disputing his promise. The warmth of his hand started to heat the ever present closure making contact with her back, but instead of adding to the burning fervor the cuffs made against her wrists, it soothed her inferno. Air started to flow back into her lungs at a relatively slow pace instead of the insubstantial drags from earlier. Her muscles relieved their tension.

Swat!

"Hmmm." Lauren rubbed her cheek against the wood.

Swat!

Amazingly, the sensations the paddle produced only ratcheted up her arousal. Lauren kept her eyes open, just as he'd ordered and found that it kept her apprehension at bay. It was still there, yet simmering under the surface.

Swat!

"Stop thinking about your fear."

"But—"

Swat!

It was as if every time her phobia crossed her mind, Connor knew and used the paddle. Was he really that observant?

Swat! Swat! Swat!

"More," Lauren pleaded, needing more of the heat and less of the mental scrutiny.

"I didn't hear a title fall from those pretty lips, Red."

"More, Sir, please."

Swat! Swat! Swat!

"Okay," Lauren gasped, trying to rear up. It was obvious his hand was on her restraints for two reasons. One, it seemed

to keep her fear at bay…but it also kept her in place. "That's—
"

"Smarting? Good," Connor said.

Swat! Swat! Swat!

"Master!"

Lauren's ass was hot. The stinging, which was morphing into pleasure, drove everything else out of her mind. Every time the paddle landed on her sensitive skin, she raised her ass higher. Was she subconsciously asking for more or trying to get away from the hard implement? At this point, it didn't really matter. Her juices were flowing and her pussy needed something to grab onto.

Swat! Swat! Swat!

"Sir, I can't—"

"You can take whatever I deem you can take," Connor replied, stopping and placing the paddle back in her line of vision. He then stroked her searing flesh. It was as if he was adding liquid fire to every inch he caressed, until his fingers dipped into her pussy. "You respond to me like…"

Lauren would have asked like what, but he'd brought his moistened finger up to her anus. When he breached her sphincter with no warning, she cried out. It was a different kind of sting than the one the paddle produced, but no less effective. A sob rose in her chest, startling her. She needed to come, and for the first time her fear was completely pushed aside.

Connor released his grip on her restraints, reaching for the button on his jeans. He tore open the button and then yanked on his zipper, pulling his jeans down around his ass. Searching for his wallet, he found what he was looking for and ripped the foil. Rolling on the latex, he couldn't get it on fast enough. He had to bury his cock in her.

"Who do you belong to?" Connor asked, already kicking himself that he allowed himself to ask that question. This wasn't supposed to be serious. It wasn't. The question was okay, he decided. Even a temporary submissive belonged to their Master, a distinction she may or may not understand. "Red, I asked you a question."

Connor used his palm to spank her already red ass and she instantly cried out.

"You, Sir. I belong to you."

Without hesitation, Connor drove his cock into her pussy. It was rare that he became immobile from the feel of a woman's cunt, but Lauren had that ability. He took a moment to savor the warmth as her miniscule contractions massaged his cock as she gained the most intimate grip possible. His breathing deep, Connor gritted his teeth to hold himself back from coming. For what Lauren had just accomplished, she deserved an orgasm.

"I'm so proud of you, Red," Connor whispered, taking additional time as he gathered her cream up with his thumb. He pressed it against her anus, loving the spasms that shot through her as he did. "Handing me total control over your body, your mind, and your fear."

"I belong to you, Master," Lauren murmured, causing his heart to twist. She repeated only what he'd asked of her, but Connor was afraid she took it the wrong way. "Please fuck me, Master."

Damn, but every time that title fell from her lips it did something to his soul. Connor pulled out to his tip, only to thrust forward. He pushed his thumb through her sphincter, mimicking his movements. Lauren's groan vibrated all the way down to his balls.

"Come for me, Red."

That was all the warning he gave her as he started pounding his cock into her pussy. Over and over, he slammed into her while hooking his thumb in her ass. Blood rushed through his ears as it sounded like an avalanche had been triggered. Lauren's cunt clamped down on his dick as she followed his command and let herself fly. He felt his balls crawl back up tight against his shaft as he felt the sparks of electricity shoot through his sac, signaling his release.

"Lauren!" Connor cried out, jet after jet of his cum shooting into the rubber.

He was so fucked.

Chapter Twenty-Eight

"**N**o."

Lauren tightened her fingers on the mug, hoping like hell she didn't crack it. Her anger was rising and Connor was acting as if she were being irrational. If he wanted to see what irrational looked like, he was one more word away. It was time to lay their cards on the table and she already knew that she held the losing hand.

"Why not? Did you run it by Crest?"

"I don't need to run it by Crest," Connor said, sitting on the stool in front of the island. "I'm not taking you to either club. I can't have you in danger."

"In danger? Let's be honest. The case has nothing to do with why you won't take me to a club." Lauren didn't need to ask if he was going to play with some of the submissives in attendance. The only threat she was in was of losing her heart. She feared the worst. Already, an ache started to blossom in the center of her chest over what she was about to do. "I don't want this to be casual anymore."

Lauren held her breath. Connor had been looking down at his coffee and her words seemed to paralyze him. If the ache hadn't just spread to an all out stabbing pain, her sob might have made it through. She just went all in and knew she'd lost everything.

"That's what we agreed on."

His words came out measured and Lauren had to bite her lip to keep from begging him to look at her. Connor was staring at his coffee as if it were a buoy in the middle of the ocean. What she didn't understand was that after the time they spent together, why he didn't feel the same.

"I know what we agreed on, but that was before—"

"Before what, Lauren?" Connor asked, his words lashing at her as he finally raised his head. His blue eyes were like ice and she felt the cold all the way down to her very being. "What you feel during those scenes is not what you think. That's why I gave you all week to assimilate what took place. We've known each other for what? Three or four weeks? That's nothing."

"Do not sit there and condescend to me," Lauren said, raising her voice. "My body might respond to you telling me what to do in a scene, but I'll be damned if I'll let you sit there and tell me how I feel. As for knowing you for only a limited period, who the hell said there was a specific time for someone to know whether or not they want something more serious than a quick fuck?"

Connor shoved his coffee away, the black liquid sloshing over the sides. He stood. Was this it? Was this where he walked out?

Knock-knock.

Connor's phone dinged the minute someone knocked on the door. Lauren slammed her coffee down as well. Damn it! While he dug his phone out of his pocket, she stomped to the door.

"Don't answer—"

Lauren threw the door open and heard him whisper the word *fuck*. She knew that she had whipped the door open partly to irritate him, knowing that he wanted her to check to see who was in the hallway first. But she wasn't feeling very gracious at the moment. Her heart stopped at seeing who was standing in front of her. Maybe she had fucked up.

"Joel," Lauren said, pasting a smile on her face. "What are you doing here?"

"You left a box at the club and since I was driving past your building anyway, thought I'd drop it off." Lauren felt her stomach sink when Joel's eyes focused on something over her shoulder—more like someone. "Whoa. Didn't mean to interrupt anything."

A million excuses ran through her mind as to why Connor would be in her apartment. Parallel to those thoughts was why Joel was at her front door. She didn't believe that he was here to deliver a box. A shiver of alarm ran through her and she wished she hadn't been so hasty in her decision to just throw open the door.

"Joel," Connor said in greeting. She tried to hide her surprise when she felt Connor's hand wrap around her waist. "I was just trying to convince Lauren to come to the club with me tonight. After meeting her last night, one thing led to another and…well, you know how things go."

"I always knew you had a wild side, Lauren," Joel said with wink. After a moment when no one said anything, he held up the box. Connor released her, taking it from Joel. "Kyle's going to be disappointed."

"I'm sure he'll be fine," Lauren responded, trying to keep her voice light. She wanted to shift her feet but didn't want Joel to see her apprehension. "Playing at home is one thing, but I'm not sure about a club if you know what I mean."

"Well, Connor knows he's permitted to bring a guest, but if you want your own membership, all you have to do is ask," Joel said.

"I'm not sure if I'm willing to share yet, so she'll remain my guest," Connor said, his words clipped.

Lauren felt her anger flare. There he went again, stressing that he didn't want her to have a scene with anyone else when that didn't pertain to him. Her initial worry of why Joel was really here got pushed aside. Impulse took over and she retracted her earlier statement.

"You know, maybe I was too hasty," Lauren said, ignoring Connor's hand slipping back onto her waist. She also disregarded the warning of his fingers pressing into her side. "Do you mind if I'm Connor's guest tonight?"

The surprise in Joel's eyes was evident, but that didn't stop a smile from appearing on his elongated face. Lauren caught movement in the hallway and was shocked to see Lach walking their way. He jiggled some keys, not looking their way as he passed by. Joel didn't look twice as Lach headed for the elevators.

"Of course not," Joel answered. He glanced at his watch. "I should be going. I'm meeting up with an old friend. I'll see you two later tonight."

Connor was the first to reach for the door and gently closed it shut. It wasn't the reaction Lauren thought he'd have and tensed, waiting for him to argue with her. Instead, he stepped away from her and pulled his phone back out. She didn't even glance at the box that he'd set on the floor.

"Connor…"

He ignored her plea and held the phone to his ear. Lauren swiped away a curl that kept falling into her eye. After such a wonderful night, this was not how she thought her Saturday would end up. Angry that he wasn't speaking with her just yet, she walked over to the kitchen where she'd set her coffee down. Getting a dishtowel, she wiped up the coffee that had spilled over the rim.

"Crest, Lach is following Joel to a meeting. I'm staying with Lauren and she's coming with me to the club this evening." Connor paused and Lauren knew that Crest was speaking. Was he also asking how this plan arose and giving it his blessing or was he going to put a stop to it? "He stopped by with a box Lauren had left at Masters last night. I got Lach's text too late. She'd already opened the door."

Lauren watched as Connor walked across her living room and into her bedroom. Apparently, he wanted privacy to finish his phone call. She leaned her elbows on the counter and held her head. What the hell had she done?

Connor sat on the edge of the bed, his forearms braced on his knees. He felt the air shift and knew she'd entered the bedroom. She didn't immediately speak and he used the moment to gather what sanity he had left. Lauren certainly knew how to drive a man crazy. Jax had warned him about redheads, but had he listened? Hell, no. And wasn't it Jax who'd actually got him into this mess to begin with.

"Being bound to your kitchen table is a hell of a lot different than being restrained on a St. Andrew's Cross in front of people." Connor lifted his head, making sure her green eyes were focused on him. "You can still back out and I can make a cover story for you. Joel won't think twice if I tell him that you were too uncomfortable playing in public."

Lauren didn't reply right away, as if she were mulling over his offer of an out. He prayed she was, because this was going too far. He'd told Crest that his relationship with Lauren wouldn't affect the case. What a fucking liar he was. She was almost pure innocence standing in front of him. Connor's chest hurt and he had to look away. He knew it was crunch time, but he simply wasn't ready to walk away from her.

"It's not in me for a serious relationship."

"It's not like I'm asking for marriage," Lauren said, her voice soft. She still hadn't moved from the doorway. "But even during casual relationships, I've never been one to be promiscuous. I won't lower myself to that type of affair now. You either play with me and me alone for however long this lasts, or we part ways."

"And what?" Connor asked, a bitterness in his voice that surprised even him. "You walk away grateful that I've erased your fears?"

"You haven't," Lauren said, taking a hold of her left wrist. "Don't feel you should take credit. They just seem to fade with you. I'm not saying that to boost your ego and it's certainly not a ploy to get you to commit to me. It's the truth."

Connor shook his head, not knowing what to say. He didn't have a lot of faith in women, but on some gut level he knew that Lauren wouldn't lie to him. But this had nothing to do with honesty. It had to do with human nature and always looking for bigger and better things.

"When you find another Dom who does that for you, you'll see that I don't have some special magic."

"Did I say you did? Could there be someone else who could make me react like you?" Lauren finally took a step into the room. "Probably. That doesn't mean I want him."

"Then what do you want?" Connor asked, already knowing the answer. "Forget I asked that."

"Let me ask you something," Lauren said, placing her hands on her hips. Connor knew that stance and finally looked her way. Her green eyes were shining with anger. "What is different today than yesterday? We had a scene. It was great. The only exception I have is you playing with other submissives while you are with me."

"Which changes things from casual to serious. I can't do that."

"If that's how you want to view it, fine. But let's not sugarcoat things. It's not that you can't, but more along the lines of you won't. Is it casual if I'm not allowed to scene with another Dom if I want to?" Lauren threw up her hands. "If I went tonight without you and played with Kyle while you had a scene with another woman…what's the difference?"

"This is the second time that I've heard about Kyle wanting to play with you at the club. Why didn't you mention this to me before?"

"Because it's none of your business. That would be the case if things remain casual."

"Something doesn't sit right about that, but we'll come back to it." Connor stood and closed the distance between them. She was so beautiful. How many times had Jax warned him that playing at home changes the dynamics of a casual relationship? He lifted a hand, brushing the back of his fingers across her cheekbone. "I know that it's a double standard, but regardless, I was also doing my job."

"That's a cop-out and you know it," Lauren said, stopping his caress. She squeezed his fingers. "You and I both know you played with that submissive to prove that I was nothing. Did it work?"

Connor ground his teeth together. Why was he surprised that she would call him out on it? That was exactly why he played with Brie and he was coming to regret every swing of that cane. Had he learned nothing from his past? He waited until she released his hand, allowing him to continue to touch her. He tucked a strand of hair behind her ear.

"My mother left my father," Connor murmured, watching her closely as he revealed a piece of himself. He didn't know why he even spoke of it or why he watched her reaction, but he did all the same. "It devastated him. It destroyed him."

Connor closed his eyes, his words taking him back to that kitchen he'd come to hate. His father still lived in that house, but it never failed to churn Connor's stomach when he walked into the small room.

"I was having breakfast when my dad came in, sat down, and told me that she was never coming back." He opened his eyes. "A woman should never have ahold of a man's soul the way my mother did my father's."

Lauren's brow furrowed, but she remained silent. He wanted to continue, but found he couldn't. Connor wasn't ready to share more than that and tilted his head, closed his eyes and tried to regain some composure. His phone rang and he'd never been more grateful. He still needed her to know one thing, though it wouldn't change things in the long run.

"No, playing with Brie didn't work."

Chapter Twenty-Nine

The rest of the afternoon had passed by in a blur. Jax had shown up to the apartment along with a petite blonde with spiky hair and black-rimmed glasses named Taryn. Both were nice enough, but they seemed to set up some mini-camp in Lauren's living room. She let them be, only making coffee when she saw they were running low. She'd kept to herself in the spare bedroom, working on smaller orders to keep herself busy.

The time away also gave her time to think things through. Lauren had handled everything wrong this morning. This wasn't a game. She didn't have the right to mess with his case. What they'd shared was completely separate from his job and needed to stay that way...if there was even a relationship to be had. He'd mentioned the timeframe in which they'd known each other, but she knew that held no bearing. What they shared *had* changed everything and he couldn't take that back. It wasn't just physical for her anymore.

The doorbell had rung twice, and both times Connor had answered it. The first person had been Ms. Finch, wanting to borrow some sugar. Lauren knew it was only an excuse to see why so many people had been stopping by. Connor was his usual and charming self, seeing to it that Ms. Finch got her sugar along with an official introduction to Jax and Taryn. The second visitor had been a deliveryman from a local upscale department store. He'd delivered a box, which Connor signed for and then placed into her hands after pulling her aside into the kitchen.

"If you are dead set on going this evening, this is your outfit," Connor said, his words coming out like gunshots. "As my submissive, you'll look the part or not go. We'll leave at eight o'clock when the floor opens for play."

"May I ask you something?"

"What is it?" Connor inquired, his resignation evident.

"What happens after tonight?" Lauren could see the indecision in his blue eyes and that was all she needed. She gently placed the box on the counter. "I appreciate the outfit and the option to attend the club tonight. I'm going to pass, so please go ahead and use the excuse that I just wasn't ready. It shouldn't come as a surprise to Joel."

"What game are you playing, Red?" His blue eyes seemed to come to life as he stepped closer. "This morning you told me that you didn't want this to be casual anymore and even finagled your way to have a scene at Masters. Now you're backing out?"

"I'm not backing out," Lauren said, correcting him. "I'm ending it. I can see that you're not ready for anything serious and I pushed the issue. You've taught me things that have changed my view on life, Connor, and I refuse to go back to the way we were before. I want more."

"I'm giving you what you want, aren't I?" Connor cradled her face, but his anger lay just below the surface. "I'm not playing with anyone but you tonight."

"Tonight? What about tomorrow?"

"Fine. Not tomorrow either." He rested his forehead against hers as if he could make her see reason. "I can't give you a time limit, but we'll keep things as is until one of us—"

"Gets tired?" Lauren pulled away and his hands fell from her face. "I am tired, Connor. Ever since I met you, it's been a merry-go-round. You make it sound like three weeks is nothing, but from where I'm standing, you've imparted a lifetime of lessons."

"What lessons would those be? Huh?" Connor ground his teeth until she could see the muscle tic on the side of his jaw. She snuck a glance into the living room, but Jax and Taryn pretended like they couldn't hear. "The fact that you can now have your wrists bound together? I didn't extinguish your phobia, for fuck's sake. Even you said the same thing not eight hours ago. You weren't blindfolded and you sure as hell weren't tied to my bed."

"You son of a bitch," Lauren murmured, feeling her back go up. She'd thought she'd been handling this just like he wanted. No strings, no fuss…just the ability to walk away. She was giving him that, yet why wasn't he taking it? "If you need to make this some type of cheap fuck, then go ahead. I obviously can't stop you. But we both know the truth, don't we?"

"And what the hell would that be?" Connor asked, obviously not caring that Jax and Taryn could hear every word they said.

"That you might have been one hell of a Marine on the field, but off of it you're nothing more than a coward." Lauren shoved the box his way, knowing she needed to leave the room before she broke. "From the sounds of it, at least your father had the courage to love a woman."

✧ ✧ ✧ ✧

Connor stood in Lauren's kitchen, hands on his hips, staring at the dark cabinets. They were the color of his soul and he'd just been damned. He knew he'd pushed her to the brink and got what he wanted when she walked away, so then why the fuck did he feel like a complete fucking asshole? The sound of a door closing, not even slamming, echoed throughout the apartment. It signaled his time to leave.

Turning, Connor walked back into the living room, ignoring Jax and Taryn and picked up his cell phone, which he'd left on the coffee table. Sending a quick text, he laid it back down while he started to gather the files they'd scattered about. They'd made good progress going through everyone's alibis and marking the ones that seemed suspicious. They'd even gathered more information on Nick Klaus and Kevin was tracking him down for an interview now.

"Connor, we've known each other a long time—"

"And you know enough when to keep your mouth shut. I don't need a lecture from you." Connor looked down at his phone, seeing that Lach returned his text. He was back in position after having followed Joel most of the day. It was safe to leave. "Let's go. We have to get ready for tonight."

"Taryn, could you give us a moment?" Jax said, standing up from the couch. His voice contained a warning, but right now Connor didn't give a fuck. This didn't concern him.

"Actually, I was just leaving. I'm heading back to the office to check on a computer program I have running." Taryn stood and shoved the folders that Connor had compiled into her satchel. She walked to the door and then stopped. He could see that she'd turned around and couldn't help the slight shake of his head. She should know to leave him alone right now. "Think twice before you burn that bridge, Connor. In our line of work, it's not every day we come across someone who really gets us."

Connor laughed, although it came across hollow. Why the hell did his chest feel like a tank was sitting on it? He waited until she left before facing Jax. His friend stood there, his disappointment evident. Jax wasn't his father or his keeper, so he could just keep his goddamned mouth shut.

"I'll say this once," Connor said, walking over to the coat rack to snag his jacket. "Lauren needs someone who hasn't seen the shit we've seen and done the things that we've done. You were the one to warn me that taking things to the next level and having scenes outside of the club was dangerous. I didn't listen. Now she's taken those intense feelings and wrapped them up with a fucking bow."

"And you feel nothing for her?"

"Three weeks, Jax." Connor shoved his arms into his coat. Walking back to where the coffee table was, he swiped his phone. "She went from casual to serious in three weeks. I'm not cut out for that shit and you know it. And what the hell is this, you standing here questioning my decision. This coming from the man who goes through subs like a pyro does matches."

"I had my chance, Connor," Jax said, looking him square in the eye. What the hell was he talking about? "So don't stand there and fucking judge me. I didn't lose it by choice. So don't throw away what she's offering you because of a fucked up mother who cared more about herself than her family. Not all women are like that and you've hung onto that excuse like a goddamned crutch."

"What do you mean, you had your chance?" Connor quickly thought back to his friend's behavior before their last tour and then took into account his comment about not losing his chance by choice. The anger, the recklessness, the desolation. Connor connected the dots and came up with something that blew his mind. "Emily—"

"Is dead." Jax slowly walked around him to the coat rack, lifting off his black leather jacket and skullcap. "We're not talking about me; we're talking about what you're about to throw away. Reconsider."

Jax walked out the door, leaving Connor standing in Lauren's living room alone. The silence was deafening and it took all of his will not to slam his fist into the coffee table in front of him. What kind of friend was he? Things hadn't been the same with Jax since their last combat tour and he'd chalked it up to too many battles in the field. They'd met Emily one week before deployment and she'd been gunned down in an attempted convenience store robbery...one week.

Connor looked toward the spare room, the door thankfully keeping him from seeing the woman who seemed to have a grip on his heart. Regardless of what Jax said, he'd done the right thing. Could he have handled it better? Did Lauren deserve better? Yes, on both counts. But that wasn't going to change the outcome. It was time he left.

Lauren swirled her wine, watching the red liquid slosh around the glass. That's what her life resembled, one big current that never seemed to settle in one place. Bringing it to her mouth, she downed the rest of it.

"Carrot Top, are you listening to me?"

"I heard you, Sue," Lauren said with a sigh, trying to sink deeper into her couch. "Want a recap? I took a chance on casual sex, fell for a guy who has commitment issues, tried to get him to see reason, and came out on the losing end. That sum it up?"

"You forget where I said at least you had good sex." Lauren could hear the kids screaming in the background and knew that she should let her sister go. It was her niece and nephew's bedtime. It was a wonder Sue had even answered the phone. "It wasn't for naught."

"No, it wasn't," Lauren whispered, looking at her left wrist. She couldn't imagine any other man trying the things Connor had. "Why did I go and give him an ultimatum again?"

"Because you had no choice," Sue said. "It was either continue on until you lost your heart and fell in love with a man who couldn't return it—in which case I'd have to kill him—or until you found out that he was a jerk. So…you discovered the second part a little early. That's a good thing. You'll get the hang of the YOLO thing. Lacey, I said to put on your pajamas, not your dress."

"My YOLO seems to be a yo-yo…just say 'in'. I'll let you go," Lauren said, finally getting up off of the couch. It was only to refill her wine glass, but it was still something. She needed to have some ounce of respect for herself. "Give the kids a big hug for me."

"Everything always looks better in the morning," Sue said. "Call me and we'll talk again over coffee."

"Bye."

Lauren disconnected the call and placed her phone on the island countertop. She swiped the bottle and headed back to the couch. Leaning forward, she grabbed her glass and filled it with red bubbly liquid that would hopefully ease the ache in her chest. Sue thought Lauren had learned the second part of her discovery when she'd really exposed the first…she'd fallen in love with a man who refused to commit.

Chapter Thirty

Connor entered Masters after having been buzzed in by Jenny, giving a cursory look around to see who was here. He had come alone, Jax having preferred to take Whip tonight. It was all good, considering he didn't need another lecture on his personal life. He also didn't know exactly what to say to Jax about Emily. That was a bit of info that Connor was still processing.

It was later than he'd intended to arrive, so the club was in full swing. Latin music spilled from the speakers, but didn't smother the sounds coming from the submissives at various play stations. He saw Brie on the St. Andrew's cross, Dante putting her through her paces. Dante was a good Dom, although he only played at the clubs every so many months. He also had an airtight alibi the night Marilyn was murdered. So did Brie, for that matter. Kevin hadn't discounted anyone.

Mistress Beverly had a male submissive lying on the bondage table, his cock and balls in a CBT cage. Connor winced, moving his gaze along. Bev had been here at the club the night of the killing. Her normal three male subs had been in attendance. Mistress Vivien was situated in one of the middle sections, comfortable in her thigh high latex boots. She didn't have an alibi, claiming she'd been home alone.

"Master Connor, would you like a drink?" Casey said, sidling up to him. The brunette placed her hand on his arm. He looked down until she removed it. That was the second time that she'd touched him of her own volition. She was a better sub than that and knew not to touch unless told. "I can bring you a club soda."

"Not tonight, Casey," Connor said, stepping away from her. He refused to believe that he wasn't going to play with her because of Lauren. She had nothing to do with his decision. Right now, he wanted to have a conversation with Joel. "I see Master Scott warming up the violet wand on one of his subs. Why don't you see if he'll play with you?"

Connor moved toward the bar, not waiting to see if she took his advice. Russell was bartending this evening and Kyle was on his usual perch. He resisted the urge to knock him off of it just because he'd offered his services up to Lauren. A niggling of doubt crowded the back of his mind. She wouldn't go for a guy like him, would she? Kyle would have no idea how to handle her fear.

"Hi, Master Connor," Shelley said, passing by him with a grin.

Connor returned her smile but not the greeting and headed for the bar. Flint must have something extra special lined up for her tonight, with the way her face had been lit up. He thought back to Kevin's SITREPs and remembered that Flint and Shelley were each other's alibi. Two people could have easily subdued Marilyn, but that would make it twice as likely they would have left behind some DNA. Taryn said those reports should be in any day now.

"Usual?" Russell said, reaching behind him for a glass.

"Yeah," Connor said, taking a stool. He leisurely looked into the mirror above the bar, assessing the area. Only when he'd acquainted himself with who was where did he spare a glance toward Kyle. He was in a conversation with a Dom on his left. No one that Connor knew. "Thanks."

"I heard you played with Brie last week," Russell said, placing a club soda in front of him. "Casey couldn't stop talking about it."

"Casey needs someone to train her," Connor replied, lifting up one side of his lip. "That disrespect won't last long in here."

"Rumor has it that CSA is helping the police work Marilyn Sweeney's murder," Russell said, leaning his forearms against the wooden surface. Connor kept a neutral facial expression, knowing that he was just fishing for gossip. "Do you know how Terry's doing? It's a shame that the police actually thought it was him."

"You had him tried and convicted," Connor said, reminding the barkeep of his initial reaction. He took a drink of his club soda. "And no, I don't know how he is. Kevin's running the case, and since I'm not allowed near it I have no access to information."

"Well, look who it is." Connor looked to his right to see Joel walking around the corner from where he knew his office to be. "Tell me it ain't so. Did Lauren back out?"

"I didn't think she was ready for a club scene," Connor replied, phrasing his words carefully.

"Those redheads have a way of being spontaneous," Joel said, walking behind the bar. "I thought she seemed a little too eager to come tonight."

"You aren't talking about Lauren Bailey, are you?" Kyle asked, butting into the conversation. Connor had to take a deep breath to keep his muscles relaxed. He placed his fingers on the rim of his tumbler. "Are you shitting me?"

"No," Joel replied, placing his hands on the bar and leaning against the surface like he was staying for a while. "Apparently she's attracted to military men. That sure as shit cuts you out of the equation, Kyle."

"Shit, if I'd known that, I would have signed up long ago," Kyle said with a laugh. He slapped the bar with his palm. "Connor, you sure know how to pick 'em. I never had a chance with that little ginger."

"Master Connor?" Jenny, the hostess, stopped the conversation. That was probably a good thing, because if Kyle kept talking, Connor knew it was only a matter of time before his fist would shut him up. "You have an important phone call."

Connor had shut his cell phone off, per the rules, before entering the play area. He could be a boy scout once in a while, but now he was regretting it. Would Joel or the members question his attendance this evening? He scanned their faces as he stood up, following Jenny to the front kiosk out in the foyer. He saw she'd set the phone down on the dark oak reception desk and picked it up.

"Ortega."

"Within five minutes, the cops will be all over that place," Jax said, his voice coming in loud and clear. "They're coming to arrest Joel Summit for the solicitation of prostitution. He and Gerry have been using the private parties to sell out the sexual services of willing submissives. Two have already been taken into custody for prostitution."

Connor took a moment to digest the news, shock rolling through his system. Out of all the shit that Joel and Gerry could have done, this one took the prize. Had Marilyn found out, and they thought death was the only way to silence her? It didn't sit right with him, but either way an arrest would be made and their investigation would suffer a few delays, but they would continue until they had their answers.

"Let me guess," Connor said, trying to look into the play area as Jenny opened the door to admit a member. Joel, Russell, Kyle, and the man who'd been standing next to him were still deep in conversation. Sweeping his eyes over the room before the door closed, he saw Mistress Bev and her sub in one of the small areas where she was administering aftercare. Mistress Vivien was nowhere to be seen. The rest of the members seemed to be accounted for. "Juliet and her little blonde friend."

"Got it in one," Jax replied.

"And Gerry?" Connor asked, able to get the name out before Jenny sauntered back to her position.

She gave him a smile and he wondered if she knew of Joel's dealings on the side. He could guarantee that there was a hell of a lot more than two subs at those private parties. Had Marilyn been privy to what was going on behind closed doors and gotten herself killed?

"His ass is already in the back of a police car. I'm heading your way. I just wanted to confirm that Gerry didn't get some message off to Joel before he was taken in."

"Negative," Connor replied, keeping his answer vague so that Jenny was kept in the dark.

Connor pulled the phone away from his ear and pressed the disconnect button. His first instinct was to check his weapon that he'd secured in his ankle holster, but he refrained. Connor nodded to Jenny that he wanted back into the main area. Once he entered he walked to the bar, taking his seat as if nothing was amiss. Conversation ceased and it was evident they'd been talking about him. If he had to guess, he'd say it was in relation to the case and not Lauren. He didn't blame them for their lack of trust.

"Everything okay?" Joel asked.

"Yes," Connor replied. "Jax just wanted to know if Casey was around tonight. He thought she'd be at Whip."

"So are you topping Lauren now?" Russell asked, placing beer on the counter for Kyle.

"What the fuck?" Joel murmured, panic coming through in his words.

Connor tensed, catching sight of two boys in blue and one detective coming through the doorway. Jenny's face was priceless as she stood in the doorway, watching the police proceed through the play area. He had to make a quick decision in whether or not to go after Joel if he decided to run. If he did, Connor would be sacrificing his position along with the trust of these members. If he didn't, would the outcome be any different? The police would eventually find Joel and place him under arrest.

He heard whispers and murmurs throughout the room and knew that everyone saw the police walking through the area. Connor was impressed with their work ethic as he watched them come closer, seeing their focus was on Joel instead of the naked subs attached to various pieces of furniture. Joel had made his way around the bar, but made the better choice of staying where he was instead of running. Defeat was written on his face.

"Joel Summit?" the officer asked, although Connor knew that he was well aware that Joel was his guy. "You're under arrest for the solicitation of prostitution."

Connor stood, moving out of the way so the police could do their job. He felt movement behind him and quickly looked into the mirror. Kyle had slid off of his stool and had lost all color in his face. Well, what do you know? This asshole was involved too. It didn't surprise Connor, but what caught him by surprise was the fact that Kyle was shifting his body toward the door. He was going to run.

Connor's gaze connected with the man who had been having a conversation with Kyle. He was watching and waiting to see what Connor would do, but Connor didn't stop to analyze it. Reflex kicked in and he turned.

"Going somewhere?" Connor asked.

Kyle sprinted for the door, knocking a plant over near one of the couches. Connor looked over at the two police officers who were now reading Joel his rights, but neither saw what was happening. Fuck. Weren't they paid to pay attention to their surroundings? And what happened to all these cops that Jax had referred to?

"You're going to let him get away?" the man asked, regarding him with curiosity. "Aren't you some type of law enforcement?"

"Aren't you?" Connor inquired, intuitively knowing this man was a cop.

"DEA. Max Higgens." Max looked toward the door, bringing his drink up to his mouth but stopping short. "Trust me. The members here won't think less of you for going after a prick that pays for it."

Connor shook his head, not wanting to cause a scene but knowing that he couldn't allow Kyle to have one more second of freedom. Fuck. He ran toward the front door, hoping that his suspect was smart enough to take off through the door and down the alleyway. At least, that's what Connor would do considering there was another police car pulling up as he made his way to the sidewalk.

Veering directly around the corner, Connor saw a shadow exiting at the other end. He took off at a dead run. By the time he turned the corner, Kyle was almost to the parking garage entrance that was situated behind the building. It wrapped around the other side of the structure, which was where members usually parked. He instinctively reached behind him, not slowing down. Shit. His weapon was attached to his ankle. No time to stop and reach for it.

Connor had managed to close the distance between them as Kyle started to run up the ramp. Kyle only managed to slow himself down by looking over his shoulder. He didn't see the car backing out. The impact wasn't as bad as Connor thought, but it did send Kyle to the ground. Connor reached him right when he tried to get up.

"I'm so sorry," a woman's voice echoed throughout the garage. She was the driver of the car and had stepped out of her vehicle. "I didn't see him!"

"It's okay, ma'am." Connor could see that Kyle wasn't injured and was, in fact, looking around in panic for a way out. "I'm working with the police and this man is being placed under arrest."

"Connor, just let me go. I wasn't part of it, I swear." Kyle backed away one step. "I attended once and that was the only time I paid for it."

"Kyle, turn around and face the vehicle, putting your hands behind your head."

"If this gets out, I'll lose my job."

"You should have thought of that beforehand."

Connor could tell by Kyle's stance that he was going to run for it again. Before Kyle had completely turned around, Connor had him shoved up against the parked Tahoe in the next stall. He heard the woman gasp behind him, but ignored her. He reached in front of Kyle and started to undo his belt.

"What the fuck, man!" Kyle started to struggle, but cried out when Connor dug his elbow into his back.

"No worries," Connor said, "I don't swing that direction."

Connor slide the leather from Kyle's waist and within seconds, had his hands secured. Whipping him around, he saw that Kyle's face was red with exertion and embarrassment. Not for a minute did Connor believe it was from the cold. Being arrested for soliciting a prostitute was the least of his worries, which Connor was privileged to hit home.

"You understand how this looks, right?" Connor said, taking him by the shirt and shoving Kyle in front of him. "Joel and Gerry selling the services of submissives, and then Marilyn Sweeney ends up dead."

"What?" All out panic and fear was evident in Kyle's voice. The word rushed out of his mouth, along with condensation from the cold air. "Connor, I swear, I know nothing about Marilyn's death. All I did was pay Joel for one of his submissives. I wanted something a little more intense than the club scene allowed, you know?"

"You can tell that to the police," Connor replied, keeping a hand on Kyle's shoulder just in case he tried to get away. Looking in front of them, he saw Max Higgens and Jax standing at the bottom of the ramp along with a police officer. "I'm sure you'll be in their company for quite a while this evening. That is, before they stick you behind bars for being an accessory to murder."

Chapter Thirty-One

Lauren didn't bother with a coat, knowing she'd be in and out of the cold within seconds. She walked down the hallway a little unsteadily and knew she shouldn't have consumed so much wine. Unfortunately, she hadn't drunk enough to put her to sleep. Work was the only thing that would keep her mind off of Connor's parting shot about her lessons learned. She'd ascertained a slew in the last month that she could do without.

Making it to the elevator, she hit the down arrow. The items she needed to work with tonight were in her van. Lauren hadn't been keeping up with her specialized orders the way she should have been, and what better time than now to start catching up? The doors whooshed open.

"Going somewhere?"

Lach stood there, his hands linked together in front of him. He didn't have his jacket on, indicating he'd been monitoring her from inside the building, and his weapon was easily noticeable as it was secured to his side with a brown leather holster. Lauren resisted rolling her eyes at his protective demeanor as it reminded her of Connor. Hell, just Lach's presence reminded her of Connor.

"Just going to get some stuff out of my van." Lauren stepped into the elevator and pressed the button for the garage. "See? I don't even have to go outside. How did you know I'd left my apartment, anyway?"

"I was monitoring the surveillance footage."

Lauren noticed that Lach kept his eyes on the doors as they closed. He didn't say anything else, but she was coming to expect that from him. He hadn't talked much at their first meeting; why should now be any different? Fine. She crossed her arms and watched as the numbers lit up in descending order above the doors. Halfway down, Lauren couldn't take the silence. She blamed the wine.

"So you're new to the area." Lauren snuck a sideways glance at him. He was still looking forward at the doors. "Do you like it?"

"It's cold."

So much for that line of questioning. Lauren remained mute the rest of the way. The doors slid open and they walked into the cold entryway that was off of the garage. She'd been lucky and gotten a parking spot a few slots away from the entrance. She put her hand on the knob to turn it when Lach stopped her.

"Let me go first and check the area."

"No offense, Lach, but if someone really thought I knew something about Marilyn Sweeney, don't you think they would have come after me by now?" Lauren let her hand drop from the metal handle. "Connor...well, let's just say we were personally involved and I think he took things to extreme. I'm sure if you call Crest, he'll probably relieve you of this boring assignment."

"A suspect stopped by your apartment today," Lach said, reminding her of the visit along with the subsequent events. "I wouldn't say that Connor took things to extreme. He's doing his job, regardless of how personal things may have gotten between the two of you."

They stared at each other for a moment and Lauren was the first to look away. He was right. She was just in a bad mood and Lach's presence didn't make it any better. He was just a reminder of what she wanted to forget tonight.

"Look," Lach said, his sigh large enough to move his massive chest. He seemed uncomfortable with what he was about to say, but that didn't stop him. "Night is when our insecurities overtake us. I don't know what happened between you and Connor, and frankly, I don't want to. But from my experience, everything always looks better in the morning. Now, let me do my job so that you can get to work on yours."

Lauren looked at him quizzically as he turned the knob, his words striking a chord. He was the second person to say that to her this evening, and both times made her feel as if she were experiencing déjà vu. She watched as Lach opened the door, the cold wind instantly wrapping its prickling fingers around her body, trying to conjure up the memory that was eluding her. Immediately, the vision struck her.

"Oh my, God," Lauren whispered, suddenly having an idea of who murdered Marilyn Sweeney.

She quickly grabbed for the handle before the door shut. She had to tell Lach right away. He would call Connor, who was already at the club. Lauren rushed through the entrance. Lach had only taken two steps when he turned back to her, a questioning look on his face. A movement behind him grabbed her attention, but before she could call out to him, a gunshot echoed through the parking garage.

✧ ✧ ✧ ✧

"Haven't seen you run that fast since Iraq," Jax said, leaning up against the wall in the hallway of the precinct. He held a Styrofoam cup and had shed his jacket a while ago, although he'd opted to keep his skullcap on. "Too bad I didn't get to videotape it. The boys from our old unit would get a laugh out of that one."

"Fuck you," Connor said, taking up residence on the other side of the door. Joel and Gerry were in separate interrogation rooms, while Kyle and the two girls were being processed. They were waiting for the detectives to get through with their interview, and since they had official clearance, Kevin would be going in next. Both men had lawyered up immediately, but they were still allowed to question them with attorneys present. He and Jax were waiting to get into the adjoining surveillance room. "If you saw me running after the asshole, why didn't you pursue?"

"Hell, I knew you had him. The day you can't take down someone eighty pounds lighter than you is the day I give up submissives. And you know I have a special relationship with my devotees." Jax's smile disappeared when he took a drink. "Have you tasted this shit? It's like sludge."

"Probably been sitting on the burner since morning," Connor said with a smile. He'd opted for a soda after seeing the corroded burner. The door opened and Crest motioned them in. "Here we go."

"Kevin is about to start questioning Joel first, although the lawyer might hamper whatever he says," Crest said, walking over to where a large desk sat in the middle of the room. A two-way mirror on the wall showed Joel looking like he'd gone to war with someone twice his size and lost. His oval face seemed longer, while bags had appeared under his eyes. "What are your thoughts?"

Connor shrugged, taking up residence near the window so that he could see Joel's expression throughout the questioning. Jax took his usual stance, leaning up against the other side of the window.

"I think if he or Gerry did murder Marilyn, it wouldn't have been staged. They would have killed her and been done."

"I agree," Jax said, nodding toward Joel. "Her murder was personal, like we all keep saying, as if she'd wronged someone."

Connor saw Kevin walk in the room, a folder in his hand. He smirked. If he knew Kevin, there was nothing in that damn folder, except maybe an old menu to the local Chinese restaurant. Everything important was stored in his brain like a computer. While introductions were made and the lawyer spewed out his *my client doesn't need to answer your questions* bullshit, Connor looked back at Crest.

"How's Terry? You said there was a change in his condition this morning. For the better, I hope?"

Crest shook his head and slipped his right hand into his dress pants pocket. "His father overreacted. Terry's fingers moved, but the doctors say that's normal. I'm heading back over there once we finish here."

"Something's been bothering me about that," Conner said, placing his soda on the ledge of the window. "Where was Terry's father during the shooting? Had he gone back up north?"

"No," Crest said, his face turning to stone. "He was staying with me."

Connor shared a look with Jax, knowing there was more to the story, but it was obviously personal and Crest wasn't about to break confidence. If anything had been pertinent to the case, he had no doubt that Crest would share that information. Whatever caused Mr. Sweeney to feel he couldn't stay with his son had no bearing on the case.

"They're about to begin," Jax said, nodding his head in Kevin's direction.

Their voices carried through the speaker. Kevin explained that he was consulting on a different case altogether, but felt that the two might be connected. He placed the folder on the table and leaned forward on his arms. Kevin's back was to them.

"From what the lead detective has told me, you're being placed under arrest for pandering. That's three to eight for each offense. A couple of days ago, I questioned you in regards to Marilyn Sweeney's death. It seems as if you're having a bad week, Mr. Summit. Is there anything you wish to share with me?"

"My client does not need to answer that question."

"No," Joel answered, ignoring his attorney's advice. "It was Gerry's idea to have the private play parties and charge for sex, but we had nothing to do with killing anyone."

For the next hour, Kevin grilled Joel. Nothing came of it; not that Connor expected it to. He was surprised to hear that because Gerry had opened up the second club, both were financially in trouble. Gerry had gone to Joel to try and make amends, offering what he thought was a viable solution. He bet Joel was regretting that resolution now considering where they'd ended up and the likelihood of both the clubs closing now.

Connor rolled his shoulder, trying to ease the tension. Kevin still had to interrogate Gerry, and then follow up with Kyle and the two girls. The night seemed never ending and his mind continually wandered to Lauren and how he'd left things.

It was in her best interest and he knew that, so why was he questioning himself? It wasn't as if they could continue on without Lauren eventually wanting more from him than he could give. Hell, she already did.

Connor glanced at his watch and saw that it was going on midnight. He found himself actually debating the risk of trying some of that sludge that Jax was choking down. They'd be here at least until three, so black tarred coffee it was. Crest's phone rang, and as he took the call, Connor reached for his. He'd turned the thing off when he'd entered Masters earlier this evening. As he pulled his phone out of his pocket and turned it on, Connor started to walk toward the door.

The sound of snapping fingers had him stopping and looking over his shoulder at Crest, who was signaling him to wait. The display on his phone loaded and he looked down, seeing three missed calls…all from Lauren. A little voicemail envelope appeared on the screen.

"I'll tell him," Crest said, reaching for his dress coat. "I'll meet you there."

"Something happen?" Jax asked, straightening from the wall.

"Yeah," Crest said, heading for the door. "Lach is being transported to the hospital now. He's been shot."

Connor felt his chest tighten and his vision dimmed. He hadn't felt fear like this since he'd been in Iraq. Crest didn't have to relay the rest of what he'd learned, as Connor knew the significance of what had happened. He looked down at his phone and forced his fingers to play the message. Slowly bringing the phone to his ear, Lauren's terrified, hushed tone came through the speaker. He closed his eyes.

"Connor," Lauren whispered, a break in her voice evident, "Connor, Lach's been shot and there's blood everywhere. I— "

The voicemail ended and it was obvious that the discon-
nection wasn't voluntary. Connor had been able to hear the
panicked gasp escape Lauren's lips beforehand. Now, there was
only silence.

"Fuck!"

Chapter Thirty-Two

"Taryn, talk to me," Connor ordered, shifting the Jeep into third. He ran the last red light that led to Lauren's parking garage, all the while keeping his phone against his ear. "What do you see on the cameras?"

"Footage is loading," Taryn said.

Jax was riding shotgun, holding onto the hand loop above the passenger door. He was also on the phone getting intel from Ethan, who was waiting for them at the scene. Connor wasn't about to wait for permission to look at the parking garage security video feeds when he knew that Taryn could hack in within a matter of minutes. He cut the corner to the entrance a little too sharp and the back tire went over the curb.

"Anytime, squid," Connor said, taking the turn that would bring them on the second level where Lauren had been taken from.

"Got it," Taryn replied, triumph in her voice. "Rewinding…rewinding…"

Coming to a stop in the middle of the garage, Connor shifted into neutral and applied the parking brake. He left the

Jeep running, knowing they wouldn't be here for long. Jax disconnected the call and rolled down his window.

"No one saw anything," Ethan said, leaning his forearm against the window. "Lach took the hit in the back, the bullet hitting his lung. They'd already taken him to the hospital before I arrived, so I didn't get to question him."

"Who found him?" Jax asked, resituating his skullcap a little lower on his forehead.

"Get this shit," Ethan said, shaking his head in disbelief. "He managed to drag his ass back into the elevator and to the lobby. He somehow indicated that the security guard should call 911 and report a kidnapping. He got out Lauren's name and the fact that his gun and phone were missing before he collapsed."

"Fuck," Taryn whispered, grabbing Connor's attention. He put his foot on the clutch, released the brake, and shoved the Jeep back into first.

"Give me something, Taryn."

"Russell Treace."

✧ ✧ ✧ ✧

Lauren rocked herself back and forth, her breathing shallow. It didn't matter how dark it was in the back of her van, because she knew her vision had tunneled. The panic attack had hit the second Russell had shoved her into her own vehicle, slamming the doors shut and locking her in. A sob rose up in her chest and she would have given anything to be able to tell Connor that she'd been right...she was only mentally stable in these situations if he was touching her. And he wasn't here.

The air felt as if it was compressing against her chest. She tried to drag oxygen into her lungs, but they didn't seem to want to comply. Her entire body was perspiring and she could feel her heart pounding against her chest, although the beats didn't seem to be normal. Lauren had no idea how long Russell had been driving, but the distance seemed endless. It didn't matter if she had a heart attack, because he was going to kill her anyway.

It took her a while to realize that the tires had a smoother tread in a way that wasn't normal, indicating they weren't on the city streets. They'd slowed down. Her mouth was dry, but she parted her lips anyway, trying to breathe. It felt like she was suffocating.

As the van pulled to a stop, all Lauren could hear was the ringing in her ears. Not knowing what was going to happen when those doors opened, she waited and tried not to instantly cry out for help. Russell might just kill her now and be done with it. How could she not have remembered their conversation and what his words had truly meant?

Keys jingled and Lauren could almost hear Connor's voice in her head telling her to breathe. She released the tight hold she had on her left wrist, ready to beg through the metal for Russell to open the doors. Instead, she bit her lip and remained silent.

She slowly picked up the gun that had been lying in her lap, trying to ignore the trembling in her hands. Hell, they were shaking so bad she was lucky the firearm didn't discharge. Lauren didn't know a lot about weapons, and hoped to God that when she pulled the trigger it fired.

She would have given anything to have her phone, but she'd dropped it somewhere in the parking garage. Lauren was relatively sure that Russell had Lach's, because she'd seen his on the ground when she'd been kneeling next to him.

When Lach had been shot, he'd still had the strength to lift his weapon and return fire. It gave Lauren enough time to run and duck behind a car. Fumbling with her cell phone that had been in her pocket, she dialed Connor. It went straight to voicemail, and through her tears she tried again to no avail. The third time she'd left a message, but when she'd heard another gunshot, she'd dropped her phone. Now she was kicking herself that she hadn't dialed 911. Maybe they would have been able to get an officer to the parking garage before Russell had found her.

All the same, after the initial shots had been fired, Lauren had remained where she was for a good three minutes before she'd decided to try and move. She had needed to see if Lach was still alive. At the time, she'd hoped he'd either scared Russell away or shot him. Slowly and carefully, she'd had made her way around the car. Not seeing or hearing anything, she'd shuffled on her knees until she'd had a clear view.

The only person she'd seen was Lach, who had managed to roll over onto his back. He'd been gasping for air. She'd known immediately that she couldn't leave him there and had scooted to the back end of the vehicle. When she saw no one else, she'd stayed low and had run over to Lach. His eyes had connected with hers, but instead of giving in to tears the way she'd wanted, he'd had enough strength to shove the weapon at her. His hand had kept trying to push it into the waistband of her jeans and trying to appease him, she did.

Lucky for her, Lach had known all along that Russell was still near. Within seconds of her having been given the weapon, Lauren had screamed when Russell had come up behind her and grabbed her hair, dragging her back to her van. She'd fought for all she was worth, but with how tight he'd had ahold of her hair and because her back had been to him, Lauren had no chance to get away.

She would say she'd never been so scared in her life as to when he held the gun to her head, demanding the keys, but that wouldn't be true. It was what Russell did afterward that escalated her fear to terror. Being thrown into the back of the van, darkness descending and confining her to be alone with this consuming panic was crushing.

The door swung open, but Lauren was ready. Pulling the trigger, she cried out, not expecting the recoil. The gun almost slipped from her fingers, and in a panicked state she tried to get the weapon back in her palm. Russell didn't waste any time and yanked her out by the wrist, snagging the weapon from her grasp.

"Bitch," Russell spat out. "I should have killed you when I had the chance."

He'd dragged her out of the van until she'd fallen on her knees. Lauren felt the cold settle over her and instead of trying to run, which would have been useless anyway since he had the gun, she took the precious time given and dragged in as much oxygen as she could. She was no longer enveloped by darkness and light now surrounded her. As the terror started to loosen its grip on her, details started to bombard her.

"One word out of you and I swear I'll put a bullet through your brain."

Lauren looked up and saw that there was nothing but irrationality within those dark eyes of his. Russell looked nothing like the young man who would bring her waters or offer to carry her stuff out to the car when he was on duty at the club. Ignoring everything, she desperately tried to focus on where they were. Someone had to have heard a gunshot.

"I want you to get up and walk in front of me," Russell said, shifting the gun toward a door on her right.

They were in the parking garage attached to the building of Masters. Had he just driven them in circles? It had felt as if they'd driven forever. Lauren looked around desperately. Was no one around to see that she was being held at gunpoint? She didn't have time to calculate her options when she felt the barrel against her head. She closed her eyes and squinted them tight when he nudged her.

"On your feet; we don't have much time before someone comes to find out who fired a gun. You've been a fucking thorn in my side from the beginning."

Lauren had no choice but to fumble to her feet. He moved the gun, but it was now directly in the middle of her back. She frantically looked around, but the lot seemed devoid of vehicles. Where was everyone? He shoved her forward to where the grey metal door was located that would lead to the stairwell of Masters. Relief swam through her. Someone would notice the gun and that Russell had brought her here against her will.

She didn't say a word as she made her way to the club, trying to concentrate on keeping her rubbery knees from collapsing. Question after question ran through Lauren's mind as to why he was doing this. Why would he have killed Marilyn?

It didn't take long for them to arrive at the entrance to the club. Russell kept the gun in place and reached around to hold the key in front of her. Why would they need a key? Shouldn't someone be here? What about Connor and Jax? It was the weekend, for crying out loud. With trembling hands, she took the key. It took her several tries to get it in the hole, but it finally slid home.

"Go stand in the middle of the play area. If you make any attempt to move, I swear I'll shoot you." Russell pushed her forward, and as she felt the barrel of the gun in her spine, Lauren knew she didn't have a choice.

"W-where is everyone?" Lauren asked, wanting to prolong the inevitable. Maybe if she kept him talking, Joel or someone would come back.

"Joel and Gerry got arrested, just like I'd planned." Russell slammed the door shut and then started to pace in front of the bar. He looked a little panicked. "But then I overheard Joel say that Connor was involved with you and I just knew that you'd remembered our conversation."

"W-why did you kill her, Russell?" Lauren asked, glancing around the room for something to use against him.

"She wanted Mistress Beverly," Russell said, spinning her way. His face was now red with anger. "No one just gets to kneel at Mistress Beverly's feet!"

Lauren felt like she was traveling down the rabbit hole. He wasn't making any sense, but then she imagined most insane people didn't. Russell took a step toward her and she instantly backed up. She calculated her odds for running toward the door, but had no doubt that he'd shoot her. Lauren looked toward the main entrance, the one that led to the foyer and then to the street, but it was even farther from where she was standing.

"Undress," Russell ordered, motioning up and down with his weapon. Where was the one she'd had?

"I-I don't—"

"I said undress!" Russell screamed, his eyes bulging out and the vein on the side of his temple protruding.

Lauren felt another sob rise up, but she forced it back. With shaking hands, she reached for the hem of her sweater and slowly pulled it over her head. She needed to ask more questions. She needed to keep him talking so that someone came looking for her. By now, someone had to know that Lach had been shot and that she was missing. Connor would find her. She just hoped like hell that it wasn't after she was dead.

"You said to me that *'everything looks better in the morning'*. Do you remember that?" Lauren asked, trying like hell to keep her words from stuttering. She managed to put the button through the denim hole, but stopped. "Marilyn had walked by my table, along with Flint and Shelley. Shelley had been angry at Flint because he'd added something to her punishment that she felt was unfair. You were bringing me water and we started to discuss how sometimes couples misunderstood each other because they weren't communicating properly. You weren't referring to Flint and Shelley...you were talking about you and Mistress Beverly. When Marilyn walked by our table, you were referring to her being dead. You knew that you were going to kill her then, didn't you?"

"What the hell made Marilyn think she would be any good for Mistress Beverly? I deserve to be her submissive. I wait on her, I serve her, I love her! Me! No one else. Not her male subs, not the female subs that covet her attention, and sure as hell not someone like Marilyn Sweeney." Russell stopped and wiped the spit that had spluttered from his mouth. He looked wildly around and then seemed to notice that she'd stopped undressing. "Keep going and shut up! I need to think."

Lauren started to shove her denim over her hips. She knew that her shivering had less to do with the temperature of the club and more to do with the fact that she was about to be murdered, but that didn't stop her teeth from chattering. She knew there would come a point that Russell would just kill her, but she had to stall him for as long as possible. Connor would come for her. Regardless how things ended between them, she knew that he would come for her.

"W-what made you think that Marilyn wanted to serve Mistress Beverly?" Lauren asked in a low voice, hoping the question didn't startle him. She needed to keep him talking. "She—"

"I said keep undressing." Russell walked over to the St. Andrew's Cross, giving Lauren pause. Should she run for the main door? If she could just get to the street, someone could help her. He turned back to face her. "Marilyn wanted Mistress Beverly. Couldn't you see that? It was in her movements and the way Marilyn looked up at Mistress like she was her savior. She wasn't! Mistress is mine and she'll come to realize it soon."

"You did a good job throwing the police off, making them think Terry did it," Lauren said, changing tactics. She slowly placed her hand on a chair that was behind her, trying to look like she needed support to kick off her boots in which her jeans were now tangled above. She really was just delaying. "The shibari was a nice touch."

"Do you know how many demonstrations that Joel has here?" Russell waved his gun around the room. "Night after night, I'm watching some goddamned demo on bondage, toys, ropes, and whatever else Joel can find someone to do. I practiced those knots over and over again, knowing that the police would look for someone with that knowledge. Imagine my luck when Terry tried to cut her loose with the knife that I killed Marilyn with. I couldn't have asked for things to go better."

Russell laughed, although it seemed strained. Lauren knew she was running out of time and kicked off her boots. She slid the jeans over her socks, taking those off too. The prickles of terror started the reign over her flesh. She knew that he intended to bind her to the cross. Russell had no idea the anarchy he was about to unleash with her phobia.

"Then why shoot Terry?" Lauren asked, unable to keep her voice from trembling. All that was left for her to remove was her bra and panties. She caught herself from laughing manically, due to the fact that she never thought her first club scene would be like this. It would also be her last. "The police thought he'd killed Marilyn. Why change that?"

"He knew," Russell whispered, looking down at the carpet as if ashamed. Lauren feared his swing of emotion. "He knew. He'd been making calls and talking to people. Joel told him that Marilyn had been talking with Mistress. I overheard the phone conversation. I knew it wouldn't be long before Terry put it together. I had to shoot him so that he wouldn't say anything."

Lauren knew that Russell was paranoid. He'd gotten so caught up in his infatuation with subbing for Beverly that his obsession had turned in on itself. He didn't know what to believe, and so he thought he could just wipe everyone out of Mistress' life, as well as his own.

"Just like I have to kill you and frame someone else. If you are involved with Connor, then he'll be the prime suspect. What better justice than to the man who would betray his friends by nosing around in their personal lives." Russell raised the gun. Lauren felt her chest constrict and knew that she'd run out of time. "Walk over to me. You're the last person with any knowledge. Once you're gone, I'll prove to Mistress that I'm the only one for her."

✧　✧　✧　✧

Connor pulled his weapon as he and Jax each took up position on either side of the door. Crest and Kevin were on their way and would cover the main entrance. They'd kept the fact that Taryn had followed the traffic cams, following Lauren's van through the city streets until it had pulled off into the garage of the club from the police. They didn't need this fucked up now. Not with Lauren's life on the line.

"A fucking romance book couldn't end better than this shit," Jax whispered, reaching for the doorknob. His fingers tightened on the handle. "You better make this good. Maybe even confess your undying love."

"Fuck you," Connor murmured, agitated that his friend would chose now to try and alleviate the tension. He used to do this shit when they were about to go on a mission, but this had nothing to do with ridding the earth of scumbags. This was Lauren. "Just do what you're trained to do."

"I'm just saying...a dedication in my name might be nice." Jax slowly turned the handle and indicated that it was unlocked. "It's not everyday a man gets to witness true love."

Connor felt the cold sweat that had broken out over his body start to dissipate. His agitation lowered, just as his friend knew it would. They were a team...a unit. They would extract Lauren using the training they had been taught, giving her back the life she was intended to live.

"On three." Connor readied his body, taking a deep breath. His heartbeat lowered and the blood he heard in his ears diminished. "One...two...three."

Jax swung the door open, entering low to the ground. Connor swept in, turning immediately to his left and surveying the club. His mind computed everything at once and instantly focused on the fact that Lauren was naked and being bound to the cross. Only one wrist was enclosed in the strap, but it was enough to have his vision darken.

"Connor!" Lauren cried out. She'd been fighting Russell like the feisty hellcat she was and Connor couldn't be more proud.

"Back away, Russell," Connor barked, aiming his weapon on the target's widest accessible area, which happened to be Russell's chest. He had to force himself to ignore Lauren's plea, knowing that if he looked away from his target that they could all end up dead. "It's over."

Jax kept moving, quickly immersing himself behind the bar. Connor knew that he would work his way to the end, giving himself a better position.

"Drop your weapon, Russell."

Connor stared into eyes that held no sanity. Russell had managed to lose any semblance of rationality. Connor's sense of morality had to try to get Russell to see reason, but Connor's gut told him that this was going to end badly. He'd seen that look before and knew he had no choice but to pull the trigger. How had Connor missed this?

Russell moved quickly, ducking behind Lauren, who had just gotten her wrist out of the cuff while Connor had held Russell's attention. Before she could run toward him, Russell yanked her naked form back against his chest. He brought the gun up to Lauren's head.

"Toss your weapon to the floor and move away from the door." Russell tightened his grip on Lauren, causing her to cry out. Connor's finger took up the slack on the trigger, waiting for a clear shot. He resisted the urge to look and see if Jax was in position. Did he have a better angle to take this fucker out? Russell looked frantically to see where Jax had gone. Connor had no idea if Russell had located him, but had no concerns. This would end, and Russell would be the one crossing over into hell. "Once I'm out, I'll let her go."

"You and I both know that you have no intention of letting her live," Connor replied, resisting the need to look into her green eyes and reassure her that everything would be all right. "I can't let that happen. Red, present!"

Connor didn't hesitate. The second Lauren used her body weight to fall to her knees, he pulled the trigger. The bullet tore through Russell's chest and that familiar wet slapping sound filled the room. Surprise flashed across his face as recognition dawned that he was dead. Russell dropped, along with his weapon. Unfortunately, he landed right on top of Lauren.

In sync, Connor and Jax darted across the carpet. Jax grabbed Russell by the jacket, pulling his body off of Lauren while Connor gathered her up into his arms. Her back and arms were covered in blood, but he ignored the slick mess with its distinctive copper smell as he held her close.

"I've got you, Red," Connor murmured, trying to shrug out of his jacket. He wanted her covered so that when the recovery team came through the main doors, she had some sense of dignity. "You're safe…you're safe."

"Got a thready pulse," Jax yelled out, digging for his cell phone in the front of his jeans.

Connor couldn't stop the irritation that he'd missed the target's heart. Connor had no doubt Russell would die. A shot to the chest from a Sig P220 firing 230-grain hydra-shock rounds had about a ninety-eight percent kill ratio. He looked down at the redhead in his arms and tried to soothe her as a sob wracked her body.

"Red, slide your arms through," Connor murmured, nudging her to shift a little. "Come on. Put this on or else my entire team will see you naked. I don't think we've quite worked our way up to that."

Her sob turned into a snort, and for the first time that day Connor felt a smile tug at his lips. No matter what happened from here on out, Lauren was safe. She lifted her upper body to where he could assist her into his coat. Her tear-streaked face finally looked up into his, and those emerald circles held such hope within them that he felt his heart crack just a little.

Chapter Thirty-Three

"Hand me that crescent wrench, mi hijo," Alberto said, his voice carrying from underneath the car.

Connor had been looking outside of the open garage, watching life pass by the old shop. Jersey never changed. He looked behind him at the ancient red tool cabinet on rickety wheels that his father refused to part with. Turning around, he closed the distance and moved around the various tools that lay in the open drawer, choosing the right one. Leaning down, he laid it in his father's outstretched palm.

"Have you called to check on her?"

"I told you," Connor replied, straightening his knees and walking over to where he'd left his can of soda. "Lauren was fine when I left. I made a couple calls since then. It's only been three weeks since the incident. She has a life to lead that doesn't include me and it was time that she got back to it."

"So you say," Alberto mumbled from underneath the vehicle. Connor resisted rolling his eyes at his father's know-it-all tone. "Maybe she wants that life to include you."

"We both know that she would have moved on if I'd decided to continue with what we had," Connor said. He brought the can to his lips and took a gulp. "I was just doing us both a favor by saving her the trouble."

"Favor, eh?" Alberto rolled out from underneath the block of metal, turning those dark eyes his way. "Not all women are like your mother."

Connor looked down at his father in surprise. It was rare that they discussed *her* and he didn't want to start now. Alberto shifted to his left and used his arm to push himself into a sitting position. He reached into the back pocket of his overalls for a rag, trying to wipe the grease from his hands. It was a useless endeavor.

"Want me to put steaks on the grill this afternoon?" Connor asked, finishing off his soda. He wasn't about to have this conversation and dredge up unwanted memories for his dad. "I can drive over to the house and get them out of the freezer to thaw."

"What I'd like is to have a conversation that is long overdue." Alberto rose from the creeper and walked over to the mini fridge, grabbing himself a water.

"Dad, I—"

"I don't think I gave you a choice, mi hijo," Alberto said, his brow furrowing. Connor sighed deeply, knowing that when his father set his mind on something, it was going to happen come hell or high water. "Why do you think I haven't remarried?"

The question came out of left field and Connor didn't quite know how to respond. What could he say that wouldn't rummage up painful memories? His father didn't seem to mind, which should have been his first clue. Alberto seemed to have an extra kick in his step this past week and thought it was because of his visit. Apparently it had to do with someone else entirely. He was a private investigator, for fuck's sake.

"Is that what this is about? You've met someone?"

"Crest has been taking it too easy on you," Alberto said, shaking his head. "My question was why do you think I haven't remarried?"

"I'd assumed because you didn't want to experience the same thing you did with—" Connor broke off, having a hard time evening saying the word mother. "Why would you want to put yourself through that again?"

"Your mother and I were young," Alberto said, a half smile on his face as if he was remembering something fondly. Connor felt anger rise in his chest, for he didn't have any of those. He checked himself before commenting, knowing it wasn't his father's fault. "I knew what she wanted out of life, and as a foolish teenager in love I thought I could give her what she wanted. Unfortunately, that wasn't meant to be."

"Dad, I really don't think we need to rehash this," Connor said, crushing the soda can in his hands and walking over to the garbage can. He tossed it inside the large rusting fifty-five gallon drum, wishing he could do the same with the pent-up wounded feelings that never went away. "Let's drop it for today."

"Why?" Alberto said, waving the water bottle in an arc. "So that you can go about life thinking that all women are like your mother? When she became pregnant with you, I was the happiest man on the face of this earth. Wherever she may be and whatever life brought her, I will always be eternally grateful that she gave me you. Her selfishness kept her from knowing you. I pity her. But you seem to think that I haven't moved on because of her actions and that is so not the case, mi hijo."

"Really?" Connor asked, turning back around to face the man who'd worked day and night to provide for him. "Then what is the case? From where I'm standing and what I've seen over the years, that is exactly the way it is. I don't blame you."

"I know that," Alberto said, looking down at the bottle in his hand. Holding it up, he moved it around and the sunlight that was bouncing off an old wreck's windshield and through the garage door caused a refraction. "And if I had had my way, I would have kept your heart as clean and clear as this water. You blame your mother. But it is she, not Lauren, that did what she did."

Connor fisted his hands and used them to lean against the wooden bench alongside the wall. His father tended to talk in riddles, much like his grandmother used to. Alberto Ortega was a very introspective man and felt the need to impart his wisdom, which Connor could do without today. He'd come home to get away from it all, not have his past rehashed.

"The one blessing that came out of your mother leaving was knowing what I wanted and needed from a woman. It was a hard lesson to learn, but one that I hold dear." Albert set the bottle of water on the tool cabinet. "I had you, so I knew that I could wait until that special lady came along. She finally did, but not until recently. I would like you to meet her this evening."

Connor knew the conversation had been heading in this direction. His father had been smiling a lot this past week and dropping hints that this New Year would bring happiness. Did his father think that he wouldn't be happy for him?

"Dad, I'm happy for you," Connor said, loosening his fist and holding out his hand. Alberto's smile grew bigger and his father drew him in for a hug. It wasn't anything that Connor wasn't used to, as his father was a very sensitive man and showed his affection. He hadn't lied either. Alberto's happiness meant the world to him. "I can't wait to meet her."

"Mi hijo, there is a difference between you and I that causes me concern," Alberto said, pulling away but placing his hands on Connor's shoulders. "I knew what would make me happy and would have continued to wait for many more years if need be. You purposefully do not seek out love for a different reason and one that will leave you very lonely, I'm afraid. You are good boy. My boy."

Alberto wrapped his fingers around the back of Connor's neck. It was his way of stressing what he was about to say. Connor could see the intensity of which he spoke.

"We both deserve happiness," Alberto said. "If this Lauren is enough woman to have you come home and hide your heart within my garage that you rarely set foot in since you left for the Marines, then she is one that is worthy to fight for. Do you have enough in your arsenal to capture her heart?"

Connor broke away, walking to the open garage door, needing a moment to himself. The cold air whipped in and he raised his face to embrace it. He closed his eyes as the deep-seated fear came over him of what could actually happen if he admitted his love for Lauren.

"What if she leaves?" Connor whispered, knowing that his father had followed him. The question was practically torn from his chest, and now that it was out in the open, a terror so vivid filled him like no battlefield ever could. "What if I invest everything I am into her, only to find that I'm stepping on a landmine? It's just a matter of time before my foot shifts and my world is blown apart. She'll slip through my fingers."

"You're already invested, mi hijo," Alberto said, placing a hand on Connor's shoulder. "Instead of viewing your relationship like a minefield, what if you see it for what it is?"

"And what is that?" Connor asked, opening his eyes. He turned his head and looked into his father's knowing eyes, looking for the security that even this wise man couldn't provide.

"The gift of love. Life doesn't come with any guarantees. You have to put yourself out there and risk being hurt to truly gain something worth keeping. It sounds to me as if Lauren warrants that. You may fail, but if you don't try, you will never achieve peace with the one person you need to make you whole."

✧ ✧ ✧ ✧

Lauren took a deep breath before opening the door to the offices of CSA, trying to slow down her heart rate. It was almost a month after Russell Treace had been shot to death in his attempt to murder her. She didn't feel an ounce of remorse for his death, but couldn't help but think that he'd gotten away from paying a price for the devastation he'd caused to his victims. What she did feel at the moment was irritation with a certain former Marine.

"May I help you?"

The woman in front of her couldn't be older than twenty-five, but there was an underlying knowledge and intelligence in her brown eyes that were rarely found in someone so young. It was also apparent this woman knew exactly who Lauren was. Her long brown hair was pulled back at her neck, similar to how Lauren wore hers when she was working. The woman gave a small smile.

"Um, yes, please," Lauren replied, pulling her purse higher onto her shoulder. "Is Mr. Crest available? I'm—"

"Lauren Bailey," the woman answered, standing from her chair and holding out her hand. "Nice to meet you. I'm Jessie, Mr. Crest's personal assistant."

"It's nice to meet you, Jessie," Lauren said, returning her smile.

"Jessie, did we receive anything from Lieutenant Commander Kryder? Ethan needs to have—" Crest broke off as he rounded the corner. "Lauren. It's good to see you again. I take it things are well?"

Lauren looked at him quizzically, not understanding why he seemed so surprised to see her. It was Crest who had wanted her to stop by the office this afternoon. She looked over at Jessie, who was now rearranging something on her desk. Why would she have left Lauren a message to be here at two o'clock to meet with Crest?

"Yes, thank you," Lauren replied. "When I stopped by the hospital to visit Lach, he mentioned that Terry was awake and responding well to physical therapy. I'm glad to hear it."

"Thank you," Crest replied, nodding his head in acknowledgment. "Lach was released a couple of weeks ago once the infection in his lung cleared up. Terry is now home with his father and is recuperating amazingly well."

"Thank you for the update. Is there a reason you wanted to see me?"

Crest looked over at Jessie and she could see irritation cross his face. His assistant's cheeks flushed, but she then seemed to get her spunk back. She straightened and she faced Crest head-on. Before either one could say anything, Jax stepped around the corner.

"Hi, Lauren," Jax said, flashing his smile. Lauren couldn't resist returning it, although she had to wonder what he was up to. His next words had her stomach sinking. "That was me

344 ✧ KENNEDY LAYNE

who had Jessie call you. I wanted to have a chat with you about Connor."

At the same moment Lauren heard Crest exhale a deep sigh, the door behind her whooshed open. Jax's smile grew larger, Jessie's eyes widened, and Crest looked downright irritated.

"Jax, in my office."

"Yes, sir," Jax replied, never once looking contrite. He leaned forward a bit, as if he was having a private conversation with her. "Lauren, Connor will have to take over our meeting."

"Now."

"Boyo, don't fuck this up," Jax called out as he led the way down the hallway with Crest two steps behind. "By the way, I've decided to buy Masters from Joel Summit. I need a partner. Let me know when you decide to come up for air and then we can head to the bank."

Lauren couldn't quite bring herself to turn around and look at the man who'd haunted her days and nights for the past month. The image of his face was burned into her mind, from the laugh lines around his eyes to the square edges of his jaw. Connor's blue eyes that so reminded her of the tourmaline gems that she hadn't been able to bring herself to use since the night he'd walked out of the hospital had preoccupied her dreams.

"Lauren?"

Connor's voice was inches from her ear, but she still needed that extra time to compose herself. After Russell's shooting, Connor had insisted she be taken to the emergency room. He'd gone with her, never once leaving her side. Of course, she'd checked out just fine and Connor had taken her home. She'd known by the look in his eyes that he was still going to walk away from what they had. And he did.

Taking a deep breath to steady her nerves, Lauren turned around. She resisted placing a hand on his chest, where his jacket was hanging open. She needed his warmth, even now. Lauren refused to make a fool of herself.

"Connor," Lauren returned the same sentiment. She bit the inside of her lip to prevent herself from saying something that she couldn't take back. It worked and she continued on. "I apologize for being here. I don't mean to interrupt your workday. I'm not sure what Jax was thinking when he had Jessie call and leave me a message that Mr. Crest wanted to speak with me."

"No one ever knows what Jax is thinking," Connor replied, not taking a step back like she thought he would. "But in this case, I'm glad he was able to get you here. I flew back from Jersey this morning and was just stopping in here for a brief moment before coming to see you. We need to talk."

Lauren's heart rate sped up, along with anger that flowed through her bloodstream. "Those two phone calls that you made since I was almost killed were quite enough, don't you think? There's not much left to say, as far as I'm concerned."

"Ah, Red," Connor said, a small smile forming over his perfectly formed lips. Lauren swore she'd awakened several times over the last four weeks having those lips on hers. "I love when you get all agitated. Your green eyes just sparkle."

"These green eyes are about to take in a beach view, so if you'll excuse me," Lauren said, trying to pass Connor.

He stepped in her way, placing his fingers lightly on her arm. "Are you heading to Florida? For a visit?"

"Does it matter?" Lauren shot back, not ready to give an inch. He still hadn't even remotely hinted as to why he felt the need to speak with her after all this time. Whatever it was, she could guarantee it wasn't the words she needed to hear. "My flight is first thing in the morning and I have a lot of packing that I need to do."

"You aren't going to make this easy, are you?" Connor murmured.

Lauren caught his eyes moving to where Jessie must still be standing. His eyes widened slightly, but enough to cause her to look over her shoulder. Taryn, along with two other men she hadn't met, stood near Jessie's desk with smiles on their faces. Lauren felt her cheeks flush, never having liked being the center of attention. She turned back around to see Connor have his hands on his hips and his blue eyes shooting daggers at the people behind her.

"We can go," Lauren whispered, changing her mind and quickly motioned with her hands that they should leave.

"No, please," one of the men said behind her. "This is a moment in history we don't want to miss."

"Fucking sharks," Connor murmured, grabbing her hand and pulling her towards the door. "Jessie, I'm still on leave. I'll be in touch in a few days. As you can see, I have personal matters to attend to."

Chapter Thirty-Four

L auren didn't say much to Connor on the drive to his house. He was starting to think that this wasn't such a good idea. He probably should have waited to talk to her until tonight, when he'd gathered up enough courage. She stared out the Jeep's window and he caught himself from saying something multiple times. One, he wasn't sure where to start; and two, he didn't want to bare his soul inside a black vehicle. His soul was already tainted enough.

Pulling alongside the curb, Connor shut off the engine and told himself to be grateful that Lauren had even agreed to come home with him. He'd kept the couple phone calls he'd made to her to a minimum, basically just making sure that she was okay after her ordeal. It was his way of keeping his distance, although there wasn't a second of the day that had passed that she wasn't within his thoughts.

"Thank you for coming home with me," Connor said, pulling the keys from the ignition. He rubbed his chin, the leather catching on his five o'clock shadow reminding him that he hadn't shaved. He hadn't expected to run into Lauren at the office. He'd been going to head home afterward to get cleaned up before heading to her apartment. "There are some things that I need to tell you."

"Connor, I'll be honest," Lauren said, finally turning her emerald eyes his way. They were filled with the pain that he'd not wanted to see, for Connor knew that he was the one responsible. But he was also the one that could make it right if she gave him that chance. "I don't think I can stay here anymore. You might view what we had as casual and be able to walk away without a second thought, but it was so much more to me than that."

"What do you mean, *here?*"

"I'm going to use this visit to my sister to look at places to live."

"Please, let's not discuss this in the Jeep," Connor said, gritting his teeth to prevent himself from reaching out to her. "Not here. Not outside in the cold, which is where I feel I've been most of my life. Walk inside my home with me and give me five minutes. If you want to leave afterward, I'll take you back to your apartment."

Lauren nodded, albeit tentatively. Connor didn't waste time as he opened the door and made his way around her side. He wasn't about to have her change her mind. Opening the passenger's side, he held out his hand and pleasure ran through him that she took it and climbed down from the runner.

They walked silently up the walk, snow still evident, and he found himself wondering what she thought of the old Victorian house. Three cement steps led up to the wraparound porch, and whereas his door was on the right, Jax's was on the left. It had three stories, although he and Jax used the third level for storage. Finding the correct key with ease, Connor opened the screen door and unlocked the deadbolt. He stepped back, making way for her to enter.

"Thank you," Lauren murmured, stepping over the threshold.

She turned and waited for him to close the door, but Connor could see she didn't know quite what to do with herself. He pulled his gloves off and placed them, along with his keys, on the side table. Lauren slowly let her purse slide from her winter coat and set it alongside his items. He would have liked nothing better than to be the one to pull her zipper down and not stop there, but Connor refrained and took a step back.

"Would you like some coffee?" Connor asked, hanging his coat on the rack situated on the opposite side of the door. The last thing he wanted to do was such a mundane task, but if it would make Lauren feel at ease, then that is what he would do. "I don't have much else available right now."

"No, thank you."

Lauren had unzipped her feather-down ski jacket, but had not removed it. Connor clenched his fists and moved into the living room. The dark hardwood floors complemented the white walls. The couch, loveseat, and matching chair were situated in front of his flat-screen, but he chose to stand. So did Lauren, who had now walked to the shelves on the far wall where he kept his personal photos.

"Your father?" Lauren asked, pointing to a photo that was taken on the day Connor went to boot camp. His father was grinning like a crazy fool. "He's a very handsome man."

"You'd like him," Connor said, putting his hands in the front of his jeans pockets. "He had a lot to say this past week."

Lauren didn't speak as she continued to look at the other pictures. For someone who was so easy to read, he couldn't tell what she was thinking. There were photos of him and Jax in faraway places, a few from when he'd served, and a couple from the past year when he would attend get-togethers at

Crest's house. He waited, hoping that curiosity would win out and that she would turn around and ask him what his father had to say. She didn't.

"He surprised me the other day," Connor said, shifting back on the heels of his black boots, "when he introduced me to the woman in his life."

"You sound surprised," Lauren said, finally turning toward him. Her hair was down around her face with the loose curls touching her cheeks. Her green eyes held the questions he'd hoped she'd be interested in. "Certainly he's dated women on and off through the years. You said you were young when your mother left."

"I was." Connor was astounded at this sudden urge to tell her everything. "I was six years old. I remember the day like it was yesterday."

"I'm sorry," Lauren murmured, slipping her hands inside her coat pocket and taking a step toward him. She was standing on the other side of the couch.

"I was eating cereal in the kitchen and Dad came in. He sat right beside me and didn't mince words. Just said that she had left. It was the first time that I'd ever seen my father cry."

Understanding and recognition for what he was telling her registered in Lauren's eyes. Connor didn't assume that a sob story would garner her forgiveness of how he'd handled things between them. He knew he had his work cut out for him and would make sure that every day for the rest of her life Lauren was well aware of how he felt about her. He was amazed at how easily the words were coming to him now.

"When I was twelve, I went in search of her. See, she'd been raised by a single mother in Hamilton Square and although she'd passed away from a drug overdose, I figured people in that area would remember the name."

"You mean she cut all ties with you? You were six," Lauren said, almost in protest. "And how did you know—"

"Even at twelve, I was good at slipping in and out of places without people asking too many questions," Connor said with a small smile. If Lauren only knew half of what he'd done in his teenage years. "I had gone to the bus station and memorized the routes. I knew which ones would get me there and those that would see me back home."

"Did you find her? Was your mother back in that neighborhood?"

Connor shook his head, remembering the devastating conversation he'd had with an elderly woman who'd been sitting on her stoop. "Apparently, this old lady who used to live next to my mother's family had heard rumors that Pamela Foust Ortega had run off to New York City to marry an older wealthy man. There was no need for me to continue. It was obvious she'd made her choice."

"What about her side of the family? Surely—"

"Her family abandoned her when she decided to take up with an immigrant." Connor started to slowly walk around the furniture, needing to be closer to her. "Why should my mother have been any different? To this day, I still don't understand how she could have done that to a six year old boy or a man as good as my father."

"I don't know what to say, Connor." Lauren looked back at the photos. "I'm truly sorry that you and your father had to go through that. I can't imagine…"

"My first serious girlfriend couldn't handle me going into the Marines. I didn't know it at the time. We'd been together all through our high school years and she never said a word to me. After boot camp, I received a letter from her stating that she'd met another boy in college and that he was going to major in accounting. She wanted that kind of life and not one where she had to worry if her boyfriend was going to be coming home in a body bag."

Connor leaned up against the back of the couch. He wanted...needed...to tell her everything. It wasn't for her sympathy, but it was for Lauren to grasp an understanding of his slanted views of what relationships were like. He just hoped like hell that she would give him a chance to prove his theory wrong.

"In my mid-twenties, I met a woman in Twenty-Nine Palms. I had a month's leave before Jax and myself headed out for a combat tour with Third LAR. We spent almost every day together and I was even thinking of taking her home to meet my father." Connor looked past her to see his dad's smiling face. "I found out that she was sleeping with a Master Sergeant who was up for promotion."

"I'm seeing a pattern here and I've got to say," Lauren said, her green eyes starting to fire up again, "that I'm not liking the comparison you're about to make."

"A few months before I met you, I'd been seeing one of the submissives at the club. Her name was Ashley. I think I was going through a mid-life crisis, because suddenly I had this urge to just say fuck it. I'm in my mid-thirties. I want a son. I want a daughter. I want to love unconditionally the way my father does me." Connor shrugged, knowing that he still wanted those things. "She ran off with another guy who was filthy rich and could offer her the materialistic life she'd wanted. Looking back, I see she did me a favor."

Connor felt the tightness in his chest and heard the blood rushing through his ears. This was it. He needed Lauren to really understand what he was about to convey. He had no doubt that her hands were fisted within those pockets of hers.

Her chin was angled, already having taken offense at the fact that he'd labeled her like those other women…like his mother.

"And then there was you. This fiery redhead that offered me what I needed at the time." Connor fought the urge to straighten and close the distance between them. This time, it was she who needed to come to him. "A casual relationship with D/s qualities in the bedroom and a chance for me to leave you with something more than what we started with. I would be able to walk away with no regrets."

"And have you?" Lauren asked. Her tone held no fear, but her green eyes radiated it. Hope started to loosen the rigidity that had settled in his chest. "No regrets, that is?"

Connor slowly shook his head. "Not even close, Red. And I'm not even sure where to begin to make it up to you. Or if you'll even let me."

"I'm not a person to play these types of games, Connor," Lauren said, not moving toward or away from him. His previous hope started to dissipate. "Regrets or no regrets, you chose to end things between us. What guarantee do I have that you won't change your mind a month from now?"

"And what's to say you won't choose to leave me a month from now?" Connor replied, comparing her fear with his. They both needed to take a chance, but how could he prove it to her? "I know that I've given you reason to distrust me. I—"

"That's where you're wrong," Lauren said. She pulled her hands out of her pockets and he saw that they were still in tiny fists. "For me to lay my fears into the palms of your hands shows how much faith and trust I have in you…in us. I don't know what all of this is about…you bringing me to your house and telling me that you've suddenly had a revelation that maybe I won't leave you like they did. Like your mother did."

Lauren backed up a step and then looked toward the door. Connor felt a cold sweat break out over his body at the thought of her walking away. The hell of it was, it wouldn't be for the reasons he'd previously feared. It would be because he'd fucked things up.

"Lauren…"

✧ ✧ ✧ ✧

"What is it that you're asking me, Connor?" Lauren asked. She knew there was a slight desperation showing in her voice, but she couldn't prevent that. He brought her here and shared his past, but for what reason? "Are you saying you want me back? Are you saying you want to pick up where we left off? You haven't stood in front of me and said that you believe I'm different. You haven't said…"

Lauren shook her head as he straightened from the back of the couch. She didn't want him touching her right now. Those nights that she dealt with her nightmares alone, the ones where she was by herself in a dark place calling out his name in sheer terror only to have him not answer came rushing back. She had no doubt resuming what they had would leave her lonelier than what she was now.

"You haven't given me a reason to stay," Lauren whispered honestly. "I'm sorry, but I can't fight your demons for you, Connor."

Lauren released a shaky breath and forced her tears back, not wanting them to fall before she was able to leave. She'd had to tear those words from her lips, not wanting to say them but knowing it was for the best. He'd given her a taste of what they could have and she wouldn't settle for anything less.

Lauren walked toward the door with every intention of gathering her purse and leaving. She'd walk to the end of the block and call for a taxi. Maybe she'd even see if she could fly to Florida later tonight instead of tomorrow. She didn't think she could take another night alone in her apartment, especially after seeing Connor once more.

"I need you."

Lauren stopped, her heart racing. Had she heard him right?

"I can't..." Connor broke off, but Lauren still didn't turn around for fear of not seeing in his eyes the one thing she wanted most of all. "I can't imagine where I would go from here if you walk out. I was so caught up in trying to give you something to have when we ended, that I didn't see what you've given me."

Lauren looked down, surprised to find that her right fingers were now closed over her left wrist. She turned around and faced him, now needing to see the honesty in his blue eyes.

"And what have I given you, Connor?"

"The promise of a future." Connor took a step forward. "Everything that I haven't let myself believe was possible. I imagine a future with you now. I imagine the rest of my days with you. A woman who is strong, yet submissive in her love. A woman who isn't afraid to know what she wants and won't settle for less. A woman who won't let me get away with only being half a man living in this goddamned civilized society. It didn't matter out on the battlefield, but it sure as hell matters here. I don't want to live in it alone."

"I didn't say I loved you," Lauren whispered, referring to his earlier statement. His image became blurry from her tears.

"I'm not saying that your independent streak doesn't drive my inner Dom to the brink of insanity at times," Connor said, as if she hadn't spoken, "but you bring it back into focus when we cross the threshold in the bedroom."

"But I do," Lauren murmured, knowing she needed to say it louder. Maybe she had needed to hear herself admit it first. A tear escaped, rolling down her cheek. "I do love you."

"I want to make you coffee every morning and see your face light up at the first sip," Connor said, taking a few more steps closer. Had he not heard her? "I want to take you back out into the snow and watch your cheeks turn red from the cold, only to bring you back inside and have them flush for a totally different reason."

"I love you."

"Fuck," Connor murmured, shaking his head and finally closing the distance between them. He gathered her up to him, coat and all, and buried his face in her hair. "You did say it. Say it again."

"I love you."

"Again," Connor ordered, his arms tightening around her waist.

"I love you," Lauren said loudly, allowing the rest of the tears to fall as she laughed.

"Christ," Connor said, finally putting her back down on the soles of her boots and cradling her face in his palms. His thumbs gently wiped away her tears. "I have never felt fear like that…in thinking I'd ruined everything. You are the air I breathe and the universe in which my body belongs. Without you, I am less than nothing."

"I am with you," Lauren whispered, tilting her head and placing a kiss on his palm.

"And I've never been so grateful," Connor replied. His blue tourmaline eyes connected with hers and Lauren swore her soul heated from the love that radiated from within. "I love you, Red."

Chapter Thirty-Five

"You said I had five minutes," Lauren said, snuggling deeper into Connor's robe as she shuffled across the hardwood floor. She tried to sound irritated, but knew that she hadn't pulled it off. Connor raised one eyebrow as she passed and headed toward the bedroom. "Fine. Two minutes. I'll be ready."

"Um, title? Have you forgotten already?"

"Sir!" Lauren yelled out laughing, knowing she'd probably pay for that slip-up later.

She closed the bedroom door, taking in the rumpled sheets and their clothes strewn all over the floor. They'd spent the entire day in bed, although not necessarily having sex the whole time, before raiding what was left in the cupboards. Finally caving in, they'd called for pizza. A lot of time had been spent talking. Several topics were covered, from the case to their families.

Lauren was honest in her summary of the night preceding the shooting. She told him of her nightmares and what she'd experienced in the van. She could see the regret in his eyes that he hadn't been there for her, but he was here now. That's all that mattered and she'd conveyed as much.

Connor told her all about his father and his new lady friend, whom Connor found to be very sweet. She sounded very nice and Lauren couldn't wait to meet them both. He told her of his trip, his walks on the beach, and the dinners with his father.

He'd also caught her up to date with the aftermath of the case. Joel and Gerry had pleaded guilty, but hadn't had to serve time in jail. Kyle's lawyer got him off on lack of evidence. Whip had closed down. They also discussed Jax's revelation at the office regarding buying Masters, and Connor said that if he went along with Jax as a partner, it would give them an entire play area to themselves after hours. Lauren liked knowing that they could play privately until she felt that she could handle a public scene. Connor had laughed, saying he would decide if they ever played publicly, because he liked the idea that she was his alone.

Now Connor was looking forward to a scene and knew that she was ready by her body's response to his suggestion. He'd asked if she'd maintained her bare pussy and to her mortification, she said yes. When he'd asked her to bare her breasts while they enjoyed their pizza at the kitchen table, she'd done so without hesitation.

By the time they were finished eating, Connor slipped his hand through the gap of her robe and then through the folds of her pussy. His finger came away glistening and when he licked it clean, stating that it was the best dessert he'd ever had, she knew her cheeks had flushed.

"What the hell can I use?" Lauren whispered to herself, glancing around the room.

When the table conversation turned to their D/s relationship within the bedroom, Lauren hinted that she'd like to take things further. Connor immediately shot her down, telling her that he would be the one to decide if and when she was ready to use a blindfold or more strict bondage implements. He'd explained that the signs would show themselves, as he would continuously watch her not only during scenes, but during regular hours as well.

When she tried to tell him that her fear dissipated to a manageable anxiety when she was with him, Connor just shook his head, stopping the conversation in its tracks. Lauren wanted to prove it to him and several ways had instantly come to mind. One of them she was about to put into action, regardless of the price. Although the expense of a pink ass might not be so bad.

Scurrying to the closet, Lauren found what she needed. The feeling of anticipation mixed with trepidation that overcame her before a scene with Connor returned full force. Dropping her robe in the midst of the other articles of clothing, she then walked to the bed and stood at the end. Before placing her arms and legs in proper position, she took a deep breath and looked at the tie in her hands. She'd retrieved it from the closet and since it was wide and black, should make for a nice blindfold. Could she do this?

With trembling fingers, she brought the scarf up to her eyes. Letting her lashes lower, she placed the fabric over them and quickly tied the ends at the back of her head. Her mass of curls kept the tight band of material from falling. It was perfect, if she discounted that her body instantly started to react as if she were enclosed in a tight space. Her breathing sounded rather shallow in her ears as she tried to lace her fingers together underneath the knot she made in the silk fabric.

"What the hell do you think you're doing?" Connor murmured in a gruff voice. She felt his hands brush up against her arm and a little bit of reason started to seep through. She grabbed ahold of his wrists. "Red, you're not ready for this."

"Please, Sir," Lauren pleaded, wanting this to be her gift to him. "Just…let me try."

Lauren could hear his shallow breathing and that ball of anxiety that was in her chest started to loosen. It didn't completely go away and her heart was still palpitating, but there was something about this that just felt right. Connor slowly pulled away and she let her fingers drift away from his skin. She then situated her hands in the proper position behind her head.

"I'm ready, Sir," Lauren said, wondering where he'd gone. She'd felt him shift away and found herself listening intently. "Sir?"

"It's a shame that my play bag is sitting at the club," Connor said, his voice coming from the left of her, where his closet was located. "We'll have to come up with something that will make a good substitute."

Lauren's senses were warring with each other, and while she thought she had a handle on her fear, she wasn't so sure that it wasn't winning out over the arousal that Connor created. She needed his touch, which seemed to ground her. Without it, she felt adrift as if she were sinking into the black depths of the sea. The trembling started to get worse and her knees felt like they were going to give.

"Here we are," Connor whispered next to her ear. Before the startled gasp left her lips, he'd pulled the tie up and over her head. She went to protest, but he claimed her lips, effectively silencing her. Pulling slightly away, his smooth, warm tongue outlined her lips in a sensuous glide. "This old crop I found is nicely broken in and will work very effectively on your ass as I remind you of who is in command when we walk through that bedroom door. Your body is mine. We have all the time in the world to ease your fears one step at a time and one scene at a time. In order for that to sink into that intelligent, keen, submissive mind, you'll turn around. Palms face down on the mattress. I want your feet spread apart, giving me access to your pussy."

A shiver traveled through Lauren's body at how deep Connor's voice had become, along with the darkening of his eyes. She wasn't so sure it was relief or regret her heart was feeling as she turned around on his command. Lauren had wanted her offering to reveal how much trust she had in him.

"Sir," Lauren said, placing herself into position, "I wanted—"

"I know what you wanted, Red," Connor said, caressing her ass with one of his hands. His voice was soft with reassurance. "But you need to understand that not everything needs to be rushed and you won't always get what you want. I'll give you what you need. As I said, each scene we have will have a purpose and right now, I will use this one to teach you your place."

It was the sound of the crop that startled Lauren more than the slight sting on her ass. She fisted the rumpled sheets as she laid her cheek against the cool material. Instead of continuing, Connor stopped and ran a finger through her folds until he'd found her clit. He rubbed the little nub in circles.

"Hmmm," Lauren hummed. She was unable to prevent her feet from lifting her up on her toes. "Sir…"

"Does that feel good?" Connor asked softly, not varying the rhythm.

"Yes, Sir," Lauren replied, now moving her hips slightly in cadence with his hand.

He didn't stop and Lauren felt her body tightening. Connor was going to make her come. Lauren let her lashes drift down, closing out the light. Instead of the confinement she'd felt with the blindfold, this type of darkness enveloped her within its warmth. Tingling sensations were starting to travel up her legs. Connor's touch was driving her toward that release and with the way her body was displayed, there was nothing holding her back.

"Did I say you could come?" Connor asked, his voice low and indicating that she was to answer immediately.

"No, Sir," Lauren's eyes popped open when she felt him pull his hand away. She wanted to cry out that he had to touch her, but knew that would gain her nothing. Her pussy was experiencing a spasm, but there was nothing to grab onto. He'd stopped just shy of her body exploding. How had he known? "But please, Sir, may I come?"

Maybe by her asking for permission, Connor would place his fingers back on her now engorged clit. She felt her juices coating her inner thighs. But when he didn't touch her again, Lauren squeezed her eyes tight as she tried to rein in her body's response to his touch.

"No, you may not. But I will take you just shy of that release several times before I decide if you finally understand that I am the one in control." Connor brought down the crop again, leaving heat to bloom outward on her left cheek. She rose up on her toes for an entirely different reason this time. "It is not the blindfold or the cuffs that bind you, Red. It is my command."

Lauren knew he was right and that when the time came for him to blindfold her, it would be magical and without fear. Until then, she did trust him to push her boundaries and expand her limits. She also knew that no matter what she said or did right now, it would not cause him to let her find relief immediately. He brought the crop down several more times until her right cheek started to feel ignored.

"You're cream is showing me that you're enjoying this a little too much," Connor said, a smile in his voice. "But that's exactly how I want it. Let's see if I can make you plead for that orgasm."

Lauren had no doubt she would be screaming for it by the time he was done. Again, his fingers slide through drenched folds, seeking out her clit. It wasn't hard to find considering it was vastly swollen. She rose on her tiptoes when the connection was made and she didn't bother to quiet her cries.

"That's right, Red. Let me hear you."

"Please, please, please," Lauren begged. Was he really going to leave her hanging again?

Connor glided his finger inside her tight channel and her sheath immediately tried to keep him there. Unfortunately, her juices made it impossible and he mimicked what he would do when he finally got his cock inside of her. In and out, there was nothing she could do but feel the heightening and swirling sensations as they spiraled out of control. Lauren's vision had just started to fade, indicating her release, when he pulled his finger out of her pussy.

"No," Lauren cried out, unable to help herself.

The crop landed again, this time to her right cheek. Several rapid successions later, she remembered his title.

"Sir!"

"Will you top from the bottom again?"

"No, Sir!" Lauren had to dig her toes into the carpet as the crop made contact with her flesh once more. The heat seemed to encompass her entire backside, but it did nothing to diminish her arousal. "Mmmmm."

Connor stroked the stinging spot with his fingers that now felt cool, when she knew they were anything but. He chuckled.

"I'm thinking you'll say anything to get that elusive orgasm that I've been holding back from you." Connor trailed his finger down her crevice and over her dark hole. "One day, I'll have you here. We'll work your body up in order to accept my cock through this tight ring. As for topping from the bottom, I'm sure you'll try again. And I'll be honored to take this crop back to your ass to show you who controls these scenes."

Connor's finger ran a circle around her sphincter and she heard another chuckle come from deep within his chest when a spasm was initiated. Instead of breaking through, his finger continued to blaze a trail back down to her swollen clit. One touch had her digging her toes into the carpet.

"That's right, Red. Time for another round."

Lauren felt tears prickle the back of her lids as his finger circled the outer area of the distended flesh. Could this break a person? She'd never been told she couldn't have an orgasm before, let alone taken to the brink twice, only to have it yanked out from under her. Now he was doing it a third time?

"Sir," Lauren breathed, tightening her hold on the covers. Her fingers felt like they could shatter. "I-I can't take any-more."

"You can take a lot more," Connor said in disagreement. "Trust me."

Connor lightly started to stroke her clit once more. Lauren continued to moan through the pleasure, feeling like her body was flying higher and higher. Her knees were locked into place, but she didn't know for how much longer. The strength it took remain in position had diminished rapidly.

"Hearing you moan like that makes my cock hard, Red." Connor finished manipulating her clit with a tap that sent electricity through her body. "I might just come from your screams."

Again, he scattered taps of the crop across her already tender flesh, leaving her suspended in the midst of euphoria. The pleasure that he'd created over and over seemed to dangle her senses over a vast void. Sure enough, when he touched her clit once more, she screamed.

"Would you like to come?" Connor asked, his voice breaking through the sound of blood rushing through her ears.

"Y-yes, Sir," Lauren said, practically chattering.

She was almost afraid to come for fear that he'd taken her body too far. Connor pulled away, causing a tear to fall. It slid sideways and landed on the bed, soaking into the fabric. Was it possible to perish from an orgasm?

"You'll come when I'm inside of you, so that I can feel the intensity from making you wait." Lauren heard a wrapper tear and felt a sob rise in her chest from relief. Connor's hands touched her hips and she expected him to slam into her with force. Instead, his words surprised her. "Crawl onto the bed and lay on your back."

Lauren turned her face into the sheets, squeezing her eyes shut. How was she going to get the strength to do that? With sluggish arms and legs, she managed what he wanted, although the entire time she worried she'd come. Her clit felt like a grenade with its pin removed.

"I want your hands wrapped around your ankles," Connor ordered, moving above her. "Don't let go."

This position opened herself up to Connor's view, as well as gave him full control over what was about to take place. Lauren was well aware that his words alone bound her to this position and she wouldn't disappoint him. He leaned over her and suckled on her right nipple. Her hands jerked on her ankles as pleasure once again took hold.

"Perfect," Connor murmured, moving to the other one. The peaked nipple got its turn as he placed his hands on either side of her. "You are still not allowed to come unless I say so."

Lauren could only watch as he rose up on his hands. She felt his cock at her entrance, which was wide open for the taking. Looking down, his huge tip seemed to be sucked into her as her pussy decided it needed him. He stretched her, sinking slowly inside of her until their bodies were one.

"Do you remember how many times the crop struck your ass?" Connor asked, kissing her jawline.

Lauren had no breath to speak, so she simply shook her head. She was trying too hard not to come, as his full width and length were testing her limits. The minute he pulled back, she knew her orgasm would strike. What had he asked her again?

"No?" Connor pulled back and looked at her with a small devilish smile. A ripple of excitement shot through her. "I wasn't keeping count either, but I'd say at least twenty."

Why was that important? And why wasn't he moving? Lauren tightened her grip on her ankles, trying to shift her lower half. His weight made it impossible.

"That is how many strokes I will have before you are allowed to come."

"But, Sir," Lauren instantly protested, after sucking in some much needed oxygen. He couldn't be serious. What would her punishment be if she did have an orgasm before he reached his last stroke? It might be worth it. "I can't—"

"You can."

With those two words, Connor didn't waste time. Pulling out, he plunged his cock back into her. She gasped, feeling a stirring in her toes. By the fifth stroke, she tried to clamp down on his dick to keep the orgasm from overtaking her. It only seemed to cause the stimulation to intensify.

Her breathing was shallow and her vision dimmed, causing his face to fade from her sight by the time he gave the command for her to come. On the twentieth stroke, Lauren screamed as her release consumed her. Her body shuddered and her pussy clenched his cock as Connor followed her to utopia.

Connor's voice reached her ears, but Lauren was still struggling for oxygen. Only when she felt his fingers enclose over hers was when she realized that she still had ahold of her ankles. He helped her release each one, kissing every knuckle. Once he had her snuggled deep into his sheets and comforter, Connor slipped from the bed. She wasn't sure how long he'd been gone, but when he did return, there was no condom and his body temperature had cooled.

"Come here," Connor murmured, gathering her up against his chest. She pulled her hands around until they were tucked under her cheek. "Feel okay?"

"Mmmm," Lauren replied, hoping he would take that as an affirmative. She had no energy left to have a full-fledged conversation. "Hmmm."

Lauren could feel Connor chuckle as his chest vibrated against her back. She let herself drift, knowing he would watch over her. For the first time since he'd saved her from Russell Treace, she slept peacefully. It was sometime in the middle of the night that a niggling thought had her opening her eyes. She smiled softly as she felt Connor move, somehow knowing that she'd awakened.

"Everything okay?" Connor asked sleepily, tightening his arms around her.

"Yeah," Lauren whispered. "I was just thinking about something you said earlier."

"What's that?"

"Do you really want children?"

"A pretty little girl, with freckles and red hair running around chasing after her older protective brother sounds like fun," Connor replied, seemingly more awake than before. "We'll have enough time for that in the future. Right now, you are in need of some more training. Are you up for it?"

"Since you've captured my heart, Marine, I'm up for anything," Lauren replied, laughing when he flipped her over.

"I think it's you who's captured me, Red."

Epilogue

Crest walked down the sidewalk after having just left Terry's place. His friend was doing well under the circumstances, but had a lot of healing ahead of him—physically and mentally. With the help of his father, he had no doubt that Terry would pull through. Family meant everything and now that Crest's obligation had been paid, maybe the three of them could move on from past regrets.

"Gavin?"

Crest had just reached his car when Kenneth Sweeney's voice had him turning back around. The biting wind had picked up this evening and Crest slipped his hands into the pockets of his dress coat. He'd left his gloves on the dash.

"Thank you for everything you did," Ken said. The older man had come out without his jacket and he'd hunched his shoulders to fight off the bitter air. "I think maybe Terry is finally coming around to forgiving me."

"There's nothing to forgive, Ken." Gavin scanned the area, as old habits were hard to break, before setting his gaze back on his biological father. "The past is the past and nothing can change the events that have led us here. Terry is my half-brother, and as such it is my duty to watch over him. I knew that he wasn't capable of murdering his wife. As for your relationship with him, Terry loves you regardless of the mistakes you made in your past and I think these events have made him realize how fleeting life can really be."

"Your mother and I—"

"Did what you thought was best," Crest said, finishing his sentence. He looked into the eyes of the man who'd had an affair with his mother without telling her he was married. While Carolyn Crest had wed another man and built a happy family, Ken had to deal with the fallout of his actions. "We've been over this, Ken. I have no hard feelings toward you. My parents raised me in a stable, well-adjusted, happy environment. Your relationship with Terry has always been tremulous, but maybe now that can heal."

"I'm grateful that he has you," Ken replied, his eyes still filled with remorse that Crest knew would never go away. "He's always had you."

"He's blood." Crest turned to his black Koenigsegg CCX and opened the door. "It's cold. You better head back inside. I'll stop by tomorrow."

Ken nodded and slowly turned, making his way back to the house. Crest turned over the engine of his most cherished possession, giving the engine time to warm up. He waited patiently for the older man to enter the front door.

Life had a funny way of making complete circles. Crest finally put the sports car in reverse, backing it out of the driveway. He knew that another storm was brewing and that he'd have to put his baby back in the garage in exchange for his four-wheel drive, but it'd been nice to take this little one out for a drive. Looking down at the passenger seat as he shifted into drive, he saw the file that would make Jax's past come full circle to meet his present. His foot pressed on the gas pedal. Crest just hoped like hell that he was ready for it.

~ THE END ~

Continue reading for a sneak peek of *Sinful Resurrection*, CSA Case Files 2...

Sinful Resurrection

CSA Case Files, Book Two

Prologue

Crest heard the telltale vibration of his phone and remembered that he'd left it on the other nightstand. Reaching carefully over the woman sleeping beside him, his fingers captured the familiar glass rectangle. He settled back on the pillow, grateful that tonight's blonde didn't stir and pressed a button on top of his cell. The screen lit up to reveal an incoming text alert. He didn't need to read it to know that the time had come to initiate a case that he wanted no involvement in, but unfortunately he needed the details. Owing favors was part of the job, but that didn't mean he had to relish the idea.

Easing the sheet off of his body, Crest leaned up on his elbow. It was rare for someone to notice he had to enter eight digits into his phone keypad rather than four. After inputting the correct sequence, he placed his right thumb in the square that appeared in the middle of the screen. On the rare occasion someone did remark, he simply commented that it was a new model.

Crest carefully read the entire message and crafted his succinct reply. He didn't want his words to be misconstrued, so he kept his response as brief as possible. That was something he'd learned as a junior staff noncommissioned officer, when his executive officer would email him another copy of the *Manual for Naval Letter Format*. The damned thing had been so big it filled up his mailbox and prevented him from receiving any other mail. The executive officer's message had always accompanied a voluminous amount of corrections and a not so subtle reference to read the fucking thing. Crest had learned early on that clear, concise messages tended to be terse but effective in conveying what his executive officer wanted to say.

This current situation was going to affect one of his team and he took that to heart, as he knew Jax Christensen would as well. Crest ran through several scenarios as to how he could contain the situation and lessen the damage it would cause, but knew it was an exercise in futility. The past, like the Phoenix, had a way of resurrecting itself.

"Leaving?"

Crest had just sat up, his feet touching the cold hardwood floor of the bedroom when she'd spoken. He held back a sigh, wishing he'd been able to find his clothes and leave before she had awakened. They'd enjoyed a few cocktails and indulged in one of his favorite proclivities, which was displayed nicely on her slightly flushed curved bottom. Both knew that this would go no further.

"Yes, I've got to head out," Crest replied softly as he reached down for his black gabardine dress pants.

After exchanging light conversation over drinks, she'd invited him back to her place. She lived in an upscale apartment building within the city of Minneapolis. It hadn't been closer than his penthouse downtown, but it did give him the luxury of leaving when the time came. It had crossed his mind when he'd accepted her invitation that she looked nothing like Jessie, but he'd quickly discarded that thought. Jessie was nothing more than his personal assistant—very young personal assistant—and he would do well to remember that. He banished her image from his thoughts once more. There was enough moonlight streaming in the window to afford him a view of the other articles of clothing that were strewn on the floor. His shirt lay on top of her dress.

"What time is it?"

Gavin shot a quick look over his shoulder at the green neon display of the clock sitting on her bedside table. If he remembered correctly, she'd mentioned that she was an attending physician and was working a twelve-hour shift at the hospital emergency room starting at seven in the morning.

"It's only four, so you have a while before you need to get up," Crest said as he finished getting dressed. The last two pieces of clothing he picked up were his Armani suit jacket and his Galco holster rig, which he swung over his shoulder before turning to face her. "I enjoyed last night."

"As did I." They hadn't exchanged more than first names as there was no need and he was relieved to see that only gratitude and fondness shone in her green eyes. She had turned slightly, making no pretense of covering herself with the sheet. There was no need. She was a beautiful woman and she knew it, although she didn't need to use it to her advantage. "Feel free to stop by anytime."

"I'll keep that in mind," Crest replied, a small smile of appreciation on his lips.

With a nod of gratitude, he turned and walked out of her bedroom. The small lamp near the couch lit a path to the door. He made his way down to the parking garage and bypassed the attendant to where his car waited in the guest parking slot, adjacent to one of the building security posts. He heard last night's game being rebroadcast on the radio from within and didn't fail to notice the attentive pair of eyes that tracked him to his vehicle.

Crest was thankful that spring was arriving, but that didn't take away the hint of chill in the night air that stole its way into his clothes and clung to his skin at the precise moment. The icy wind outside would be brutal. Old habits died hard, so Crest took in his surroundings as he walked across the cold cement. It didn't surprise him to see Schultz Jessalyn leaning up against his vehicle.

"I thought you might make an appearance," Crest said, coming to a stop in front of his old friend. Schultz was currently a Special Assistant to the National Security Advisor to the President of the United States. He was far away from home, but the mission that he wanted Crest and his team to take was not. He had to wonder how far this friendship extended. "I guess it's futile to ask how you located me. My GPS *is* encrypted."

Schultz laughed and extended his arm. They shook hands and then Crest used the opportunity of silence to shrug into his shoulder holster and suit coat. He continued to scan the area, knowing full well that Schultz would never arrive here on his own. The question was how many agents were now in the immediate area.

"Don't worry," Schultz said with a smile, "they're around."

"I wouldn't want you to scratch your knee on my watch, Schultzy," Crest replied, using his friend's old nickname. "The President and his cronies might take issue with that. Speaking of protection, where's the witness?"

"Safe," Schultz replied, the condensation of his one word drifting in the air and then disappearing. He gave no outward appearance that the cold affected him in any way. "We'll make the transfer in five hours. Your team checks out, but I am still concerned about Jax Christensen. Do you think he'll be a problem?"

"What about your witness?"

"No. She only agreed to protection if it was under your firm and that of Mr. Christensen"

"Then you have your answer," Crest said, crossing his arms and shifting his stance. "Who will be accompanying you?"

"It will just be me and the witness." Schultz looked around, as if assuring himself that he had enough protection even though Crest knew of his background and was confident he could take on an opponent or two without additional support. Lifting one side of his long black dress coat, Schultz pulled out a manila folder. "This is everything we deemed necessary for your need to know with regards to her protection. The Attorney General is in the process of verifying the evidence that our witness provided."

Crest took the folder but didn't glance at it. He'd take his time before their nine o'clock morning meeting to ensure he had all of the facts pertaining to this mission. There was one thing that bothered him about the scenario that Schultz was presenting.

"You mean this folder contains what I'm cleared to know, not necessarily the truth." Crest had made sure upon retirement that he kept certain clearances active. It had only helped his firm. The government contracts that his business was allotted paid him and his team a handsome salary. The assignment that Schultz was giving him superseded most clearances due to the involvement of the United Nations. "How do you know her?"

"I'm not sure I know what you're talking about," Schultz replied with a tilt of his head.

"Don't bullshit me, Schultzy." Crest held up the folder. "You told me that she has evidence that Grigori Alekseev, the United Nation's Secretary-General, has his finger in the sale of WMDs to mid-eastern countries. You also revealed that the former Secretary-General was murdered, leaving pertinent facts out. I'm assuming they're tied together, but your information is scarce. How is it that she knew she could go to you, let alone trust you?"

"Because I'm that kind of guy?" Schultz asked, raising an eyebrow. With a small salute, he stepped away from the car. "Review the file and have your men triple check the location you'll be transporting our witness to. And as I stated previously, trust no one that you wouldn't trust with your life."

Crest despised that gut feeling he got when things were about to become some half-assed cluster fuck. He was feeling it now and didn't like being kept in the dark. His 'need to know' for compartmentalized information required advancing a notch or two and he knew just the person to make that happen. Unfortunately, Crest didn't hold all the power here and had no choice but to see this assignment through. As much as he would like to prevent it, Jax was about to come face to face with his past.

About the Author

First and foremost, I love life. I love that I'm a wife, mother, daughter, sister…and a writer.

I am one of the lucky women in this world who gets to do what makes them happy. As long as I have a cup of coffee (maybe two or three) and my laptop, the stories evolve themselves and I try to do them justice. I draw my inspiration from a retired Marine Master Sergeant that swept me off of my feet and has drawn me into a world that fulfills all of my deepest and darkest desires. Erotic romance, military men, intrigue, with a little bit of kinky chili pepper (his recipe), fill my head and there is nothing more satisfying than making the hero and heroine fulfill their destinies.

Thank you for having joined me on their journeys…

Email:
kennedylayneauthor@gmail.com

Facebook:
https://www.facebook.com/kennedy.layne.94

Twitter:
https://twitter.com/KennedyL_Author

Website:
www.kennedylayne.com

Newsletter:
http://www.kennedylayne.com/newsletter.html

Books by
Kennedy Layne

KENNEDY LAYNE

CAPTURED
INNOCENCE

CSA
AGENCY CREST SECURITY

CSA CASE FILES 1

Captured Innocence
(CSA Case Files 1)

When former Marine, Connor Ortega, was ordered into the offices of Crest Security Agency on a Saturday morning, he didn't expect the latest case to hit so close to home. A submissive has been murdered in a particularly vicious manner and to bring her killer to justice, he must go undercover. Not hard to do considering he's already part of the BDSM lifestyle.

Lauren Bailey, a local vendor of bejeweled erotic implements, lives vicariously through her clients due to her fear of bondage. When Connor's dominant side can't resist trying to ease her anxieties, she accepts his proposal and agrees to his one stipulation…keep things casual.

When the killer sets his sights on Lauren, Connor is forced to rethink their relationship. He has the training it takes to catch a murderer, but does he have the courage to escape his inner demons and capture Lauren's heart?

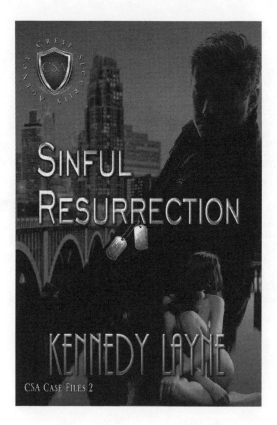

Sinful Resurrection

Kennedy Layne

CSA Case Files 2

Sinful Resurrection
(CSA Case Files 2)

Sins of the past have been resurrected, predetermining their path to love. Can they overcome the treacherous obstacles set before them?

Jax Christensen likes his life just the way it is. He has his work, his club, and the occasional naked submissive to take his mind off everything else. He doesn't talk about the past, as there is no point in reminiscing about things that cannot be altered. His chest has an empty hole where his heart used to be, but he's grown accustomed to the constant pain. It's become the only thing that reminds Jax that he's alive.

Emily Weiss has never forgotten the one and only man she's ever loved. She's hidden for two long years in an attempt to protect Jax and herself, desperate to try and stay one step ahead of those who want her dead. She has information that could destroy the United Nations. Unfortunately, they want to eliminate her first. Emily's exhausted and wants more than anything to feel safe once more. That was how she felt in Jax's strong arms and she longs to be there again.

When Jax sees that Emily has risen from the grave, his heart and soul are full of anger and regret. He'll never forgive her lies and deception. He will, however, keep her safe. He hates her for what she's done, but he doesn't want her death on his conscience. He'll protect her and then walk away.

Secrets are revealed and the danger is more sinister and deadly than anyone could have guessed. Jax and Emily are forced on the run and the passion they once felt for one another burns even hotter and brighter the second time around. Jax doesn't know how he'll walk away this time or if he even wants to. Emily is determined to expose a high-level official within the United Nations and walk away unscathed. She wants a second chance with her first love—even if it kills her.

Made in the USA
San Bernardino, CA
21 April 2014